Intruders
Flight of the Kestrel book 1

A M Thomas

Alina Publishing
Swansea

Published by Alina Publishing
45 Rhondda Street, Mount Pleasant
Swansea SA1 6ER

ISBN: 978-0-9571988-7-6

Printed by Kindle Direct Print

Available from Amazon
Also available on Amazon for Kindle and
Smashwords.com for multiple ebook formats

Kestrel artwork by Brett Buckle
http://brettbuckle.co.uk/
Cover design by Steve Jones

Dedication
To my husband Michael who has encouraged me all the
way, even though he doesn't like science fiction

Acknowledgements
I want to thank my editor Gail Williams
(https://thewriteroute.wordpress.com/), and my beta
readers Lisa Higgins, Dawn Smith and Anna Ingram for
all their superb advice.
I am grateful to Brett Buckle (http://brettbuckle.co.uk/)
for making real the image of the Kestrel that I had in
my head, and my son Vincent Thomas for finding Brett
and working with him. Thanks to Steve Jones for
designing the cover. And last but by no means least,
thanks to
Swansea & District Writers Circle
(http://www.swanseawriters.co.uk/) for all their advice
and support.

Among the stars
Who knows what friends we'll find
What mind
Will reach us from afar
And teach us things
Like how the universe sings?

About the author:

Writing poetry and making up stories since she was a child, she only started to write seriously when her children were grown. Her main ambition was to write science fiction, but along the way she got fascinated by local history and distracted by a major stroke. However, she wrote poetry about her stroke and spent her recovery writing a local history book. Taking early retirement gave her more time to concentrate on her writing.

Connect with the author online:
Website: https://annmariethomas.co.uk
Mailing list: http://eepurl.com/bbOsyz
Email: amt.tetelestai@gmail.com

Twitter:
https://twitter.com/AnnMThomas80
Facebook: http://on.fb.me/1P9OkCu
Amazon: http://amzn.to/1EjoBAZ
LinkedIn: http://linkd.in/1MUdsAv
GoodReads: http://bit.ly/21nG4Jv

FREE BOOK!
Join her mailing list and receive this free book and monthly updates
http://eepurl.com/bbOsyz

Chapter 1

When Tabitha Enns was called to the Principal's office, her first thought was it was related to her being top of the class. But then she had already received a presentation in front of the whole academy. Next year she would be going on to the Academy on Earth for final training, her first time off-planet. So she wondered if she had done something wrong. Maybe she wasn't going to Earth after all. But why? She was still frowning when she knocked on the door.

'Come in, Enns sit down.' Principal Hernandez was as stern as ever, her black hair captive in a tight bun and her green uniform not daring to crease.

She never asked students to sit down. This must be serious. Tabitha's worry increased as she automatically thanked the Principal and sat, clasping her hands to keep them still.

'What do you know about the PACT Fast-Response Fleet?'

'What?' Tabitha blinked, reddening at her uncontrolled reaction. She caught herself and took a deep breath. 'I know the Planetary Alliance for Co-operation and Trade, of course, but I didn't do much study on the Fast-Response Fleet.'

'Well, you're about to learn first-hand.' The Principal smiled. 'One of their ships has offered you some work experience.'

'What?'

'Enns, there are better ways to request clarification. This is a wonderful opportunity for you.' Tabitha's heart leapt; then sank as she thought of her mother's reaction.

'But - my parents, they won't let me.'

'I have spoken to your father, and he has given his permission.'

'What about my mother?'

1

The Principal offered a half-smile. 'She wasn't there. Your father's permission is enough.'

Tabitha's heart pounded as the news started to sink in. One hand escaped the other and rose to her face.

'You mean I'm actually going into space? What will I have to do?'

'The Fast-Response Fleet is a diplomatic and emergency service. They deal with incidents outside of local planetary space where jurisdiction may not be clear. The Kestrel is a crewman short due to a medical emergency, and the Captain is offering a place until the crewman recovers. You won't be asked to do anything you're not ready for, though you will have to share a cabin.'

'So what do they deal with? Where do they go?'

'I'm sure Captain Darrow will answer all your questions when he arrives in an hour.'

'An hour? Is that all the time I have?'

Hernandez stood and leaned on her hands on the desk. 'Tabitha Enns, do you want to go or not? If you don't want this opportunity, I can talk to Paul Sung's parents.'

'No! I mean, yes, I do want to go. Yes, please!' Both hands took on a life of their own.

The Principal tapped the keypad before her and Tabitha's pad chimed. 'Here are the dimensions of the standard crew container for your things. Go and get ready, Captain Darrow will bring one with him.'

Tabitha's head was spinning as she left the office. She stepped across the corridor and leaned her forehead against the window. The PACT Training Academy stood on a hill overlooking the city. She looked down on the familiar sight. The original living pods had long been extended to create sprawling, low houses made from local wood. As long as she could remember, she had wanted to get out and see other worlds, meet real-life aliens, find out what it was really like out there. But as she looked out, the prospect of leaving was suddenly, unexpectedly hard. Alpha was all she had ever known, and if her mother had her way, it was where she would stay. Her father though, had seen her longing, had repeatedly fetched her from the spaceport fence so her mother wouldn't find out, and supported her desire to join PACT.

'Aliens mean trouble,' her mother always said. 'That's why the Alpha colony is for humans only. We need to look after our own.'

It was lucky her mother hadn't answered Principal Hernandez's call. Even now, she was still trying to persuade Tabitha to take an admin post on Alpha when she qualified. The thought of the final training year on Earth filled her mother with dread, and she constantly reminded Tabitha to keep away from aliens while she was there. Now she might be meeting aliens on a mission in the - what was the name of the ship? The Kestrel. A thought struck her. Were there aliens in the crew? After all, PACT was an alliance between the seven species with warp drive technology. Did they mix the crew? She raced to her room to look it up as she got ready.

Tabitha looked like a typical Alphan girl of eighteen. Stocky and short from evolution in high gravity, but with intelligent green eyes and shaggy brown hair that flopped in her eyes. But physicality was where the similarity ended. A typical Alphan girl wanted nothing to do with anything outside her own planet, but ever since Tabitha saw her first spaceship trail in the atmosphere, space was where she wanted to be. Her friends thought she was weird and her parents tried to dissuade her, but she would not budge. Now her chance had come.

* * *

Principal Hernandez called Tabitha back to her office when the Kestrel's Captain arrived to collect her. Captain Joseph Darrow seemed friendly enough, with dark curly hair and warm brown eyes. He seemed very thin compared to Alphan men, she had to remind herself that most human men would be of a similar build. His rank was marked by the yellow armband on his green uniform and Tabitha made a mental note to brush up her knowledge of the rank colours. He smiled as she saluted then shook her hand.

'Nice to meet you, Trainee Enns. Principal Hernandez says you have some questions?'

'Yes sir, I wanted to know what my duties will be, and where we'll be going.'

'Don't worry; we simply need an extra pair of hands. We'll work to your strengths, and give you some training as well. As to where we're going, we patrol a designated sector of the galaxy and ferry some light cargo, but we're on call, so it could be anywhere. Here's your personal container. I'm afraid you can't bring any more than that, and check the prohibited items list.'

'Go and pack, quick as you can,' the Principal said.

To Tabitha's great relief, what she had put aside fitted easily into the container, so she was back in the Principal's office quickly. She had said her goodbyes while she was waiting for the Captain. Her classmates were shocked but jealous - most of them were at the Academy because they were "weird" by Alphan standards too. Captain Darrow was in a hurry, though he moved slowly in the higher gravity of Alpha. She caught a glimpse of a back brace under his jacket. He ushered her into a ground vehicle and they left immediately.

'Our helmsman was promoted to another ship and Personnel were unable to find us a replacement.' Darrow briefed her as they travelled to the spaceport. 'This damned Bokan situation has everyone tied up on the border. They sent us on patrol with one crewman short, and then Lieutenant Balitoth fell ill. He's being treated here on Alpha, but if we get a call-out we can't cope two crew down, so that's why you're here. You won't be expected to cover his duties, the crew are all multi-skilled. But we need an extra pair of hands. Do you know about the Fast-Response Fleet?'

'Only what I managed to look up, sir. You have a crew of eleven normally, don't you?' She took a deep breath. 'Sir, are any of them aliens?'

'Are you against that?' he said sharply.

'No, no. I don't agree with Alphan isolationist policies. It's just that I've never met one. I wouldn't want to cause offence.'

He laughed. 'No need to worry, Ensign Reuel is gentle. He's the only non-human on board, now Lieutenant Balitoth's in the hospital. I expect all the men to be patient and accommodating. I understand you've been told you have to share quarters. You'll be in with Lieutenant Andrew Chambers. Any questions, he'll see you right.'

Tabitha suppressed a gasp. Sharing with a man! Studying with boys was one thing, but sharing a cabin - she hadn't expected that. She hadn't thought about it at all. Too late now.

* * *

It was the first time Tabitha had been inside the spaceport. She had spent many hours watching ships through the fence, but now she was inside, actually going on board a ship. She spotted the Kestrel right away, with its green and gold livery and low, horizontal triangular shape. Captain Darrow smiled as he saw her reaction.

'I remember my first time in a spaceport,' he said. 'I was only a child at the time. I'm amazed you're eighteen and never been in a port before.'

They were waved through check-in when the Captain showed his pass, walked to the ship and in through the open airlock. He took her to a cabin on the lower deck and introduced her to a man in his thirties with fair hair and freckles, wearing a dark blue armband.

'Lieutenant Andrew Chambers, this is Trainee Tabitha Enns. Help her settle in, and once we're underway, Commander Holland will be along to take charge.'

'Yes, sir.' Both saluted as the Captain left.

Chambers looked her up and down, particularly down, as he was a head taller than her.

'Well, I can see you're an Alphan. How much do you weigh? Sorry, don't answer that. Let's get you settled. The bottom bunk is yours, and this is your locker. The head is through here. When you get changed, either go in there, or if I'm not here, lock the cabin door. But don't forget to unlock it afterwards, I don't want to sleep in the corridor,' he laughed.

The cabin was small, just bunks, lockers, a desk with a computer console and one chair, and very little floor space.

It'll be hard not to get in each other's way if we're both in here at the same time, she thought.

Chambers seemed friendly and helpful, and was doing his best to put her at ease. Her container slotted into the locker, but needed repacking for the vertical position. While she was repacking, Kestrel prepared for take-off. A red light blinked on the wall, and the intercom barked, 'Take-off in thirty seconds!'

Chambers sat down and indicated to her to sit on the bed. The engines whined, there was a slight jar, the artificial gravity kicked in, and Tabitha slipped from the bed.

'Steady on there!' Chambers tried to help her up. 'Have you done acclimatisation?'

Shamefaced, Tabitha shook her head and scrambled to her feet. Her heart was pounding. Things were going wrong so soon. Maybe she wasn't up to this.

'The gravity on board is 1G - Earth-normal,' Chambers said. 'Ensign Reuel has the opposite problem. He's Altairian, and has to wear a back brace as he's used to much lighter gravity. He couldn't cope at all on Alpha, had to stay in bed. You'll get used to it, you won't need to work so hard to move things on board. Just take things slowly and be careful not to slam or break things.'

This last was said as the locker catch came off in her hand. Everything felt light and she was so much stronger than usual.

As if I don't have enough to get used to, she thought.

As she finished putting her things away, the door chimed and Chambers opened it to reveal a tall, good-looking man with dark hair, wearing a green armband. Chambers snapped to attention and saluted. Tabitha attempted the same, but lost her balance again. Her heart sank. They both helped her up.

'Stand easy,' the officer said.

'Commander Holland, Trainee Enns,' Chambers introduced them.

'Welcome to the Kestrel,' said Holland. 'I'm the First Officer. I'll be responsible for your duties and training. Report to me at 0900 tomorrow and we'll see what you know and how we can best use your skills. Do you have any questions now?'

'Er, will I get a uniform sir?' she asked.

'No,' He frowned. 'We don't want you being mistaken for someone qualified, do we? No, your school uniform will do fine. The blue tunic and trousers are similar to our green ones, but lose the neckerchief - health and safety - it might get caught on something. You need to tie your hair back too. Right, Lieutenant Chambers, will you give her the tour? Message me if any issues come up.'

With that, he was gone. Barely time to salute before the door closed. Tabitha let out a long breath and clasped her hands nervously.

'Don't worry about Commander Holland,' Chambers said. 'He'll go easy on you. It's the Captain who's a real stickler for protocol. Don't try to bend any rules or Captain Darrow will throw the book at you. Commander Holland just got promoted to Captain. He's waiting for his new ship, the Falcon, to be refitted. Then he'll be off to the Bokan border with the rest of them, I expect. I don't know what Kestrel will do when he goes. There are no spare staff anywhere.'

'What's happening on the border?' she asked, tying back

her shaggy brown hair, which seemed even wilder than normal.

'Don't you know?' he asked in surprise. 'I suppose Alpha doesn't bother itself with interplanetary politics. The Bokans developed warp drive, and were invited to join PACT. Only they're a suspicious lot, and thought the observers who spotted their craft were spying. They've threatened war. So while diplomatic talks are going on, PACT have all available non-military ships patrolling the border, guarding against any incidents that might scupper things, like any rogue ships that decide to start the war on their own. It's a very prickly situation, but it's left the rest of the PACT fleets seriously undermanned. Anyway, let me show you around. Got your balance all right? Just take your time.'

The tour didn't take long. The ship was quite compact. Their deck had two shuttle bays, a small cargo bay half-full of supplies, and three cabins, including theirs, with a central corridor running fore and aft. She had to hold on to the hand rail inset into the corridor wall, as the lighter gravity gave her vertigo. Her ears felt funny, sloppy, as if she were sailing rather than flying. It had all happened so fast, she felt a bit queasy, and she was sure she wouldn't remember everything.

'The rail is for getting around if the artificial gravity goes,' Chambers explained. 'There are handholds scattered about as well.'

Then Chambers took her up to the main deck. There were stairs at either end of the corridor, and she had a peep through the bridge door.

'You probably won't be allowed in there,' he whispered. 'Only those on duty are. During patrols it's usually just one man looking after helm, navigation and comms. But we have two consoles round the walls for when we're fully manned, to cover scanners and weapons too. That's Lieutenant-Commander Hoy, the Second Officer, on duty.'

They worked their way back through the central corridor and Chambers pointed out the officers' cabins, sick bay, hydroponics and the mess hall.

'It's a joke to call it a mess hall. There are only seats for eight people. It's more of a cupboard really. Now, this is the business end.'

He opened a door to reveal a huge room full of machinery, cables and blinking lights. Chambers saluted a burly older man with a ruddy complexion. He was wearing a green armband.

'Commander Blackwell, this is Trainee Enns, I'm giving her the tour.' Blackwell looked her up and down, snorted and turned back to his console. Chambers turned to Tabitha, 'This is the engine room. It takes up the full width of the stern and both decks. The Kestrel can make three times the speed the big gunships and pleasure cruisers can, that's why they call us Fast-Response. That's it. Let's get something to eat.'

As soon as she entered the mess hall and smelled the food, Tabitha thought she was going to be sick. She ran into the head, but nothing happened. Chambers helped her back to their cabin.

'You've been through a lot today,' he said. 'Lay on the bed and rest. You haven't got to do anything until tomorrow, so just relax.'

'I can't be ill,' she said. 'What good am I if I'm ill? I don't know what's the matter with me. I was all right until take-off.'

Chambers jumped to his feet. 'Space sickness! That's what it is! You've never been out before, have you? Lots of people get it.' He dragged her to her feet and headed out the door. 'You need to see Quack, he'll put you right.'

'Who?' As Tabitha struggled along, she tried not to lean on him.

'Doctor Robinson, our Medical Officer, or MO. He wears his hair long, like doctors in the history books. Back then people who set themselves up as doctors without any training were called quacks, so someone nicknamed him Quack, and it stuck.'

'Does he mind?'

'Of course he minds! We never say it to his face. Here we are.'

As the door opened he handed her over to a man wearing a white uniform with a blue armband.

'Trainee Enns, Doctor. Space sickness, first time out.'

Chapter 2

Tabitha was so relieved someone was going to fix her, she relaxed onto the arm the doctor offered her. He yelped and flinched.

'Sorry,' she mumbled, taking her own weight. 'I'm not used to this gravity. It's so light.'

'It's all right,' he said. 'I'm Dr Robinson. Sit here.'

As she complied, she noted the MO was an older man with a large nose and shoulder-length black hair gathered at the nape of his neck. He was slim and looked very fit.

'Space sickness, undoubtedly,' he said after examining her. 'It's most likely the gravity difference. What's the gravity on Alpha? 2.5G? Come over here and lie down inside this pressure pod.'

He helped her into the pod and fetched her a phial and a leaflet.

'Sip this anti-emetic when you feel queasy, and read this - you'll need to do these exercises three times a day until you acclimatise.' He pulled the clear canopy down. 'I'm going to set this to 2.5G to give you relief. It will reduce gradually over the next three hours. Then you can go back to your cabin and straight to bed. You'll be much better by the morning. I'll let Commander Holland know -'

Tabitha shot up in bed, shaking her head, and nearly fainted. Robinson chuckled, raised the canopy, and pushed her down again.

'Don't you worry, you won't get into trouble. Relax now and let the machine do its work.'

As she lay there, Tabitha reflected on the events of the day. She had started off as Tabitha, top student, and ended up as Trainee Enns, who hadn't a clue what she was doing and couldn't even walk straight. All her life she had dreamed of being in space, and now she was, but she hadn't imagined it like this. She thought of her parents. Dad would be proud. Mum would be horrified. *I got away without having a scene with Mum,* she thought with relief. *I'm going to make the most of this chance while I can.*

As she dozed under the canopy, Tabitha could hear the MO and another man checking off the inventory of medical supplies, a gentle drone in the background. Then there was a knock at the door.

'That'll be Reuel,' said Robinson. 'He's so eager to learn human customs, he's the only one who knocks.'

Tabitha raised her head a little to see. Reuel was the Altairian, she remembered. This would be the first alien she had seen in the flesh. He was a tall, slender pink humanoid without hair, spines ran down his head like a coxcomb. He was wearing a violet armband. *Ensign,* thought Tabitha. His cranial spines writhed and his expression looked anxious.

He gave a little bow. 'I apologise for my intrusion. Is there any news of Balitoth? Will the operation be over yet?'

'As promised, I will tell you as soon as there is news,' Robinson said. 'I'm sure he will be fine.'

Reuel frowned. '*Fine*, I must research this word more fully. Humans seem to use it in so many situations.'

'I mean that everything will be done under the best possible practice and Balitoth will recover as well as can be expected under the circumstances.'

'Under the circumstances, yes.' Reuel gave another bow. 'Thank you for your time.'

As the door closed behind him, the other man chuckled.

'He's so gentle, it's hard to believe how fierce he can be when roused.'

* * *

After a good night's sleep, Tabitha felt much better. She was starting to get the hang of the gravity. She was hungry, having missed food the day before, and breakfast in the mess hall gave her a chance to meet two more of the crew. The

Second Officer, Daniel Hoy, was the smallest man she had ever seen. She hadn't noticed his size when she saw him on the bridge. About her height but slim, he had almond-shaped eyes and pale skin. Chambers introduced them.

'Lieutenant-Commander Hoy is of Oriental descent and proud of his heritage.' Chambers said. Hoy smiled and gave a little bow. 'Because of that he's learned ancient martial disciplines,' Chambers continued, 'so he's really useful in a fight because people don't expect his style of combat.'

Hoy moved away and sat down to eat. Chambers introduced her to the other man with less enthusiasm.

'This is Ensign Roy Stubbs, the assistant Engineer.'

Stubbs was a skinny, rough-looking young man, and she was taken aback when he winked at her. Chambers scowled at him.

'Don't take any notice, Enns. Ensign Stubbs doesn't know how to speak to a lady.'

Stubbs stiffened, and then noticed Hoy watching them. He turned away and went to fetch his breakfast.

'Come on,' Chambers said. 'Hurry and finish eating. It's time for you to meet with Commander Holland.'

Holland's cabin was at the rear of the main deck, with a corner screened off as an office. He reviewed her school records and asked her lots of questions about her studies. Then he assigned her to work in a different discipline each day, with a review after a week.

This is worse than school! She thought.

The first person Holland sent her to meet was Ensign Reuel who was going to show her the scanners.

Maybe he's deliberately putting me with the alien, she thought, *to see how I react.*

'Thank you, sir,' she said, straight-faced, 'I've been hoping to meet him. Is there anything I should know, not to cause offence?'

Holland looked impressed. 'Yes, don't ask him about his family. It's a private matter for Altarians, they don't talk about it.'

'Yes, sir, thank you, sir.'

She saluted and made her way to Engineering to properly meet her very first alien. He was sitting at a console displaying schematics. As she greeted him, she quaked despite the air of confidence she tried to project. She needn't have worried; Reuel was as kind and gentle as Chambers had said. He offered her his hand to shake, but it looked so frail she was afraid she might break it, so she just touched it with her fingers.

'I'm sorry about the handshake,' she said, 'I haven't got used to my increased strength yet.'

'Thank you for your concern,' he said. 'Please sit down. Welcome to the Kestrel, I hope we shall be friends.'

'That would be great,' she smiled. 'My first name is Tabitha. You can call me Tab if you like.'

'Oh no, that would not be appropriate until we are much better acquainted. We are not so free with our privacy on Altair.' He patted her hand. 'But I am gratified at the offer.'

She pulled a face. 'I'm so excited to be here, but I'm nervous I'll mess up.'

'Do not worry. The rules are simple - the senior officers tell you what to do and you do it, and in between, you study. It is the same for us all. Now, examine these schematics and see if you can find the places where we can calibrate the scanners.'

They worked through the schematics together, with Reuel explaining the parts she didn't understand. Later they took a break and Tabitha told Reuel the story of getting the call to work on Kestrel.

'It is good that Lieutenant Chambers is looking after you,' Reuel said. 'Perhaps it will take his mind off his new responsibilities.'

'What new responsibilities?'

'He has just been promoted to helmsman. Our previous helmsman Grey Lanx was promoted to another ship, but there was no replacement available. The Captain made Chambers helmsman, but Chambers is not convinced, he

14

does not think he is ready for it. We need to give him our encouragement. He is a qualified helmsman, but I believe there was a serious accident. I do not know the details.'

'Thank you for telling me,' Tabitha said. She remembered she had seen Reuel before. 'I was in sick bay when you came to ask about Lieutenant Balitoth. Is there any news of him?'

Reuel's cranial spines leaped up from his head, and he smiled. She tried not to stare at the spines.

'Oh yes!' he said. 'The operation was a success! He must have time to recover, but he will be … fine.'

Ensign Stubbs was passing and heard the last remark.

'Is that news of Balitoth?' he said. 'When will the old lizard be back with us then?'

Reuel stiffened. 'It is inappropriate that you speak of him in that manner. Dr Robinson says he will monitor the situation and let me know, but not less than a week.'

'Just friendly banter, no offense.' Stubbs turned to Tabitha. 'How are you settling in, Sweets?'

'Fine,' she said, looking away.

When Stubbs had gone, Reuel remarked, 'Ah, another use of the word 'fine'.'

* * *

At the end of the day, Tabitha was allowed to call home. Chambers showed her how to log on to the external communications system from the console in the cabin and pick up the designated channel. Then he left her to it. She waited for the call to be answered and one of her parents to appear on the screen. It was her mother, who immediately burst into tears.

'Oh Tab,' she said, 'How could you?'

Tabitha was used to her mother's tricks. She was determined not to be swayed.

'It was too good an opportunity to miss, Mum. Don't cry. Principal Hernandez wouldn't have let me come if it wasn't safe. Anyway, I'll probably be back in a week or two.'

'You said you wouldn't go into space.'

Tabitha gritted her teeth. 'No, you asked me not to go into space. I never agreed. No, Mum, don't. We can't talk about this now.'

'What about aliens? Will you have to meet aliens?' whispered her mother, shuddering.

'There's an Altairian on board,' she said, deliberately brightly. 'He's really nice.'

Her mother became angry. 'You just remember where you're from, and what they did to us.'

'Mum, I don't want to argue with you. I'm here and I can't come home. I want you to be proud of me.' She had a sudden idea. 'This is my chance to experience life on a serving space ship. Maybe I'll find out I don't like it.'

Her mother brightened. 'Well, just you behave yourself. I hope you make some nice human friends.'

'Yes, Mum.' She decided it would be unwise to mention there were no other girls on board. 'Give my love to Dad.'

The screen went blank and she closed the connection. *Thank goodness that's over,* she thought. *I think I'll just send messages from now on.* She switched the screen to write up what she had learned that day. Later she wrote in her journal.

Tabitha's Journal:

Well, I'm here. There was a bit of a hiccup getting used to the lower gravity, but it's been treated and I'm OK now. Still a bit unsteady on my feet - yet another chance to mess up. I just have to remember to take it slowly, and use the handholds, which is hard when you're nervous. At least the ship is small, so I won't get lost. I don't know how they don't go crazy, cooped up for months at a time.

The crew are all men, which is a bit daunting, and the Engineer doesn't approve of taking me on, but everyone's been kind. Andrew Chambers has taken me under his wing and gives me advice, and Commander Holland, though he gave me an interrogation about my studies, has been good about my work. I'm learning so much - it makes such a difference to see things in real life.

I've met my first alien, Shom Reuel, he's Altairian and really nice. He has these spines down the centre of his scalp instead of hair, and they move! He was such a help, as I was so nervous. He said working on the Kestrel is just like school - just my luck! You see, there's not much to do in between missions. It doesn't take many people to run the ship, so the ones on duty do maintenance or study. Everyone is working for promotion, qualifications, or just a field of interest. I hadn't expected that!

Something else I didn't expect was to find one of the crew coming on to me - Roy Stubbs. At least, I think he is, it's hard to tell. The boys back home didn't behave like that. It's hard to know whether he's just being friendly or something more, but I could really do without it right now.

Chapter 3

The next day, Captain Darrow was alone on the bridge when a Priority One call came in. There had been an accident at a razor quartz mine on Pallas, an asteroid, and Kestrel was the closest ship for emergency response. The mission seemed straightforward, but the details were encoded, which puzzled him, so he decided to open it in his office. He changed course then called Lieutenant-Commander Hoy to take over the bridge.

Hoy arrived and saluted.

'What's up, sir?'

Darrow raised an eyebrow.

'Sorry sir. Lieutenant-Commander Hoy reporting for duty.'

'That's better. Now, "what's up" is a mining accident on Pallas. I've already changed course.'

Hoy frowned. 'Pallas, that's an asteroid isn't it? A razor quartz mine - unusually large crystals.'

Darrow was impressed. He got up and Hoy took the seat.

Hoy's face fell. 'Will I have to go underground, sir?'

'That will be up to Commander Holland. He'll be drawing up the assignments.'

As Darrow took the few steps to his office behind the bridge, he reflected on Hoy's claustrophobia. Hoy had struggled the first time he donned a space suit, but had managed to concentrate on the view, and the panic had passed. He had fought the claustrophobia because of his desire to work in space, and, with counselling, he made it. But how would he cope underground?

Once in his office, Darrow entered the security code and unpacked the data burst which had arrived with the accident report. The report came via Chert, the mining company, and the reason for the security was the suspicion of sabotage.

The report included several reports regarding missing razor quartz. The company was suspicious that the explosion was staged to cover up the thefts. The word that caught Darrow's attention was "mystery" - the miners claimed it was a mystery how the quartz disappeared. Darrow had always had a fascination for mysteries and collected stories from across the galaxy. He mentally added this one to the list, as he called Holland and Robinson to his office.

The office had a chair either side of the desk and drop-down seating for another four around the walls, plus another console that pulled out from the wall as well as the one on the desk. As the senior rank, Holland took the seat across the desk, while Robinson pulled down a seat. They both carried electronic pads for taking notes.

'We've been ordered to assist with emergency aid after an accident at a razor quartz mine on Pallas, an asteroid,' Darrow said, once they were seated. 'What we know so far is there was an explosion and a cave-in, and there are casualties.' He brought up on screen the pictures and schematics from the data burst.

'We'll need to programme the maintenance 'bots for digging,' Holland said, making notes, 'and we'll need the force lifters. I'll speak to Commander Blackwell.'

'We may need EVA suits as well,' Robinson said. 'The dome may have been damaged in the explosion.'

Darrow checked the report again.

'They reported a crack, but they'll fix that first. Unfortunately their comms are down, so we can't ask. They got the mayday out via the direct line to Chert, the mining company. Chert alerted PACT. Best check out the suits just in case.'

'That razor quartz is nasty,' Robinson said, 'it didn't get its name by accident. What races are the personnel?' he asked, leaning forward to scan the report. 'I need to know what medical aid to prepare.'

'Human only, to make facility provision simpler.' Darrow zoomed in to the relevant details on screen. 'There are 25 personnel - 12 miners, 3 support staff and 10 family members.'

'At least it will give the crew something to do,' Robinson said, tucking a stray lock of hair behind his ear. 'With all this personnel trouble the crew are quite unsettled. I know this trainee will be an extra pair of hands, but I'm not sure it's wise.'

Darrow stiffened. *Is that a criticism?* he thought. 'She will also give the crew something to do,' Darrow said. 'There's no better way of testing your knowledge than trying to explain it to someone else.'

Holland and Robinson sat back and looked at Darrow in expectant silence.

'So what's the mystery, sir?' Holland said when Darrow didn't respond. 'Why the security coding?'

Darrow sighed and turned his thoughts away from the crew problems. 'Over the last few weeks the miners have reported several incidents of quartz going missing, quartz they say they didn't steal. Chert aren't convinced, and now with this explosion, they think it may be sabotage to cover up the thefts. They want me to investigate. Don't tell the crew about this; just tell them to keep their eyes open and report in detail. Let them think it's for the accident investigation.'

'Maybe it'll take the crew's mind off all the upset,' Robinson said. 'Two gone and Mike going - that's a big hole.'

Back to the crew problems, Darrow thought.

'Yes, it's unfortunate it's all come at the same time,' Holland agreed. 'It was bad timing, my promotion coming straight after Lanx's, but with Balitoth's emergency as well …' he leaned forward, 'You're going to need a good First Officer to make them a team.'

'*If* Personnel can get their act together and find us another First Officer,' Robinson interrupted. 'I'm sorry Mike, but they shouldn't have promoted you without a replacement available.'

'Now now, Doctor, let's avoid insurrection,' Darrow smiled, 'you could be court marshalled, and then we'd lose another crew member.' He became serious. 'And it's Commander Holland, not Mike.'

He turned to Holland. 'I'm relying on you to help them through it, and to help Trainee Enns get settled. Make sure she's well supervised if you let her help.' On seeing Holland roll his eyes, Darrow added, 'Were you hoping for an easy ride before you leave us?'

Robinson interrupted, 'Not Mike - Commander Holland, he loves to be in the thick of it. I wouldn't be surprised if he goes looking for trouble on his new ship.' He slapped Holland on the shoulder, who gave an embarrassed grin.

'I'm not that bad, but I must admit I was hoping for some action. And there's a puzzle to solve too.'

'Not for you, Commander, leave that investigation to me,' said Darrow.

'*Captain* Holland is just looking for some excitement before he leaves,' said Robinson with a grin.

'Well, Captain Holland is still *Commander* Holland at the moment,' smiled Darrow. 'You two take charge of the mine rescue and leave me to handle the mystery. Dismissed.'

* * *

With preparations underway, Darrow turned again to the mystery. The details were sparse: The miners had reported two incidents of quartz missing from the stores. The inventory was correct one day and out the next, with no sign of tampering. Everyone was denying responsibility, the base had been searched and the men were angry. They had put a guard on the stores who had foiled a third attempt, but there was no sign of the culprit. The guard said the electronically-locked door opened on its own. He claimed he saw a shimmering figure in the dim light, which disappeared when he shone a torch in its direction. The mining company didn't believe a word. Quartz does not disappear on its own.

Actually, Darrow was inclined to believe the miners, because he had heard of such things before. Among his collection of mysteries he had spotted a pattern. Raw materials were disappearing all over the galaxy, but because it never happened in the same place twice, no one else seemed to have made the link. In some instances the thefts were associated with an equally mysterious death - and the cause of death could not be determined.

Darrow had contacts on many planets and had asked them to investigate the incidents. He was convinced the incidents were linked, and his contacts were starting to agree with him. He thought the galaxy was being raided by an unknown race invisible in normal spectrum light. He thought of them as "Intruders". But when he submitted a report to his superiors, they were not convinced. Procedure was procedure, but he was being knocked back by his superiors, and however much it grated with him, he had to follow this through.

He contacted his Kohathi friend, Calneh, from planet Dedan with this latest piece of news. The Kohathi looked like old human men, but lived much longer than humans. On screen, Calneh's bewhiskered Kohathi face was beaming.

'Joseph my friend, good to hear from you.' Calneh's soft voice rose in pitch. 'I have some news!'

'So do I,' said Darrow, 'that's why I called. How are you?'

'All is well here. You must tell me your news first. Has there been another incident?'

'Yes, and more than one. They've tried to steal razor quartz crystals from a mine on three separate occasions.' He couldn't keep the excitement from his voice. 'And I get to investigate myself this time.'

Calneh smiled, then became serious. 'They must want those crystals badly. I fear this is an escalation of their campaign. Be careful Joseph.'

Darrow nodded and changed the subject. 'What was your news?'

'There has been another incident here too. Well, not here, on Kohath. The search engine picked it up. There was a death, and maybe because it was someone known to him, the pathologist was more diligent in determining the cause of death. He still does not have a cause, but an unknown enzyme was found in the body.'

Darrow became even more excited. 'That's great news! I'm going to be tied up with this mission for a few days, so can you circulate it to the others and ask them to recheck the post mortems?'

'Certainly. Maybe your "Intruders" have finally left a clue.'

'Yes. Maybe these two things will be the proof we need of the "Intruders"' existence and the threat they pose. You chase up the enzyme and I'll be in touch when I finish my investigations.'

'Farewell my friend.'

'Goodbye.'

Darrow sat back with a smile on his face. Maybe this was the breakthrough he had been hoping for.

* * *

Holland came to see Darrow to discuss the initial crew assignments.

'With no communication we don't have the latest update, so I may have to make adjustments depending on what we find when we arrive,' Holland said. 'I think we should leave someone on board Kestrel during the rescue. If there *is* a saboteur, we have to protect the ship.'

'Good point. Commander Blackwell spoke with me and we've agreed Stubbs won't go underground. There's something in his past apparently.'

'Claustrophobia?'

'No, just a fear of going underground. So leave him on board.' He paused while Holland made alterations to the notes on his pad. 'Do you plan to send Hoy underground?

23

He *is* claustrophobic.'

'He's overcome it before. If he's going to be an officer, he has to get over it, or at least learn to deal with it.'

'You could assign him to co-ordinate the rescue work, while you go down to assess the situation underground.'

Darrow smiled to himself as Holland squirmed. He knew Holland would want to be in charge at the pithead.

'There'll be no need for that,' Holland said. 'The miners are the experts; they'll be able to tell us what the situation is and what's needed. I thought Dr Robinson should meet with their doctor and Commander Blackwell with their engineer, to assist them, and the rest I'll take to the mine. I'm not sure what use Reuel will be, he's not strong, so I was planning to leave him on board. He and Stubbs can stand guard. I can always call on him later if necessary.'

'So that means you'll be taking Hoy, Chambers and Ryan with you. Are you sure that will be enough?'

'I won't know until I speak to the miners, but I've checked and Pallas isn't very big, so the mine may not have a lot of room to move in.'

'What about Trainee Enns?'

'I'm not sure. She's enthusiastic and works hard, but she's barely had time to settle in. I could take her along for the experience I suppose.'

'Don't forget she grew up under 2.5G, so she's strong in standard grav. What's the gravity like on Pallas?'

Holland consulted his pad. 'Minimal on the surface, but they live under a dome with artificial gravity. So she'll seem even stronger there.'

'I've hardly spoken to her since she came on board. Let's call her in, see how she's getting on, and assess whether she could help.'

Tabitha arrived, nervously tugging her tunic straight.

'Trainee Enns reporting, Sir.'

'At ease, Trainee. Commander Holland tells me you've been working hard.'

'Yes sir, I want to make the most of my time here.'

'You know where we're going?'

'Yes sir. Pallas, it's an asteroid full of razor quartz crystals. There's been an accident at the mine, so there's liable to be severe lacerations as well as blast and crush injuries.'

'You've been doing some research.'

'Andrew, I mean, Lieutenant Chambers, has shown me how to use the console in our cabin.' She frowned. 'Will there be any gravity sir?'

'The domed base has artificial gravity,' Darrow said, 'unless it was damaged in the explosion. We'll be docking with the dome airlock, so you won't be out on the surface. The gravity will be set to 1G, since the miners are from Earth. How are you coping with 1G?'

Tabitha paused a moment, looking unsure. 'Dr Robinson is helping me … adjust.'

Careful choice of word there, Darrow thought.

'I just need to remember everything's so light.'

Holland smiled. He too had seen the hesitation, but didn't pursue it.

'Sir, if there's been a cave-in,' Tabitha continued, 'we'll have to dig them out, won't we?'

'Think you could help?'

Her face brightened. 'Yes sir, I used to help my Dad with the logging, so I'm used to heavy work.'

Darrow and Holland exchanged glances. Darrow nodded.

'Very well,' Holland said. 'Report to Lieutenant-Commander Hoy in fifteen minutes. Dismissed.'

So, Darrow thought after the others had left, *not only is Hoy going underground, but he's going to be babysitting.*

Chapter 4

Since Chambers had his own duties to take care of, Tabitha didn't see him until they met at the airlock after landing at Pallas. They were in the rear of the assembled crew.

Biting her lip in worry, she looked up at Chambers beside her. 'The Captain said I could help,' she whispered, 'but I'm not sure how useful I can be.'

'Don't worry,' Chambers said quietly, offering a reassuring smile, 'just stay alert and do as you're told.'

'I'm glad we don't have to wear suits.'

'As long as the dome is intact, they can control the atmosphere and gravity inside. You'll be fine.'

'This is my first alien soil, you know.'

'You mean you've never left Alpha?'

'Don't forget that Alphans don't want anything to do with the rest of the galaxy. I've been trying all my life to get away from there.'

'Now here you are - and here we go!'

The outer airlock doors opened and Chambers gently nudged her forward.

Her first sight of "alien soil" was a bit disappointing. Inside the dome the ground was rock, dry and dusty, and they were surrounded by low block buildings. The lighting obscured the sky, so there wasn't much to see, really. They could be in an industrial complex anywhere. *Even back on Alpha*, Tabitha thought. She couldn't entirely contain her disappointment, but she managed to internalise it.

The crew were met by an older man, grey haired and slim, but his musculature proved he was still fit. Recognising Darrow's yellow armband, he shook his hand.

'Wil Jones, Base Administrator. Excuse the dirt, Captain, we all muck in here. I'm glad the message got through.'

'I'm Captain Darrow. This is my MO, Dr Robinson, and

my Engineer, Commander Blackwell. If you direct them, they can help your doctor and engineer. This is my First Officer, Commander Holland and most of our crew. We've brought digging and lifting equipment. If you brief Commander Holland, they are at your disposal. Then I'd like to meet with you and get an overview of the situation.'

Jones introduced the younger man with him.

'This is shift leader Gareth Davies,' Jones told Holland, 'He'll take you to the mine and brief you.'

'Do you have a scanner that detects life-signs?' Davies asked. 'Huw and John are missing, and we don't know if they're under the cave-in or beyond it.'

Holland indicated Ryan's backpack. 'In here,' he said.

* * *

Davies led everyone away and Jones gave directions to Robinson and Blackwell before inviting Darrow into his office.

Jones' office was utilitarian, but Darrow noticed the personal touches - a family photograph, a trophy, a child's drawing. Jones moved a pad off a chair and they sat down. Everything was covered in a fine layer of rock dust.

'There was an explosion on Level Three,' Jones began, 'which caused a cave-in, bringing down Level Two above. The explosion also damaged the communications array and cracked the pit dome. We had to repair the crack before anything else, so the mine rescue has barely started. The men on Level Two sustained minor injuries, but Elwyn on Level Three was badly hurt. Luckily he was this side of the cave-in, so we managed to get him out quite quickly. John and Huw are missing. We don't know if they're under the rubble or beyond it. Our scanners are set to detect the quartz voids, not life-signs.'

'We have a scanner that will do that. I'm sure Commander Holland is seeing to it already. Any idea what caused the explosion?' Darrow asked, watching for Jones' reaction.

'Not so far, we've been concentrating on the results, not the cause. Razor quartz grows into a void, you know, and sometimes when we break through there's a pocket of gas. The gas can be highly volatile, but the men carry meters and dispersal equipment. We'll need to check the meters once we get them out.'

'Let's hope we find them safe. What's the progress on the rescue?'

Jones sighed. 'Slow so far. We all had to wear suits in case the dome went, and there's not much room in the shaft.'

'Hopefully progress will be swift now we're here to help.' Darrow paused. 'Chert asked me to look into the possibility of sabotage.'

Jones swore. 'It's because of the missing quartz, isn't it? I told the men if we were honest, it would prove our innocence. The company has made me a liar!' Jones' Welsh accent got stronger.

Darrow watched him closely. 'Look, they sent me your reports, but why don't you tell me in your own words?' He leaned back and put his foot across his knee.

Jones took a deep breath.

'Sean Parry, the Stock Controller, came to see me and said the tally was out. I thought he meant there had been a miscount or an inventory error. But a whole container of the stuff had gone. That's impossible. A cubic metre of razor quartz weighs over two and a half tonnes at 1G. The stores is in the pit dome, but even at one quarter G it's quite a weight, and awkward. How do you move that much quartz without being seen? And where would you put it? We can easily see ships approaching, and there hadn't been a single one. We hushed it up, but most of the men found out. Less than a month after, it happened again. I had to question the men, do some sort of investigation. There was a riot. You must understand, Captain, we only get a basic wage, a pittance. We earn our money on the bonuses for the tonnage mined. We're a close-knit community - have to be, stuck out here. I've sacked people just for not fitting in. No one would do that to the others. If we can't rely on each other, the whole operation falls apart.'

Jones stood up and paced while he continued the story.

'Everyone denied all knowledge, of course. We searched the base for any trace of quartz outside the stores and the pit. There was none. We even searched the old opencast workings. Nothing. The men wanted me to keep quiet, but the carrier is due soon, and what if we can't replace the quartz in time? No, I insisted the only way to show we had nothing to do with it, was to report it. We wouldn't report ourselves for theft, now would we?'

'There was a third incident,' Darrow prompted.

'Ah yes, now that was different. Sean decided to set a guard on the stores. The men took turns, and one night the guard heard a sound and saw the stores door seemed to be opening by itself. He shone a light, and whatever it was, vanished.'

'"Whatever it was"?'

'He said he saw a figure, like an angel.' Jones waved his hands in exasperation. 'But there's no sign of it on the video records. Probably sleeping at his post and he dreamed it.'

'You've got video records? Wasn't it dark?'

'It's never completely dark here, we keep a low level of lighting even on the off-shift for the benefit of those who have to be about. We only work two shifts here, there's not enough men for three, and not enough accommodation for more men.'

Darrow leaned back in his chair. 'Sit down, Mr Jones, I want to tell you something.'

Jones raised an eyebrow and sat down. Darrow leaned forward and dropped his voice.

'I need your word you will keep confidential what I'm about to tell you.'

Jones nodded.

'Your incidents appear to fit into a pattern I've discovered.' He raised a hand. 'Nothing's proven yet, but my investigation here may give us something. There have been raw materials disappearing all over the galaxy with no evidence of what happened. So, while my crew helps with the rescue, I'm going to look into this missing quartz and see what I can find.'

Jones considered for a moment, then gave a curt nod and got to his feet.

'It's time I checked on progress.'

'I'll come with you.'

* * *

As Gareth Davies led them to the mine, Tabitha looked him over. He was ruggedly built, a perfect specimen of the manual labour involved in mining, yet he moved with grace. On Alpha, the men were cumbersome and awkward. She was fascinated and tried not to stare.

'Can you explain the setup here?' Holland asked as they made their way across the dome, followed by the diggers and lifters.

'The pit is in a separate dome attached to this one,' said Davies. 'It means we can keep the air separate in case of a gas release from a new void, and we can have different gravity too. We maintain 1G in the main dome, because that's what we're used to, and it means there's no adjustments when we go home on leave. But in the pit dome it makes sense to reduce the gravity to make the machinery and the quartz easier to handle. We keep it at one quarter G, just enough to stop things floating about, so you'll feel it change in the airlock.' He looked around. 'I hope you all know what you're doing in low gravity.'

Tabitha caught Chambers' eye and shook her head, her eyes wide.

'Just take things slowly and listen to Lieutenant-Commander Hoy,' he whispered.

'Lower gravity in the mine is a great idea,' Holland was saying to Davies. 'Does it take long to get used to switching gravities all the time?'

Davies smiled, 'It can take a while. We have bets on how quickly new guys will adapt.'

'Well, we've brought you some new people to bet on.' Holland grinned.

'Now you're here we can give some of the men a much-needed break,' said Davies, 'and if necessary we'll be able to operate round the clock.'

They crowded into the airlock, and Tabitha's heart sank as she read the warning signs about the gravity. *I'm still trying to cope with 1G,* she thought, *what will this be like?*

As the airlock cycled and the gravity reduced, Davies pointed out the handrails. 'There are handrails and grip points everywhere. Let's get you kitted out and get that scanner down to find those men.'

Davies stepped out of the airlock without a second thought and launched himself in a graceful leap towards the pithead. Tabitha understood why he was so graceful. The rest of the Kestrel crew were more careful, moving with varying degrees of confidence. Tabitha felt so light she was afraid to move. Chambers took her arm and stabilised her as they followed the others.

Davies handed out breathing masks, goggles and heavy gloves. 'The air can get full of dust when we're digging, so these are mandatory - these razor quartz crystals really are razor sharp. Before you go down, there is something important you need to know: the crystals respond to noise, and certain frequencies of sound can cause a resonance overload. The whole mine rings with it. So keep the noise down when you're underground. Here we are.'

"Here" was a hole in the ground with a winch at one side. There were rungs set in the shaft wall.

Davies introduced two men. 'This is Dai Williams. He's organising work on Level Two above the cave-in. Arwel Hughes is on Level Three starting to dig into the rubble. The two levels run almost parallel, so if, as we hope, the men are beyond the cave-in, we should be able to reach them from above.'

'Ryan, you go down to Level Two with the scanner,' Holland said. 'Chambers, you're with him. Hoy, take Enns down to Level Three with Mr Hughes.'

Dai Williams stepped over the rim of the shaft and allowed himself to fall, controlling his descent by tapping on the rungs.

Ryan looked back and grimaced. 'Forget it,' he said, and used the rungs as a ladder. Chambers followed suit.

Tabitha held on tightly to a handrail and hung back while the first team descended.

Meanwhile, Davies took Holland to a console and hooked his feet under a bar at the base. Holland did the same. Davies called up a 3D map of the mine. Tabitha craned to see.

'When it was surveyed this asteroid was found to be a honeycomb structure. Every void has huge quartz crystals growing on the walls.'

'So this place is full of holes,' said Holland, with a smile.

Davies didn't get the joke. 'Exactly,' he said. 'Originally they mined the quartz using opencast methods, but it was too awkward, so they sank a shaft and worked from that. It also meant we could have a dome and not work in suits.' He pointed to the map. 'There are three levels which run almost parallel, although, since we go from one void to the next, the tunnels are not straight. We've got a man on Level Two who has scrambled across the cave-in and is drilling a pilot hole at the place where the tunnels next cross. Let's hope he's not wasting his time.'

Chapter 5

Once the rescue team had left the Kestrel, Reuel and Stubbs settled down together on the bridge, watching the external cameras. Reuel turned to the communications console.

Stubbs reached out and stopped him. 'What are you doing?'

'I must have news of Balitoth.' Reuel's cranial spines quivered with his distress. 'I thought I would contact the Alphan medical facility myself to find out how he is.'

'You'll only get yourself into trouble. Do you think Dr Robinson is hiding something?'

'Oh no. The doctor has been kind to me, but I cannot bear the waiting.'

'It's strange, you know, how you two have become such good friends. It seems so unlikely a Zoan and an Altairian would have anything in common.'

Reuel laughed and his spines quietened. 'What we have in common is being on a ship full of humans! And an interest in football.'

'What? You like football - is that an Altairian or Zoan game too?'

'Certainly not. Altairians would not demean themselves and Zoans would probably kill each other. No, we discovered we both liked watching the human game. It is a strangely bonding experience.'

Stubbs snorted. 'You could say that.'

Reuel frowned. 'I just did. You must not stereotype the different species, Roy. Commander Holland decided not to send me down the mine because he didn't think I would be strong enough. But I am strong in lighter gravity, which they have in the mine. Why are you not with them? You are strong, are you not?'

Now it was Stubbs' turn to be agitated. 'I can't go

underground.'

'Is it … what is the word? Fear of enclosed spaces?'

Stubbs hesitated. 'No. It's … my brother. He worked underground. There was an accident -'

'Say no more my friend, I understand.'

Reuel began to make a crooning noise in his throat. Stubbs had never heard it before, and he found it strangely soothing.

*   *   *

In the mine, when Ryan and Chambers reached Level Two behind Williams, he took them to the edge of the cave-in and looked them over sceptically.

'You don't look much. Are you going to be able to handle the heavy work?'

'Actually Mr Williams, I come from Orion 3, a reversionist colony,' Ryan said. 'They don't use technology if they can do without. I grew up on a farm, so I'm used to heavy work.'

Williams looked at Chambers.

'Let's just get on with it shall we?' Chambers said. 'How heavy can it be, in low gravity?'

Williams grunted. 'The cave-in below brought down their roof - our floor, in mostly one great slab,' he said. 'It's dropped about two metres, but it's not level, and there's a lot of rubble. Which one of you is going to scramble over to Rhys Jenkins with that scanner?'

He pointed to a hunched figure further down the tunnel, who was working with a small drill.

'I'll go,' said Ryan. 'I know the scanner best.'

The nearest end of the slab was nearly three metres down, but Ryan sat on the edge and dropped, falling slowly enough that he landed easily. He then scrambled over the rubble to the other end, about six metres away. He jumped up and caught himself with straight arms on the tunnel floor and levered himself up. He immediately got to work with the scanner and soon reported life signs below where Jenkins was drilling.

'Right,' said Williams after he had radioed the news to the pithead. 'You start clearing any rubble that end - throw it down onto the slab to make a way down. We'll do the same this end.'

Ryan's end of the cave-in didn't have much rubble, and it hadn't dropped as far. Once he had cleared most of it, he climbed down onto the slab and tried to arrange the rubble into a crude set of steps. Williams came over with a gun-like implement which melted the rock and made it smoother. Then Ryan joined Chambers at the other end.

They had been warned about the danger of noise and reverberation, but the noisy machinery, they were reassured, didn't emit the right resonance for long enough bursts to start a resonance overload in the crystals. What it did do was spit plenty of rock dust into the air, dust that reduced visibility and soon covered them all in a fine layer that seemed to pass through the fabric of their clothes and act like sandpaper in the creases of their skin.

Chambers wasn't used to manual labour and the low gravity meant he sometimes moved himself instead of a rock. He had to concentrate on bracing himself before he pushed.

'How's it going?' Ryan whispered.

'OK, but I'm not used to this sort of work. Luckily in this gravity things aren't so heavy.' He scowled. 'They should have sent Stubbs down. I'll bet he's crowing over it while he puts his feet up on board.'

'What is it with you and Stubbs? Why don't you get on?'

'It's not me, it's him. He found out about my accident and asked for a transfer. Says he doesn't feel safe with me at the helm. Jumped-up little grunt! The Captain refused.'

'To me that says he doesn't trust the captain's judgement, which is dangerous territory,' Ryan said.

'Captain Darrow's been good to me - gave me a chance when no one else would. But I don't like being made helmsman so soon. It puts me under pressure, and Stubbs doesn't help, with all his digs.'

'Well, you're not at the helm now, so enjoy yourself. Admire the scenery.'

Ryan swept his hand around and Chambers took in the view for the first time. The voids were roughly spherical, and the miners had levelled the floor by melting compacted rubble. The rubble included tiny pieces of quartz, so it glittered in the lights. The curved walls and ceiling ranged in height and width from two to four metres, as the voids varied in size. The cave-in had broken through into new voids, and there the quartz crystals glittered like diamonds, glinting in the light like sharpened razors.

Chambers found himself breathless at the strangely beautiful sight.

* * *

As Hoy and Tabitha prepared to go down the shaft to Level Three, Hoy kept up a running commentary of advice.

'Don't make any sudden or extreme moves. Do everything gently, and ensure you are braced before you push or lift anything. Otherwise you'll just push yourself backwards.'

Arwel Hughes, the miner they were with, grabbed one of the maintenance robots in one hand and stepped over the edge. The other machines were fixed to the hoist and sent down. Tabitha was grateful that Hoy opted for using the rungs as a ladder. She followed him down, praying that she wouldn't make a fool of herself on her first mission.

As they made their way down the rungs Tabitha said, 'I feel sick.'

'Don't you dare,' said Hoy. 'Vomit can travel a long way in low gravity. Concentrate on what you're doing and you'll be fine.'

The trip down the shaft only took a few minutes, but Tabitha worried Hoy would be angry with her as she had to take it slowly. He did seem rather agitated, and breathed deeply through his mask. Despite the filter he still managed to draw dust in, which made him cough. With every cough from Hoy, Tabitha felt her own stomach clench, her palms sweat. She felt as if the shaft got narrower as it dropped, she feared they would get stuck any minute. This only passed when they reached the bottom and there was room to move. When they entered Level Three visibility improved and Tabitha stopped and gasped.

'It's beautiful! It reminds me of pictures I saw once of a cathedral.'

'You're not here to admire the view,' said Hughes. 'Come and see the problem, and keep your voice down.'

Tabitha ducked her head to hide her red face. Hughes led them down the tunnel to the cave-in.

'Level Two have reported that their floor has dropped in one great slab,' he said, 'so for the moment we're not going to try to clear it. They are using it to reach the place above where the men are trapped. What's needed is to clear the loose stuff and put in more supports so no more comes down.'

Tabitha thought she and Hoy made a strange looking pair, but with his guidance and her strength they were able to accomplish a lot. She was puzzled why Hoy kept talking all the time, while they shifted rubble and put in shoring posts, but just assumed he was being helpful to her, and was grateful.

'You're getting the hang of it now.' Hoy said. 'Gently and slowly, that's it. How's your sickness?'

'Actually, sir, it's gone. It's strange, but being down here in such a small space makes me feel heavier. Do you know what I mean?'

Hoy took a deep breath and coughed in the dust. 'Let's get a move on. The sooner we finish, the sooner we can get out of here.'

As they worked, Tabitha was amazed at Hoy's size and his elegance. He was only a little taller than her, but much less broad. Yet he was strong, quick in his movements, and graceful in the low gravity. They discovered that the end of the slab was unsupported. Tabitha suggested they use a lifter underneath to try to raise the slab a little, but Hughes wouldn't allow it.

'We don't know what pressure the slab is under. Best pack rubble under it and stabilise it.'

Hoy looked at the spare roof supports.

'Can you cut these down without weakening them? We could use a couple and crank them up to support the slab.'

Hughes nodded. He took his hand cutter from his belt and cut one to size.

'This needs to be as far under as we can get it.'

Someone had to wriggle under the slab to put the support in position. Hughes looked at Hoy, the smallest of the three. There was a moment's hesitation, then Hoy sighed and took the support. Once the supports were in place and cranked up, they packed the rubble around them. It didn't take long. When Hughes was satisfied, they reported to Holland, who ordered them back to the Kestrel for a break.

Chapter 6

Following directions to the medical centre, Robinson introduced himself to a young man and asked for the doctor.

'I am the doctor!' the man laughed. 'Maybe I should grow a beard! I'm Dr Simon Thomas, and I'm really glad you're here.'

They shook hands.

'When the explosion went off, I rushed down to the pit, but they ordered everyone into suits in case the dome ruptured. Only then could I do anything for the injured, and it's hard in a suit. I've treated the two miners from Level Two - they only had minor injuries, and we had two casualties outside the mine - little Rhi fell down the stairs in the rush, and landed on her Mum. Rhi broke her arm, and Mum has concussion. But then they got Elwyn out and he was badly hurt. Really pushed me to my limits treating him. I had to get creative, which is why I'd be grateful for your advice. Come and see him, and I'll explain on the way.'

To Robinson's surprise, Thomas handed him a breather and led the way out of the medical centre.

'Where is he?' Robinson asked.

'In the stores airlock,' Thomas laughed. 'I told you I had to get creative. Elwyn had contusions and lacerations, as you'd expect, but he also had severe blast damage to his lungs and a broken spine. He will probably need new lungs, and I don't know whether his spine can be repaired. This is beyond my expertise. I've no stasis chamber, and I needed to ease his breathing and the pressure on his spine. I could have put a mask on him, but what about his spine? So he's in the airlock, where I can increase the oxygen content of the atmosphere, introduce medication including sedative for him to breathe in, and reduce the gravity, to ease the pressure on his spine. What do you think?'

'I'm impressed,' Robinson said.

They reached the airlock that led into the mine dome. Robinson was alarmed when he saw the signs about the low gravity, but followed Thomas' lead and used the handrails as they came out. Immediately on the left inside the mine dome was the quartz stores, a warehouse-like building with a pressure door. The man on duty keyed the door open for them and closed it behind them. Large containers were stacked in rows from floor to ceiling, filling more than half of the space. They walked down the central aisle.

'Why is there an airlock at the back of the stores?' Robinson asked.

'That's how they collect the ore. It doesn't make sense to take it through the main dome. The carrier lands on the surface, links to the airlock and takes it out that way. We'll have to take Elwyn out that way too.'

Robinson stopped walking. 'What?'

'You do have a stasis chamber, don't you?'

'Yes, but...'

'We can't move Elwyn to your ship through the main dome, because he can't take normal gravity. We'll have to take him round the outside.'

Robinson was appalled. He had had low gravity training of course, you couldn't avoid it, but he hadn't enjoyed it one bit. Since then he had always made his medic do that sort of thing, and treated the casualties when they reached normal gravity again.

'My medic, Sam Ryan, is down in the mine.' Robinson said quickly, as they set off again. 'When I've examined Elwyn I'll contact Commander Holland and get Ryan sent over to help you.'

'Very well.' Thomas shrugged. 'I just hope he's experienced enough. I'm really nervous of moving him and causing more damage.'

They reached the airlock door.

'You'll need to wear the breather in the airlock, otherwise you'll get a dose of medication too.'

The gravity in the airlock was low, but not zero.

'I wanted some gravity, otherwise I'd have had to tether him down, and he's got enough equipment on him as it is,' said Thomas, as he tucked his feet under the bar at the base of the bed.

Robinson did the same, and examined the injured man.

'You have real skill with a regenerator. I can barely see the scars where you've repaired the lacerations, and I can't see any trace of bruising.'

'Thank you. I get plenty of practice with the miners. Razor quartz crystals are like scalpels, you know. One slip, and it can slice right through your glove. And there are always bumps and bruises. With the low gravity in the pit it does minimise broken bones, but we do get a few, especially with new arrivals, until they get used to it. What's your diagnosis?'

Robinson sighed. 'You were right. You've done a good job, but he's going to need stasis and transport to a specialist medical facility. Where can I contact Ryan?'

* * *

Captain Darrow went to see Sean Parry, the Stock Controller, in his office adjacent to the pithead. He was not welcomed.

'Wil Jones asked me to help you, but I don't have to like it. There's none of us thieving here, Captain.'

Darrow withdrew his outstretched hand, since Parry was ignoring it.

'I'm on your side, Mr Parry. If I can show I investigated fully and found no fault with anyone, it will go in your favour with Chert. I've read the reports. I want to hear your view on things.'

Parry looked at him for a long moment, while Darrow waited. This was his chance to search for evidence first hand. Parry grunted, but he sat down at a console and waved Darrow to a chair. Darrow smiled to himself.

'What do you want to know?' Parry asked.

* * *

Before Darrow went to the old mine-workings he wanted to talk to Stefan Kozlik. At his apartment, Kozlik's wife opened the door. She recognised Darrow's uniform.

'You must be the Captain from the rescue ship.'

'Yes, Mrs Kozlik, Captain Joseph Darrow. May I speak to your husband?'

'He's asleep at the moment, but come in and let me make you a cup of tea. He won't be long.'

The apartment was like Mrs Kozlik - neat as a pin. Not a thing out of place, and everything that could shine, shone. She was a tall woman and carried herself stiffly, and watching her bustling about, Darrow wondered if she ever kept still. Such constant movement would drive him mad. He wondered what Kozlik was like, and how he coped.

'I'm looking into the disappearance of the quartz. I understand your husband saw something.'

She turned to him with a fierce look. 'I hope you've not come to mock. If my Stefan says he saw something, then there was definitely something there, whatever they say.'

'What's all the noise, woman? Can't a man have peace to sleep?'

A square-cut, muscular man came into the room wearing only trousers, rubbing his hand across his short hair. Darrow rose to his feet.

'Mr Kozlik, I'm Captain Darrow. I was hoping to speak with you about the missing quartz.'

A shadow crossed the man's face.

'I have an open mind,' Darrow said. 'I just want to hear your side of the story.'

Kozlik motioned him to sit down, took a freshly-pressed shirt from a hanger and put it on.

'Make us some tea, Mother, and some of your cake.'

He sat down and pulled his chair closer to Darrow's.

'I was on guard at the door to the stores, while my arm was mending.' He flexed his wrist. 'It was night period, but I wasn't sleeping - I had slept in the afternoon, so I would be fresh for the night shift. We only run two shifts here, as there aren't enough men for three, but we keep the lights on low during night period, for those who have to work.' He took a mug from his wife and drank, then continued. 'I heard the door open - it's well-maintained, but you can't move something that heavy without some noise. I looked up and there was a figure by the door. It kind of shimmered, so I couldn't make it out clear. It looked sort of human, but with something from the shoulders, like small wings, but I can't be sure.' He grabbed Darrow's shoulder. 'But it wasn't a ghost, I swear!'

The grip on Darrow's shoulder demonstrated how strong this man was. 'Calm down Stefan, I'm not making any judgments, I'm just gathering facts. I want to know exactly what you saw and heard. Was there any indication someone was there before the noise of the door lock?'

'No, nothing.' He stopped and took a bite out of his cake, watching Darrow.

Darrow drank his tea, and simply nodded, but his heart leapt.

'When I turned my torch on it, the figure instantly disappeared,' Kozlik continued. 'I shouted and activated the lights in the stores, but there was no sign of anyone and no sign of tampering. So I called Sean Parry, and he came running. He checked, but there was nothing missing. I can show you if you like.'

'That would be great,' Darrow said, getting to his feet. 'Thank you for the tea and cake, Mrs Kozlik.'

Kozlik put his boots on and led Darrow to the mine dome, navigating the airlock and the change in gravity without a thought. Darrow scrambled to keep up. At the stores a man got out of a chair and came to meet them with a smile on his face.

'Someone new to tell your ghost stories to, eh Stefan?'

Before Kozlik could react, Darrow said, 'Actually, I think there might be something in it. Were you sitting here Mr Kozlik, when it happened?

'Yes. The figure was over there, to the left of the door.'

Darrow turned to the guard. 'Have you seen or heard anything unusual Mr - ?'

'Pavel Patla,' the guard replied. 'No, everything's been boringly normal. Hey, Stefan, don't take it so hard, I was only joking.'

'Well the joke's wearing a bit thin,' said Kozlik. 'Captain, do you really think there was something?'

Darrow tried not to show his excitement. *After all,* he thought, *I still don't have any evidence.* 'I've still got an open mind. Mr Parry gave me a copy of the video record, and I'm going to get my Engineer to examine it, to see if we can find anything.'

He had brought an electron scanner, which he passed over the lock. 'Maybe this will tell us something. Thank you for your help.'

He left the men and contacted Commander Blackwell.

'How are the repairs going on the communications array?'

'They won't take long, sir. The damage wasn't much, but it's fiddly to replace.'

'I've got a video record I want you to take a look at. See if anything else shows up under a different light spectrum, and anything else you can think of trying. There's an electron scan too. I'm going back to the Kestrel now, so I'll leave them in Engineering for you.'

'Yes sir. I'll get to it as soon as I finish here.'

Chapter 7

Dr Robinson went to contact Ryan about the casualty transfer, when the call came that Level Two had broken through to the trapped miners and established communications. A doctor was needed urgently. Since Dr Thomas was treating Elwyn, Robinson responded, thinking he could send Ryan back once he got there. He fumbled his way to the pithead and carefully climbed down the rungs in the shaft, much to the miners' impatience. On Level Two he was met by Dai Williams who helped him over the rubble steps, across the slab, and up the other end to where Ryan crouched with a monitor and a microphone. Ryan covered the mike and reported.

'They've drilled a pilot hole down to the void where the men are trapped, and lowered a camera and microphone. The dark-haired man is Huw and the fairer one is John. They've got contusions, and severe lacerations from the razor quartz - they fell into a new void. But Huw says John hit his head. When you finish, they'll start enlarging the hole.'

'Thank you, Ryan.' Robinson took the microphone. 'Hello there, I'm Dr Robinson from the Kestrel. Now we know where you are, we'll have you out as soon as we can. Now, John, can you tell me about your injuries?'

At the sound of his name, the fair haired man opened his eyes.

'It's hard to hear you from so far away, and I've got this headache. I'm awful uncomfortable, I think I'm bleeding on my back and legs. A bit bashed about too. Can you get me out?'

He started to move, but gasped in pain and fell back. The dark haired man spoke.

'You lie still John. Hello, Dr Robinson, I'm Huw. John

45

hit his head when we fell. I cut up my jacket and bandaged it. We're cut up pretty badly - John's arm is the worst, but I put a tourniquet on with my belt.'

'Where did you learn to apply a tourniquet?'

'My father was a miner, his friend died from loss of blood, so he taught me. We're bleeding from too many places, Doctor. You have to get us out fast.'

'I'll leave that to your colleagues. They're all prepared. As soon as the hole is large enough, we'll get pain relief and bandages down to you.'

Robinson turned away from the mic to speak to Ryan. 'There's a casualty needs taking to the Kestrel via the outside, not through the dome. I want you to assist Dr Thomas and I'll stay here.'

Ryan's eyes went wide and he shook his head. 'I've little experience in zero gravity, sir, I don't know if I can do it. What's wrong with the casualty?'

'Lung and spine damage, that's why he can't take the gravity in the base.'

'Sir, I'm not qualified for that. The base doctor will have to be responsible for the patient, I'll just try to assist with the transport.'

Robinson paused for thought. Ryan was right, he wasn't qualified to go. Robinson would have to go himself, much as he feared it. He put his hand on Ryan's shoulder, shook his head and turned back to the mic.

'Huw, I'm leaving my medic, Sam Ryan to monitor you both. Is there anything else you want?'

'A stiff drink would be my favourite, but I guess it has to be water.'

'I think we can manage better than that, but alcohol wouldn't be a good idea right now. Any changes, or anything you need, tell Ryan straight away. I have to go and help Dr Thomas with Elwyn's treatment.'

He gave Ryan instructions before he left.

'I'll get supplies sent over from the Kestrel, including a life signs monitor - get it on John straight away. I'm going out on the surface, so I won't be available, but keep me updated on progress and I'll be back as soon as I can. Try to keep them talking, we don't want them losing consciousness.'

* * *

Nervously Robinson followed Thomas back into the stores and got dressed in a suit. Thomas saw his hesitation.

'Bit rusty, eh? Don't worry, it's something you never forget. It'll come back to you once we get out there.'

Thomas helped him with the fastenings and checked everything was working. Robinson in turn checked Thomas' suit, and they were ready.

'Now, there is some gravity out there, caused by the spin of the asteroid,'Thomas said. 'Just enough so you won't float away, and your boots are weighted, so that helps you stay upright too. Just one word of warning, keep watch, because the voids come up close to the surface in places, and the crust can get quite thin. Let's go.'

The airlock cycled and the door to the outside opened. Robinson was captivated by the desolation. The surface of the asteroid was barren, gently undulating, and covered in dust. While Robinson was contemplating the view, Thomas set off, so Robinson's first step was a stumble, as his hold on the stretcher pulled him over the threshold.

'Watch out there,' Thomas called, pausing.

Robinson grabbed the stretcher and carefully regained his balance. *It did come back to me after all,* he thought, as he automatically didn't flail about, but slowly brought things under control.

Thomas led the way, the stretcher carried between them. They kept close to the dome, and after a short time the Kestrel came into sight around the curve. Robinson was eager to get back inside, and began to walk faster, swinging the stretcher round until he was walking almost parallel with Thomas. His eyes were on their destination and he failed to see a dark patch ahead. It was a hole. Robinson's right foot went in, he sank past his knee and a sharp edge cut into his calf. The other knee wrenched as it hit the ground, and pain juddered through the joint. He cried out and fell forward.

Thomas pulled the stretcher from Robinson's grasp and guided it to the ground, then came to Robinson's side.

'Are you all right?' he asked. 'Can I help you out?'

Robinson reached out to him.

'Get me out quick. I think I've dislocated my knee, and I'm bleeding.'

'Bleeding?' Thomas drew back.

Robinson couldn't think for the pain. 'Yes, something sharp cut my leg, I can feel the blood running. Give me a hand here.'

Thomas laid a restraining hand on his shoulder. 'Sorry. If you're bleeding then your suit is punctured. The sharp edge must be blocking the hole. It's vital you keep still. You'll have to stay where you are until I can get help. Let me see your oxygen reading.' Thomas checked. 'You *do* have a leak, but it's slow.' He spoke into the comm unit. 'Mayday, mayday! Kestrel do you hear me? Doctors Thomas and Robinson out on the surface near the dome. Assistance needed urgently!'

* * *

A melodious voice replied. 'This is Ensign Reuel on board Kestrel. What do you need?'

'Dr Robinson has had an accident. I need help to get a patient to your stasis chamber so I can bring the stretcher back for him.'

'I can give you that assistance. I have located your position. I will be with you shortly. Reuel out.'

Reuel was as good as his word. Within a few minutes Thomas saw a lithe figure almost flying towards them, as he pushed off the ground in huge strides. Reuel was in his element.

Thomas directed Reuel to take one end of the stretcher, but as they lifted it, Robinson panicked.

'You can't leave me!'

'We have no choice,' Thomas said. 'We have to get Elwyn off the stretcher so we can use it for you. We'll be as quick as we can. Try to stay calm and slow your breathing.'

And they were off. Reuel slowed down to accommodate Thomas, but went in front, so he pulled him along with the stretcher.

'Dr Thomas, this is Ensign Stubbs on the Kestrel. I see your approach. I have cycled the airlock and put our stasis chamber inside so you can transfer your patient without coming on board. The airlock will be open for you in one minute. Notify me when you have left again. I will take the chamber back to sick bay and leave the airlock open.'

'Message received, Ensign Stubbs, and thank you.'

* * *

Darrow returned to the Kestrel and was displeased to find the bridge empty.

'Captain on board!' he said over the intercom. 'Report!'

'Ensign Stubbs here Captain. Dr Robinson has had an accident out on the surface and Ensign Reuel is assisting Dr Thomas with the rescue. I'm waiting at the airlock.'

'Very good. Is anyone else on board?'

'No sir.'

'Very well. I'm going out to the old opencast mine workings. I'll be using that airlock myself. There may be a problem with communication if I go underground, so consult Commander Holland at the pithead if you need advice. I'll notify him now.'

'Yes, sir.'

Darrow notified Holland and returned to his office. Urgent messages were waiting for him and he paused to check them. His contacts had gone to unexpected lengths checking post mortems on the unexplained deaths that coincided with the other suspicious incidents. Calneh had shared details of the "unknown" enzyme. The others had not only looked for it, but had circulated its details and compared them. Of those post mortems they had managed to access, fully half had identified the same enzyme. Darrow gasped in astonishment, he felt a growing sense of vindication. The evidence was mounting.

He pulled his attention back to the situation in hand and went to put on his suit and gather his equipment. He took a powerful torch to supplement his helmet light and a rope and grapple in case he needed help to climb down into the workings. He also took his walking pole. He loved hill walking on verdant planets, but he had found the pole equally useful on other terrain. Jones had warned him about the patches of thin crust, so he planned to use it to probe the ground ahead of him, to test the safety of each step.

He went through the cargo bay and out of the airlock and stepped into the shadow of the ship without turning on his helmet light. The light from the stars was dim, but he wasn't looking at his surroundings, he was looking up. He loved the feeling of being in space without a ship. No atmosphere between him and the stars. His imagination soared into the black as he slowly turned on the spot. His turning brought him back to face the Kestrel with the dome behind, and brought his mind back to the task in hand. He switched on his helmet lamp and turned left around the ship until he reached the dome and then followed it.

The ground was undulating, covered in fine dust, and in places it became uneven. Darrow used his pole to test the ground and to boost himself over rough patches. He weighed almost nothing in the minimal gravity, but there was enough to keep him upright at least. The gently rolling landscape soon became rough. Piles of spoil were dotted around, and he struggled on for some distance until he found a path between them. The workings had obviously not been approached from this direction. Soon he saw ahead a large dark patch, even in the dim light from the dome. The mine workings. Reaching the edge, he shone his hand lamp down into the hole. It was about ten metres deep and thirty metres across at the widest part. The inside of the pit looked like broken eggshells: the remains of voids, some shallow, with most of the walls removed to gain access beyond, some like caves with just a small opening. Where to start? How long would it take to search for hidden quartz?

If it's hidden, then it must be in one of the caves, he thought, *so that narrows it down a bit. But how to organise a search methodically?*

He played the light across the workings and saw a disturbance in the layering of dust at a cave entrance.

That's as good a place to start as any.

He shone his lamp around the rim and found some crude steps a few metres away. He worked out a route to the cave, put his torch on his belt and climbed down to the bottom of the pit. Once there, he used his torch to relocate the cave. It was dark in the pit, with only the light from the stars to see by. As he drew near he saw the dust was disturbed along a track from the cave entrance to the pit wall. He ducked his head and went inside, where he was met with a blow to his leg from inside an alcove near the entrance.

Darrow stumbled, shocked by the unexpected attack. As he fell, he instinctively swung his walking pole at his assailant, who dropped his weapon - a torch - which went out. The force of the blow pushed Darrow down into the cave. He thumbed his comm unit and shouted 'Mayday, mayday!' but there was only static.

Damn! he thought. *Too far underground.*

Hearing his call, the man turned towards him. Darrow let his torch drop so he had two hands for his walking pole, which he used to halt his progress. He got his feet under him and pushed off, launching himself back towards his assailant. As he brought the walking pole round to use as a weapon, the man wrenched it out of Darrow's grip and threw it out of the cave entrance. They grappled, and the man grabbed Darrow's arm and smashed his comm unit against the rock face. Now he would be unable to call for help.

The man's helmet light was off and his face plate was polarised, so Darrow could see nothing of his features. Darrow turned his own helmet light off, so the only light in the cave was his dropped torch, shining against the back wall. It was likely the man could see nothing through his darkened face plate. While the man was disoriented, Darrow reached down and turned off the man's air supply. As the man let go and scrabbled for the control, Darrow de-polarised the man's face plate and then turned his own light on. Both men stopped in shock. The man because he was discovered and Darrow because of what he saw. Not that he recognised the man, but he was green.

Chapter 8

Dr Thomas and Reuel arrived at the airlock, put the stretcher beside the stasis chamber and lowered the stand. Thomas turned to Reuel.

'Don't close the outer door, Ensign. I'll keep the gravity low when the airlock pressurises, so I can transfer Elwyn to the stasis chamber on my own. Will you return to Dr Robinson?'

'Yes sir, what should I do?'

'Talk to him. Keep him calm and make sure he doesn't struggle. Any movement could open that cut in his suit.'

'I will do my best, sir.'

Reuel sped off to return to Robinson, and Thomas set the airlock to pressurise so he could open the stretcher.

When Reuel got back to Robinson, he found him very tense.

'Ensign Reuel reporting sir!'

'Yes, yes, check my air supply, will you? I can't see from this position.'

Reuel started when he saw how fast the display was going down. He quickly recovered, took a deep breath and said, 'Do not worry, Doctor, you will be fine.'

'Fine? What does that mean?'

Reuel got down to Robinson's level by lifting his feet to the side and gently floating to the ground.

'Doctor, you told me yourself it means "as well as can be expected under the circumstances". Is that not sufficient?'

Robinson groaned and closed his eyes.   Reuel remembered he was supposed to talk, and racked his brains for what to talk about. Then he remembered something he had heard about a typical human subject.

'The weather is good is it not?' When Robinson didn't respond, he tapped gently on the top of his helmet. 'Doctor?

Is not the weather acceptable?'

'What? What are you talking about? And don't bang on my helmet!'

'My apologies, Dr Thomas told me I should talk to you. What would you like to discuss?'

Robinson was spared Reuel's conversation by a call from Dr Thomas.

'Ensign Reuel? Can you return to help me bring the stretcher?'

'At once, Doctor.'

With a casual push of his hand on the ground, Reuel floated to his feet and disappeared at speed. Soon he and Thomas were back with the stretcher. The first thing Thomas did was to check the readouts. He looked at Reuel in alarm.

Reuel understood the unspoken enquiry, and said, 'I have informed Dr Robinson he will be fine.'

Thomas nodded and turned to Robinson.

'How are you?'

'A bit light-headed,' Robinson replied, 'I think I've lost a lot of blood. I don't know if the pain has subsided or I'm just getting too woozy to feel it.' He gave a wan smile.

'Well, don't you pass out on us. We need to get a tourniquet on that leg as soon as it's out of the hole.' Thomas reached into a bag hanging from the stretcher, pulled out a bandage and shook it free of its pack. 'Once we get you into the stretcher you need to open your helmet, to use the internal air supply.' He turned to Reuel. 'Your hands are smaller than mine, Ensign. Will you try to work your hand down into the hole and see if you can free the doctor's leg? Be careful, the crystals are sharp.'

Reuel laid down and worked his hand into the hole as Robinson moaned with the pain. He found the crystal jabbed into the hole in Robinson's suit and leg.

'I will pull his leg free and cover the hole with my hand. It will not be a perfect seal, but should be enough until you get the tourniquet on. Are you ready Doctor?'

Thomas bent and took hold of Robinson under the arms. It was awkward, with them both in space suits. He said to Robinson, 'You need to take a deep breath and hold it while we get you out. Try not to let your breath go when it hurts. That will help to protect you against the loss of air. Now, everybody ready to go on a count of three. One, two, three!'

With Thomas pulling and Reuel pushing, Robinson came out of the hole with a cry. They laid him on the ground. Reuel put his other hand on top of Robinson's leg so he could exert more pressure.

'Don't let go!' shouted Thomas, as he saw the blood running between Reuel's fingers. 'If we don't stem that bleeding, he could bleed to death before we get him to the ship.'

Thomas wrapped the bandage below Robinson's knee and pulled it tight, knotting it. He inserted a piece of metal and twisted it to tighten the bandage. Robinson cried out. Thomas opened a second bandage. As Reuel let go and Thomas wrapped the bandage around the wound, Reuel was showered with a spurt of blood as the air rushed out of the suit. Quickly Thomas bound it tight, and he and Reuel lifted Robinson into the stretcher and slammed the canopy shut.

'Robinson! Open your helmet! You need to breathe the air from the stretcher. Robinson!'

Groggily Robinson responded and fumbled with the catch as he gasped for air. Finally the helmet seal cracked and Thomas and Reuel released the breath they hadn't realised they had been holding. They rushed him to the airlock. As the airlock re-pressurised, it also came up to normal on-board gravity. Reuel slumped against the wall. When the inside door opened, Stubbs was standing there with Reuel's back brace in his hand.

'One moment Doctor. I just need to help Ensign Reuel. The lift to take Dr Robinson up to sick bay is over here,' Stubbs said, pointing. He dodged past the stretcher. 'Are you all right, Reuel? What's all this blood?'

'It is well, Stubbs. The blood is not mine. Come, help

me out of my suit.'

As soon as Reuel could manage, Stubbs helped Thomas take the stretcher to sick bay.

* * *

Hoy and Tabitha returned to the Kestrel from the mine.

'You've worked hard, Trainee,' Hoy said. 'I'm impressed. Get cleaned up, get something to eat, then rest, prepare in case you're needed again.'

'Yes sir.'

Tabitha felt as though she grew several centimetres under Hoy's praise. As she headed for her cabin, she met Stubbs by the sick bay door.

'Sounds like you did all right,' he said.

'Yes sir.'

Stubbs laughed. 'You don't need to call me sir, I'm only an Ensign. We've only met briefly. I'm Roy Stubbs, Assistant Engineer.' He shook her hand, but didn't let go. 'If you've got any questions, you can always ask me.'

'Thanks.' She withdrew her hand. 'Don't let me keep you. I wouldn't want you to get into trouble.'

'That's good to know.' He smiled. 'See you later.'

He went into sick bay, and Tabitha continued down the corridor, muttering, 'Not if I see you first.'

* * *

Hoy cleaned up and went to the bridge. Holland notified him that Chambers was returning, so he sent Reuel out to replace him. A short while later the comm station sounded.

'Kestrel, this is Commander Blackwell. We've received a scrambled message - sounds like a mayday call. It may have come from underground. Has Commander Holland reported anything?'

'No sir, Lieutenant-Commander Hoy here. 'The Captain has gone to investigate the old opencast workings. He said he may go underground.'

'They have a booster here for underground communication, which we were working on. I'll see if I can get a location. Stand by.'

While Hoy was waiting, Chambers arrived. He was telling Hoy about the work on Level Two when Blackwell's voice was heard again.

'Kestrel, the call came from the opencast workings. The Captain needs help. I'm sending the co-ordinates now.'

'Thank you, Commander, I'll investigate myself. Can you advise Commander Holland, ask if he can release someone from over there to meet us at the opencast workings too?'

'Will do. Out.'

Hoy left Chambers on watch, while he went to put on his suit and go out to the Captain.

At the pithead, Holland received the message from Blackwell just as Reuel arrived.

'I know you've just got here, Ensign, but you're the fastest in low gravity. Will you go?'

'Yes sir. I am most willing,' Reuel said, removing his back brace. 'I will need a suit from a tall man, and is there a weapon?'

Gareth Davies sent a man for the suit, and produced something that looked like a hand gun. 'We have no weapons, but you could take a hand cutter. It's got no range but it cuts through rock up close.'

He showed Reuel the operation of the hand cutter while the suit was brought. Within minutes Reuel left the stores airlock and was speeding round the dome towards the opencast workings.

* * *

Tabitha crept through the bridge door.

'Psst! Andrew! Can I come in? There's no one here.'

'What about me?' said Chambers. 'Am I "no one"? You know you're not allowed on the bridge.'

She hesitated and decided to take her chance. 'So report me!'

She came in and sat boldly in the nearest chair.

'First you come on the bridge unauthorised,' Chambers smiled at her, 'now you're sitting in the Captain's chair!'

She scrambled out of the chair like it was burning and sat down beside Chambers.

'Is this all right? Whose seat is this?'

'Weapons station. Don't touch anything.'

Chambers laughed as her eyes went wide and she squeezed her arms in tight to her body. 'I'm only joking. It's all offline.'

She looked around the bridge and wrinkled her nose. 'It's not as impressive as I expected, there's not a lot of room, is there?'

'What more do you need than three workstations?' He pointed them out. 'This main one is the helm and navigation, beside this is scanners and weapons, and the one at the back is for the bridge officer, when we have a full complement, and he takes comms as well.The fourth one's spare, in case of malfunction. Of course, most of the time there's only one on duty, the helm. All functions can be operated from here. It's a working environment, not a pleasure cruise.'

'I suppose so. It's not like the simulators, is it? In fact, nothing is as I expected it.'

'You've only been here five minutes, give it a chance.'

'Where's the viewscreen? This window's all right on planet, but what about long distance?'

Chambers laughed. 'This "window" is the main viewport. It polarises, to be clear for take-off and landing, then to show a visual display of any screen on the bridge. So how was your first mission?'

'Not at all what I expected!' she laughed. 'When you sign up to serve in space, you don't expect to end up down a mine.'

'In the Fast-Response Fleet you have to expect anything. I've slogged through jungles and deserts on planets, done spacewalks for repair and rescues, and coped with refugees and all sorts on board. It's certainly not dull. How did you get on?'

'All right, actually. We were mostly heaving rocks around. Wasn't it dusty though?'

'That's one of the disadvantages of low gravity. When you disturb the dust it just floats about for ages. It was pretty much the same for us on Level Two - heaving rocks around.'

'You didn't have the cave-in to deal with. Once we found it was mostly one big slab, they didn't want it touched too much in case it broke, though I did manage to raise it a few millimetres. We just moved the other debris and put in roof supports.'

'A few millimetres? What are you - supergirl?'

'Don't be daft, I used one of those lifter things,' she laughed. 'What about you?'

'The scanner confirmed the missing miners are trapped in a void beyond the cave-in, and they drilled a small hole to communicate with them. Dr Robinson spoke with them then left Ensign Ryan to monitor their condition while they drilled a bigger hole to get them out. Once we'd tidied up, there wasn't anything else I could do, so Commander Holland sent me back here. Hey, did you hear about the Captain? He sent a mayday. Lieutenant-Commander Hoy's gone out to him on the surface. I hope he's all right.'

'What's he doing outside the dome? We're here to rescue the miners aren't we?'

'He knows what he's doing, there must be something else going on. He doesn't tell us everything you know. Maybe we can get Lieutenant-Commander Hoy to tell us when he gets back.'

'He's a talkative one, isn't he? He gave me some really good advice about low gravity and stuff, but he never stopped talking.'

'Hoy? He's not usually like that. How strange. Maybe he was nervous about baby-sitting.'

'Shut up! I'm no baby. I bet I could show you a thing or two, even about piloting.'

Chambers face fell and he turned away.

'Oh no! Andrew, I didn't mean … I wasn't thinking. Look, I don't know what happened, but you must be a good pilot or Captain Darrow wouldn't have made you helmsman. My Dad says the past is a bucket of ashes. It's gone and there's nothing you can do about it. But the future is a promise built from all our todays.'

'Quite the philosopher, your Dad.'

'Yes, and he's usually right.'

They sat in silence for a while. Then Tabitha remembered.

'Oh, did you hear about the MO's accident? Ensign Stubbs told Lieutenant-Commander Hoy when we came back.'

'No, what happened?'

'Dr Robinson and the base doctor were bringing a casualty here via the outside for some reason, and Dr Robinson had an accident. Ensign Reuel went to help bring the casualty in and then go back to rescue the doctor. Ensign Stubbs has gone to sick bay to help.'

'I wondered where everyone was. I thought Stubbs and Reuel had been left on board. So let's get this straight,' he counted off on his fingers. 'Hoy is out on the surface helping the captain, Reuel and Stubbs are in sick bay with the MO, Commander Blackwell is with the base engineer, and everyone else is still at the mine.'

'No, wait.' She frowned in concentration. 'I heard Lieutenant-Commander Hoy sent Ensign Reuel to the mine to relieve you. Wow, this is complicated!'

'But it's important, do you see? If we don't keep track of everyone, how will we make sure they're all right?'

'In that case, would it be a good idea to check in with Commander Holland to see if he knows where everyone is?'

Tabitha felt warmed by Chambers' look of approval.

'Now you're thinking!'

Chapter 9

On Level Two all work on the cave-in had stopped as they concentrated on digging to the trapped miners. Using the camera they had lowered through the pilot hole to survey the shape of the void, the miners had determined the best route to enlarge the hole. As the hole was enlarged, dressings, fluids and pain killers had been lowered. Under Ryan's instructions Huw Thomas had treated both himself and John Rees. Now the hole was big enough to pass down thinly rolled blankets to put across the quartz crystals to make them more comfortable. The next plan was to get an armoured blanket and roof supports down there to protect them and try to prevent another collapse as work proceeded. As it was, they couldn't prevent pieces of rock and crystal falling on the men as the hole was enlarged, however carefully they worked.

Ryan crouched at one side, trying to keep out of the way of the drilling, monitoring the condition of the trapped men. He kept them talking so he could monitor their level of consciousness, but also, to take their (and his) minds off the situation. He only had a microphone, and it was hard because of the noise of the drilling machine and the extractor brought in to try to keep the dust down. He felt under pressure from all sides, but tried not to let it show.

'Tell me Huw, have you always been a miner?' Ryan asked.

'Never wanted to do anything else.' Huw replied. 'Runs in the family. My father, my grandfather, and several uncles were all involved in mining in one way or another. It's not such backbreaking work as it used to be, of course. Now, John's story is very different, isn't it John?'

'What?'

'Ryan is asking if you've always been a miner. He'd never guess would he?'

The monitor showed John's grin. 'Not a hope. I sort of fell into it, you might say.'

'What did you used to do?' said Ryan.

'Accountant, I was.'

'Bean counter, you mean,' said Huw. 'They sent him here to check the books, and we lured him underground.'

John nodded. 'Most people hate being under … I loved it. Hated counting. Applied for the job straight away.'

'We were short staffed,' said Huw. 'Glad to have him, even though he was a rookie. Still keeps an eye on the accounts, though. What about you?'

'Me?' said Ryan. 'I come from Orion Three. It's a reversionist colony. They do things the old way, sweat of the brow and all that. Trouble is, there's some technology that shouldn't be abandoned. My brother lost his leg in an accident and it ruined his life. I saw traders with prosthetic legs living a normal life, but we had no doctor skilled enough to fit one. Skilled medical staff don't want to work in a backwards society like Orion Three. I decided to go and get qualified as a doctor and go back to help my people.'

'What are you doing out here then?' Huw asked.

'Once I got away from home and saw what life was like outside, it made it hard to go back. I had the chance of a posting to the Fast-Response Fleet as part of my training, and I jumped at it. Do you know, I'd never even seen an alien until I left home?'

Huw laughed and nudged John. 'What about you, John? Had you ever seen an alien before you left home?'

'What?'

'Pay attention, man! Have you ever seen an alien?'

'I don't know,' said John with a wan smile. 'You look pretty weird. I feel pretty weird too.'

Ryan wasn't happy with John's vital signs. He had lost a lot of blood and his lack of concentration indicated concussion at least. He turned to Dai Williams and covered the mic.

'John's not doing well. We need to get him out quickly.'

'We're doing our best, but the drilling is loosening crystals that fall on them, and if we rush we might bring the roof down.'

'I'm not telling you how to do your job, but I think you should take some risks if you want to get them out alive. I need to get a message to the doctors.'

* * *

Following Ryan's advice, Dai Williams called for another drill. This made conversation impossible. Ryan now had to rely on the sensors for monitoring the miners' vital signs, the video screen showed them only faintly through the shifting and increasing dust. As the hole was enlarged Williams planned to try to rig up a canopy to protect them from falling rock and crystal shards.

I dreamed of going into space, Ryan thought ruefully, *and now here I am: underground, cramped, dirty, and deafened. Still, it looks as though they're enlarging the hole much faster, maybe I'll be back on the surface quite soon. I wonder why Dr Robinson hasn't returned.*

As the dust increased the extractor began to labour, then clogged and began to whine. Within seconds the crystals began to vibrate and the tone spread through the mine.

Williams shouted, 'Shut down!' and made cutting motions across his throat.

They cut the power but the sound was self-sustaining. Soon everything was shaking, as the crystals amplified the sound and reflected it back and forth. The noise was deafening.

There was a crack and a large slab of the floor gave way, taking a machine and Jenkins with it. The reverberations died. The dust hung suspended in the air as everyone stared in shock.

'Told you I'd be first here, didn't I boys?' Jenkins' voice broke the silence.

'Good of you to drop in.' came Huw's reply.

Ryan joined in the great cheer that went up and rushed to the edge of the hole, to see that the slab had missed Huw and John, and also provided a bridge, the perfect means of rescue. Williams radioed the pithead with the news.

Ryan didn't wait for permission, but jumped down beside Jenkins on the slab and crawled over to Huw and John. He laid a blanket beside John and crawled on to it.

'I'll take John, Huw, so they can get you out first. Mr Jenkins,' he said, 'help Huw up, would you?'

Huw pulled his arm out from under John. It was dripping red. Huw paused in alarm.

'I didn't know...'

'It's okay, leave it to me,' said Ryan gently to reassure him as he took John. He reached for a dressing with his free hand and John's monitor gave a continuous tone. Ryan checked John, as though he didn't believe it, and Huw struggled to escape from the rescuers' grip.

'No John, not now! We're saved, can't you see?'

'Turn that thing off!' Williams shouted, and silence fell.

Ryan shook his head. 'I'm sorry, his head injury is worse than we thought, and he's lost so much blood. I can't save him.'

They all bowed their heads in the silence.

Chapter 10

In the abandoned opencast workings, Darrow's assailant pushed him away and desperately scrambled for the entrance to the cave. Darrow recovered his balance and pursued. At the entrance, where the attacker had scrambled out, he emerged cautiously, on the lookout for another attack, but there was no sign of the man. Darrow stood up, and a large rock landed on the top of his helmet. The force drove him to his knees and sent a shock through his spine and shoulders. His heart leaped in fear. If his helmet was damaged, he could run out of air before he reached the airlock, but to his relief, his helmet was undamaged. The man was above him now, scrambling up the face of the cliff.

Darrow took his grapple off his belt and swung it round, looking for a place to land the hook. Looking upwards in a suit wasn't easy at the best of times, now a shaft of pain coursed down his neck. He found a likely spot and launched the hook, which landed too far to the right. He stepped carefully to the left, pulled on the rope, and the hook slid sideways and caught. He pulled himself quickly up the rock face, but his attacker reached the top first, looked down and saw him.

The man walked over to the hook and kicked it repeatedly with his heavy boot until the cliff edge gave way and the grapple fell. The shaking of the rope when he kicked the hook had alerted Darrow, who threw himself on a ledge at the last minute as the grapple fell past him.

Darrow scrambled up the rest of the way and looked cautiously over the edge. The man was heading for a buggy with balloon wheels parked behind a spoil heap. Darrow boosted himself to his feet and followed. He reached the buggy and leaped on the back just as the man started it. Various tools on arms projected from the back, and as Darrow and the man struggled, they knocked a switch, starting some of them.

It's not easy to fight wearing a space suit, Darrow wasn't getting very far. As they grappled, another switch was knocked and the buggy started forward with a jerk. The man grabbed the steering wheel but Darrow wasn't so lucky. He fell sideways off the back of the buggy, towards a spinning circular saw. There was no way he could avoid it. Darrow gasped in surprise as he was pulled backward by the suit and swung clear, then dumped on the ground as the other man sped away.

Darrow sat for a second in astonishment. *Why would he save me?*

* * *

On the surface, Hoy and Reuel arrived at the opencast workings, from opposite directions. Reuel started after the buggy, but Darrow called him back. He could identify the man later. When Reuel didn't stop, Darrow remembered his comm unit was broken. He waved his arms to attract Hoy's attention, pointed at Reuel and his comm unit and signalled negative. Hoy understood and called Reuel back, and they both made their way round the edge of the workings towards the Captain. By putting their helmets together, they could talk directly to each other, the contact of the visors allowing the transfer of some of the sound, lip reading helping with the rest.

'Are you all right sir?' Hoy said. 'Who was that?'

'Don't know,' Darrow said. 'He attacked me when I stepped into the workings. I can deal with him later. Right now I want to see what he was up to.'

'Excuse me sir,' Reuel said. 'If it was in the pit, should you not say "see what he was down to"?'

Darrow and Hoy smiled.

'I'm afraid it's another phrase you just have to learn, Ensign,' Darrow said. 'Let's find a way down to the cave.'

They climbed down to the cave Darrow had found. In a narrow space at the back they found some small rocket-shaped cannisters and a large net on a collapsible frame. Reuel identified the net.

'We use these on Altair, Captain. In low gravity, a capsule can be dropped from a ship and caught with the net. It can also be used to launch a capsule into space, to be caught by a ship.'

'Here's what they were sending,' called Hoy, who had opened one of the canisters. Reuel relayed it to Darrow. The cannister contained what at first looked like grit, but they realised it was razor quartz micro crystals. 'Tiny quartz crystals. A few at a time would be easy to conceal, coming from the mine. The tiny ones are quite valuable. They're used in computer circuits, so they're in high demand.'

'So someone is smuggling micro crystals off the base, out to a ship, and getting the empty capsules back,' said Reuel.

Darrow looked around. 'This isn't just opportunistic, it's organised. The miners, however many are involved, smuggle the crystals out of the mine and store them in these canisters. At pre-arranged times the canisters are put into the capsules and propelled into space, where they are collected by a waiting ship, and the empties returned to the surface ready for next time. I wonder how long it's been going on?'

Hoy jumped. 'Sir, a message came in - the miners have been rescued!' His shoulders sagged. 'Oh, one didn't make it.'

'Check if Commander Holland needs help,' Darrow said.

'No, he says it's under control.'

'You are not to say anything about this,' said Darrow. 'I don't want anyone to know what we've found. Lieutenant-Commander, take the net and a full capsule back to the Kestrel and leave them against the ship near the starboard airlock. I'll see they get to Mr Jones, the Base Administrator. Now you two return to your posts. I'll follow you back after I retrieve my walking pole.'

Reuel turned back and put his helmet to Darrow's. 'Sir? You have a pole that walks?'

Chapter 11

When Darrow returned to the Kestrel, Commander Blackwell reported he had checked the video record from the stores door. He was able to confirm that a figure did indeed show up under infrared light. Darrow drew in a breath, to control his thumping heart, this was good news, very good news. Proof at last! The Intruders he had speculated about were now on record. At that moment a call came through from Holland.

'Captain, there's been a death.'

'Yes, I heard one of the trapped miners died.'

'No, sir. The stores have been raided again, and the watchman, Pavel Patla, has been found dead.' Holland was interrupted. 'Oh! Yes, Mr Jones. I'm sorry sir, I'm not allowed to say any more. Mr Jones wants to see you immediately.'

'I'm on my way.'

Darrow headed to Jones's office, his emotions conflicted. It was strange, to be glad about someone's death. Darrow told himself he wasn't glad the man had died, just excited about having real evidence. It was particularly exhilarating to know that he was on the spot during the incident - the trail couldn't get much hotter than it was right now.

Outside Jones's office, Holland attracted his attention from around a corner.

'Captain, I'm not supposed to talk to you, but I wanted to warn you. Because everyone from the base rushed to the mine when they heard the trapped men had been reached, they're all accounted for. Our crew are also accounted for. You are the only one missing at the time Patla died. Jones is very angry.'

'Thank you, Commander.' Darrow thought fast. 'Take an electron scan of the stores door and get a copy of the stores video record. Get them to Commander Blackwell, he'll know what to do.'

For a moment, he was more concerned about the evidence he was seeking for his own investigation, than the current situation. Of course the evidence could help solve both enquiries. Holland's look of surprise brought Darrow back to the present.

'Just get that evidence. It may be exactly what I need.'

When Darrow knocked, Jones hustled him inside, locked the door, and sat in front of it.

'No more mysteries, Captain. I want answers, and you're not leaving until I get some.'

Darrow took a chair away from the door and sat down. He leaned back and breathed deeply, trying to look calm and unthreatening.

'You know where I was Mr Jones, I was out at the old opencast mine workings, looking into the thefts of quartz you reported.'

'Waste of time,' Jones scoffed, 'and you could have been anywhere.'

'I wasn't alone and I wouldn't say it was a waste of time,' said Darrow. 'I didn't find anything to help my investigation, but I did find evidence of smuggling, and a smuggler.'

'What?'

'Someone is smuggling micro crystals. I've got some of their equipment, in case they try to clear it out.' He rushed on, before Jones had time to take it in. 'That's not the important issue right now. What happened to Pavel Patla?'

'He was found dead by the stores door, and there's more quartz missing! How am I supposed to explain that to the mining company?'

'Where is the body now?'

'In sick bay. Dr Thomas has finished with Elwyn and your doctor and is doing a post mortem now.'

'Would you mind asking him to check the enzymes in the body? Advise if there are any he hasn't encountered before.'

'Why?'

'Just ask him, please, then I'll explain.'

Jones went to the comm unit and called Dr Thomas.

'Hello Wil, you must be calling about Huw. I can patch him up, but I recommend leave. It's going to take a while to heal the psychological trauma.'

'Thanks Simon, that's good to know. We'll use the accident fund to send him home. Now then, I've got the Kestrel's captain here, and he has a strange request for you. When you do the post mortem on Pavel, will you check for all enzymes? Known and unknown.'

'What do you mean, unknown?'

Jones looked quizically at Darrow.

'Something that's not on record, Doctor,' Darrow said, loud enough to carry. 'I'll have details sent to you when I can get back to my ship. But trust me, the tests are vital.'

'Very well. I'll let you know.'

Jones sat behind his desk, Darrow leaned forward.

'Do you know the funny thing about all this? The things that looked significant, turned out to be irrelevant, and the things that looked irrelevant, turned out to be significant.'

'I wouldn't call Pavel's death irrelevant,' Jones bristled.

Darrow raised a hand. 'Sorry, that's not what I meant. We came here looking for sabotage and found an accident. I discovered smuggling, but it's got little to do with the theft of the quartz. But Kozlik's ghost, who everyone laughed at, may turn out to be very significant indeed.'

* * *

Jones crossed his arms and waited.

Darrow took a deep breath.

'My engineer examined a copy of the video record of the night Mr Kozlik saw his ghost. He tried changing the lighting, and under infrared light a figure appears. I don't have the details yet, but Kozlik was right. I told you earlier there have been thefts elsewhere, but this is the first time we've found proof of a figure. The aliens can't be seen in normal light, so no one knows they're there. Now, what else can you tell me about this latest incident?'

'I haven't had time to speak to everyone yet,' Jones frowned, 'but there was something. I don't know if it's relevant. Pavel wasn't dead when he was found. Apparently he said 'butterfly' before he died. Have you heard of that before, Captain?'

'Not that I recall. I'll check the records.'

'Now, what am I going to tell the men? They're not likely to believe in invisible aliens.'

'You can't tell them anything. They don't know I'm investigating, and I need to pull my evidence together.'

Jones snorted. 'You've spoken to Parry, Koslik, and Koslik's wife. Your investigation won't stay secret for long.'

'I can't help that.' Darrow thought for a moment. 'Admit it if you have to, but don't release any details. I'll see you get a copy of my report. You could always blame the thefts on the smugglers.'

Jones paused to consider the idea. 'That'll frighten them! We can keep asking them where they put the missing quartz, and then accuse them of Pavel's death.'

'At least it will buy time for me to put this new evidence with my other findings and take it to my superiors.'

'Wait!' said Jones. 'Who are the smugglers?'

Darrow smiled. 'Have you heard of Ochrans?'

'The lanky green-skinned guys? What have they got to do with it?'

'Ochrans are tall, but they're not all taller than humans. Their atmosphere has less oxygen than earth, and Ochran green skin goes pink in an oxygen-rich atmosphere. You've got at least one Ochran posing as human here.'

'That's impossible! We all know each other.'

'Well, maybe there are a few people vouching for each other. All you have to do is get everyone together and reduce the oxygen until your smugglers appear.'

Despite himself, Jones laughed. 'This I've got to see. At least it will give everyone something to focus on.'

Chapter 12

Sam Ryan returned from the mine tired, dirty, and mourning the tragedy of John Rees's death. He stepped into sick bay and stopped, hit by another shock to see Dr Robinson on a bed and the place in a mess. Apparently Dr Thomas had made sure the stasis chamber was running correctly and treated Robinson, but it seemed he'd returned immediately to the base. No one else had thought to clear up sick bay, but why would they? That was Ryan's job. Jaw slightly slack, not knowing what to say, Ryan turned to Robinson where he lay in bed. Robinson instantly ordered him to his bed for rest. Ryan figured the man must be unwell, Robinson was usually a stickler for a clean and tidy sickbay, but Ryan was too tired to argue. So he went to the cabin he shared with Stubbs, removed his filthy uniform, letting it drop to the floor, and flung himself into bed. He was asleep before his head hit the pillow.

* * *

Darrow was eager to get back to the Kestrel and find out what Blackwell had to say about the scans and video record. When he came through the airlock he was met by Holland.

'Glad you're back, Captain. I was worried we may have to launch a rescue attempt.'

Darrow smiled. 'Against regulations Commander, but most welcome. No, I was able to convince Mr Jones I'm not the enemy. I revealed what we'd found out about the smuggling, so he's going to be occupied with that for a while.'

They walked together down the corridor and up the stairs to the main deck.

'Jones says they can manage on their own now, sir,'

Holland said. 'They're not going to shift the cave-in, just work around it. They were on the verge of moving sideways from the tunnels into other voids anyway.'

'Are all the crew back on board?'

'Affirmative, and, with the exception of Dr Robinson no injuries.'

Darrow didn't mention his neck and shoulders. They were still painful, but there would be time for that later. *I'll just ask Ryan to give me pain killers,* he thought. 'Did you get the scan and video record I asked to be sent?'

'Yes sir. Commander Blackwell is analysing them now in Engineering. I think he wants to see you. Are you aware that when they attempted to open the stores door to check if there was a theft, the airlock door was open? There's an automatic safety mechanism that won't allow both doors to be open at the same time, and the attempt to open one door closed the other. The quartz was taken out through the airlock.'

Darrow was mentally fitting the pieces together. If Blackwell told him what he expected, his case was solid.

'Thank you Commander. Prepare for take-off. I'm going to check on Dr Robinson, then I'll see Commander Blackwell.'

Although he was impatient to hear the results of Blackwell's investigation, the health of his crew came first. While Holland headed to the bridge, Darrow went to sick bay, where he found Robinson in bed with both legs bandaged and his left leg in a splint. Darrow was relieved to see the medical display above his bed showed his vital signs were normal. Stubbs was tidying up.

'Sorry I can't stand to attention Captain,' Robinson said with a wan smile. 'I've made rather a fool of myself.'

'At ease, Quentin. Do you feel up to telling me what happened? I'll read the reports later, but I'd appreciate a summary.'

'The short version of what happened,' said Robinson, 'is I stepped in a hole and dislocated my knee. The asteroid's crust is thin in some places, and I strayed too far from the safe ground near the dome. I broke through to a void of quartz crystals, and got cut pretty badly too. I'm comfortable now. Dr Thomas looked after me well, but he didn't have time to use the regenerator on anything but the incision. He's good for one so young. Ensign Reuel was a great help too. Have you seen him in low gravity? The way he moves is incredible. Unfortunately, I'm not going to be fit for duty for a while, sir. The damage to my knee is too severe. It feels strange, being a patient in my own sick bay. I'm afraid I've made your staffing problem worse.'

Darrow frowned. 'So we're yet another crewman short. Ryan will have to take charge in here on the journey home. Stubbs can cover when Ryan's off duty - at least he knows how the machines work, since he services them. You can give him advice if needed - but no exertion. We won't be responding to any calls. I want to get all the casualties safely transferred and then we're not going anywhere until we've got a full crew complement.' He felt a load lift as he made the decision. He looked round. 'Where is Ryan?'

'I've sent him to get some rest,' said Robinson. 'He looked exhausted. He had quite a time of it, down in the mine, and he's bound to be upset by the death of one of the trapped miners.'

'Very well, but work is probably the best cure. Take his mind off it. He's going to have to be on call anyway. With luck there won't be a medical emergency in the next 24 hours. You make sure you rest and don't try to do anything until Ryan gets to work with a regenerator.'

Darrow left, entering a reminder into his pad to speak to Ryan in a few hours. Then he headed for Engineering.

'I'm glad to see you, Joe,' Blackwell said, 'this is really fascinating.'

Darrow ignored the informality. John Blackwell was old enough to be his father, and sometimes acted like he was. As long as it wasn't in front of the crew, he could put up with it. Right now, he could call Darrow anything, as long as he told him what he wanted to hear.

'What did you find on the new video record? Is there a figure?'

'Absolutely.' Blackwell played the adjusted images on screen. 'The figure killed the guard and opened the door. It's all there, once you change the lighting to infrared.'

'Yes!' Darrow pumped his fist in triumph. 'They'll *have* to listen to me now.'

Blackwell turned to face him.

'What's this all about? Who are these people? Sounds to me as though you were expecting them.'

Darrow wasn't ready to talk about his conclusions yet.

'It's something I've been looking into privately that dovetailed with the investigation on Pallas. I'll let you read the report when I get it together. What about the scan on the lock?'

'Electrical interference, definitely. Whatever this figure is, it can generate an electrical pulse. It would have seemed to anyone watching that the door opened by itself.'

Darrow clapped Blackwell on the shoulder.

'Thank you, Commander Blackwell, thank you very much. Forward your report to me as soon as possible, but keep it separate from the mission report.'

* * *

Tabitha was desperate to know what the captain's mayday call was all about. As soon as Chambers returned to their cabin, she bombarded him with questions.

'Did you find out what happened to the captain?'

'Well, he's safe now, but I don't know what actually happened,' he said. 'It's all very secretive. Lieutenant-Commander Hoy came back alone, and Ensign Reuel went back to the mine. Then the Captain returned and rushed straight off again to meet with Mr Jones, the Base Administrator.'

'Did you ask Lieutenant-Commander Hoy or Ensign

Reuel about it?'

'I tried. When he came back and relieved me, the Lieutenant-Commander just said "No problem, the Captain is fine."' Chambers climbed up to his bunk and lay down. 'I haven't seen Ensign Reuel yet.'

'Maybe I'll ask him.'

Chambers looked over the edge of his bunk. 'You can't do that! You weren't supposed to be on the bridge, and any command talk not aimed at you, you're supposed to ignore. If you start asking about, you'll get yourself and me into trouble.'

'But you put it in the duty log, didn't you? What went in afterwards?'

'I haven't looked, it's nothing to do with me.'

'Surely you want to know?'

He shook his head and lay down again.

'You're hopeless!'

Tabitha felt a glow of satisfaction. Although she had only been shifting rocks, she had, at least, been useful, and Lieutenant-Commander Hoy had praised her. She reflected ruefully that the last thing she envisaged when serving in space was to end up shifting rocks underground. Still, she now had experience of low gravity, and before any of her classmates.

Commander Holland came to the cabin and Tabitha jumped to attention.

'As you were, Lieutenant.' Chambers lay down again. 'At ease Trainee, how did you get on?'

'It was good, sir, once I got the hang of it. I even got used to the gravity.'

'Good. Now, we need a report. Document everything you did on this mission. The trick is to get the level of detail right - somewhere between "down mine, shifted rocks" and a description of every rock. It's a skill to be learned, like any other. I expect you're used to writing reports for school. They can have a copy too, once I've approved it. There's a template on the computer to give you an outline.' He turned to Chambers. 'And you're not to help her - I want to see her first attempt. Carry on.'

When Holland left, Chambers made for the door.

'I'll leave you to it. I've got to prepare for take-off.'

Tabitha paced up and down while she thought about the report. *Should I include my impressions of the crew? How the Captain likes things by the book, but Commander Holland tries to cut people some slack. How Hoy talked all the time underground.* She shook her head. *Probably not, but I might put it in my own journal. There's more than rules and procedures you can learn by watching people. Should I include what I heard about the mysterious goings-on over the missing razor quartz? Probably not - that can go in my journal too, along with the Captain's absence from the mine rescue. What was he doing? He didn't stay on the ship, so where did he go? No, 'document everything you did' the Commander had said. Now, what did I do first?*

* * *

Tabitha's Journal

Well, I've served in my first mission - not what I expected at all - and I've started to get to know some of the crew - also not what I expected. The trouble is, when I joined a ship I expected to be older, more experienced, and on more of an equal footing. The crew are so far beyond me in experience that it's hard to relate to them. It's more like being on a ship full of school teachers. Andrew is being a real help, even though he's nearly twice my age. Roy is nearest my age but he creeps me out a bit. I don't know what it is - he's always friendly and helpful, but he keeps watching me and winking, and he stands too close. Maybe I'm being paranoid, but I don't know how to respond to him.

My first mission saw me underground in a razor quartz mine, with hardly any gravity. Very weird. I sort of enjoyed it - it was good to help people, but it wasn't what I expected from life in space. And I got filthy. That dust gets in everywhere! Things weren't all they seemed either. The

Captain went missing, apparently investigating some missing quartz, but they had to rescue him. I'm itching to know more, but no one's saying. Captain Darrow seems really nice, but I've had to swot up the rules - I've been warned he's a real stickler. I got told off for walking on the wrong side of the corridor, would you believe. You have to keep to the right, so in an emergency people don't bump into each other. Trouble is, my balance is still off, and sometimes I'm all over the place.

I haven't had much formal training yet, because of the mission, but Commander Holland has worked out a programme for me. I expect it will start properly now we're back on patrol. I'll be spending time with various crew members, learning what they do. Lieutenant Commander Hoy was great in the mine. He explained everything and gave me lots of advice, especially about working in low gravity. It's quite easy once you know the tricks, like bracing yourself before you push.

I've just written my first mission report - I don't expect they mark it, like in school, but I'll be happy once Commander Holland has seen it and told me if it's OK. Or not. But if it's not, I won't mind him telling me, because he's good about explaining things too. Perhaps I can ask him about the Captain and the missing quartz.

* * *

Tabitha wasn't the only one writing reports. Fleet procedures stated everyone should record their version of events after every mission. Darrow was writing two reports: the official one and his Intruders dossier one. His superiors *had* to take notice now. They might settle the Bokan situation and find another crisis knocking on the door.

Chapter 13

Once the Kestrel had taken off, Darrow called Holland to his office.

'I'll read the detailed reports later,' Darrow said, 'but what are your overall impressions as to how the crew dealt with the situation on Pallas?'

'Very good overall, Captain. Everyone played their part, even though conditions in the mine were difficult. Enns did better than expected. Lieutenant-Commander Hoy said she was useful, obedient and didn't complain.'

'We must make sure she gets some real training,' Darrow raised his hand to stop Holland's protest. 'I know there hasn't been time, but I want you to see to it that the schedule you drew up gets implemented right away. I don't want Principal Hernandez complaining that we misled her. It strikes me that work experience would be beneficial for all the trainees and we can prove that. We want to create a good impression. Now, I'm contacting Personnel and telling them I'm taking Kestrel off-duty until we get crew replacements.'

Holland whistled. 'They're not going to like that. They need all the ships out on patrol.'

'That's what I'm counting on. They sent us out with one short, which is against regulations. Then we lost Balitoth, now Robinson. I'm putting my foot down.'

'Good luck.' Holland left.

However, when Darrow tried to put his foot down he discovered he was out-manoeuvred.

'Captain Darrow, I was just about to transmit your new orders,' said the administrator he got through to. 'You are to proceed to T'Lon Space Station immediately.'

'Now wait,' said Darrow. 'I've got an injured MO as well as two other crew missing. I'm not going anywhere but base.'

'Captain, T'Lon is no further from your present position than Earth is, in fact you may get there sooner.'

'I have two casualties on board, who need medical attention.'

'The medical facilities on T'Lon are excellent, and the Falcon is there too, waiting for Captain Holland. His orders will be sent today. He is to report as soon as you arrive.'

'What?! He's not due to leave the Kestrel for another nine days. I presume you have a new First Officer lined up for me?'

The administrator shifted uncomfortably in his seat. 'Not as yet, Captain. One thing at a time.'

'Then can you inform me when new crew will be available and we can be operational?'

There was an awkward pause. 'We're working on it.'

'Then I must inform you the Kestrel is off duty as of now, and will not be leaving T'Lon until she has a full crew complement.'

'Duly noted Captain. Out.'

Darrow was frustrated. He couldn't even give the crew leave because there was nowhere to go that didn't involve arranging passage on other ships, and no guarantee they could get back quickly for duty when new crew were finally assigned. He ordered the course change and called Holland back to his office to break the news.

* * *

When Ryan awoke, several hours later, his clothes were clean and folded, and there was a cereal bar and a drink on his bedside cabinet. He discovered that normal routine had been re-established and to his surprise the Kestrel was en route to T'Lon and not Earth.

When he had eaten, showered and dressed, he went to sick bay, where he found Robinson sleeping and the whole place clean and tidy. His head was still in a whirl from the events at the mine and he struggled to process it all. Had he imagined it? To add to his confusion, he realised with a shock there was now no Medical Officer on duty. Did that mean he was the acting Medical Officer? Or was Robinson going to run things from his bed? Just then the Captain arrived.

'Ah, good, you're awake. I see Ensign Stubbs has finished. He asked permission to clean up while you were sleeping. You'll have to check he put things in the right place. How are you feeling?'

'A bit confused right now sir. It was tough down in the mine, and I didn't know about the Doctor's accident. Is he still MO?'

'He'll probably think he is,' Darrow smiled, 'but he can't do much from his bed. Can you cope for now? It won't be long - we're going to drop off the casualties then we'll wait for new crew.'

'Yes, sir. I'm sure I can manage.'

'Good man. You'll need to treat the Doctor with the regenerator too. Ask him what's needed.' He paused for a second. 'While I'm here, can you give me some pain relief?'

'What's the problem Captain?'

'Oh, it's nothing serious, I'm sure.'

Ryan took a deep breath. 'I think that's for me to say Captain. You did just ask me to take charge, so I think I should examine you.'

Ryan saw the captain's hesitation, but after a moment he gave in with good grace. After all, even an Acting Medical Officer had the authority to order a Captain off duty in the right circumstances. When done, Ryan was buoyed by his first success as temporary MO.

* * *

To take his mind off the crew problems, Darrow went back to his dossier on the missing raw materials and added his new evidence: image analysis from Pallas and post-mortem enzyme reports from his contacts. He contacted them to share the latest information about the ghostly figure, asking them to check the video records for their local incidents under infrared. As he looked at the growing body of evidence, he decided to make a new attempt to convince his superior officer, Commodore Michel, of the threat. He wrote a report, attached the relevant files, plus a copy of the original report outlining his suspicions, and transmitted it to Commodore Michel.

* * *

The following morning, Darrow received an incoming call. He responded eagerly when he saw it was from Commodore Michel. The Commodore was an older man whose sandy blond hair had not yet turned grey. He was smiling but his brown eyes were serious.

'I read your report Captain. Fascinating, fascinating. I agree it's worth looking into.'

'I'm glad you can see it, sir. The threat is escalating, as the timeline shows.'

'Oh, I'm not sure about that. I called to tell you I've passed your data on to Intelligence, it's in their jurisdiction now.'

'But sir, my contacts on the other worlds agree -'

'Better to let the experts look at the evidence. Don't worry, it's all in hand. Thank you for bringing it to my attention.'

'But sir -' The Commodore had gone. Darrow slammed his fist on the table.

Intelligence! He may as well have buried it, he thought. *I'm right! I know I am. Why can't he see? What has to happen before they take it seriously?*

His office door buzzed, then Holland entered.

'The crew's reports are all in, sir, if you want to see them… Captain, are you all right?'

Darrow paused. 'I've just had an infuriating conversation with Commodore Michel.'

'Is there anything I can do, sir?'

'Maybe a reality check.' Darrow said. 'Sit down Commander. You know I've got a hobby of collecting mysteries. My contacts have contributed to my collection with mysteries from their worlds. I recently found a pattern in some of them. Raw materials have been disappearing without a trace from all over the galaxy.'

Holland sat forward, 'Like the quartz from Pallas?'

'Yes and no. Pallas is the first place that multiple incidents have been recorded, though it's unclear if that's linked to the smuggling or not. Do you remember the video records and scans I had Commander Blackwell look at?'

Holland nodded.

'He found that under infrared light a figure could be seen.'

Holland considered for a moment. 'Invisible aliens? At least invisible to the visible spectrum. Are they just helping themselves to the raw materials they want?'

Darrow slapped his hand on the desk. 'Exactly! How come you can see it and Commodore Michel can't?'

Holland leaned back in his chair and paused for thought. 'Do you have solid evidence from elsewhere or just Pallas?'

'I've spoken to some of my contacts and their checks are turning up similar results. They've found the same unknown enzyme in the bodies of some of the victims, each death otherwise unexplained, and Dr Thomas found the same enzyme in Pavel Patla.'

'So they are stealing *and* killing. They have to be stopped.'

'I'm afraid that's not going to happen. Commodore Michel has passed my findings to Intelligence, where they'll sit on the pile indefinitely.'

Holland leaned forward. 'You know Admiral Keever?'

Darrow nodded.

'He's my uncle.'

'You kept that quiet! But what's that got to do with it?'

'Well, if I give him a friendly call, and just happen to

mention what you've discovered, you can't disobey if he wants to see your findings, can you?'

Darrow slapped the desk and smiled broadly.

Chapter 14

Within a few hours, everything changed, but not in quite the way Darrow had hoped. He was convinced that the Intruders were a real threat, and an expedition should be sent to gather information and locate them. What he had wanted was to provoke the investigation into action. When Admiral Keever called him, action had indeed been provoked. Without any formalities, Keever got down to business as soon as Darrow switched on the screen.

'Captain, thank you for your report.' Darrow could see the family resemblance with Holland, despite the silver hair and the paunch. 'I did some investigation myself, talked to my contacts on other planets, and I think you may have something.'

'Thank you, sir. Will you be sending an expedition?'

Keever raised an eyebrow. 'Let's think this through, shall we? Where do you propose we send them?'

Darrow frowned. *Had he overlooked that?* 'Well sir, initially to investigate the incidents more fully and to look for evidence of which direction they went.'

'Since they appear out of thin air in the planet's atmosphere, that's going to be difficult, don't you think?'

Darrow was thrown for a second, then his mind locked on to something the admiral said.

'Sir, did you say they appear in the planet's atmosphere? How do you know that?'

Keever smiled. 'There have been further developments. A military ship was scanning an area when one of your alien ships attempted a theft. I have video records which I'm sending you. It appears they have a warp drive which can operate within a planet's atmosphere, since the ship was not seen approaching or leaving - it just appeared above the planet's surface.' He paused. 'They also leave a distinctive "wake."'

'So we now have the means to follow them.' Darrow felt vindicated.

'I agree,' Keever continued, 'an expedition needs to be sent. I have given orders to Commodore Michel to organise it.'

'Thank you sir.'

'Keever out.'

Darrow's spirits sank. Commodore Michel, who had rejected his claims, was now aware that Darrow had gone over his head, and Admiral Keever had dumped it back on him. Darrow didn't relish the next time he had to speak to his commanding officer, he hoped he'd have time to forget this incident. Darrow's wish didn't come true, as Michel called him only an hour later.

'Captain, I believe Admiral Keever has spoken to you about these Intruders of yours.'

'Yes sir. He asked to see my report -'

'I'm not interested, Captain. The Admiral wants me to send an expedition. However, as you know the Bokan situation is a big drain on our resources at the moment and there are no ships available.' The Commodore smiled, but it didn't reach his eyes. 'I believe there is no one better qualified to lead that investigation than the one who did all the research. No one knows these Intruders, as you call them, like you do.'

'You're taking me away from the Kestrel to join an expedition, sir?'

'No Captain, you and the Kestrel *are* the expedition.'

'But we're not equipped, we're too small - '

Michel raised his hand. 'I know all your objections, Captain, and you're absolutely right. But there is no one else. If this situation is as urgent as you indicate, you have to do this.'

Darrow was shocked. 'Sir, as you know, first contact regulations state that -'

'I am fully aware of what the regulations state,' Michael frowned, 'but in an emergency, regulations sometimes have to be set aside.'

Darrow set his jaw. 'This is not an emergency, sir, just urgent. We can't go.'

'That sounds like insubordination, Captain.'

'We don't know what we're facing, sir. Our armaments -'

'We're not asking you to fight them,' Michel interrupted, 'just find out about them, *if* they exist. Figure out where they come from if possible. If you can safely talk with them, all well and good, otherwise run. Send back any information you gather - on a secure channel of course.'

Darrow's mind was in a whirl. He grabbed at another objection. 'Sir, I don't have a full crew.'

Michel wasn't phased. 'What crew do you need?'

Darrow struggled to concentrate. 'First Officer, Medical Officer, and two other crew.' A daring thought occurred to him. 'Commodore, I know of a man who would be available as First Officer. Nathaniel Parks is working in PACT Security on Earth, so it won't deprive another ship. He is an experienced First Officer, but has a weak shoulder. I worked with him before, which would be extremely useful, make the transition easier.'

'I'll put my aide on it, and let you know. Michel out.'

Darrow sat there stunned. This was not what he had in mind at all. He couldn't believe Commodore Michel would disregard so many regulations. It made him feel very uncomfortable. The Admiral had put the Commodore in a difficult position, and he was passing it on. The door chimed and Holland came in at his call.

'Captain, I was wondering if you've heard from my uncle Admiral Keever yet?'

'Unfortunately, yes,' Darrow said, waving him to a seat.

'Why "unfortunately"? Was he not convinced?'

'He was convinced all right, but he tossed it straight to Commodore Michel. So the Commodore knows I went over his head and is mad as hell.'

Holland winced. 'Ouch! The Commodore's been in touch then?'

'Just now, and guess who he's sending on an expedition to find these aliens?' Darrow paused for effect. 'The Kestrel!'

'He *is* mad, and I don't mean angry. We're neither equipped for exploration nor armed for infiltration. And with the MO and I off at T'Lon, you'll only have half a crew.' Holland said wryly. 'I know my uncle, he's playing politics.'

'They both are.' Darrow said. 'The Admiral is looking for glory for ordering the expedition, and putting one over on the Commodore. The Commodore is squeezed, so he takes it out on me.' Darrow folded his arms. 'Well, I have registered my objections, and if he does find some more crew, I'll be putting my objections in writing.'

'*If* he finds more crew. Personnel say there aren't any.'

'We'll just have to wait and see.'

* * *

By the time the Kestrel was approaching T'Lon space station, Commodore Michel had found solutions to the crew shortage, though not optimal ones, Darrow thought. Nathaniel Parks was appointed as First Officer and Dr Matthew Ky, a doctor from the T'Lon space station, placed as MO, but no additional crew was available. So Balitoth would return, cutting short his recuperation period, and Tabitha would stay on. The Commodore himself had called Tabitha's Principal at the training school. Parks and Balitoth would rendezvous with the Kestrel at T'Lon. Despite Darrow's objections, the Kestrel was indeed going on this mission.

Darrow briefed his senior officers and then summoned Tabitha.

'Stand easy, Trainee. We've been assigned a new mission. I still need a crewman, but I don't want a passenger. If you're willing to work, Commodore Michel has arranged with Principal Hernandez for you to stay on with us.'

'Really, sir? Oh thank you sir!' Tabitha started forward,

and Darrow felt sure she was going to hug him, but she recovered herself just in time and saluted instead. Thankfully.

* * *

The captain gave Tabitha permission to call her parents and asked her to reassure them that she was and would remain all right. She used the screen in her cabin, after authorisation. There were the usual delays in connection to allow for the relays, but this time she was lucky enough to catch her father, so the conversation went much easier.

'Hi Dad, how's Mum?'

'She's calmed down, don't worry.' He smiled. 'How are you?'

'I'm great, I've been on a mission already!' She laughed at his look of surprise. 'We went to help with a mine rescue on an asteroid. We were in one quarter gravity and underground!'

'What? I thought you were going into space!'

'I am, but this is a Fast-Response ship - we're like the emergency services. We never know what's next.'

'Do you realise you're saying 'we' already?'

She drew back. 'No, am I? I'm still settling in really. Anyway, we've got a new mission now and it might be a long one. Did Principal Hernandez call?'

'Not just your Principal, the Commodore's aide called too. Seems it's an emergency,' he paused. 'This is more than you expected, Tab. Are you sure? You can get off at the space station, and they'll send you home. They can't make you stay, and there's no shame in coming home if you don't feel up to it.'

'No Dad. When I heard about the new mission, I was sure they'd send me home, and I was so disappointed. The fact that they want me is wonderful. I'm so glad you said I could stay.'

'Didn't think we could say anything else really. I know

it's what you want. Well, you take care, and keep in touch.'

'I will.   Love you. Try to break it to Mum gently will you?'

Chapter 15

Having never been on a space station, Tabitha was a bit nervous when she was told she had free time and could explore if she wanted. She called up a map of the station. It reminded her of a spinning top she'd had as a child. The gravity, created by the station's spin, meant you walked with your head always pointing towards the centre and your feet towards the rim, so all the floors and ceilings were curved. *It must feel like constantly walking uphill*, she thought. The floors nearer the rim spun faster, so had higher gravity, those nearer the centre, had lower gravity. Earth-normal gravity of 1G was halfway out. The central column's spin produced just enough gravity to be able to stay upright.

Chambers had to run an errand, so he offered to show her the way onto the station.

'Ships dock at a non-rotating ring at the base of the station,' Chambers said, 'so your first challenge is to negotiate your way to the centre and through the doorway between the stationary ring and the rotating central column.'

'What? There must be an easier way. What about people with no experience in zero gravity? They don't just push them out of the airlock do they?'

'Well, no,' Chambers laughed. 'There are pods. You can get someone to push you about like a parcel, but you don't want that do you?' He looked at her.

'Is that a challenge? I suppose experiencing one quarter gravity on Pallas prepared me a bit. I would like to have a go. You'll be there to rescue me, won't you?'

Without further ado, Chambers grabbed Tabitha's arm and they launched themselves out of the airlock. It was like flying. Tabitha had never felt so free, she couldn't keep the smile from her face. She soon found that any movement affected direction of travel, so she let Chambers do most of the steering. There were rails in the ceiling and floor, so

Chambers was able to pull them along and keep them on course. Part way to the centre she noticed large boxes being expertly guided. Most were cargo, but one or two had windows in and carried people. *Those who can't cope with zero gravity,* she thought, feeling a surge of pride that she was giving it a go.

As they neared the centre of the ring, Chambers pointed to the doorways labelled IN and OUT, to prevent those arriving from colliding with those launching themselves out into the zero gravity. They waited for the doorways to line up then went through into the rotating central column, and found maps and lifts.

'I think I'll head for a cafeteria first,' Tabitha said. 'There's one on the map here, out towards the rim. It would be comforting to be back in my own gravity for a while.'

'That means you have to go up to the right level and then transfer to a lift going outwards,' Chambers said, pointing to the map. 'Gravity will increase as you go.'

Chambers left her when she changed lifts.

* * *

Tabitha's Journal

Wow! I feel like I'm on a roller-coaster. It's less than a week since I left Alpha, and things have changed again! I was excited to come, but I thought it would be routine, just on patrol, with plenty of time to settle in. After the mine rescue, we've been diverted to a space station and there's to be a new mission. They haven't told us what yet, but it's going to extend my stay, which is a bit scary, but I wouldn't back out for anything.

The space station is called T'Lon. It's like an interchange point for interstellar travel. It spins to create gravity, so I've now been in zero gravity and 2G, all within minutes! You know what? Zero gravity is great fun! Andrew helped me the first time, on the way onto the station, but coming back, I did it on my own. I loved it!

It was a strange experience, going on the outward lift. I

actually felt heavy as I passed the halfway mark. I must be getting used to 1G. I decided to get off when the lift announced they were approaching 2G. The map outside showed the cafeteria down the corridor to the right. Within a few steps, I adjusted to the gravity and felt really comfortable. I didn't realise how much I missed this, and started to feel homesick. I hesitated, uncertain whether to go on or go back, and a man shouted at me and made me jump.

'Oh, sorry!' I said, turning to find a man who was unmistakably Alphan. 'I wanted a taste of home, but ... but now I'm not so sure.'

'How long have you been away?'

'Only a few days.'

He looked me up and down. 'First time?'

I nodded.

'Look at it this way,' he smiled, 'if you don't go, you'll regret it. What are you going to do - skulk around the lighter levels?'

'Since you put it that way, now I have to go!'

He offered me his arm. 'Permit me to escort you. My name is Vaughan Gibson, I'm the Engineer on the freighter Lincoln.'

I took his arm and introduced myself. I said I was hungry, so we had a meal and then spent a pleasant couple of hours touring the station before it was time for me to return to the Kestrel. Well, I've seen so many alien races, I think I had my mouth open most of the time. I took loads of pictures.

'Thanks so much for looking after me,' I said. 'I definitely owe you a favour.'

'Don't worry, I was new once. Just paying it forward. Now it's down to you. Best of luck.'

I got in the lift, the lift doors closed and whisked me down to the docking ring. This time there was no Andrew to help me, and I hesitated near the doors.

'Oh heck,' I said, 'go for it!' and launched myself.

When I came back to the Kestrel I had to go and lie down for a bit, just to take it all in.

This is more like it!

* * *

Admiral Keever's contacts on the other PACT worlds had alerted their governments, and an urgent meeting had been arranged at T'Lon for representatives of all the species to meet Captain Darrow. Darrow arrived at T'Lon to find orders from the Admiral to brief them personally on his investigations and discuss how to proceed. Darrow was not looking forward to dealing with so many different species at once - they rarely all agreed. He waited nervously in the small conference room for the representatives to arrive.

The Zoan arrived first: stocky, dark and reptilian. He bowed formally to Darrow and took a seat. The Casparan arrived next: the size of a ten-year-old human, with green skin and an imperious air. Seeing that the table was arranged with three seats either side and Darrow at the end, the Casparan moved one of the chairs to the far end, gave Darrow a curt nod, and sat down. The Altairian and the Ochran arrived together, both tall, but one pink and fragile looking, the other robust and green. Both nodded to the others and sat, the Ochran being careful to sit next to Darrow, as far away from the Casparan as possible. They may be in alliance, but some of the species were still suspicious of each other.

Darrow, who had risen when they came in, sat down and shifted in his seat while he waited for the others. The Kohathi bustled in, her grey whiskers and wrinkled face making her seem like a little old human man - it was impossible to tell how old she actually was. Since Kohathi males and females dressed alike, the only visible evidence that she was female was the bow in her hair. Before she had time to take her seat, the last one arrived. The Anak, though still humanoid, facially resemble Earth lions, with bushy hair, long jaws, and large canines. This one was tall too, but carried himself gracefully as he took the last seat, next to the Casparan, who shifted further away.

Darrow stood.

'Ladies and gentlemen, thank you for coming to this meeting. I am Captain Darrow. My ship, the Kestrel, has been given the task of finding the aliens referred to as Intruders. Have you all read the information sent to you?'

There was a general murmur. Darrow decided to accept it as a 'yes'.

'The incidents I have collated stretch back nearly three years, but they are increasing in frequency, suggesting a full-scale raid may be imminent. I have just come from a razor quartz mine where they had four incidents in as many months, suggesting that razor quartz is something they are in urgent need of.'

'The problem for us,' said the Zoan, 'is the unrest on some of the colony worlds. The incidents you have identified have been associated with this. Now these aliens have been identified, we are working to separate the incidents out, but telling the difference is rather difficult.'

'We believe we may have found incidents even farther back,' said the Ochran.

'Can we get on with where we are now?' snapped the Casparan in his high-pitched voice. 'We can all compare notes later.'

'Let me bring you up to date,' Darrow raised his voice to regain their attention. 'At the quartz mine a man on guard claimed he saw a shimmering figure in dim light, which disappeared when he shone a light on it. No one believed him until we adjusted the light on the visual record to infrared.'

Darrow activated the projection on the wall behind him and stepped to the side. The best video record from Pallas played in split screen, one side with normal lighting, the other in infrared.

'Figures have been seen on other adjusted video records too,' he continued. 'And now - we have video record of a ship. This,' he changed the display, 'is it in slow motion, as the shot only lasts a few seconds.'

He had only seen this briefly. What he saw still astonished him. In a clear blue sky a shape suddenly materialised - the shape of a butterfly. Now Pavel Patla's dying word made sense. Its iridescent sheen made it look even more like a butterfly, until a bird flew nearby, giving a sense of the scale of the ship. It was easily three times the size of the Fast-Response ships. Then, as quickly as it appeared, it disappeared. Darrow turned off the projector and sat.

'Is it a cloaking device?' the Casparan asked.

'No. It seems they can operate their warp drive within planetary atmosphere. I don't understand how it works, but it obviously does - they must have an incredible braking system and inertial dampers. There was another important facet to this appearance. We discovered they leave a spacial disturbance in their wake, something we can scan for and therefore follow. That is Kestrel's mission.'

'Which way did they go, Captain?' asked the Kohathi female, her soft voice trembling. 'Whose world is nearest to their incursions?'

'We have only their initial direction to go on so far - but if they flew straight, they went through Altairian space.' There was an uncomfortable silence.

'In that case, Captain,' the Altairian said, his cranial spines lifting, 'I insist a representative of the Altairian government go with you. If we are nearest, it is only right we have a say in the decisions of the mission.'

Darrow was far from comfortable with the suggestion. It could be difficult having someone on board not technically under his command.

'What about the new technology they have?' the Casparan demanded of the Altairian. 'You want first pick of that too, no doubt. If an Altairian is going, I insist on a Casparan also.'

'There is no question of new technology,' Darrow said. 'We are simply on a fact-finding mission. If we find them amenable to dialogue, a diplomatic team will be sent.'

'There will be no time,' said the Zoan. 'If they want to talk, we must talk. I think there should be a representative of all the PACT species. This is far too important to allow just one race to take the lead.'

This was getting ridiculous. 'My crew does include a Zoan and an Altairian,' said Darrow.

'But they are subject to your commands,' said the Casparan. 'They will not stand up for the rights of their people.'

'And what about the other species, Captain?' said the Kohathi.

'My ship is not big enough,' Darrow said.

'You carry cargo, do you not,' the Ochran said, 'and occasional passengers?'

'Yes, I'm sure you can make room,' the Zoan said.

The Casparan raised his voice. 'Casparans are known for their fairness, because of our long history of oppression,' he glared at the Ochran. 'I am sure we could represent you all.'

The chorus of voices rose in discord. For a moment it seemed that Darrow would lose control of the meeting. He was appalled at the suggestion he should take more people, especially people with no practical function. He raised his hands, prepared to shout them down. The Anak, who had been silent thus far, rose to his feet and roared. That got everyone's attention. When they had all fallen silent, he looked at each one in turn and nodded. Then he turned to Darrow.

'Captain, I know it will be difficult for you, but we must insist on representation.'

'It's not difficult, it's impossible,' Darrow said. 'Permissable occupancy regulations state that overcrowding is not allowed except in an emergency. There are all sorts of risks …'

As they went to make objections, the Anak roared again, stunning them all into silence with their mouths open. But when he spoke it was in a soft voice, still somehow chilling. 'I'm afraid we outrank you Captain. Do you wish to refuse the mission and go back to your superiors?'

Darrow weighed up the options, thought about giving up the once-in-a-lifetime opportunity, the urgency of the mission, and came to a decision. He stood up and locked eyes with the Anak until he sat down. 'I understand your position, but you must understand mine. On the Kestrel *I* am Captain, like it or not I am the one in command and I will not take passengers.' He looked around the table. 'Each representative you send, no more than one per race, must have skills that contribute to the mission and the running of the ship. They must be willing to carry out any assigned duties *under my command.* And they must be aware they will not have a comfortable journey: the Kestrel is a small working vessel, we have no diplomatic or even passenger quarters, they will be sharing the accommodation on a ship that is already cramped. The Kestrel leaves in twenty hours.'

Darrow left before his temper got the better of him. *First Michel and now them! Did they know what they were asking? How could he ask his crew to undertake such a mission?*

* * *

As Darrow made his way down the corridor, he spotted a tall blond human figure up ahead, carrying a kit bag.

'Nate!'

The figure stopped and turned.

'I was worried they wouldn't let you come,' Darrow said as he caught up to the man. 'You have no idea how much I need a friendly face right now.'

Nathaniel Parks turned round, dropped his bag, and enveloped Darrow in a bear hug. Almost 20 centimetres taller than Darrow, broad with straight blond hair, the higher head was a distinct contrast to Darrow's own slim figure and curly dark crown.

'I wasn't sure either,' he said. He held Darrow at arm's

length. 'It's so good to see you. How did you swing it, with my dodgy shoulder?'

'Desperate times require desperate measures,' Darrow's smile slipped under a frown. 'Do you mind? What did Greta say?'

'She was pleased for me. It's been great to be around for the children but they're growing up now, and she knows how much I've missed Fast-Response. I never thought I'd get the chance for active service again.'

'Just be careful not to put that shoulder out again. Greta will kill me if you get hurt.'

Now it was Parks' turn to become serious. 'Any chance of that? I don't really know what we're going to do. Some kind of long range expedition, the Commodore said.'

'Commodore Michel spoke to you personally?'

'Yes, I was very surprised. He asked me nicely if I would go, too. They must be desperate,' Parks laughed. 'The Commodore really hates the Admiral you know. He must have been livid when he dumped the mission on him.'

'I'm even more desperate now,' said Darrow. 'I've just come from a meeting where the PACT members insisted on each sending a representative along on the mission. I nagged for a full crew complement, and now I've got to fit in six extra!'

Parks whistled. 'Kestrel is a standard Fast-Response ship isn't she? It's going to be a squeeze.'

'Yes, and as First Officer, you can work out where to put everyone.'

'Oh thanks, *Captain*.' Parks gave him a mock salute. 'I'm not on duty yet. See you later.'

Chapter 16

The Kestrel seemed deserted when Parks boarded through the airlock, which opened into the cargo bay. The crew were taking the chance to stretch their legs and get a change of scenery while they could. Station personnel were loading supplies and equipment and checking the ship over. He found a slight figure watching over them, consulting a pad. The difference in their heights was even greater than with Darrow. Parks saw the man's blue armband, and when he looked up noted the Asian features and straight black hair.

'Are you Lieutenant-Commander Hoy? I'm Commander Parks, the new First Officer.'

Hoy snapped to attention and saluted.

'As you were,' Parks said, and sat on a large container so he wasn't overshadowing the man. 'What do I need to know?'

'I've prepared briefing files for you sir, but the main thing at the moment is the crew are unsettled and under stress,' Hoy sighed. 'We were sent on patrol one crewman short, then Lieutenant Balitoth fell ill. So the Captain roped in the top trainee from the Alphan PACT Academy. She's had to stay on, because we're still one short, she's been good though. You'll be responsible for her training and supervision. Balitoth is coming back to us after a major operation, so he's still convalescing and needs to be on light duties. Commander Holland just left for his own command, though he's a Captain now of course, and Dr Robinson got injured on our last mission. So out of eleven crew, we've two new - yourself and the MO, one trainee, and unfit. Until Balitoth fell ill the crew had been together for six months, many of us for at least a couple of years, but now we're a practically new team.'

Parks nodded. 'I'm afraid it's going to be even more

stressful. The Captain will hold a crew briefing, so keep this confidential for now, but we're taking on six extra passengers.'

'There's no room!'

'We're going to have to make room. I'm seeing the Engineer next to find out if we can build cabins in the cargo bay. I thought I should give you advance warning - I will need your help to keep order.'

'Yes sir, I'll do my best.'

* * *

Parks went to Engineering in search of Blackwell. He found a skinny pair of legs sticking out of an open panel.

'Excuse me, I'm looking for the Engineer.'

The legs wriggled until a body and then a grimy face appeared. 'Commander Blackwell is on the station, and you shouldn't be in here.' Stubbs finally spotted the green armband and jumped to his feet and saluted. 'Sorry sir. Ensign Stubbs sir.'

'As you were,' Parks smiled. 'Commander Parks, First Officer. I see Commander Blackwell is keeping you busy.'

'Yes sir, but I'm off duty once I finish here.' He indicated the panel. 'Sir, would you be able to assist me in getting a part? I need a series T flow integrator, and the stores are being so slow in responding. It's me the Commander will shout at if it's not installed by tonight.'

'I'll see what I can do. It might put me in the Commander's good books. Do you know where on the station he is?'

'No sir,' he checked his watch, 'but he'll be back here in an hour.'

'Thank you. Carry on.'

Stubbs got back inside the panel, but not before Parks noticed his hopeful smile. Parks headed off to the stores.

* * *

An hour later Parks returned to Engineering, a T flow integrator in his hands. No harm in making a good first impression. He found Blackwell at his desk. The burly man looked up and then went back to studying his computer screen.

'Brought a sweetener have you, Commander Parks?' Blackwell said. 'Trying to impress me?'

Parks played along. 'Absolutely. I'll take all the help I can get.' He offered his hand. 'Do you need sweetening, Commander Blackwell?'

Taking Parks' hand, Blackwell smiled, as they shook. 'Definitely.'

'I thought I should speak to you, since the engineer usually knows most of what's going on. You already know who I am, for example. What do I need to know?'

'That this is a good ship, and the crew mostly get on with each other, so don't go upsetting things.'

'Mostly?'

'It's not all plain sailing. You wouldn't expect it to be, with eleven people cooped up together for weeks at a time. Balitoth doesn't show emotion, which you already know about Zoans, and some of the crew haven't got over that yet. And the Captain has probably told you not to put much weight on Chambers' record. He's a fine helmsman, but he's still insecure.'

Parks mentally filed that away for later.

'Noted,' he said. 'I'm afraid I *am* going to upset the crew, as I've got to figure out how to fit six new passengers in. The Alliance worlds are each sending a representative. It won't be easy.'

'Well, it never is,' Blackwell said. 'They make these decisions without a thought for how it's going to work out in practice. Stubbs can move into Engineering, if it helps. I can make a room for him in one corner. We can also create an extra cabin or two in the cargo bay, though we'll need to carry extra food supplies, so it'll be tight. If you don't mind some advice?' He paused and waited for Parks to nod. 'Make sure the extra people are crew, not passengers, and do their share of the work. That will help reduce any resentment. The crew won't give you any trouble, if you treat them right.'

'Thanks. I'll draw up some plans and come and discuss them with you, once I've had a look around.' Parks left.

* * *

Later Parks was called to the airlock to meet the new doctor. He found a plump older man with caramel-coloured skin and straight black hair touched with grey. He was surrounded by boxes, bags and crates.

'Is anyone about?' he said. 'I can't hump all this stuff myself.'

'Can I help Doctor? I'm Commander Parks, First Officer.'

The Doctor looked him up and down. 'I suppose carrying boxes is beneath you.'

'No,' Parks said, ignoring the insubordination, 'but I'm afraid you can't bring all that on board, there's not enough room.'

The Doctor looked from the pile to the ship in consternation. 'Oh! I thought... No, I didn't think actually. I haven't served on a ship for decades.' He sat down on a crate. 'Sorry, I didn't even introduce myself. Matthew Ky.'

They shook hands.

'Look,' said Parks, 'why don't you come and see your quarters, then you'll get a better idea of how much room you have.'

As they walked, Ky looked around.

'I'm only a few months off retirement. This is insufferable! Sending me on some damn fool mission, with no warning! What do I want, gallivanting off across the galaxy at my age?'

'We all have to obey orders, I'm afraid,' said Parks.

'Think of it as a last challenge to round off your career.'

'Hmph!'

Parks left him inspecting sick bay and his quarters and went to find someone to help him sort out his boxes and bring on board only what he decided to take. A miserable MO was the last thing they needed.

* * *

Ryan arrived back on board and bumped into Parks.

'Sorry sir.' He saluted, looking up at the big blond man. 'Ensign Sam Ryan sir, Medic and Comms.'

'Commander Parks, your new First Officer. Are you on duty, Medic?'

'We're not working to set shifts at the moment sir. I'm off duty until I'm needed.'

'Well, you're needed. The new MO just arrived, Dr Ky. He needs help with his stuff and a detailed familiarisation with sick bay.'

'Yes sir.'

Ryan headed for sick bay, where Dr Ky was opening and shutting cupboards and drawers.

'Medic Ryan reporting sir. Commander Parks notified me you were on board.'

'About time too,' Ky replied. 'Who organised these cupboards?'

'Dr Robinson had a system, sir. Supplies are organised into categories of injuries, so everything for treatment is together.'

'Hmph! That's all right for emergencies, but it will not do for my sick bay. I want everything alphabetical. You can do it once you've brought my things aboard.'

Ryan's heart sank. *What a job!*

'Yes sir. I'll go and fetch your things now sir. Are they outside?'

'You can't get them yet, I've not sorted through them. Damn accommodation's not big enough!'

'Sir, if I may suggest, why don't you go and see to your things, and I'll start in here? You can call me when you're ready to have them brought on board. I'll work off the inventory - get the computer to sort it alphabetically.'

Ryan turned to the console and called up the inventory.

'I think I should review the inventory before we leave, to ensure the supplies are adequate.'

'Yes Doctor.'

Ky said, 'Carry on,' and left to sort out his belongings.

Ryan groaned and rolled his eyes.

* * *

Darrow called the whole crew to a meeting room on the station, to brief them on the mission. Chambers brought Tabitha, whose eyes were like saucers from exploring the station's size and facilities. Darrow looked the crew over with a frown on his face as if he was trying to anticipate future problems. Tabitha looked round in the same way. She had met everyone except the two who were consulting pads as each crewman came in. When they were all seated, Darrow called the meeting to order.

'I know there's been speculation as to what's happening, but I'm now in a position to brief you fully. I didn't want to say anything until all the arrangements were made. We now have a full crew complement, albeit rather rushed.' He nodded to the two men with the pads. 'This is Commander Parks, our new First Officer, and Dr Ky, our new MO. I expect you to give them every assistance. The only crewman still missing is Balitoth, who is on his way from Alpha after his operation, and will be checked over by PACT doctors before he is allowed to resume his duties.' There was a collective sigh of relief. 'Dr Ky will receive a full report and recommendations for his continuing care. He will be on light duties for the first few weeks.'

He paused until everyone gave him their full attention.

'There have been a number of unexplained thefts of raw

materials across the galaxy. I've been looking into these incidents, and evidence is accumulating of a previously unknown alien race being responsible. They appear to be energy beings who are invisible in normal light. I'll put all the details on the database, but Admiral Keever is convinced they are a serious threat. Since there are no other ships available, Kestrel is being sent to investigate them. The scanners will be adapted to follow the spacial disturbance their ships leave in their wake. We're to gather as much information as we can about these beings and send it home, to enable plans to be made to meet this threat. We're not expected to engage them, except to defend ourselves. However, if an opportunity comes for peaceful dialogue, I mean to take it. Now, this is all confidential, so you're not to mention it on the station or when you contact home. Are there any questions?'

Tabitha nervously raised her hand.

'Captain, how far is it? How long will we be gone?'

'I can't give any guarantees, except to say their home world is obviously not in known space. So I expect to be heading out to the edge of the galaxy. It may take some time.'

Tabitha swallowed as she digested that. This little bit of work experience was getting bigger and bigger. She looked up to find Stubbs watching her. He smiled and winked as their eyes met. She quickly looked away.

'What about weapons, sir?' Hoy asked. 'We're not equipped for any major fighting.'

'We're hoping to avoid that,' Darrow replied, 'but if it comes to it, we'll have to manage with the weaponry we have. There is no time or funds for enhancements.'

They were all silent. Tabitha looked around. Only the doctor seemed unhappy with the prospect. The rest of the crew seemed to take it in their stride. Darrow spoke again.

'There is more news. The Alliance races have insisted on each sending a representative with us. So there will be six extra crew members.'

He waited for the unhappy murmuring to die down.

'I have insisted they are not passengers, and will be assigned duties, so it will lighten your loads, but it's going to be a squeeze to accommodate them. Commander Parks has been working out where we're going to put them. Commander.'

Tabitha's throat was suddenly dry. More aliens? Parks called up a file on his pad.

'Thank you Captain. Now, I don't know any of you, so if these arrangements cause anyone serious problems, let me know. I have discussed it with the Captain and I consider it best if most of the crew share a cabin with one of the representatives. Your duty will be to help them to fit in with us. Commander Blackwell is creating extra cabins where he can. Ensign Ryan will be moving into sick bay and Trainee Enns into Engineering - they're going to make a corner for each of you.'

Dr Ky interrupted. 'This is unacceptable! The quarters are small enough as it is. If Ensign Ryan is living in sick bay, where will we put the injured?'

'We rather hope there won't be any, Doctor,' said Parks. 'However, if anyone needs to be in sick bay for a long period, Ryan can take their bed.'

Both Ryan and Ky looked equally unhappy with that suggestion. Parks continued.

'Ensign Reuel will share with his fellow Altairian in his cabin, likewise Lieutenant Balitoth will share with the Zoan in Stubbs and Ryan's cabin. Lieutenant Chambers will share his cabin with the Kohathi, and Ensign Stubbs will move to a new cabin set up in the cargo bay, and share with the Ochran.'

Stubbs was shocked. 'The cargo bay?' he said.

Parks grimaced, 'Sorry Ensign, you get the short straw.' He turned back to the rest of the crew.

'Lieutenant-Commander Hoy will share his cabin with the Casparan, since they can be a bit prickly, and I will have the Anak in with me. They can be pretty scary, so I won't inflict him on any of you. Commander Blackwell is providing beds, etc., and you all need to move today, before the new ones arrive. Any questions?'

Chambers spoke up. 'What if we don't get on?'

Parks frowned. 'You'll just *have* to get on. Each of you is to play host to your assigned representative. Do everything you can to make them feel comfortable and welcome - but you are not their servants.' There were frowns on every face. 'I know it's difficult - just think of it as experience in diplomacy and inter-racial relations.' He sighed. 'I'll be seeing each of you individually in the next few days to get acquainted and see how your room-mate is getting on. In the mean time I suggest you research any of the races you don't know so we don't cause any unintentional offence.' He turned to Darrow. 'Anything else Captain?'

Darrow shook his head. 'Dismissed.'

Chapter 17

Ryan and Stubbs were in their cabin packing.

'It's not fair that I have to go into the cargo bay,' Stubbs grumbled, slamming his locker door. 'I think it must be against health and safety regulations or something.'

'I'd rather babysit a representative than sleep in sick bay,' said Ryan, as he threw clothes in his container. 'Have you met Dr Ky? I thought working with him was going to be torture. Now I'm going to sleep outside his door.'

'What sort of cabin can they make in the cargo bay?' said Stubbs. 'We'll probably be sleeping on the floor behind a pile of crates.'

'You know Commander Blackwell. He'll do the best job possible making that cabin decent. If not for you, then for the representative. I'll bet they'll be quick to complain if it's not good enough.'

'Serve them right for pushing themselves on us. I think it's a stupid idea.'

'Look at it from their point of view.' Ryan sat down. 'The burden is all on the Captain to decide what to do about this new race of aliens. His decisions may have far-reaching consequences. The other races want to have someone to watch out for their interests. I think the Captain is going to have his hands full.'

Stubbs looked up from the container he was packing. 'I'm hoping to have my hands full before long.' He smiled. 'That new trainee is going to be in engineering. I'll be there with her all the time I'm on duty.'

'Steady on, Roy. She's only 18, and they're conservative on Alpha - she probably hasn't had a boyfriend yet.'

'Oh, I'm going to be the perfect gentleman. This is too good an opportunity to miss.'

'Well you be careful.' Ryan laughed. 'She's Alphan, and very strong. She just might break you.'

* * *

'Why do I have to go into Engineering?' Tabitha said to Chambers as she packed. 'I'm sure Commander Blackwell doesn't approve of me.'

'Don't worry, Tab,' Chambers said, 'His beef is with the Captain. He doesn't think it was a good idea to take you on. Commander Blackwell's manner is abrupt, but he's fair. He'll look after you. Stubbs is the one to be careful of.'

'Stubbs? Why?'

'He's the youngest member of the crew, that's all, not much older than you. Thinks he's a ladies man. Don't let him take advantage of you.'

She raked her fingers through her untidy hair. 'At least I don't have to share a cabin with an alien.'

'Now, now, your Alphan prejudices are showing,' Chambers laughed gently.

'No,' Tabitha protested. 'That's not what I mean. I've got no experience of aliens. Having all these new ones on board is really scary. If I had to share a cabin with one, I'd be certain to make a mistake.' She could feel her panic rising.

'Listen,' Chambers stopped her packing for a moment and turned her to face him. 'They may look different, but they're just people. Of course you should research their characteristics and their culture, but they're all individuals, just like us. We're all going to need time to get to know each other. Maybe you can even do it as part of your training - ask Commander Parks. You've already met Reuel, and he was alright, wasn't he? Balitoth's the same.'

She sat down on the bed. 'I feel strange with him coming back. It's because of his illness that I'm here.'

Chambers sat beside her. 'It was no one's fault, and he'd like to meet you, I'm sure. Not that he'll show it, of course - remember Zoans don't show emotion, but it doesn't mean they don't feel it. Balitoth has developed ways of expressing himself to help us humans understand him, but the new Zoan might not do that.'

'See what I mean? I didn't know that. And what about these Ochrans and Casparans? I looked them up and they look the same when you see them separately on screen. They're just different sizes.'

'Don't ever say that!' Chambers said, jumping to his feet. 'There's no love lost between them.'

'I thought they were two variations of the same people, because they live together too.'

'Where've you been? The Ochrans conquered Caspar, and they didn't live together, the Casparans were in servitude. The Casparans only gained independence a few decades ago. My grandfather told me about it, he was there.'

Tabitha bristled. 'That's why I'm out here! They don't tell us *anything* back home. I've never even *heard* of some of these aliens.' She dropped her voice. 'I'm afraid I'm going to say or do something to offend them.' The panic rose again. She felt so naive.

'Hey, don't worry about that, just be polite, and if you don't know, ask them.' He playfully punched Tabitha on the arm. 'I'm sure they won't bite - most of them, anyway.' He laughed at her alarm.

She sighed and resolved to make the best of things. *I'm stuck here anyway, so I'll just have to find a way to talk to them,* she thought.

'Remind me not to ask you for advice again,' said Tabitha. 'Maybe I'll ask the Anak guy, just to show you.'

* * *

Ryan was still reorganising sick bay when a message arrived from T'Lon's medical section.

'Doctor, Balitoth's file and the medical report have just been sent. He has been cleared to join us. He is on his way over.'

Ky came over to the console. 'Go and meet him while I read his notes. Bring him straight here.'

'Yes, sir.'

Ryan was delighted Balitoth was okay, and grateful for the respite in emptying and filling drawers and cupboards. Balitoth arrived at the airlock with his bag on a suspensor.

'Hello Ryan,' he said. 'would you carry my bag for me? I am not allowed to lift anything.'

'Good to see you,' Ryan said, taking his bag, switching off the suspensor and leaving it against the wall.'Dr Ky wants to see you straight away.'

'Where is Dr Robinson?' Balitoth asked as they walked.

'He had an accident on our last mission. He's going to be fine, but not quickly enough for this mission, so PACT drafted in Dr Ky.'

'I see by your face that this is not a good thing.'

Ryan looked around. 'I can't say more, just wait til you meet him.'

'I wish to leave my bag in my cabin before going to sick bay.'

'You're not in your old cabin, I'm afraid. The captain will explain, but we're having six Alliance representatives join us, so you'll be in my and Stubbs' cabin with the Zoan. Here.'

Ryan opened the cabin door and left the bag inside. Balitoth looked in and saw the empty lockers.

'So where are the two of you sleeping?'

Ryan grimaced as they started walking again. 'I'm in sick bay and Stubbs is in the cargo bay.'

'That is most curious. I appear to have missed a lot.'

'You bet! Captain Darrow wants to see you as soon as the Doc finishes checking you out.'

They arrived at sick bay and Ryan introduced Balitoth to Ky. Balitoth saluted.

'Never mind the saluting,' said Ky, 'come and sit here and lift your tunic. I see you still have the scar - I'll have to sort that out.'

'That would not be advisable, Doctor,' Balitoth said,

'unless you have a regenerator calibrated for Zoan physiology. Dr Robinson didn't have one.'

Ky looked sharply at Ryan. 'Well?'

'We don't have one, sir,' Ryan confirmed.

'Well you'd better get one. We're going to have two of them on board, so add it to the list.'

'Yes, sir.'

Ky continued with his examination, insisting on performing scans, even though the doctors on T'Lon had done them. Ryan went back to the reorganising.

'Right, you're done,' said Ky eventually. 'I expect you're tired after your journey. Go to your cabin and rest.'

Ryan intervened. 'The captain wants to brief him, sir. He instructed that Lieutenant Balitoth report to him as soon as he arrived.'

'I'm the MO and I say he is to rest. I will inform the captain myself.'

Ryan and Balitoth exchanged glances as Ky turned away to the intercom.

* * *

Tabitha moved into her makeshift cabin in a corner of Engineering. Blackwell had strung plastic sheeting on a wire and anchored it to the floor and one wall. She had a locker and a bed and access to one of the Engineering consoles. As she put the last of her belongings away, she was surprised by a visit from Parks. She'd only seen him at the staff briefing and wasn't sure what to expect. The presence of the much taller, senior officer had her stomach in knots.

'As you were, Trainee. Please, sit down.'

He indicated the bed and Tabitha was glad to comply to save her knocking knees.

'How are you settling in?'

'OK I guess.'

'Only OK? I heard you were excited at this chance to get out into space before your classmates.'

'Yes sir.'

Parks sat in the chair by the console.

'I'm sorry you're not happy here. At least I found out before we leave. There's just time to arrange to leave you on T'Lon and get you shipped home.'

Tabitha was shocked. She jumped up. 'Oh no sir! Don't send me away!'

'Look,' Parks said, 'I'm new here too. It's my job to look after you and make your time here valuable to you and us. You need to be honest with me.'

Tabitha looked at him doubtfully for a long moment, could she trust him with the honest answer? She sat down again with a sigh.

'I suppose I'm being unrealistic, sir, but all my life I've dreamed of going into space. When I was offered this placement, I thought my dreams had come true. But first I'm down a mine, now I'm stuck in Engineering, and soon I won't be able to move for aliens, and we don't even know where we're going…' her voice tailed off.

'The way I see it,' Parks said with a smile, 'there are two main problems we need to overcome: unrealistic expectations, and fear of aliens. Don't deny it, I've dealt with Alphans before. Anyone who is not Alphan is suspect, and although you've obviously tried hard, you can't help having absorbed some of your parents' prejudices. Well, here is the perfect opportunity to overcome them for good.'

Tabitha's stomach was doing somersaults.

He stood up and tapped his foot while he thought. 'First,' he began, 'your expectations. The stories always show the glamorous side of working in space. But even the heroes have to get down into the engines now and then, or fight through the vegetation on some strange world. You had the privilege, on Pallas, of helping a community to deal with a disaster -'

Privilege? She thought. *I never thought of it like that.*

'You made a difference,' Parks was saying. 'It could have been very different if you'd refused or panicked or just not made an effort. I've read the report about you. Your parents and your Principal will be proud. You should be at least a little pleased about it. Second, you won't be stuck in Engineering most of the time. This is just somewhere to rest and sleep. You'll have duties and studies, which I will plan. By the time you get back here, you'll be glad to put your head down!'

I don't know if I'm pleased about that! She thought.

'Third, people are just people, whatever shape or colour they are. They have hopes and fears the same as you, and traditions and customs and the way they like things done.'

Hope began to rise. Chambers had said the same thing.

'To them, you're the alien,' Parks said, pointing. 'Research what you can, ask questions, be considerate. Once the representatives arrive I'll arrange for you to meet each of them and see what they can teach you. Don't worry, they won't bite! Oh, I see someone has worked that one on you already. They really won't bite. Even the ones who can. They'll be on their best behaviour - I'll see to that.'

Tabitha began to see a way through.

'So here's your first project, I want you to write a report on each of the races, based on what you learn from them directly - no research. When we see what skills they have, there may be things they can teach you as part of your training too. In fact, it will help me if you keep them occupied. This ship is in good condition, so I fear there won't be enough maintenance work to go round, and everyone will get bored. Now, are you staying?'

Tabitha jumped to her feet and saluted. 'Oh yes sir!'

Parks smiled. 'Best if you drop the "Oh" in future, it's more professional.'

* * *

Tabitha sat in her makeshift cabin, behind the flimsy curtain, and read over her journal entry.

I thought the new mission was going to be something like

delivering medicines to a remote colony or something, but it's much more than that. We're off to the edge of the galaxy to look for a new race, and we're going to have representatives of all the PACT species on board. I've been shunted behind a curtain in Engineering to make room, and most of the crew have to share with a representative. I'm glad I don't have to do that, but I was really upset at all the changes.

I've been very confused lately, but I think I'm a bit clearer thanks to Commander Parks. Going out into space has been nothing like I expected. I can see I've not really stopped to think it through. It was so hard back home, all I could think of was getting away, not what I would be doing. I certainly didn't expect this! Space is starting to look very empty and cold. It's going to swallow me up if I let it get to me.

Now I've talked to Commander Parks I can see I have to concentrate on the positive things. This is turning out to be a once-in-a-lifetime opportunity. I will be able to spend time with all the allied species and learn from them first-hand. And how special to be part of the discovery of a new race! At least, that's what I keep telling myself - I'm not sure about these invisible aliens. How are we going to find them if they're invisible?

I was just getting to know Andrew too, and now I'm on my own behind a curtain in Engineering. I don't like it at all! Engineering is where that Roy works. I hope he doesn't try anything!

Chapter 18

The Altairian representative was the first to arrive. Darrow and Parks went to the airlock to meet him.

'See me once all the representatives have arrived,' Darrow said, 'I'd like to compare notes on first impressions.'

Like Reuel, the representative wore a back brace, but his was more elegant, as were his robes. His jacket and trousers were of shiny red material trimmed with dark pink braid, and he wore a short red cape. His manner was stiff and formal.

'Welcome to the Kestrel,' said Darrow as he introduced himself and Parks. 'I trust you have been briefed on the situation, specifically regards the accommodation and the need for you to share the workload while you're here.'

'Yes Captain. I am Madai Rendor.' He handed him a data stick. 'Here are my credentials. I have extensive knowledge of Altairian space and beyond. I understand that is our direction of travel.'

'Thank you. There will be a briefing as soon as all representatives are on board. Commander Parks will show you to your cabin.'

Rendor looked from Parks to his luggage and back again.

Start as you mean to go on, Parks thought.

'Bring your luggage, Mr Rendor,' Parks said with a smile, 'it's this way.'

There was a moment's hesitation, then Rendor complied.

Round one to me, Parks thought.

'Your cabin is on the lower deck,' Parks said as he led Rendor out of the cargo bay and down the corridor. 'You are sharing with our Altairian crewman, Ensign Shom Reuel. The mess hall, sick bay, and the Captain's office are all on the upper deck. Here is your cabin. This is Ensign Reuel. Reuel, this is Mr Rendor.' Parks turned and left them to it.

* * *

Rendor stepped inside the door and looked Reuel over.

'You wear no clan insignia on your uniform,' Rendor said.

'No,' said Reuel, 'I find it unnecessary. Your insignia, however, tells me we are the same clan, which makes things much easier.'

Rendor relaxed. 'That is good. These humans fight among themselves, but never seem to think we might do the same.'

'I find it simpler not to make a fuss over the distinctions,' said Reuel, taking Rendor's bag.

'But the distinctions are important! How can you give respect to the ancestors if you are sharing with someone with different ancestors? Who may have fought with your ancestors. No, it is quite impossible!'

'Normally, I share with a Zoan, so that doesn't arise.'

Rendor didn't respond, but his cranial spines registered the shock.

* * *

The Kohathi's name was Tofi Dathan. As with most Kohathi, it was difficult to determine his age, because he looked like a bewhiskered old human. The impression was enhanced by the fact that he appeared to be wearing a grey cardigan over his grey shirt and black trousers. He was introduced to Chambers.

'I am very pleased to make your acquaintance,' Dathan said, bowing. 'You will please excuse me, as I have never met a human before, and I do not know the protocol. I hope I will not be an annoyance to you.'

Chambers relaxed at once. 'I'm sure you won't be, but I'll tell you if you are.' *Oh no,* Chambers thought, *that sounded rude.*

Dathan didn't seem to notice, so Chambers hurried on. 'I have never spent much time with a Kohathi, so we can learn from one another. Let me help you with your bag.'

'Thank you. I hope to make my master proud and bring back much data.'

'You're an apprentice, then?'

'Yes, my master grows older, and feels it is time to pass his knowledge on. He has allowed me to be the one to learn of these new beings. This is a great honour, as I am young.'

Chambers made a mental shift of his picture of Dathan. 'Can I ask how old you are? I know Kohathi live much longer than humans.'

Dathan smiled. 'It is impertinent, but I will tell you. I am one hundred and twelve years old. My apprenticeship only began five years ago, so I have much to learn.'

'I'm sorry, I didn't mean to be impertinent, it's just that to human eyes, you look old. In human terms, you *are* old. I, for example, am thirty two years old, and have been considered an adult since I was eighteen.'

'I had read such a thing, but it is amazing to me. Why, you are just a baby!'

They both laughed.

* * *

Balitoth welcomed Hazeroth, his fellow Zoan, to his cabin. Hazeroth's scaly skin was darker than Balitoth's, indicating his greater age. He wore a jacket and trousers made of dark leather, with a tunic underneath that looked like wool. As the younger man, Balitoth bowed deeply.

'May the tribe smile on your endeavours, and may you bring them great honour,' Balitoth said.

Hazeroth acknowledged him and gave a smaller bow.

'May your tribe be gratified at my report.'

'May your family be my family, and my home your home,' said Balitoth, looking around, 'such as it is.'

There was a moment's silence, then Hazeroth spoke again.

'Now the formalities are over, where do I sleep?'

* * *

Stubbs had never considered himself particularly tall, but as he was introduced to the Ochran he felt particularly short and rather pink in contrast to the man. At over two meters tall, Merari Two could only just about stand upright in the room and he was certainly the greenest non-human Stubbs had ever met.

'Hello,' said Stubbs. 'Er, greetings.'

'Ergreetings? I am not aware of these,' said Merari with a frown. 'I do not wish to cause offence.'

'Oh no, I didn't mean… that is, well, just greetings. Come in, sit down. Let me take your bag.'

Stubbs rushed forward and took Merari's bag and waved him to a seat. Merari removed his finely-embroidered forest green coat, revealing a tunic and trousers exactly the same shade of spring leaf green as his skin.

'You seem nervous, my friend,' said Merari. 'There is no need, I assure you.'

Stubbs sat down heavily on his bed. 'I'm sorry. I've not met many aliens before.'

'I am only alien to you. To me *you* are alien.'

'Oh, I'm so sorry. I didn't mean…'

Merari laughed. 'Please, relax. I am not offended. Let us speak as friends.'

Stubbs sighed. 'Perhaps I shouldn't speak at all.'

'Certainly not. I suggest we begin by introducing ourselves. I am Merari Two, which means I am the second son of my father. I am a linguist, though my study of Earth Standard has not been extensive. I hope to learn more while I am here. Now it is your turn.'

'Oh, right. My name is Roy Stubbs, I'm the assistant engineer, and I don't have a father.'

'Really? How is that possible?'

Now it was Stubbs' turn to laugh. 'I did have a father, biologically, but I never knew him. My mother refused to tell me who he was. It's a long story.'

'No doubt there will be time for long stories during the mission. Now, I should unpack.'

* * *

A message came through that the Anak representative was going to be late, and would meet them the following day en route. There was no word from Caspar. Darrow decided he was going to be true to his word, and gave orders for the Kestrel to leave the station, even though the Casparan representative was missing. The Kestrel received permission to leave, disengaged from the docking port and began moving away from the station.

'T'Lon station to Kestrel.'

'Go ahead T'Lon.'

'You are required to return to the docking port to collect a Casparan gentleman. He is threatening a diplomatic incident if you do not.'

Darrow raised his eyebrows, but gave the command, and called Parks to the airlock. They re-docked to find a small green man at the airlock almost jumping up and down with rage. His long purple tunic that reached below his knees and his shoulder-length wavy hair made him look like a little girl having a tantrum. Darrow struggled to keep the smile off his face.

'This is an insult to the Casparan people! How dare you attempt to leave without me! We will not be excluded from this mission!'

Darrow waited calmly until the Casparan paused to take a breath from the mask he wore around his neck.

'The time of departure was clearly stated at the meeting. It is unfortunate that you were not able to arrive in a timely manner. I am Captain Darrow. This is my First Officer, Commander Parks. He will take you to your cabin while I arrange our departure. Again.'

Darrow turned to leave and the man came on board and

walked past Parks, pausing to look pointedly at his luggage.

'Excuse me,' Parks said, walking past him as he stopped and winking at Darrow, 'you forgot your luggage.'

The man drew breath, then thought better of it, and picked up his cases. Darrow hurried to leave before the representative saw his grin.

* * *

Parks escorted the Casparan to Hoy's cabin and made the introductions.

'This is Lieutenant-Commander Hoy, our Second Officer. This is our Casparan representative, who has not, as yet, given us his name.'

The little man drew himself up to his full one-and-a-half-metre height. 'I am Ser Desmar Barok, son of the Casparan Prime Minister. You may leave now while I unpack.'

'I recommend you sit down first,' said Parks, pulling a face at Hoy behind Barok's back, 'and brace for takeoff. It might get bumpy. I have to return to my duties, but Lieutenant-Commander Hoy will help you settle in.'

Parks left abruptly and Hoy and Barok sat down in silence until the word for normal operations came through.

'I should like some refreshments,' said Barok, lying on the bottom bunk and breathing from his mask. 'It has been a stressful time.'

'The mess hall is just down the corridor,' Hoy said. 'Turn left outside and it's on your right. Do you want to unpack first or later?'

Barok considered. 'I think you should bring my refreshments first and then unpack.'

'Excuse me?' This time it was Hoy who drew himself up. 'I am Second Officer on this ship, not your servant. You are to share this cabin with me and look after yourself. That is your locker, your cupboard, and the head is through there. I'm sure you would prefer to be alone if you're stressed, and I have better things to do.' He abruptly turned and left.

* * *

The following day the Anak ship arrived, and attempted to dock with the Kestrel. There was a crunch as it missed and had to pull away and try again. The second attempt was successful, and inspection showed only minimal damage to both ships, but Parks was called to sick bay. He found Dr Ky treating an unconscious human woman with a head injury while the Anak stood by. A head taller than Parks, the Anak was wider too, and his muscular physique and dark skin was apparent as he wore only a short kilt and a brightly-coloured cloth draped across his torso from one shoulder. He appeared rather ferociously feline with his long jaw, prominent canine teeth and thick wavy hair. He introduced himself.

'Greetings, I am Ehu Pathrusim.'

'Welcome. I am Commander Parks, First Officer. Should I call you Mr Pathrus?'

The Anak raised an eyebrow. 'Thank you for the correct adaptation, but Pathrus is my clan. You may call me Ehu.'

'Are you injured?'

'Fortunately, no. Only this human woman. The pilot's career will however, not remain uninjured for long once this is reported.'

'Accidents do happen,' said Parks.

'Docking is a basic manoeuvre, is it not?' Ehu growled. 'And this woman was injured because an unsecured crate fell on her. Such incompetence is unforgiveable!'

'Who is she? Were you bringing her here?'

'I do not know who she is, because she does not know who she is. We rescued her from the debris of a ship, which had crashed on a planetoid. She was not badly hurt, but could tell us nothing, until she heard our destination, and then she insisted she must come here too. We were planning to let her speak to someone here and then take her to where she could be assisted. Thanks to that idiot pilot, she now needs treatment, and he has fled. I apologise for the trouble.'

Ky interrupted. 'Do you mind talking elsewhere? I'm trying to treat this patient.'

Parks led Ehu away.

'My equipment and personal luggage is still in the cargo bay. Would you help me with it?'

As they went, Parks said, 'You are sharing with me. I hope it won't be too difficult for you.'

Ehu tilted his head at Parks. 'Are you intending to be difficult?'

Parks laughed. 'While sharing with an Anak? Definitely not.'

Ehu looked surprised and a little pleased. 'I think we will get along well. It is so tiresome when people are always afraid of us.'

Chapter 19

Now the last representative had arrived, Darrow called the first mission meeting. *Now we'll see what skills we have and whether they're all going to get on,* he thought. *Please let them get on, I've got enough on my plate.*

The biggest place available was the mess hall, with seating for eight. Darrow decided to meet the six representatives with just Parks and Hoy. That way, everyone but him had a seat, and it wouldn't be too cramped. If they needed more crew members present in future, it would be a problem. Darrow wondered if he should get the tables unscrewed from the deck to make more room.

When he entered, the others were already gathered. The representatives' bright clothing contrasted with the plain green uniforms of the crew, but the looks on their faces were not so bright. He noticed the Casparan still had the mask round his neck and breathed from it every now and then. *We need to find out what that is,* he thought, *I'm not having recreational drugs on board.* He swallowed hard and called the meeting to order.

'Good morning gentlemen. You have already met my First Officer, Commander Parks, and this is my Second Officer, Lieutenant-Commander Hoy. I have met most of you briefly, but you have not met each other, so I would like to begin by having each of you introduce yourselves and stating what you bring to this expedition.'

He turned to the nearest representative, the Kohathi, whose voice was soft and hesitant, and whose eyes fixed on the table in front of him.

'My name is Tofi Dathan. I am a xenobiologist. My master has taught me all he knows of the biology of the major species, now it is my turn to go out and gather more knowledge to pass on.' He looked up at Darrow. 'I am especially keen to learn more of humans, while we conduct our search, and excited about what we shall find out about these energy beings.' His eyes flicked round to see the others' reactions and then returned to looking down at the table. 'I offer my services to your doctor, to assist him.'

'Thank you,' Darrow said, and mentally catalogued Dathan as *nervous and inexperienced*. Darrow indicated they should go round the room. Sitting next to Dathan was the Zoan.

'My name is Hazeroth,' he said in a firm but sibilant voice. 'I have expertise in inter-racial relations and first contact. I offer my services should we be able to meet with this new race.'

The Casparan spoke up. His voice sounded childish after Dathan and Hazeroth, and the petulant tone increased the impression. 'I thought the goal of this mission was to find out about them and return, not attempt to engage with them, since they appear hostile.'

'They may not be hostile,' Darrow said, cataloguing Hazeroth as *calm and confident* and the Casparan as *full of his own importance - and probably scared stiff*. 'We know nothing about them or their interactions, in all likelihood they know as little about us. If the opportunity for dialogue arises, I intend to take it. In that case Mr Hazeroth's expertise will be an asset. Perhaps you would like to introduce yourself.'

The Casparan took a breath from the mask round his neck. 'My name is Desmar Barok,' he said. 'I have been sent by the Prime Minister, my father, to observe the mission and report on everything.'

Darrow was annoyed, but took advantage.

'Thank you. Your skills of observation should make you an excellent record keeper for the mission, be sure to see everyone has a full copy of all observations.' He looked round the table. 'All reports are to go to Mr Barok for collation.'

'My title is Ser,' Barok said. 'You will address me as Ser Barok.'

'For simplicity, I suggest that we use the human title "Mister" for everyone,' Darrow said. 'That way we can all show respect without having to worry about different forms of address and accidental racial insult.'

'My title,' said Barok slowly, 'is Ser.' He breathed from his mask again.

Darrow just looked at the other man, his eyes tight, there was a very slight curl to his lip as he looked away.

'Let's continue with the introductions,' said Darrow, nodding to the Ochran. His skin was already turning pink in the oxygen-rich atmosphere on board. Now Barok's mask made sense - he apparently wanted to stay green.

'My name is Merari Two. I am happy to be called Mr Merari.' He smiled condescendingly at Barok. 'I speak several languages, but my main skill is linguistics, the study of the structure of language, including non-verbal ones. Like Mr Hazeroth, my skills may be useful should we attempt a dialogue with these beings. I also offer my services should there be any communication problems, with any members less skilled in Earth Standard.'

He bowed his head. Darrow thanked him, and thought *We'll have to watch those two.* The Anak spoke next, his voice a low rumble and carefully pronounced.

'I am Ehu Pathrusim, and should be addressed as Mr Ehu. I am an expert in scanners and weapons - after all, you have to find your enemy before you can shoot him.' He bared his fangs, the action momentarily alarmed Darrow until he realised it was a smile. 'I have brought refinements for your equipment which my people have only recently developed, and have agreed to share for this mission.'

'That is more like it,' said Barok. Darrow ignored him but mentally agreed and put Ehu down as another *calm and confident.* He nodded to the Altarian, whose cranial spines stirred nervously.

'My name is Madai Rendor, Mr Rendor.' His voice was of a higher pitch, but more confident than Barok's. He inclined his head towards Darrow. 'I have been a navigator for 80 of your Earth years and have spent the past 40 years exploring to the edge of the galaxy from Altairian space. Since that appears to be the direction the alien ship travelled, I humbly offer my star charts, which I hope will prove useful.' His voice hardened. 'However, I was not aware we were going to try to make contact with these Intruders. I thought this was just a fact-finding mission. We already know they are dangerous. Any attempt at contact is liable to put us in extreme danger.'

'It is not my intention to take us into danger, Mr Rendor,' Darrow said, thinking *I hope he's not going to be as bad as Barok,* 'but I will take advantage of every opportunity that presents itself. We need to find out whatever we can about the Intruders, and what better way than to ask them? I doubt that such an opportunity will arise, but I will not ignore the possibility.'

'I for one am not happy with this,' said Barok. 'I was not aware this mission was dangerous.'

'Perhaps you should leave now,' said Ehu, 'while you can. I am sure your government would understand your weakness.'

'We are dealing with an unknown race,' Hazeroth said quickly. 'So we cannot know what will happen. We must be prepared for any eventuality, but be wise in our decisions. I am sure Captain Darrow is wise, or he would not have been entrusted with this mission.'

If only you knew, Darrow thought. He decided to take control of the meeting again before the discussion got out of hand.

'Thank you all,' Darrow said. 'I look forward to working with you. We will be establishing duty rotas - if you have any other areas of expertise, please let Commander Parks know. Duties will include maintenance, hydroponics, food preparation and cleaning. I want two people on the bridge at all times, with all stations manned during any incidents. We also have a Trainee on board, Enns. You will recognise her by her blue uniform. She is an Alphan, and not used to other species, but willing to learn. It would be good if you could each spend some time with her, to teach her about your species and assist her studies, but please be mindful of her youth and lack of contact experience.'

He scanned their faces for reactions to the idea of work, but except for Barok, they showed no signs of objecting. Barok may have a rude awakening when he had to do his part. Darrow made a note to ensure that Parks treated him the same as the others, not letting up.

'We aim to follow the wake of the Intruder ship and see what we find,' he continued. 'It may take some time, so it's important we all get along. If you have any problems or queries, please talk first to the crewman you are sharing with. Then see Commander Parks, Lieutenant-Commander Hoy or me. Now, Lieutenant-Commander Hoy will take Mr Dathan to meet Dr Ky, Mr Ehu to meet Commander Blackwell our Engineer, and Mr Rendor to meet with Lieutenant Balitoth, our navigator. Commander Parks will meet with Mr Hazeroth to discuss first contact, since his time working in Security has given him some experience in dealing with inter-racial contact. Mr Barok and Mr Merari will come with me. I will show you our computer system so Mr Barok can begin setting up folders for his record keeping and Mr Merari can check out our linguistic databases. You may go.'

* * *

The casualty from the Anak ship had been treated and was being monitored in sick bay. She woke to a confusion of lights: bright lights overhead and small, winking lights in displays around her. She didn't know where she was, couldn't remember what had happened to her. She tried to look around and found she was restrained. Her head and shoulders were strapped down. The confinement brought back the terror.

'No! No more! Don't do any more!'

Her cry brought a figure running.

'It's OK, I'm a doctor. You're going to be all right.'

'Let me go! Let me go!'

Her distress increased.

'Don't be afraid. You suffered a head injury in the accident. I need to keep you immobile for a while.'

But the terror wouldn't listen. The impressions were only vague: strange faces bending over her, doing things to her. Restraints. Pain. She had thought it was over. Something sharp pressed into her skin and oblivion enfolded her again.

The next time she awoke it was dark. It seemed less threatening somehow. They left you alone at night. Maybe the terror was sleeping too. She tried to gather her thoughts, to remember. There had been friendly faces too. Helping hands that took her aboard their ship. They were curious, but didn't press her with questions, which was just as well, because she didn't know too much. She had a purpose to fulfil. Somewhere she had to go, something she had to do. Now her head hurt and she wasn't sure.

She was afraid.

* * *

Ehu entered Engineering carrying a crate and wearing a tool belt, he was immediately intercepted by Blackwell.

'And what are you proposing to do with that?'

Ehu put the crate on a workbench, bowed his head and shaded his eyes with one hand, the Anak sign of respect.

'I thought you might like to discuss some modification to the weapons and scanners, and see if there is anything you can use.' Ehu held out his hand. 'I understand it is your custom to grasp hands on meeting. I am Ehu Pathrusim. You will please call me Mr Ehu.'

Blackwell shook his hand and grinned.

'John Blackwell, Engineer. What makes you think you've anything new?'

'Because it took me two days and a lot of roaring to

persuade my government to release these.'

Blackwell bowed his head and shaded his eyes.

* * *

'Lieutenant-Commander Hoy reporting, Captain. You asked me to look into the injured woman from the Anak ship.'

'At ease, Lieutenant-Commander. What did you find out?'

'The Anak picked up her distress beacon and found her by her crashed ship. It wasn't an inter-planetary vessel, so it's a mystery how she got there, but until she recovers her memory, she can't tell us. She told them her name was Anna, and when they said they were coming here, she said she needed to come here too. When they pressed her, she said she didn't know why. Dr Ky has examined her and reports she is human, and has had some sort of brain surgery. Unfortunately, the crate that fell, cracked her skull at the point of weakness caused by that surgery, so he can't say any more about what was done. He can't say whether it was the surgery or the injury in the accident that caused the amnesia. He's having to keep her sedated as she is very distressed.'

I hope she's fit enough to be moved before we leave Alliance space, so we can drop her off somewhere, Darrow thought. *There are enough extra people on board without dragging along a casualty.*

'Thank you. Ask Dr Ky to keep me informed, will you? By the way, what was the cause of the Anak accident?'

'Pilot error, sir. Mr Ehu has confirmed it. The damage to Kestrel was minor, it will not affect our operational capability.'

'That's good. Dismissed.'

Chapter 20

Anna regained consciousness and found herself unrestrained. She stirred and reached a hand up to the bandage on her head, attracting the attention of a young blond man in a white tunic.

'Hello, please don't be afraid, you're safe.' His voice was soothing. 'I'm Sam Ryan. How are you feeling?'

'My head doesn't hurt so much now.'

'Good, the regenerator work we did must be taking hold. Can I get you anything?'

'Water please.'

He lifted a beaker to her lips while she drank.

'Thank you.' She looked around at the other bed, the monitors and the equipment. 'Where am I?'

'In sick bay on board the Kestrel. Do you remember being on the Anak ship? It brought you here, but you were injured in a docking accident. Do you remember?'

She frowned. 'All my memories are hazy and mixed up. I remember pain...' she faltered, 'b-but not where or when.'

'Do you know who you are?' he asked gently.

She shook her head, then something stirred in her mind and she looked up in alarm.

Ryan laid a hand on her arm. 'Don't distress yourself, it'll come back in time. I'll tell the doctor you're awake.'

He walked over and knocked on the door of Ky's cabin, which led off sick bay. Ky opened the door and Ryan started to tell him, when Anna screamed. They ran to her bedside.

'They're here! They're here! Help me.'

Anna clutched at Ryan's tunic, eyes wide with terror. She shook with fear and pointed out of the view port across the room. There was nothing to see but stars, then suddenly, faintly, an iridescent butterfly. Ryan couldn't believe his eyes.

'What the --'

'Never mind that, see to her while I alert the Captain.' Ky dived for the intercom. 'Captain! Red alert! An Intruder ship! We can see it from sick bay!'

The red alert sounded and there were running feet as the crew jumped into action. Ryan tried to calm Anna. She closed her eyes and turned her head as if listening for something.

'It's too late, they're on board! Oh help me, please don't let them take me!' She cowered against him and pointed.

Ky looked where she was pointing and thumbed the intercom again. 'Captain, they're in Engineering!'

There was a jolt, as the Kestrel suddenly dropped out of warp speed. Almost immediately Anna slumped back on the bed and gasped, 'They're gone.' She was pale and bathed in sweat.

Darrow came back on the intercom. 'Doctor, how in Heaven's name did you know about the Intruders? Our scanners picked them up just as you came through, and Engineering didn't even have time to signal.'

Ky looked at Anna and dropped his voice. 'She knew. The casualty, Anna. She was terrified they'd take her. She knew they were here even before we saw them.'

'I'll be right there,' Darrow said.

'No Captain,' Ky said, 'she's too distressed. Let me treat her first. I'll let you know when she's fit to speak to you.'

* * *

Tabitha was in her makeshift cabin in Engineering when she heard the red alert. She came through the curtain and saw Blackwell thrown to the floor by a bolt of light from nowhere. She screamed, just as the ship jolted and the lights dimmed.

She heard Stubbs shout, 'Get back!' She threw the curtain aside and dived under her bed.

There were more shouts and then only the klaxon. A voice said, 'They've gone Captain,' and the klaxon ceased, but her ears were still ringing. Footsteps approached and she jumped when Stubbs called, 'Enns, are you all right?'

'Yes, thank goodness,' she called. She got up and pulled back the curtain a little.

Stubbs' hand, as he reached for her, had a livid mark across the back.

'Oh, you're hurt!'

'The doc will fix that for me. Come here.'

He stepped through the curtain, put his arms around her and held her tight. Tabitha relaxed a little, but she felt awkward. *He's so thin, I might break him if I hug him back - not that I want to,* she thought.

'Stubbs, where are you?' Blackwell's voice rang out.

Stubbs cursed under his breath and let her go. 'I'm here, sir, seeing if Enns is OK.'

'Commander Parks wants your account of what happened.'

'Yes, sir.' He smiled and touched her cheek. 'It's safe now.'

He left, and Tabitha peeped round the end of the curtain. Blackwell had a large burn down the front of his tunic, and sat in front of a console. Parks still had a laser pistol in his hand.

'How is Trainee Enns?' Parks asked when Stubbs appeared.

'A bit shaken up, sir,' Stubbs said. 'She saw the attack on Commander Blackwell and retreated to her room. The first we knew was the energy discharge. Commander Blackwell dimmed the lights - that's when he was attacked. I came running but they disappeared - just got this.' He showed his hand and looked sideways at Blackwell.

'Any idea what they were after?' Parks asked.

'No sir, I didn't even see which machine they were looking at.'

Blackwell waved his hand, which made him gasp. 'Warp drive. Shorted a couple of circuits, but it's mostly shielded.'

'You two get to sick bay,' said Parks. 'I'll keep an eye on

things until you get back.'

As they left, Parks noticed Tabitha behind the curtain.

'Are you sure you're OK?'

She opened the curtain to see him properly. 'Yes sir, I think so. It was a shock, that's all.'

He looked at the shorted circuits. 'In more ways than one.'

* * *

Stubbs came back from sick bay before Blackwell. While he made a start on the repairs, Tabitha stepped out of her room. She needed to talk to someone, but didn't want to bother the senior officers. Stubbs would have to do.

'Stubbs, can I ask you something?'

'Sure.'

'Were those the aliens we're looking for?'

'I guess so.' He shrugged. 'Looks like they found us first.'

She chewed her lip. 'Can we fight them?'

Stubbs spoke over his shoulder. 'Doesn't look like it, does it?'

She stepped closer. 'Don't you care? Aren't you afraid?'

He stopped what he was doing, and took her hand.

'You and me, we'll be okay. They're going to enhance the shields, that Anak bloke has some new equipment to install. Then, using the sensor data, he'll set it up so they can't get on board again, you'll see. Probably enhance the weapons as well. You should see the ideas Mr Ehu's got.' He paused and looked in her face. 'It won't come down to a space fight anyway. The Captain's got orders not to fight them. Then, if we have to go planetside and fight, they'll send the senior staff, not us.'

He put his arm around her. 'You'll be safe, don't worry.'

Uncomfortable with his closeness, she wriggled free. 'I'd better let you get back to work. Thanks for reassuring me.' But was she reassured? She wasn't sure.

* * *

Darrow, Parks, Ky and Anna sat on soft chairs in sick bay. Darrow wanted it to feel more like a friendly chat than an interrogation, though Ky seemed nervous. He forced himself to lean back in his chair and take things slowly. Ky persuaded Anna to sip from a small glass. Darrow began.

'The Doctor tells me you are recovering well. How do you feel?'

'Much better physically, but I'm a bit confused.'

'Why don't you start at the beginning, and we'll see if we can fill in some gaps?'

She closed her eyes in thought, then said, 'Well, I remember the accident, though not clearly, but nothing before that.' She looked up. 'How did I get here?'

'The Anak picked you up on Mok.' Darrow said. 'They followed your distress signal and found you near your crashed ship.'

'What's Mok? I've never heard of it.'

'It's an obscure planetoid, an abandoned mine. Are you sure you don't know how you got there?'

Anna blanched and looked away, then abruptly changed the subject.

'Why is this ship called the Kestrel?'

'Because it's small, fast and dangerous,' Darrow replied. 'All PACT Fast-Response ships are named after birds of prey - why, is that important?'

'Yes,' Anna frowned, 'but I don't know why.'

Parks said, 'Look, we don't have time for this. What we really want to know is how you knew the Intruders were here.'

Anna started as if he had slapped her.

'Is that what they're called?'

'That's what we call them.' Parks said. 'We don't know anything about them except what they've been doing to our people. What's your link with them?'

'Link? Oh God!'

She put her head in her hands. Ky motioned Parks to wait and offered Anna the glass.

'Drink this, it will calm you down.'

Darrow was just as impatient, but he shook his head at Parks and spoke softly to Anna. 'You're safe with us, but we need to know.'

After a few moments she raised her head and took a deep breath. She spoke with difficulty.

'Someone ... did ... something to me. It causes a ... fear in me - a terror. It was just a vague memory, a nightmare, until today. I don't know who they were. Maybe they gave me the terror so I would know when the Intruders were near.'

'The things that did this, they weren't these same beings, the Intruders?'

Anna looked worried and shook her head. 'I don't know - I don't think so.'

Darrow leaned forward. 'Did they send you to us?' Anna nodded. *Yes!* he thought.

Parks rolled his eyes. 'So we may have two sets of unknown aliens. Great!'

Anna cried, 'I just want to know why they did this to me!'

Ky made her sip the drink again and her eyelids began to droop.

'That's enough for now, Captain. She's still weak, and needs rest. Some more of this relaxant and she'll sleep for a few hours.'

He gave her another sip and helped her into bed.

'I'll send Ryan to sit with her,' Ky said. 'Can I speak to you, Captain?'

Parks left, Ky called Ryan, then drew Darrow into his cabin. He seemed uncertain how to begin. He clasped his hands and raised them to his lips.

'Captain, I have treated Commander Blackwell and Ensign Stubbs ... These aliens, these Intruders ... Is it true they are invisible?'

'Yes, in normal light. They show up best under infrared. Doctor, are you all right?'

Ky was wringing his hands and muttering. 'Tokoloshe! They are Tokoloshe!' He looked up. 'Captain, they are evil spirits! We must have nothing to do with them.'

'Control yourself, Doctor! What do you mean, Tokoloshe?'

Ky was shaking. 'Tokoloshe are invisible water sprites who make people sick or die. The only way to get rid of them is the n'anga, the witch doctor, but we have none. It is too dangerous!'

Darrow couldn't believe it. This man of science was referring to old superstitions.

'Doctor, our mission is to find them, don't you understand?'

Ky looked away. 'No, I wasn't told, I didn't know. It is too dangerous, Captain! I have examined Commander Blackwell and Ensign Stubbs most carefully, and prayed to the ancestors for them. I do not think they are possessed. But I recommend they be watched carefully.'

Darrow knew he had to get this man under control. He held Ky by the shoulders and made him look at him.

'Doctor, in PACT each man's religion is his own private concern, but it cannot be allowed to interfere with his duties.'

'It never has before, Captain. We've never encountered spirits before!'

Darrow shook him. 'You were assigned to serve this mission, Doctor, and you will do so.'

Ky came to himself and suppressed his fears with a struggle. 'Yes, Captain.'

'You are not to mention this to anyone, is that clear?'

Ky nodded.

* * *

Tabitha's Journal

Eek! The alien representatives came on board and I've got to meet them all and write reports. But we've met the other aliens too, and it wasn't pleasant. I was wondering how we could find them if they're invisible, well they found us, and they boarded us! I was terrified, especially because you don't know where they are. They weren't here long, so I don't know if they found what they came for or did what they came to do. No one seems to be asking why they boarded. They took the engines off line though. Roy says we'll be safe, he says the officers will see to it. It's strange, but he did try to comfort me after the attack, and I was grateful. I wish I understood the signals he's giving me. Maybe he's being friendly after all.

Chapter 21

The representatives all wanted to know what had happened, and Darrow assembled them in the mess hall with Parks, leaving Hoy and Reuel on duty on the bridge. The realities of the mission had suddenly come home to them.

'Silence please!' Darrow raised his voice. 'You will be given all the data we have on the attack. The short version is, the Intruder ship materialised alongside. We attempted to communicate with them - they either didn't receive our message or ignored it. The next we knew, they were in Engineering and took our warp drive offline.'

'They were on board?' Barok articulated the shock on their faces.

'They must have some kind of teleport,' said Ehu.

'Since they are composed of energy, such technology may be possible for them.' said Darrow, addressing the less emotive comment, 'or they can pass through solid objects and don't need an atmosphere,'

'What did they want?' Rendor asked.

'We don't know,' said Darrow. 'They're invisible under normal lighting, but Commander Blackwell had the presence of mind to dim the lights in Engineering. As soon as they could be seen, they left.'

'You say "they",' said Merari, 'there was more than one?'

'Commander Blackwell and Ensign Stubbs reported seeing two figures,' Parks said. 'Humanoid in shape, with an appendage on each shoulder that looked like small wings. The Intruders are able to fire an energy discharge - both Blackwell and Stubbs were burned - but it seems to drain them, as neither of them fired a second bolt.'

Darrow watched the representatives' faces, trying to judge who might be a problem.

'The good news,' said Ehu, waving his pad, 'is I think we can calibrate the sensors to detect their ships, to give us some warning of their approach. I have not had time to study the sensor logs in detail, but I believe it can be done.'

Darrow jumped on the good news. 'Since Commander Blackwell is injured, I suggest you work with Lieutenant-Commander Hoy,' said Darrow. 'He has considerable experience of sensor arrays. I want this done quickly, so Lieutenant-Commander Hoy will be relieved on the bridge as soon as we finish here.'

'Do you think the Intruders know about us, our mission?' asked Rendor. 'Do you think this was an attempt to stop us?'

'We *are* following the wake trail of one of their ships,' said Ehu. 'Maybe this one. It was always likely we would encounter them.'

'But if they *do* know, they will attack us again,' said Rendor. 'We may have to fight all the way.' He turned to Darrow. 'Are we equipped for that?'

Before Darrow could reply, Barok said, 'We are not supposed to fight them, just follow them. Perhaps Mr Ehu can tie the weapons into the sensors, to fire the moment we encounter a ship.'

Dathan said quietly, 'Is not all life sacred?'

They all turned to look at him.

He took a deep breath. 'Our mission is to find out about these people. How much will we find out if we destroy every one we meet?'

Darrow was glad of Dathan's input. 'I am prepared to assume for the moment,' Darrow said, 'that this was a chance encounter, and their only object was to prevent us from following their ship. They probably don't know we are following their wake. We are going to continue and see what happens, but be on our guard.' He paused, but raised his hand to forestall any comments. 'There is, however, another matter to inform you of. When the Anak ship arrived it carried a human woman they had rescued. She says her name is Anna but she remembers nothing of who she is or any of her past. She was injured in the docking accident, and was being treated in sick bay until she was fit enough to drop off somewhere.'

'That is not important to us,' interrupted Barok, preparing to leave. 'I know we insist on knowing every detail of the mission Captain, but surely that is irrelevant?'

'Which is why you have not been informed of her presence before,' said Darrow, pressing on. 'But she sensed the presence of the Intruders before we detected them, and also knew when they boarded, even though she was in sick bay and Engineering is shielded.'

The representatives all spoke at once, and Barok sat back down. Darrow allowed them to talk, until they all realised they weren't getting anywhere and turned back to him. Barok took it on himself to speak for them all.

'Captain, you must put her under guard until we determine she is not an agent for the Intruders.'

Just the reaction Darrow had feared. 'I am certain,' he said carefully, 'she is not an agent. The experience of sensing the Intruders terrifies her, and the Doctor was forced to sedate her. She says she thinks someone operated on her to give her this ability, but it has traumatised her.'

'In any case, Captain,' said Hazeroth, 'I think you must give up the idea of sending her away. We need every advantage we can get.'

'But it's important we get her co-operation,' said Darrow, raising his voice over the hubbub this caused. 'I will not force her to help us. She has already been traumatised, and is recovering from a head injury. I will not do her more harm.'

'Captain,' Barok said, rising to his feet and gesturing to make his point, 'if these aliens are not stopped, the future of all our worlds is at stake. The life of one individual is nothing compared to that.'

Darrow took a deep breath and looked around the room. 'These Intruders have been taking what they want,' he said, 'without a thought for the people they are stealing from. If we take what we want from this woman without her consent, how does that make us any better than them?' He waited in the silence while they thought. When Barok moved to speak, he stopped him with a raised hand. 'Now then, the scanners will be recalibrated, full reports will be written by everyone involved in this incident and forwarded to Mr Barok for collation and distribution. I see we are under way again, so let us return to our duties.'

As the meeting dispersed, Darrow sighed with relief. He wondered how many more of these confrontations were ahead, and whether he would always be in command of them.

* * *

Ehu's words were muffled, as they came from inside a panel in a corner of Engineering.

'This ship is impressive for one so small. I find more and more of interest to me.'

Hoy checked his readout before replying.

'The Kestrel is named for an Earth bird of prey. It's small, fast, and armed. She's designed for quick response, mostly for emergencies rather than war, but we never know what we'll find in some of the situations we get sent to. I think that coil needs further adjustment. The frequency is still out of alignment.'

'I shall adjust it. We must have the sensors at their most sensitive to give us every advantage when the Intruders appear.'

They worked in silence for a while, adjusting each of the sensors in turn. As they were replacing a wall panel, Hoy nervously asked, 'I know very little about the Anak, can I ask you some questions?'

'So long as I do not have to reply if the information requested is too personal. I would hate to have to kill you afterwards.'

He waited for Hoy's shocked reaction and then laughed, displaying his long canines.

'I am sorry, my friend, that is how most people see us. As you humans say, I could not resist the temptation!'

'That was one of my questions. Are your people really dedicated to conquest and bloodshed? You hear the rumours, and you do look like lions, one of our largest beasts of prey on Earth. But I have never heard of anyone the Anak have conquered.'

Ehu moved to the next wall plate and frowned as he considered where to start his explanation.

'The Anak are warriors by necessity. Our world is rich in resources and treasures and my people were peaceful, so other worlds believed our riches would be easy to take. We have needed to fight to survive. But we do not wish to be aggressors. I am of the clan of Pathrus, and we are renowned for our bravery and loyalty but also for our fairness. There is a story in my family of the warrior Tarn who threw away his weapon in a fight because his enemy was unarmed and he refused to take an unfair advantage!' He laughed. 'I do not think I would go that far myself!'

'Me neither,' Hoy agreed. 'My people were warriors too, you know. To honour my ancestors, I have learned the traditional ways of fighting.' He drew himself up to his full, small stature and took a stance.

'Well! You and I have more in common than I thought. But tell me, Commander, were you disappointed Commander Parks was given the position of First Officer? Did you hope to be promoted?'

'Oh no, I've been with Captain Darrow for three years now and he's been good to me. I was only made up to Second Officer six months ago, so I knew it was too soon for another promotion. I'm looking forward to working with Commander Parks, he has quite a reputation. I looked up his record. He was invalided out of active duty because of damage to his shoulder, but he puts the shoulder out again about once a year because he won't stay behind a desk.'

'I think I shall enjoy working with these warriors.'

Anna woke from her sedated sleep, and dozed again. She saw the lights, felt the terror, the pain. Her scream brought Ky running.

'Oh Doctor! Thank God it's you. I keep reliving it in my dreams. I'm so confused. Who has given me this ability, to sense the Intruders? Why would they do that to me?'

'That's something only you can answer,' he said. 'You're safe here. They're recalibrating the sensors now so we'll get more warning next time we encounter a ship.'

She shuddered.

Ky turned away. 'I'll give you something to calm you down.'

'No, no more drugs. Please.'

Ky considered. 'Perhaps we can use a cortical suppressor to prevent the dreams.'

Anna scrambled out of bed and backed into a corner. 'No! First *they* do something to me, to my head, and now *you* want to! Leave me alone! I want to leave. You've got to let me go!'

Ryan, who was off-duty, heard the noise and came out of his curtained-off corner of sick bay.

Ky said to him, 'Anna is distressed and saying she wants to leave. Try to calm her down. I'm going to see the Captain.'

'But sir, I'm off duty.' But Ky left. Ryan approached Anna slowly. 'We're trying to help, not hurt you. They won't keep you here if you want to leave. Dr Ky is just concerned you're not well enough.'

To his surprise, she came into his arms. She was like a frightened child, in her rumpled sleep-suit. He sat down on the bed with her and stroked her hand. She started to cry, silent tears that dripped on his tunic.

'Oh Sam, where can I go if I can't remember who I am? How can I live if at any moment I might encounter one of these Intruders and be paralysed with fear?'

'But they're not - you don't know, do you?' He held her by the shoulders. 'You don't know about the mission we're on, who these Intruders are. Wait there.'

He got up and went to the intercom. 'Ensign Ryan to Captain Darrow.'

'Darrow here.'

'Sir, I need to speak to you.' He glanced across the room and kept his voice low so not to disturb Anna. 'I know you think Anna can help us in our mission, but she doesn't know anything about it. She doesn't know who the Intruders are or why they attacked us.'

'You're absolutely right, Ensign. Dr Ky and I are discussing now the best way to explain it to her. Will you reassure her until we come?'

'Yes sir.'

* * *

They set up a screen in sick bay. Anna sat amazed as they showed her the video records and other evidence of the Intruder raids. Ryan sat with her, and seemed to be almost as amazed as she was.

'I had no idea,' he whispered.

Darrow turned off the screen and sat down.

'Do you see now why we need your ability so much?' he said. 'We seem to be outclassed, and you might just give us the edge we need.'

'But why me?' Anna said. 'If these other aliens wanted to help, why didn't they pick somebody heroic?'

Darrow smiled at her. 'With no memory, who's to say you aren't heroic?'

Anna shook her head. 'I don't feel it. There should be a reason.'

'Who knows?' Darrow said honestly. 'Maybe you happened to be in the right place at the right time, or maybe you were especially picked for some reason we don't yet understand. All we do know is you're here and we need you. What do you say?'

There was a long silence. Anna sighed and looked out of the viewport.

'Where are we, right now?'

'In Altairian space. Would an exact position make any sense to you?'

Anna smiled. 'I suppose not. I don't remember any of it, even if I've been there. The point is, how far are we from the nearest inhabited planet?'

'About 10 light years from some outlying colonies.'

'So how long would it take to get me there, if I wanted to leave?'

'But we need…'

Anna gestured to interrupt him. 'What I'm trying to say is it's not possible for me to leave now, really, is it? It would take too long, and you would lose the trail.'

Darrow looked uncomfortable. 'It would make things difficult for us. We have no right to keep you here against your will, but there wasn't time to consider that when we set out.'

Ryan said, 'We could try keeping you sedated.'

'No, that won't be necessary.' Anna gave a small smile. 'It seems between one set of circumstances and another, my fate has been determined for me. I don't feel very brave, but I don't seem to have any choice.'

There was an audible sigh of relief in the room. Ryan took Anna's hand.

'We'll do everything we can to help you and protect you,' he said. 'I promise.'

Chapter 22

Once there was more time for talk, Darrow invited Parks to his quarters to catch up. They sat together at the table in his office and Parks grinned and produced a bottle of dark liquid.

Darrow raised an eyebrow. 'You know intoxicating liquor is against regulations.'

'Don't talk to me about regulations,' Parks said, opening the bottle. 'This whole mission is against regulations.'

Darrow frowned. 'I tried to refuse ... I seem to have been overruled at every turn.'

Parks poured the liquor into two glasses. 'Well, one more breach won't hurt. Cheers.'

'That's what's worrying me,' Darrow said, but took a slow sip of his drink. 'Once you start disregarding regulations, you're heading for disaster.'

'It doesn't have to end in disaster, Joe. The death of your friend was a long time ago. He stowed away and the cargo got dumped into space - you couldn't have known that would happen when you helped him. You've come so far since then. We'll whip this lot into shape between us.' He sipped his drink. 'Before anything else, I want to know how you had me posted here. Since the accident I'm not fit for space flight duty, that's why I've spent all these years in Security on Earth. How did you swing it, and why?'

'You don't think I'd miss the chance to have you with me, do you?' Darrow laughed and gripped Parks' arm. 'You've always looked after me ever since the Academy. No, seriously Nate, I recommended Mike Holland's promotion, but it didn't make it any easier to lose him. He was a good First Officer. I've plenty of experience of emergencies and dangerous situations, but the only dealings I've had with alien races have been within PACT, and the few individuals we've had on board from time to time. With the postings you've had in Security, you've dealt with aliens up close and personal. I told the brass I needed that, and with no qualified First Officer available, I needed someone I knew and trusted, whatever the regulations say. This is no time to start rubbing up against different personalities and getting used to one another. There will be enough of that with the rest of the crew.'

'Are most of the crew new, then?'

'Not all, I managed to keep most of the existing Kestrel crew, but some of them are relatively new, and haven't had time to settle in. Enns hasn't even finished her training yet, she was dropped in the deep end at Pallas but did well, so I kept her on rather than be one short.'

'Yes, I've spoken to her. She's feeling out of her depth but I think I've convinced her not to waste this opportunity. I'll be keeping a close watch on her, and Chambers seems to have taken her under his wing.'

'Good. Chambers has only been with us six months, although he's had plenty of experience, but he needs careful handling. Did you read his file?'

Parks nodded. 'I've had a quick look at all their files. That was quite a tragedy he was involved in. The way I read it, it wasn't his fault.'

'He doesn't see it that way. He's a gifted helmsman, but he blames himself, and it's really shaken his confidence. I persuaded him to come here, and he improved a lot under the supervision of Lanx. Now Lanx is gone, I'm hoping Chambers will step up to the responsibility. He's certainly capable, he just has to believe in himself.'

The conversation paused while they drank.

'The MO is brand new,' Parks prompted.

'Yes. Dr Robinson wasn't fit for duty after his accident on Pallas, so they landed me with Matthew Ky as MO. I don't think he was very happy about it, he wanted to sit it out until he retires next year.'

'He made it quite clear to me he wasn't going on any landing parties. He's staying on board.'

'Don't push him. You'll find Ensign Ryan is always up for an excursion, and he's good too.'

Parks nodded, and said, 'Then we have all the crewmen from the allied worlds. I'm concerned there'll be cultural misunderstandings in addition to the problems of the cramped conditions.'

'I was amazed when I was assigned this mission. I mean, I would love to solve the mystery of all these thefts and deaths, but it doesn't make sense, sending a small ship on a mission like this! But I had made such a fuss about the urgency of the situation, I couldn't get out of it. Then the allied worlds insisted on sending their people. It's crazy. That's another reason I need you. You always were an excellent peacekeeper.' Darrow saluted him with his glass.

'Well, I'm really grateful,' Parks saluted him back. 'Security has been great, but I miss being out here in space. I didn't believe it when they first told me. The Admiral called me personally to confirm!'

'How're you getting on with everyone?'

'It takes some adjustment being the new First Officer, and I gather Mike Holland was popular, so he's a hard act to follow. But the crew are professional. Even the ones who aren't comfortable are getting on with the job. I thought I'd take time over the next few days to have a chat with each of the crew members and the representatives. Check out if there are any potential problems. I'm going to make Desmar Barok my first priority. Can you believe those Casparans, sending him?'

'He reminds me of that cadet you had the feud with in the second year at the Space Academy. He wouldn't let it go, do you remember?'

* * *

Ky was checking an inventory when Dathan came to sick bay.

'Would it be acceptable to begin working together now?'

he asked. 'We have had little time so far.'

'Yes, all right,' said Ky. 'Come in. This is Anna.'

Dathan bowed to her. 'It is good to meet you,' he said. 'Please excuse me, I do not wish to cause offence, but you do not seem to have a patronymic.'

'A what?' Anna said.

'A family name. It is not respectful to use first names with new acquaintances.'

'I'm afraid I don't remember my, um, patronymic.' Anna smiled. 'Can we not be friends from the start?'

Dathan looked a little uncomfortable, so Ky said, 'I suggest Anna calls you Dr Dathan, and you call her Anna.'

'That would be most acceptable,' said Dathan. He turned back to Ky. 'Now Doctor, I have brought some of my data on the biology and medical care of Alliance species, that I hope you will find useful. Have you much experience of treating other species?'

'Not much,' said Ky, taking the offered data stick and putting it into the console. 'I spent the last fifteen years working on a space station in the Sol solar system, so most people passing through were human. We did have some casualties from the other species, but since I was part of a team, we had the expertise between us. I was expecting to finish my days there, away from crises, until I retire next year. This reposting has come as quite a shock, so your assistance would be welcome.'

'What is this "retire" you speak of? Is it a position of honour?'

'Not exactly. We humans set a limit on the length of time a person must work, and then they are free to enjoy their old age as they wish.'

'I have never heard of such a thing,' said Dathan. 'I cannot imagine how it would be to work all your life and then be deprived of the satisfaction of continuing. In my culture, we revere our long-lived ones and continue to consult and use them in all fields of knowledge and endeavour. When someone becomes older, they take apprentices and pass on their knowledge. I myself began as an explorer. I always had an insatiable curiosity about the stars. As I ventured out, I found myself drawn to help those who were suffering, which is why I turned to xenobiology. Now, wherever I go, I can help others as well as discover new worlds and new species. Although we live longer than humans, there is not enough time to learn all there is to know. So our apprentices take our knowledge and continue the work after we are gone. I have only been an apprentice for five years and am greatly honoured to be allowed to come on this mission and bring back data on a new race.'

Ky frowned. 'Well I expected to retire, and that's what I'm going to do, the first chance I get.'

* * *

Tabitha approached Dathan in the mess hall. 'Mr Dathan? I'm Trainee Enns. I'm supposed to be with you now.'

'Welcome Trainee Enns, I am most happy to meet you.' Dathan bowed his head and patted the bench beside him. 'Please sit down.'

'Thank you. I - I don't know much about Kohathis, only what I've read, and I can't remember it all. Commander Parks says I will understand the races better if I meet them.'

'Commander Parks is wise, that has been my experience also. Our time together can be mutually beneficial, if you are willing. I have little experience of humans, and want to learn more. You are not from Earth?'

'No, I was born on Alpha. It's the first Earth colony. The gravity is much higher than on Earth, which is why I'm shorter and wider than ordinary humans,' she laughed. 'It's nice to meet someone my height.'

'Yes, we are not a tall people, I am average height for a Kohathi.'

'Oh, I'm sorry. I didn't mean to cause offence.' She put her pad down with a thump. 'Oh, I'm going to make such a mess of this. I've got to meet with each of the representatives, and I just know I'm going to do or say something wrong.'

'May I give you some advice?'

'Please do.'

'Let us agree not to take offence at anything the other does or says. Then we will both feel safe when we are together. When we have learned a little, the other races won't be so daunting.'

'That's kind of you, thank you.'

'Now, since we have agreed not to take offence, would you be willing to allow me to examine you? I am a doctor, and would like to see the effect of high gravity on your body, so I may compare it with earthly humans.'

Tabitha thought for a moment. 'I think that would be OK. I don't mind, and it would keep me busy so I don't get more homework from Commander Parks.'

'Homework?'

'When we study in school, we are given extra work to do at home. The word means any work outside of lessons.'

'Ah, I see. Commander Parks is trying to keep you busy, and you can be busy with me.'

'You've got it! Now, where do you want to start in telling me about Kohathis? Perhaps, as well as your own race, you can tell me a bit about the others too.'

'That can be my homework - to prepare some of my notes for you.' Dathan looked around. 'Another piece of advice - if you are to spend time with each of the races, leave the Casparan until last.'

'Why? Are Casparans unfriendly?'

Dathan looked around nervously. He lowered his voice. 'I would not want to be heard disparaging another representative, but I would prevent trouble if I can.' He stood up. 'Why don't we continue our conversation in sick bay while I begin my examination?'

In sick bay, Tabitha lay down as Dathan prepared the scanner.

'What can you tell me about the other representatives?' she asked. 'I've never met any ali - non-humans before. It's all a bit daunting.'

'What have you read about Caspar?'

'They were occupied by the Ochrans until they gained independence about seventy years ago, that's all I know.'

'Think for a moment. How would you feel if your whole life was controlled by another, and then you were free?'

'Happy, but nervous, I suppose. I'd be wary of anything that looked like oppression again.'

'Good. And how do you feel being so much shorter than others?'

'What have my feelings got to do with it? Oh, I see. Casparans are little, aren't they?'

'Exactly. Now lie still please.' Dathan began the scan. 'Mr Barok is an extreme example of the Casparan need to assert themselves, watching for any suggestion of … what is the word?'

'Denigration?'

'Exactly. If you accord him respect and ignore his belligerent manner, you will have no problem.'

'Phew! I hope they're not all like that.'

'On the contrary, most of the representatives have been chosen because they are adaptable and sociable, as well as having skills to contribute to the mission. This is interesting. I expected your bones to be thicker, but the adaptation of the joints is fascinating.'

'Tell me about the others please. What about the Ochran representative?'

'Mr Merari is especially wary of Mr Barok, but treating him in a civil manner. The old attitudes linger on.'

'Tell me about it.'

'I am doing so.'

'Sorry,' she laughed. 'It's an expression that means I know what you're talking about. On Alpha the vast majority are isolationist and suspicious of aliens. Oh sorry, there I go again!'

Dathan smiled. 'No offence, remember? I will scan again, this time looking at muscle and circulation.'

'Fine. My mother especially was opposed to me joining PACT. She doesn't even want me to go off-planet. I only got permission to come because Principal Hernandez spoke to my father, not my mother. Are there any other species like that?'

'There are factions among all species that distrust other races, but in general we all see the benefit of collaboration. The Anak, for example, have a fierce reputation to match their appearance, but in fact have no desire for warfare. They realise a treaty that respects their autonomy means the mineral wealth of their planet can be fairly traded.'

'So Mr Ehu is really a pussy cat?'

'"Pussy cat"? What is this?'

She frowned, thinking of the best way to answer. 'They are domesticated pets, who, although related to wild cats, are smaller and no longer dangerous. Mr Ehu looks like one of the bigger wild cats, an Earth lion to be exact, and they are dangerous beasts.'

Dathan laughed. 'What a wonderful picture you have created! A pussy cat. I must remember.'

'What about Zoans? I'm here because the Zoan crewman, Balitoth, was taken ill, so I didn't get to meet him. Now there's Mr Hazeroth as well. Is it coincidence their names end the same way?'

'It probably means they are from the same tribe. Your blood circulation is enhanced in a most interesting manner. I must store these scans for later study. I am grateful for your cooperation. Now, it is time you should go.'

Dathan switched the scanner off and helped her up.

'Can you tell me more?' she asked, a bit frustrated at his interruptions.

'I am aware of the time,' he said, 'and you are supposed to be learning about Kohathis. I think it would be best if you study for yourself and ask me questions at our next session. I will do the same with these scans.'

A M Thomas

* * *

As soon as he had the opportunity, Stubbs went to see Tabitha again. She was not pleased to see him. He hadn't done anything overt she could put her finger on, but he made her feel uncomfortable.

'How are you, Enns?'

'I'm fine thanks,' Tabitha said, shifting awkwardly in the gap in the curtain. 'It was a scare, but soon over.'

'I can't keep calling you Enns, what's your name? I'm Roy.'

'Oh, um, my name's Tabitha. People call me Tab.'

'Tab, that's lovely. Or Tabi. Sounds like a fluffy kitten.' He edged closer.

Tabitha tensed. She didn't know how to get rid of him.

'I can't talk now. I've got to study.' She retreated.

'Perhaps I can help. What's the subject?' His hand was on the edge of the curtain. Tabitha started to panic.

'Stubbs, where are you?' Blackwell's voice rang out.

Stubbs clenched his teeth. 'Coming sir!' He turned back to Tabitha, 'See you later.'

'I hope not,' she said, behind his back, and breathed a sigh of relief. *I wish we'd been allowed to mix with the boys more at home,* she thought. *I don't know what he wants. Is he just being friendly?*

Chapter 23

Parks settled in and tried to get to know the crew. It wasn't easy to talk to them because of the overcrowding, but Ehu spent a lot of time in Engineering, so Parks was able to see some of them in his cabin. The trouble was, it sounded too much like a disciplinary summons, and they tended to arrive looking nervous. That didn't apply to Blackwell, who didn't seem to recognise authority, though he certainly wielded it.

'Sit down Commander. Thanks for coming. Would you like something to drink?'

'Would that be alcoholic?'

'I'm afraid not. Can't be setting a bad example, can we?'

'I won't mind if you won't, just between us, of course.' The older man winked.

Parks guessed it was a test and refused to be drawn in. 'Sorry, I got sent here so fast I had no time to pick up any little comforts. How are things going?'

'In Engineering, things are great. That Ehu knows so much, I could talk to him for hours. Before long he will have wheedled all my secrets out of me, but I'm returning the favour. Between us we're getting Kestrel finely tuned. It's keeping Stubbs busy too. You know he's sweet on the Trainee?'

'Is he?' Parks frowned. 'Inappropriate behaviour?'

'I haven't given him the chance. Especially with her having the cabin in Engineering. We should look over the rotas - see if we can keep her out of there when Stubbs is on duty.'

'Good idea. Anything else you've noticed?'

'Well, you're not popular.' Blackwell laughed. 'Being the new guy is always tricky, and then you turfed them all out of their beds, so you haven't got off to a very good start. Treat them right and they'll come round. How are you getting on with the Captain?'

'We go way back - we were in the Academy together, but I haven't seen him for years.' Parks paused. 'He's done well. I'm impressed with how he handles the crew, but it'll be interesting to see how he handles all these representatives. He was always a stickler for the rules, and we're breaking a few already on this crazy mission.'

'Why do you call it crazy?'

'Well, we're the wrong ship, we've got a patched together crew, and we're overcrowded with extra people. He doesn't like it one bit.'

'He may not like it, but he's loving the chance to chase down one of his mysteries. You ask him about his collection of mysteries - he'll keep you for hours!'

'Seriously Commander, I hope I can rely on you to keep me up to speed about the regular crew - you know them, and I don't. Will you do that?'

'No problem. I'm grateful you asked. I'd better get back now. Ehu wants to adjust the inertial dampeners.'

When Blackwell left, Parks found Ryan waiting outside.

'Could you spare me a moment sir?'

'Yes Ensign, come in.'

'Sir, I need your advice. It's Dr Ky - he's so … bad tempered. I'm trying to please him, to make things easier for him, but nothing works. I don't know what to do, sir.'

'Is he like that with everyone?'

'When he's treating someone he's kind and considerate. He's good with Anna, but even she prefers to be looked after by me. He's polite to Dr Dathan, but all he does is moan to him while they're working.'

'I'll see what I can do, Ensign. Just make sure you give him no reason to be angry with you, and I'll try to mitigate the rest. Are you on duty now?'

'No sir, I've just finished.'

'Fine. You go to the mess hall and eat and I'll go to see Dr Ky. Dismissed.'

Ky was in sick bay. Parks hadn't managed to speak to him properly yet.

'Good afternoon, Doctor. I came to see how you're settling in. You must find it hard, not knowing anyone.'

Ky shook his head.

'Oh, I'm doing all right. I'm used to keeping to myself. I've read everyone's files, of course, and Dr Dathan is being extremely helpful discussing the various alien physiologies.'

'At least I know the Captain, but you didn't have that advantage.' Parks said. 'Have you worked on a ship like this before?'

'Not for a long time. My post on the space station lasted fifteen years, and before that I was at the Moon colony. I got used to having more room to move around.'

'It can feel a bit claustrophobic.' Parks saw his opportunity. 'I hope there's no problem having Ryan in here. There really isn't anywhere else to put him.'

Ky sighed. 'I suppose I've taken it out on him a little. With Ryan and Anna, sick bay is full. I don't know what we'll do if there are casualties during the mission.'

'Don't worry, we'll just swap them with Ryan. Poor guy won't know where he is.' Parks smiled, then leaned forward and spoke quietly. 'You have to learn to live inside your head on a small ship, you know.'

For a moment, Ky lost his frown.

* * *

Parks finally found the opportunity to speak to Barok, the Casparan, though it was not the casual occasion he had hoped for. Barok came to Parks' cabin to complain.

'Commander, I do not believe that I am receiving all the information I was promised. I overheard the Captain this morning referring to this woman Anna's telepathy, and I have seen her about the ship. How do we know she is not reading all our minds?'

Parks took a deep breath and suppressed the urge to shake him.

'Mr Barok, since Anna's telepathic ability was

discovered, we have not had time to prepare any reports, but believe me, you know as much as we do. You must therefore be aware that she can only link with the Intruders, and only over short distances. Your secrets are completely safe.' Parks had an inspiration, and made the Casparan sign of obeisance. 'While you are on board the Kestrel, we are pledged to protect you.'

To Parks' relief, Barok relaxed and sat down. His green face took on a paler shade, and he took a breath from his mask.

'I am sorry, Commander Parks. My suspicion is inbred. We Casparans were oppressed for so long, that even in our independence we do not feel safe.'

'I'm not familiar with your history, how long have you been an independent world?'

'Only seventy years. The Ochrans controlled our world for centuries, and treated us as servants. They always looked down on us as inferior. Even since independence we are still dependent on them because they control our trade routes. A nebula blocks other routes, unless we go round, which is counterproductive, so we have to fly through their space. Over the centuries they used many inducements to informers, and we are still not free of them. I am afraid we still treat everyone with the same suspicion. Perhaps this journey will be an opportunity for me to learn otherwise.'

He smiled, and Parks warmed to him.

'I had no idea your people had had such a raw deal. Let me give you some advice. If you treat people well, they usually respond in the same way. Try to be a little friendlier and it will go a long way.'

'Thank you, Commander. I am in your debt, and Desmar Barok does not forget.'

He held out his two palms and bowed, in the traditional Casparan manner, and left. Parks smiled, and reminded himself not to pass judgement so quickly in future. His reverie was rudely interrupted however, by the sound of raised voices in the corridor. He rushed out of his cabin to find Barok confronting Merari. His small green figure looked almost childlike beside the tall, now-pink Ochran.

'What were you doing here, spying on me? You have no power over my people now, and you will not gain any here!'

'We have no further use for you, nor any interest in your business, my dear *Desmar*.' Merari sneered the name, as if it was an insult.

Which it probably was, thought Parks, to use Barok's given name in public that way.

'And what use are you to this mission?' Barok snapped, his face darkening. 'You may be a linguist, but you will not know their language if we have never met them before. What is your name? Merari Two? Only the second son. They sent you out here to get rid of you!'

The Ochran pulled a wicked looking dagger, but Parks stepped in quickly and took it away from him.

'I don't intend to get involved in your internal quarrels, but I will not have them disrupting this ship or this mission. You're to stay away from each other, and I'll consult the Captain about banning all personal weapons on board. For everyone's safety.'

Merari scowled and stormed off. Barok sighed and turned to Parks.

'I am sorry things spoiled so soon after our conversation. Please do not ask me to make any promises regarding Merari. I must defend myself and my people. The hatred is deep and long held.'

* * *

Balitoth came off duty and returned to his cabin. Hazeroth was there.

'Do you mind, my friend,' said Hazeroth, 'if I ask you about your friendship with the Altairian?'

'Reuel?' said Balitoth warily. 'You disapprove?'

'Not at all. I am fascinated. Altairians are known to be secretive, and your friendship is remarkable.'

Balitoth relaxed. 'Initially it was simply because we were the only non-humans on board. We compared notes and advised one another on their customs and speech idioms and such. Then we discovered a mutual interest in the human game of football. The humans take it very seriously, and are almost tribal in their devotion to their chosen team. We thought if we learned more, it would help relations with the rest of the crew, so we watched some games together. That is a bonding activity for the humans also, but we were surprised it broke down some of our cultural barriers too.'

'How interesting. I would like to know what you found out, but would not expect you to break a friend's confidence,' he said. 'I have noticed you have been unable to spend time together recently.'

'No, sadly. Even the mess hall is often full or used for meetings. Reuel is ... sensitive. He misses our companionship. Also I have been seriously ill, so he is concerned for my health.'

'It seems he is not getting on well with his compatriot either.' Hazeroth stood up. 'In the interests of crew morale, I propose to spend the next hour elsewhere, and I happen to know Reuel is off-duty.'

* * *

Working in Engineering, Tabitha ran into Stubbs. Her heart sank.

'Hello, Stubbs. I can't stop, I've got to clean up.'

'Hi Tabi, I'll walk with you.'

Tabitha rushed ahead, but didn't manage to lose him. She could feel the panic rising. She wasn't ready for this, why couldn't he leave her alone? She plucked up courage and turned to face him.

'Look, Roy. I'm grateful, but I don't want to get involved with anyone. I'm so new, and there's so much to learn...'

'Get involved?' he cut in. 'You've got the wrong

impression, Tabi. It can make things difficult if ship mates get involved, but we can all use a friend.'

Now she was panicking. All worked up, but she'd got it wrong! 'Oh, I'm sorry. I didn't mean to offend you.' She laid a hand on his arm. 'I'd like us to be friends.'

'That's great, really great.'

Tabitha was so relieved.

'Now you go and get cleaned up.' Stubbs said and turned away, so Tabitha didn't see him smiling to himself.

Chapter 24

The days settled into an uneasy routine. The kind of monotony where the smallest incident is an event. One day the Altairians, Reuel and Rendor, were working together in the mess hall and began their strange crooning sounds, much like a human might hum to himself. In some circumstances this can be very soothing, but Barok didn't find it so. He was eating his lunch and, after huffing and puffing for a bit, finally exploded.

'Will you cease that awful noise!' he shouted, jumping from his chair.

Rendor jumped up in turn and Hoy quickly put himself between them.

'Mr Rendor, you will kindly consider others before you make that noise. Some of us are not used to it.'

There was a tense moment, and then Reuel apologised. Rendor sat down and Hoy breathed a sigh of relief. He turned to Barok, who inclined his head and gave a rare smile to thank him.

Life was boring and it was easy for people to get on each other's nerves. Ehu went out of his way not to intimidate Barok - every time they were in the same room, Ehu sat down. Everyone smiled when they saw it, but Barok was totally unaware. Darrow and Parks devised drills and extra duties to keep people busy. They managed to rearrange the cargo, which was mostly food and spare parts, to make room in the cargo bay for exercises and an occasional film show, though some had to sit on the floor.

Anna worked with Ryan on meditation and breathing exercises to control her fears. Ky was nervous around her so once he had done all he could with the regenerator to heal her head injury, Ryan took over her care, under Ky's guidance. Ky watched them carefully though, and was concerned about their growing closeness. He warned Ryan not to take advantage of her vulnerable state.

Tabitha got into the schedule of her duties and studies. Parks took full advantage of her presence and much of the routine maintenance and cleaning was combined with teaching Tabitha how to do it. The duties took longer to do, but that occupied more time and kept everyone busy. Most of the representatives were happy to spend time with her, and were quite relaxed without the usual time constraints. Even Barok, who had no useful skills, found he could get her to do a lot of his record keeping in the guise of lessons. Her meeting with Merari, however, caused unexpected trouble.

* * *

Tabitha was in the mess hall having lunch one day, when Merari approached with his plate.

'May I sit here?'

'Yes sir, of course.'

'We have not met yet. I am Merari Two, from Ochra. You are the trainee, are you not?'

'Yes sir, Tabitha Enns. I'm from Alpha, the first Earth colony. I will be spending some time with you as part of my training. Commander Parks wants me to meet all the representatives, to learn about the different species first-hand.'

'I have never met an Alphan before. I have heard Alphans are insular.'

'They are, that is, we are, but I don't agree with it. That's why I joined PACT, for a chance to get away out into the stars. I think we're missing out on so much by not dealing with the other species.'

'I commend you for your attitude. Do you have questions you would like to ask me now, while we eat?'

'Thank you, sir.' She paused. 'Would you be offended if I asked about your skin colour?'

Merari laughed. 'You noticed the loss of green? My atmosphere has less oxygen than on board this ship. The atmosphere here is most suitable for humans, because the crew are mostly human. The other species can breathe it, but Ochran skin goes pink in an oxygen-rich atmosphere. So does Casparan skin. You notice Mr Barok wears a mask around his neck which he breathes from occasionally? It is to keep his skin colour pure. I decided not to bother, being pink is a new experience.'

'I'm afraid I made the mistake at first of thinking you and Mr Barok were the same, but Lieutenant Chambers put me right. He told me about Casparan independence from Ochra. His grandfather was there.'

Merari stopped eating. 'Chambers?' he said. 'I did not make the connection before. Who would think I would end up on the same ship as a descendant of Christopher Chambers?'

He banged his fist down on the table, rose to his feet and rushed out.

What did I say? thought Tabitha.

* * *

When Anna was sufficiently recovered from her head injury, Darrow arranged for each of the representatives to meet her. They all wanted to send their own reports back to their governments. With the exception of Barok. He was convinced she could read his mind, and stayed well away. Dathan had already met Anna, from working with Ky, so Darrow arranged for the other four to spend time with her, individually, one afternoon. Ky insisted on being present to monitor her health, but agreed to do so from across sick bay. They drew lots, and Hazeroth won the first visit.

He came into sick bay and stopped just inside the door.

'Hello,' he said softly, 'I want to give you time to look at me and ask me any questions, before you are happy for me to come and sit down. Take your time.'

Anna looked at his lizard-like features and large teeth, but took a deep breath and smiled. 'Thank you for being so considerate. Please sit down. Can you tell me a little about your race?'

'I am from Zoa, a planet much warmer than your Earth.' He indicated his thick jacket. 'Though I hear there are places near the equator which would be more to my liking. We have a tribal culture and our government is co-ordinated by the tribal leaders. We founded PACT. There is much I could say - what would you like to know?'

'I'd like to know a lot, since I can't remember anything, but I think you would rather talk about me.'

'Indeed. Can you remember nothing at all?'

She shook her head. 'Nothing about me or my life or the outside world. It's strange to have no reference points. I have vague memories of the...' her face clouded, 'the surgery, but no details. Then I woke up here. I'm sorry.'

'What about your link to the Intruders?'

'I know it's connected with the surgery, because it brings back those memories, and makes me so afraid.' She shuddered, and Hazeroth laid his hand on hers.

'Please don't distress yourself, but anything you can tell me would be valuable.'

She shrugged. 'I call it "the terror", and all I know is when it comes, they are near.'

Hazeroth turned the conversation to easier topics for a few moments, thanked her and left. Ky looked over at Anna but she waved him away, saying she was fine.

Rendor was next, and not so diplomatic as Hazeroth. He came straight in and sat down, but was taken aback when Anna laughed.

'Oh I'm so sorry,' she said, controlling herself with an effort. 'I've never seen hair like that. Oh, it moves!'

Rendor's cranial spines had writhed, and now lifted at the affront. 'My spines are not hair, and are not to be mocked.'

'I'm sorry, I wasn't mocking you. It's just I've never seen anything like it. At least, I don't remember...'

'So what do you remember? Who altered you?'

'I don't know. I just remember the pain.' She faltered,

but Rendor took no notice.

'Can you not describe them at all?'

'No! I told you, I don't remember anything!'

Ky called from across the room. 'If you distress her, I'll stop the interview.'

'I am entitled to gather information, as much as the others,' replied Rendor. He turned back to Anna. 'Tell me what you know about these Intruders.'

'A little more courtesy and consideration, please,' Ky called, but Anna raised a hand and shook her head.

'I want to get it over with.' She took a deep breath. 'All I know about the Intruders is that when they're near, I feel terrified. It brings back the memories of the pain.'

Rendor was exasperated. 'I want to know what you told the others. There must be more than this!'

'No, I'm sorry. There really isn't any more.'

'I do not believe you. What have you told the others!'

Anna sat back, her face white, her eyes wide.

'Mr Rendor, that is enough,' Ky intervened, stepping between them. 'You will leave now.'

Rendor stomped out, his spines stiff. Ky checked Anna's vital signs.

'Come and lie down. I will not have you put under such strain.'

Anna obeyed, but said, 'Mr Hazeroth was so nice, I didn't mind talking to him. Can you ask the others not to be so aggressive?'

'I certainly will,' Ky replied, 'but no one is coming to talk to you for at least an hour. Your blood pressure has spiked.'

While Anna rested, Ky contacted the other two representatives, Merari and Ehu, and made it quite clear how they should behave. He also notified the captain what had happened.

When Merari's turn came, he obviously had other things on his mind. He didn't even sit down.

He bowed to Anna and asked, 'Do you have any

information which is not in the reports?'

'N-no. I've told them everything. Not that I can remember much.'

'Why can you sense the Intruders?'

'I don't know. I...'

'Thank you.'

Merari bowed again and left. Anna raised a puzzled face to Ky, and then burst out laughing.

'What was that?'

Ky shrugged then turned serious. 'Now, Anna, don't be alarmed by Mr Ehu. He is not as fierce as he looks.'

The sick bay door opened, and there was a pause. Anna was beginning to wonder if anyone was coming, when Ehu shuffled slowly into view. He bowed, and waited. Anna took in the height, the mane, the jaw, the eyes. The eyes did it. Anna smiled.

'Please, come in and sit down. Thank you for taking time for me to see you.'

Ehu smiled and sat down. Anna looked at the large canines that were revealed, but decided to trust the eyes.

'I suppose you know you look like a lion,' she said. 'But I had a book as a child about a friendly lion, and I think that's you.'

'I understood you had no memory of your past.'

'I don't... oh, how do I know that?'

Anna gasped, the colour draining from her face. Ky rushed over with a med scanner. Ehu looked around uncertainly, not sure whether to stay or go. Anna reached out and grabbed his arm.

'Please stay, I might remember more.' She smiled. 'You must be a lucky lion.' She turned to Ky, fussing with his scanner. 'I'm all right, Doctor. I was just shocked. Please, I want to carry on.'

Ky nodded. 'Very well, but not for long.'

Ehu asked, 'Are you certain?'

'Yes. I'm sorry I got upset. Can you tell me a bit about you first?'

'My name is Ehu, from the clan Pathrus. I come from Anak. My world is rich in resources, and others thought they could help themselves. My people had to learn to fight. Even though we look fierce, at heart we are peaceful. So when the news came about the Intruders, we had to respond. And now there is you.'

'And I don't know who I am, or where I'm from. I have no people to save.'

A tear ran down her cheek. Ky rushed over, but before he could intervene, Ehu took her in his arms.

'You may be the salvation of all of us,' he said.

Chapter 25

Chambers was accosted in the corridor by Merari, raging.

'As soon as this mission is over, you will be imprisoned and returned to Ochra. You are a terrorist and must be punished for war crime.'

Chambers had no idea what was the matter, and shrank against the wall. Merari was a head taller than him.

'What are you talking about? I haven't done anything!'

He could only think of the instructions not to upset the visitors, and didn't know what to do. He tried to walk away, but Merari grabbed his arm roughly. Instinctively Chambers reacted and punched him. Merari bellowed and reached for his knife, no longer on his hip. The shout attracted attention. Hazeroth and Ehu rushed to separate them before any serious damage was done. The moment Hazeroth grabbed Chambers he went limp and looked down. Ehu grabbed Merari and growled low in his ear. Parks was called and arrived at a run.

'Take them both to the mess hall, now.' He ordered. 'Mr Hazeroth and Mr Ehu, keep them apart, while I clear the room.'

They stumbled into the mess hall, alarming the occupants, one of whom was Tabitha.

'Andrew! What's going on?' She rushed to her friend's side.

'Not now, Trainee,' snapped Parks. 'Everyone leave.'

He sat down and got Merari and Chambers seated as far apart as the room allowed. Chambers was red in the face. Merari held himself stiffly.

Parks began. 'I want to discuss this privately. Will you both give me your word there will not be any more trouble, or do Mr Hazeroth and Mr Ehu need to stay?'

Chambers and Merari nodded. Parks motioned to the others to leave and asked Ehu to guard the door. When the door closed he turned to Chambers.

'I hope you have a good reason for attacking one of our guests.'

Chambers shouted, 'He accused me of terrorism!'

Parks put his hand on Chambers' arm but he wasn't ready to calm down. Parks turned to Merari.

Merari drew himself up. 'His grandfather was one of the terrorists who caused much damage and killed many Ochrans before Caspar was granted independence. Ochra demands justice!' He thumped the table with his fist.

'What?' Chambers said. 'My grandfather? I knew he was there, but he never told us any details. Anyway, it's too late. He died ten years ago.'

To his surprise, Parks didn't look relieved. He turned to Merari.

'Surely you understand that the human legal system doesn't recognise family responsibility?'

Before Merari could answer, Chambers said, 'What are you talking about? My grandfather is dead!' His voice rose and he leaned across the table.

Parks motioned to Merari not to speak and reached out and grabbed Chambers by the shoulder. 'Keep calm, Lieutenant, let me handle this, you don't understand.' Chambers sank back into his chair, and Parks turned to Merari.

At that point, the red alert klaxon went off. Parks warned Merari not to take things any further and rushed Chambers out of the mess hall.

* * *

A few minutes earlier Anna had felt uneasy and called to Ryan.

'Sam, can you help me? It's faint, but I'm certain I can feel them.'

Ryan paused only to alert the doctor and the captain, and rushed to her side. He was pleased to see she had started the breathing exercises he had taught to help her focus and stay calm. She opened her eyes and gave him a troubled look.

'It's getting stronger, so we're heading in the right direction. Why hasn't the alarm gone off?'

'It seems you're more sensitive than the sensors. Don't worry, I've told the captain and everyone is on alert.'

A few seconds passed, then Anna sighed.

'I'm so sorry. I must have imagined it. The feeling is fading.'

Ryan thought for a moment, took her arm and turned her around.

'No, wait. Face the direction the ship is travelling. Where are the Intruders?'

She pointed to her right and slightly behind. Ryan thumbed the intercom. 'Captain, we've passed them! They are to the rear of starboard.'

He heard the captain give the order: 'Helm, come about, 100 degrees. Scanners on alert.'

Anna soon began to get a stronger signal. One minute later, the red alert klaxon went off.

Ryan was pleased with the way Anna was handling it. Ky wasn't so sure.

'You're doing fine, but it's going to get stronger as we get nearer,' Ky said. 'Do you want me to give you a sedative until it's all over?'

Anna stiffened. 'No, I want to face it. I need to face it. I can't be unconscious if those things get in here.'

* * *

On the bridge the scanner alarm went off and the scanners confirmed a single ship heading *into* the galaxy. Darrow turned to Hazeroth, who was on duty with him.

'I don't know where it's going,' said Darrow grimly, 'but if it's heading inwards it must be going to cause more trouble. I'm setting an intercept course, maximum speed. Sound the alert!'

The klaxon sounded and the designated crew began hurrying to Engineering and the bridge. Parks and Chambers arrived on the bridge, but so did the representatives, and Chambers had to squeeze past to get to the helm. The bridge became crowded, so Darrow assigned Ehu to the scanners and weapons station and gave up his seat to Hazeroth to take on comms. He dismissed Parks, but kept Chambers at the helm, unaware of the state he was in. The rest he asked to stand back out of the way.

It was lucky the sensors had been adapted, as there was no visual contact. The sensors told them they had caught up with the Intruder ship, but they were staring at empty space. Darrow ordered the universal first contact message in every language to be transmitted, which was ignored. As they came closer they matched course and speed with the Intruder vessel. They were ignored. The representatives' advice was conflicting.

'I suggest you fire a shot across their bow, Captain,' said Barok. 'That should catch their attention.'

'Absolutely not!' snapped Hazeroth. 'You don't handle a first contact situation by shooting at them!'

'Drop our shields and power down our weapons to show that we are not a threat and come in peace,' suggested Dathan.

'What?' Barok snapped. 'Leave us vulnerable to attack? Don't do it, Captain!'

'Can we fly towards them and see how they react?' asked Merari.

'I don't think we should provoke them,' said Hazeroth. 'Just follow them and see where they are going. We could get valuable information on the way they operate.'

The Altairian, Rendor, was looking at the navigation display.

'Captain, one of our colonies is the nearest inhabited planet on this course. Are you suggesting we stand by and make observations while the Intruders attack?'

Darrow was calling for order when Ky came through on

the intercom. 'Are we in communication with the Intruders Captain?'

'No Doctor, they are unresponsive.'

'Well, we have contact down here! It's not exactly communication, but Anna appears to be sensing their thoughts! It only works at this range, she didn't get anything until the last few seconds. Have we been flying parallel?'

'Yes we have. I think you should bring Anna to the bridge.'

'Immediately, Captain, I'll send Ensign Ryan with her.'

While they waited for Anna, Darrow announced, 'I would remind you all that I am the captain here, and I will have order. Your advice is welcome, but if you interfere with operations, you will be removed.'

Anna was as amazed as the rest of them at this new ability. The terror was still there, but as time passed, and with Ryan's help, she was getting used to it. It grew in strength as they drew nearer the Intruder ship, and that became harder, but suddenly she had ideas in her head. At first they were a distraction, but as she tried to concentrate, they grew clearer. Not words, just feelings and impressions, hard to express. Having to go to the bridge was difficult, it interfered with her control. When they arrived she had to sit for a few seconds before she could refocus.

'It's hard to explain, Captain. I just sense ideas and feelings. They know we're here, they just don't think we're important enough to bother with. They're heading for a planet they call four-five-oh point two. They need … liquid metal … I think it's mercury, for … I don't understand.' She shook her head.

'It's OK Anna, you're doing fine.'

Darrow silently thanked whoever had altered Anna for giving him the edge, when there was so little information. He was in charge and would insist on making the decisions, but he didn't want to cause a diplomatic problem later by upsetting one of the representatives. If only they didn't all disagree.

Rendor spoke up. 'Captain, the Altairian colony Jacs mines cinnabar ore for mercury, and it's the second planet in that solar system.'

'How long before we could get there?'

Chambers, at the helm, replied. 'Two hours at maximum speed, sir, but we don't know the Intruders' maximum speed.'

Rendor turned to Darrow with a grave look on his face, his crest raised.

'You have to do something Captain. There are 10 million colonists on Jacs. The mercury is their main export.'

There was a troubled silence.

'Mr Rendor, we know they steal, but so far deaths have been minimal, please don't panic yet.' Darrow said as he came to a decision. He turned to Hazeroth. 'Send this message to the Intruder ship: "This is the Planetary Alliance ship the Kestrel. We cannot allow you to continue raiding the planets in this galaxy." Weapons, fire across their bow. Shields up.'

Ehu, on the scanners, said. 'Captain, they have raised their shields and are powering up weapons.'

Anna spoke. 'They think we are a nuisance. Like a fly to be swatted.'

She gripped Ryan's hand tightly.

The Intruder ship fired a single bolt that passed through their shields and immediately knocked out the warp drive. The engines fell silent and there was a jolt as they dropped out of warp, and the Intruder ship was gone. There was a sick, sinking feeling in Darrow's stomach, and it wasn't just the effect of the sudden deceleration.

'Damn! We have to find a defence against that, or we'll never be able to fight them.' He reached for the intercom. 'Engineering, let me know as soon as warp power is restored.' He gave commands to the bridge. 'Link sensors to navigation to follow their emissions trail. Comms, notify Jacs about that ship. Tell them to be prepared and secure their mercury stocks. Anna, can you still sense them?'

'Yes Captain, but fading fast. They weren't angry, they just wanted us out of their way.'

She was trembling, and Ryan cut in. 'Anna should rest now, Captain, that was quite an ordeal.'

'Take her back to sick bay,' Darrow said.

The Intruders' weapon did no direct damage, but it took critical minutes to restart the engines and achieve warp speed. They would not be in time to help defend the colony.

* * *

The moment the alert was cancelled, Tabitha rushed to find Chambers as he left the bridge.

'What was all that about?'

'We encountered an Intruder ship -'

'Not that.' She lowered her voice. 'Why was Mr Merari shouting? What did you do?'

'Nothing! He charged up to me and said I'm to be put on trial for war crime. I haven't done anything! He was raving about my grandfather, but he's dead. Commander Parks seemed to think it was serious, but the alert started and we had to leave it there.'

Tabitha said nothing. She was remembering her conversation with Merari.

'What's the matter?' Chambers asked. 'Do you know what he's on about?'

'No, no.' She pulled him to the stairs, out of sight of the corridor. 'But it was me who told him about your grandfather.' She turned away, feeling awful. 'I'm so sorry. I didn't think it would cause a problem.'

Chambers turned her back to face him. 'Don't blame yourself, I don't see the problem either.'

'What did your grandfather do, anyway?'

'I don't know. I knew he was there, he told us about it. But he only told us about the people, not what he did. Merari said he was a terrorist.' Hazeroth appeared on the stairs and they stopped talking until he had passed them.

Chambers continued. 'There's no way to find out, either. My grandfather died years ago.'

Tabitha thought for a moment. 'What about the records? We could research the fight for independence and see if he gets mentioned.' She cheered up at the thought. 'That's how I spend my free time, finding out all the stuff they never told me back home. Think of everything you remember from your grandfather, and we'll look it up as soon as we get some free time. Did Mr Merari say anything else?'

Chambers frowned, trying to remember. 'Commander Parks said something about family responsibility.'

'I've got a study period now, if it's not cancelled with this emergency. I'll look up Ochrans and family responsibility. What was your grandfather's name?'

'Christopher Chambers.'

'I'll see what I can find, then when you're free, we'll look it up together.'

'Thanks. I'd better get back to work.'

* * *

Darrow was surprised when Parks requested a word with him while they were waiting for the engines to come back online. The representatives had left the bridge, but Parks kept his voice low.

'Sir, we have a problem with Lieutenant Chambers and Mr Merari. I'm handling it, but I thought you should know.'

'Come to my office. Let's keep this private.' Once the door was shut he asked, 'What has Chambers done?'

'The problem's not Chambers, it's his grandfather. It turns out he was involved in the fight for Casparan independence. Merari is claiming family responsibility.'

'Damn! Chambers is under enough pressure as it is without this. I thought Earth courts didn't recognise family responsibility.'

Parks rolled his eyes. 'We're not on Earth and PACT is an inter-species alliance. It's a bit difficult in space. I'm going to have to do some digging in the regulations.'

'Yes,' Darrow agreed. 'Outside local space is where Fast-Response comes in. Deal with it first, and sort it out later.'

Parks nodded. 'It needs to be sorted out, for Chambers' sake. He can't be a helmsman if he can't leave Earth.'

'Is Merari demanding justice now, in the middle of a mission?'

'No, thankfully, but if we can't resolve it, Chambers is going to have the threat hanging over him the whole time. We also have to consider whether Merari can work with him. It's just going to increase the tension on board.'

Darrow shook his head. 'It's such a shame, he's a damn good pilot. If he can get his confidence back he'll be a real asset to this crew.'

'I'll do my best to find a way out for him.'

Chapter 26

By the time Kestrel reached Jacs, the Intruders had been and gone. The planetary defences were heaps of molten metal and rubble, but there seemed to be no other damage. They landed at the little spaceport and Darrow sent Parks with some of the crew to help with the clean-up. Blackwell met with some of the colonists to discuss repairs to the systems and what would be needed in order to rebuild. Dr Ky refused to leave the ship, as he had said he would, but was happy to treat any colonists who came to him. Darrow figured that at this point they probably had the best facilities on board so he let the point slide. Stubbs and Hoy were tasked with checking over Kestrel's engines while they were shut down. Darrow wanted to make sure there were no hidden problems before they set off again. They were going a long way and they would be a long way from help.

Once the emergency was over, Darrow and the six representatives met with the Altairian leaders in the colony meeting hall. Jacs had lower gravity than Earth-normal, but the representatives all wanted to hear the colonists' report first-hand. Some of them managed better than others, yet still there was a general relief when they were all seated.

'The Intruder ship dropped out of warp directly in our atmosphere,' said Nobah, the colony leader. 'We barely had time to prepare after we got your message, and the sudden appearance of the ship so close to the planet meant our defences fired few shots before the ship fired back. The beam completely destroyed the defence system. The beam itself did not cause much physical damage, but the short-circuit of all that power, collected ready to fire, was what caused the destruction. All those manning the system were killed, but luckily we had got everyone else away from the stores and the processing plant, so casualties were limited.'

'We were hit with a similar weapon, which took our

engines offline,' Darrow said. 'How many people did you lose?'

'Ten,' Nobah said. 'Ten good people this colony can ill afford to lose. The ship landed beside the mercury storage tanks, extended a drill hose which bored into them, and siphoned it all on board. We tried to attack the ship on the ground, but no one could get near. They had some sort of force shield round the ship which extended around the tanks. Some of us got burned by it.' He held up a roughly-bandaged hand. 'Then they disappeared as suddenly as they had come. But not before leaving a message - in standard language.' He pushed a button and the message played.

'We do not wish to communicate with you solids. We merely wish to avail ourselves of the materials your worlds provide. You are of no interest to us. You cannot resist us. The harvesters are being prepared.'

There was a stunned silence after the message was played. The cranial spines on the head of every Altairian were raised in anger and fear.

'Harvesters!' Nobah shouted, his spines quivering. 'We are nothing but a new source of materials to them! And they are right - we cannot resist them. They did not attack our people, but we cannot survive without the income from our mercury. They took everything we have processed for the last 3 months.' He slumped in his chair.

'It is interesting that they did not take the raw material this time,' Hazeroth muttered to Darrow, who nodded.

Rendor stood, his crest quivering.

'If all they want is materials, at least they are not likely to come back here for a while. As a representative of Altair I have already contacted home on your behalf, and made an initial report. You must give them the details of what has happened.'

One of the other colony leaders said, 'We need to build storage tanks at other sites, and not ship all the ore to the spaceport. That way it cannot all be stolen at once.'

'We should build underground shelters for the women

and children,' another voice said.

'And Altair must rebuild the defence system for us.' said Nobah.

Rendor turned to Darrow. 'Captain, we have to stop them!'

All eyes turned towards Darrow. It truly hit home for him what it could mean if the Intruders carried out their threat. He realised what a huge burden had been placed on his shoulders, and for a moment his anger rose again at the lack of vision of Commodore Michel and the lack of PACT resources assigned to the mission. Suppressing the reaction, he drew his attention back to the expectant crowd. He rose to his feet and looked around the room.

'We have prepared a report giving details of everything we have found out so far, including the scanner modifications and the developments we are working on right now to protect our engines against their weapon. Send it to all the worlds in the Alliance. See it reaches everyone. That ship must have returned by another route, as it didn't pass us on our way in. We have to find their home world as soon as we can, and do whatever we can against them. But we have to leave soon, while we can still follow the wake trail.'

Later Darrow spoke to Merari, the Ochran linguist.

'How do you think they know our language, when there is no record of any previous contact?' he asked him.

'It would seem to me,' Merari said, 'that as well as the incidents you and your contacts have discovered, they have been monitoring our communications.' He paused for thought. 'They do not seem to speak as we do. I would suggest they have found a way of converting their form of speech to ours.' He smiled. 'I wonder how they do communicate? Telepathy?'

Darrow said, 'Maybe you'll get a chance to find out. Safely, I hope.'

* * *

While Captain Darrow and the representatives met with the colonists, Parks led some of the crew to help with the cleanup, including Tabitha. She knew she was just another pair of hands, but she was delighted and nervous. This was her second experience of a new world, though arguably this was the first new planet she'd ever been on. Jacs was very different to Pallas. The settlement was in a tropical valley below high volcanic peaks, and the mist that hung in the air turned out to be from geysers that erupted at regular intervals. The smell of sulphur increased when the wind changed. Tabitha looked in horror as they passed the twisted molten mess of the defence system.

'Sir, if they've got a ray that does that,' she said to Parks, 'what chance do we have if we meet them?'

'Every encounter gives us more data,' he said, 'and we're using that to develop defences and counter measures.'

'We are not going to fight them anyway,' said Reuel. 'Our mission is to locate their home world and find out as much as we can. Then our worlds can prepare a defence, to fight them if we have to.'

'That's right,' said Parks. 'There's no cause for concern. By the way, just a reminder that you can't mention this in your communications back home. This mission has to be secret until it's resolved. We don't want to scare people.'

Tabitha sniffed. *We don't want to scare people,* she thought, *but there's no cause for con*cern.

The wind shifted and there was a reek of sulphur. The Kestrel crew reacted, but the colony members accompanying them took no notice.

'You get used to it after a while,' said one.

Down a short path through the trees they came to the processing plant, and beside it, the ore storage and mercury tanks. Masks, gloves and goggles were issued from sealed packets.

'Cinnabar ore and mercury are both toxic,' the Altairian said. 'You must keep these on at all times and hand them in afterwards.'

The cinnabar stores had minor damage from the fighting, and Tabitha, with her strength, was assigned to tidy up there. While she worked, she chatted with one of the Altairian colonists. He told her his name was Eber.

'The colony's main income is the processed mercury,' he said, 'and the attackers took it all.'

'At least they didn't touch the processing plant. You'll be able to process the rest of the ore.'

'What is to stop them coming back to get more mercury every time we produce some?' His cranial spines writhed. 'This colony was such a peaceful place. We dreamed of a bright future.'

Tabitha tried to encourage him. 'I'm sure it still can be.'

'My son was killed when the defences blew,' he said, his spines limp. 'We have not even had time to grieve.'

Tabitha's voice caught in her throat. 'I'm so sorry.'

'I have a daughter and a younger son. If we cannot be protected from these attackers, I will have to take them away, for their own safety.'

'It would be a shame to give up all you've built here.'

* * *

On her way back to the Kestrel after helping the colonists, Tabitha encountered Merari. The others were ahead of her. She had been dreading it, and trying to avoid him. She turned away, then stopped, took a deep breath, and came back.

'Look Mr Merari, I know I'm supposed to be respectful, but you're wrong about Chambers. You can't blame him for something his grandfather did.'

'Family responsibility is a defining principle in Ochran culture,' Merari said stiffly. 'Fathers teach their standards to their children, so they grow up and behave the same way.'

'No they don't.' Tabitha stepped forward, frowning, then checked herself as Merari moved back. 'My father believes Earth and its allies turned their backs on the Alpha colonists, and many others feel the same. They've turned inward, and have as little contact as possible with the outside. I was taught that version of history in school and at home. But I don't think that way. I fought to get out.'

Merari sat down on a fallen tree. 'Then you are a rare exception. Tell me, how many of your classmates feel like you?'

Tabitha's face fell. 'But that's not the same as blaming someone for something his father or grandfather did!'

'I know you want to defend your friend, but tell me this: If a child grows up and decides his father or grandfather was wrong, why does he not report him to the authorities?'

'Because Andrew doesn't even know what he did!' She clenched her fists in frustration. *Why didn't he understand?*

Merari shook his head, as if he knew what she was thinking. 'Ignorance is no excuse under the law.'

'Then it's a stupid law!'

Tabitha turned and hurried back to the ship. She couldn't believe she had just shouted at one of the representatives. She would probably be in trouble if Merari complained. She couldn't get her head around the argument. Other cultures had different ways of doing things, but this didn't make sense. Family responsibility just had to be wrong, but an entire species believed in it. How many other people had been punished for things their fathers or grandfathers did? She was appalled. As she entered the airlock she pulled up.

How can I work here if I think like this about a whole race? But if I can't stay, I can't go either. Where can I go?

She fought the rising panic, and then stamped her foot.

Enough! What a stupid way to behave, getting in a sweat! I don't have to like people, I just have to do my job.

She set her jaw and went back to work.

* * *

Tabitha's Journal
I've finally been on my first alien planet, but not for a

good reason. The Intruders we're looking for attacked the Altairian planet Jacs and stole the mercury which they had mined and processed. I helped with the clean-up. The colonists are lovely people, it would be such a shame if some of them left. It makes me more aware of the importance of our mission.

Jacs was very hot and very smelly. It's volcanic and there are geysers throwing out steam and boiling water, all reeking of sulphur. But it's very beautiful too, very lush and green, with bright flowers. I've never seen anything like it, except on vid shows. It's different in real life. I wish we could have spent more time there.

I've met all the representatives now, and they're teaching me the maintenance and cleaning of ship systems, along with talking to me about their cultures. It's fascinating, but I have to write reports on <u>everything</u>. Still, it helps me remember. Unfortunately there's been a big stink with Mr Merari, the Ochran. Not sulphur this time, but threats. He accused Andrew of war crime for something his grandfather did! They have this law about family responsibility. I told Mr Merari it was a stupid law, and was afraid he would report me for insubordination, but nothing's been said. I'm really worried for Andrew. As soon as I finished on Jacs, I looked up family responsibility, but even after research, I still don't agree with it. And as for Andrew's grandfather, I've only found some cryptic references. I'm waiting for Andrew to be free to look further.

I saw Anna for the first time today. She's a woman who arrived with the Anak but was injured. I don't really understand it, but Andrew says she has some kind of mental link to the Intruders, when they're near. Why would anyone want that? She usually stays in sick bay, but Sam brought her into the mess hall. I didn't speak to her as Merari came in so I left to avoid him.

Chapter 27

Dr Ky decided it was not good for Anna to be cooped up in sick bay, so Ryan took her to the mess hall for meals, and sometimes they stayed a while. It gave them the chance to get to know one another.

'My planet is a colony world, but with a difference,' Ryan said one day, after he cleared the table. 'The first colonists were quite happy to use technology to get there, but wanted to do without it as much as possible. They thought civilisation had lost its core values. They wanted to return to a time when people lived by "the sweat of their brow and the strength of their arm."' He gave a bitter laugh. 'The trouble is, they gave up the benefits along with the problems. People suffered, people died.'

'So you tried to make it better,' Anna said.

Ryan scowled. 'I'm not doing much, am I? I was so full of plans to get qualified and go home, but then I saw what life was like outside. I grabbed the chance to do a year out here … and now I don't want to go back.' He hung his head.

Anna took his hand. 'You shouldn't be so hard on yourself. You need to make your own life. Now me, I don't even have a life.'

Ryan put his hand over hers. 'I'm sure you will one day, when this is over. Right now your link to the Intruders is vital to us.'

'It's so strange, it's like telepathy, only with someone so different that it's hard to understand the way they think.'

'We would have been much worse off if you hadn't been able to tell us what they were up to. With practice, you might become even more accurate.'

'I'm not looking forward to that.' She sighed. 'Oh Sam, why me? I don't remember who I am, and I feel like a nobody. Why did they have to do this to me?'

'It seems to me that whoever "they" are, they knew these

Intruders were a threat and wanted to help us without getting personally involved. Maybe you were the first person they found, or maybe you are, and always were, more special than you know.'

When she turned to face him, the vulnerability in her eyes pulled at his heart. A part of him needed to make the same connection she was obviously craving. Leaning in to kiss her felt like the most natural thing in the universe.

'Oh, I'm sorry, I shouldn't have …' he blushed.

Anna laid a finger on his lips and smiled.

Ky and Dathan arrived in the mess hall, and Ryan sat back in his seat. 'Oh no,' he said to Anna, but looking to Ky, 'He's probably got another job he wants me to do twice. I never seem to satisfy him. Sometimes I think I'll never be good enough to become a doctor, if his opinion is anything to go by.'

'You're supposed to be on duty, young man,' Ky said. 'I need you to help me with some samples I'm testing.'

'Sorry, Doctor. I was giving Anna a change of scenery, as she's not allowed out of sick bay unattended.'

Dathan spoke up and bowed to Anna.

'I am on my way to the hydroponics lab. I would be most honoured to escort Anna there, if that is permitted, and then I can return her to sick bay.'

Anna turned to Ky, and when he smiled agreement, she accepted Dathan's offer. Dathan bowed to Anna and offered her his arm. She nervously took it, and he escorted her from the mess hall. Ryan gazed after her and touched his lips.

* * *

It is impossible to keep secrets on a small ship, and soon everyone had heard what happened between Merari and Chambers. When it reached Desmar Barok, he was delighted, and sought out Chambers as soon as possible.

'My dear young man!' he gushed, 'I understand your grandfather was a hero. May I shake your hand?'

'No!' Chambers stepped back, and then remembered his manners. 'I mean, it's not necessary. It's a long time in the past, and nothing to do with me.'

'But - family responsibility…'

'I've never heard of such a thing. I'm not responsible for what my grandfather did, good or bad. I don't even know what he did.' Hope rose in Chambers that Barok might be able to tell him, but it was dashed.

'I am sorry I cannot help you, there are few records from that time on Caspar, but we are in your debt.'

Chambers didn't know what to do. He was as unwilling to receive Barok's friendship as he had been to receive Merari's condemnation.

'If you'll excuse me, I have duties to attend to.'

As he turned to leave, Barok bowed deeply in the Casparan manner.

'If there is any service I may render, you have only to ask.'

* * *

Tabitha's Journal

Well, my feared confrontation with Roy has finally happened. As part of my duties, I was assigned to work with Roy in Engineering. Although he had said he wanted to be friends, I've been trying to avoid him, but now I had no choice.

'Hello, Sweets,' he said (I hate it when he calls me that), 'we have to work in very close quarters today. Won't that be fun?'

My heart sank. 'Let's just get on with it, shall we?'

We had to check some relays. He handed me a pad with a list of numbers on and opened a service panel. Each number indicates the location of the relay. I did a couple, and then I came to a panel I couldn't open. He reached round me, and seemed to lean in unnecessarily close as he opened the panel. I thought his lips brushed my cheek, but I wasn't sure. I told myself not to be silly, we're working. We continued to work our way along until we reached a hatch, which Roy opened.

'The next one is in here,' he said. 'After you.'

The space was very narrow. I said, 'We can't both get in there.'

'You go,' he said, 'the junction is only about two metres in. Call the reading back to me.'

I climbed in on hands and knees and worked my way into the crawl space. I found the relay and sat down to free my hands for the work. As the panel came open, I heard the noise of the hatch closing, and looked up to find Roy in the space behind me.

'I told you we would be in close quarters, didn't I, Sweets?' he said. 'We won't be disturbed in here. How about a little kiss?'

I felt my face go red. 'Don't Roy, I'm not interested.'

'Oh, come on,' he said, drawing nearer. 'I'll bet you've had lots of boyfriends. Aren't you missing them just a little bit?'

It was awful. I didn't want to admit I didn't know. I said, 'Please don't. We'll get into trouble.'

'Not if we don't tell. It can be our little secret.'

He made a grab for me and I panicked and kicked out.

'Watch it!' he said. 'What do you think you're doing?'

'What do you think you're *doing?' I said. 'Don't you blame this on me!'*

I wriggled to one side and, grabbing his arms, dragged him further into the crawl space. Then I pushed the hatch button with my foot and scrambled out, closing the hatch after me and leaning on it. My face was red and my hands trembling, I ran into my cabin and wished I could lock the door, wished there was a door to lock. What made it worse was knowing I haven't had any boyfriends, so I'm not sure I understood his intention right. I just panicked. The boys back home seemed so immature, and I was so focussed on my studies, I took no notice of them. Maybe I should have paid more attention. Suppose a kiss was all he wanted? Would it have hurt?

I heard Roy come out of the hatch, and tensed as I waited to see what he would do. I relaxed when he moved away.

What now? *I thought.* If I stay in here, I could be in trouble for not working. If I go back, what will Roy do? *Then I decided,* No, it's about what I'll do. *I had an idea, so I gritted my teeth, and went back out.*

I said, 'I'm sorry, Roy, perhaps I misunderstood. You said you wanted us to be friends.' I smiled at him, but it was strained. 'I'll discuss it with Commander Parks on my next report. He'll tell me the rules on crew relationships.'

'There's no need for that,' Roy said quickly. 'I was only teasing. Friends is fine.'

So my guess was right. We went back to work, but I made Roy go into the hatches. But it didn't end there, because Andrew caught on, and he doesn't like Roy already. At meal break, I saw Andrew in the mess hall, and sat with him. He asked me how things were going.

'Don't ask.' I said. 'I've been working with Roy.' I pulled a face. Big mistake.

'Did he try something? Where is he?' He made to get up, but I put a hand on his arm.

'No don't, Andrew. You'll only make it worse. I'm stronger than him - he can't do anything.'

'You shouldn't have to fight him off. It's unprofessional conduct.'

'Oh please, leave it.'

Andrew went back to his food. I talked about other things, but the look on Andrew's face said he wouldn't let it go. As we were leaving, Roy arrived. What bad timing! Andrew appeared to stumble in the doorway and knocked into Roy, who went sprawling. I was mortified. I leaped forward and went to help him up, but lifted him bodily off his feet - in front of everyone!. I pushed him in through the door and dragged Andrew away from him down the corridor.

'Leave it!' I hissed. 'I can handle it.'

Andrew pulled his tunic straight. 'I reckon you can,' he said with a grin.

Oh boy.

* * *

Darrow was reading the latest collection of reports from Barok when Hoy called from the bridge.

'Meteor storm dead ahead, sir, picked up on the long range scanners. It looks like comet debris. Commander Blackwell does not believe the shields will withstand attempting to pass through. He recommends we go around.'

Damn! thought Darrow. *More delays.* 'Won't we lose the trail?' he asked.

'We will lose it in the meteor shower anyway,' said Rendor, from the navigation console. 'The trail has been a straight line, so I can plot where it should be on the other side.'

'Very well, plot a course around the storm and see if we can pick up the trail again. Notify me as soon as we do.'

That's all we need, Darrow thought, *to lose the trail this far out and have to go back and search for another one.*

Chapter 28

Hazeroth approached Parks in the hydroponics bay and asked to speak to him privately.

'Commander, I wish to offer my services in resolving the issue between Mr Merari and Lieutenant Chambers. I have experience in conflict resolution.'

Parks sighed. 'Thank you. I don't see a solution. There's no way that Earth would permit Chambers to be prosecuted. Most of the humans who were involved were dealt with at the time. It's history now, and family responsibility doesn't hold up on Earth.'

'But Chambers is not on Earth is he? We have a vital mission, which must not be jeopardised. Would you trust a helmsman whose mind is not on his job?'

Parks only reply was a momentary glance to the floor.

'So will you let me speak to Mr Merari on his behalf?'

Taking a deep breath Parks considered. 'I'm grateful for your help, but don't promise Mr Merari anything without discussing it with me.'

* * *

Hazeroth waited for Merari to be alone in his cabin in the cargo bay, and went to see him. Like most of the cabins, there was only one chair, which Merari was using, so Hazeroth remained standing. After the polite formalities, he came straight to the point.

'It seems to me that you are trying to start a war with Earth. Do you not think you should discuss it with the other species before you take such drastic action?'

Merari was shocked, and then angry. He jumped to his feet. 'I am trying to get justice for my people, not start a war!'

Hazeroth backed away. 'After so long? When will repercussions end? The peace plan which created Casparan independence provided for justice for both sides, but laid down a limitation on seeking recompense.'

'This is a personal matter between my family and the family of Christopher Chambers.'

'You call for justice, what about justice for Lieutenant Chambers? What has he ever done to your people?'

'Family responsibility - '

Hazeroth interrupted. 'Can you tell me what Chambers' family passed down to him?'

'What do you mean?'

'How did he regard you when you first met? Did he say anything against your people?'

'No, but - '

'Surely his grandfather told him about Ochra and Caspar?'

'Chambers told the young woman Enns that his grandfather was involved in Casparan independence.'

'So Chambers was hateful towards you because of what his grandfather told him?'

Merari paused and sat down. 'No. He was always courteous towards me. He showed no animosity.'

Hazeroth softened his tone. 'But he told Trainee Enns about the Casparan struggle for independence.'

'No. Enns was excited to learn about our two species, and didn't know anything about the struggle.'

Hazeroth said nothing. He sat on the lower bunk and waited for Merari to think about what he had just said. Merari looked at him, puzzled, and then understood.

'So his grandfather never said anything to prejudice him one way or the other,' Merari said slowly. 'He never told him.'

Hazeroth nodded. 'How much damage could Christopher Chambers and his family have done over the years if he had spoken out? Can you not see he made sure there was no responsibility on his family?'

Merari looked a little uncomfortable. 'I shall consider what you have said,' he said.

Hazeroth rose and bowed. 'I am at your service should you wish to communicate with Lieutenant Chambers again.'

* * *

A short while later Parks came to see Darrow.

'Good news, Captain. Mr Hazeroth has talked Mr Merari round about Lieutenant Chambers.'

'How?'

'Mr Hazeroth offered to try to mediate. He has experience in conflict resolution, so I gave him permission. It appears to have worked.'

'What happened?'

'Mr Merari wouldn't say, he was a bit stiff. He just came to see me and said he won't be taking the matter any further.'

'Did you press him?'

'I didn't have a chance, he just bowed and left.' Parks laughed.

Darrow became serious. 'I need to tell Chambers, ease his mind.' He reached for the intercom, but paused. 'No, if I summon him to the office, he'll probably expect the worst. Is he on duty?'

'He's rostered for the night shift, sir, you should find him in his cabin.'

Darrow dismissed Parks and went to Chambers' cabin.

'Lieutenant, can I have a word? I've got some good news for you.'

'Captain! Come in!' He jumped to his feet.

'As you were, Lieutenant.'

Chambers shifted from foot to foot while Darrow sat down.

'The subject of family responsibility is not going to be mentioned again,' Darrow said. 'Mr Hazeroth spoke to Mr Merari and helped him see things differently.'

Chambers slumped on the bed. 'What a relief! Trainee Enns looked it up - can they really prosecute family members?'

'Only within their own people, or in space.' Darrow got up to go. 'But I recommend you avoid Mr Merari as much as possible. We don't want to risk upsetting him further.'

'Yes, sir. Thank you sir.'

* * *

When Dathan was out of Chambers' cabin, Tabitha and Chambers took the opportunity to search the history databases. Even though the Captain had said Merari was going to drop the issue, Chambers wanted to know. Tabitha felt for him, and wanted to help. She knew there was something in his recent past, and his position as helmsman worried him. Now with this on top of the general tension, he was looking very strained. Research was difficult because the Casparans viewed the events as freedom fighting, but the Ochrans viewed them as terrorism. There was significant loss of life on both sides, until representatives from Anak and Zoa persuaded both parties to talk to each other. The Zoans could be persuasive and were adept at seeing situations from both sides. The Anak had many years' experience in negotiations for their own situation, and could stop any discussion from getting too heated, with one roar.

'Let me show you what I've found so far.' Tabitha grasped Chambers' elbow and lifted him out of the seat, and took over the keyboard. She called up an entry and Chambers leaned over to read it.

"Christopher Chambers was a vocal supporter of the independence of Caspar from Ochra. He took part in many marches, wrote many articles, and was part of the delegation to the early peace talks. There was no evidence of his being involved in terrorist activities, until the infamous Jokti incident, after which he disappeared."

Chambers looked up at Tabitha, ashen faced. This was what he had dreaded finding. But what did it mean? Tabitha took control.

'Don't panic yet. I haven't had time to look up the Jokti incident.'

Chambers backed away. 'I don't know, don't show me.'

It was too late, Tabitha had already entered the search - but it came up blank. She frowned and tried a different approach. The best she could get was a couple of further mentions of "the infamous Jokti incident" and one mention of "the dreadful Jokti incident", but nowhere could she find any explanation. Chambers, unable to bear the suspense, drifted back again and looked over her shoulder. Tabitha abandoned the search and rose to grasp his arms.

'I'm sorry, Andrew, there's no further information. I can't understand it. You should be able to find out everything from here.' She paused. 'Do you think it was deliberately deleted?'

Chambers howled, 'But what did he do?'

* * *

Chambers was torn. He wanted to know what his grandfather had done, but he didn't want to find out he was a terrorist or a murderer. He didn't know which was worse - knowing or not knowing. The only way to know was to speak directly to Merari, which he had been told not to do. He spent days in indecision. Twice he met Merari in the course of his duties, and both times he opened his mouth to ask, then his courage failed and he turned away. Eventually he could stand it no longer, and went to Merari's cabin. At least if he was refused, it wouldn't be public. He spoke into the intercom.

'Mr Merari, sir, it's Chambers. I need to talk to you about my grandfather. Please let me in.'

There was a long silence. Chambers was about to turn away when the door opened.

'I was expecting you. Now it has been mentioned, you want to know what happened. Come and sit down.'

Chambers had prepared himself for Merari to be angry, but he looked sad.

'I - I don't want to upset you, but I've searched the

197

databases, and all I can find is reference to the Jokti incident, but there's no trace of anything more. I don't even know what Jokti was. I always thought my grandfather was a good man, but now I'm afraid...' his rush of words faltered. 'I need to know.'

Merari had winced when Jokti was mentioned, but now he smiled gently.

'It seems there has been family responsibility after all. You have been suffering with your thoughts. If you really want to know, I will tell you, but you must promise me never to tell anyone else.'

Chambers nodded. He could hardly breathe as he waited. Merari leaned his hands on his knees and bowed his head as he thought how to begin.

'Jokti was a school near the main government complex on Ochra. There was a protest march and your grandfather Christopher Chambers was one of the leaders. The military were marshalling the protesters towards the school. It was after hours and they thought the school was closed. Your grandfather attacked one of the military vehicles and the driver lost control and crashed into the school. There was an explosion. There was a class which had stayed late at the school to work on a class project. Seventeen children and their teacher died that day, along with the driver and two Casparans who were working there.'

Chambers was ashen faced, and he thought of his own niece and nephew. Merari paused and shook his head.

'Men and women had died in the struggle, but this was children, and Ochrans do not have large families. The Jokti incident was so shocking that it brought both sides back to the negotiating table, but it also drove a wedge between them. Both sides blamed the other for the tragedy. In the end it was agreed that the whole issue of independence was the ultimate cause, and for the sake of both species, it was agreed to wipe Jokti from all records and never mention it again. Then there could be peace, and independence for Caspar, as their legacy.'

Chambers whispered. 'He never spoke of it, but was always at pains to tell us how good both species were at heart. He would never allow anyone to speak badly of any of you.' He saw the grief on Merari's face. 'But why did you bring it up, if it is supposed to be forgotten?'

Merari sighed. 'I never thought I would meet any of his family. I thought I had buried it until I heard his name. You see, the teacher was my mother.'

Chambers felt his throat constrict, and his own mother's face sprang to his mind. He fell to his knees. 'I am so so sorry, I don't know what to say.'

There was silence for a short while, and neither of them moved.

Then Merari lifted his head and gave a small smile. 'I think that is enough,' he said, then dropped his head and was silent. Chambers quietly left.

Later, he told Tabitha he had spoken to Merari and it was all right, but he wouldn't tell her why.

Chapter 29

The scanner alarm sounded. Darrow scrambled out of bed and raced to the bridge. There, on the screen, was an Intruder ship. The butterfly shape could be clearly seen, but the iridescence was gone. It was badly damaged and drifting.

'Engines all stop! Cancel forward motion; maintain relative position with that ship.'

Chambers brought the Kestrel to a halt, then said, 'Captain, request permission to stand down.'

Darrow saw the fear on Chambers' face and his hands shaking.

'You stay where you are, Lieutenant. Your skills are perfectly adequate to hold relative position to the Intruder ship. We're not planning to dock, so you can keep a safe distance.'

Chambers had no time to protest as, responding to the alarm, the representatives began arriving on the bridge, in various states of dress. As Darrow's brain whirled with possibilities he noted the representatives' reaction as they took in the view on screen. Merari and Ehu both growled, which alarmed Darrow more than what he saw. Dathan seemed pleased, and although Zoans show no emotion, Darrow was sure he detected a light in Hazeroth's eyes at the prospect of first contact. Rendor's cranial spines stood straight up with shock as he registered what he was seeing. The small bridge became crowded. Barok pushed his way to the front.

'Destroy it Captain! We can't take any chances. It might be a trap.'

'I don't think so, Mr Barok,' Darrow said, 'it seems their ship is badly damaged. Our mission is to find out as much as we can about the Intruders. We won't do that by blowing them to pieces.'

Barok was insistent. 'They have made it clear they do not care about us - why should we care about them?'

Dathan placed his hand on Barok's arm. 'They are sentient beings, Mr Barok, and we have a duty to preserve all life. Otherwise we become as bad as them.'

'Exactly,' said Darrow. 'This is too good a chance to miss.'

The representatives jockeyed for position, trying to see the view screen and the readouts.

Darrow looked around. The three bridge stations were manned by Kestrel crew, he, Parks and the six representatives were all standing. 'Mr Rendor please relieve Ensign Reuel on scanners and Mr Ehu please take over comms. Ensign, Lieutenant-Commander, you are both relieved of duty. 'The rest of you, move away from the consoles, or I shall clear the bridge.' *We don't want someone jogging an elbow and firing a weapon,* he thought.

'Now, what do the scanners tell us?' Darrow asked.

Rendor spoke up from the scanner console. 'Based on the readings from when they boarded us, I believe there are four life forms, one faint. The ship appears to be silicon based. You can see the structure clearly without the glow.'

On the screen they saw that what had appeared to be butterfly wings were two web-like structures on either side of the main hull. Both were damaged. Darrow took a deep breath to calm his excitement. He hadn't expected a chance like this. He made his decision.

'Hail them and offer assistance,' said Darrow.

'Captain!' The representatives spoke almost in chorus. Darrow silenced them with a look.

'They are responding to our hail, Captain,' Ehu said from the comms station.

The faint, glowing shape of a humanoid head and shoulders appeared on the screen. There were no facial features, just a rippling pale green surface difficult to focus on. The background was dark. The voice was melodious and low.

'Why do you offer assistance? You have no bond with us, and we have … damaged your kind.'

There was a gasp from everyone on the Kestrel bridge when the Intruder used Standard language, but Darrow raised a hand to still the questions. There were more important things to deal with first.

'Because we value all life and seek to alleviate suffering,' Darrow said. 'It seems from our scans that one of your crew is injured.'

The glowing figure flickered yellow and then blue. 'Yes, and two have ceased to be. Your technology is primitive, but it may be of some use until our craft regenerates. Do you have means of transportation?'

'We can send a shuttle over. Can we dock with your ship?'

'I will activate the entry port.'

Barok pushed forward.

'Captain, this is madness! You are putting us all in danger!'

Darrow said to the Intruder, 'Excuse me one moment,' and turned and moved out of view of the screen, signalling to Ehu to cut the sound. Parks came to stand beside Barok and nodded briefly to the Captain.

'Mr Barok,' Darrow said, keeping his voice low, 'you are here to advise and assist, but I am in command of this ship, and this mission. We will take every precaution, but we *must* find out about this species, and I will not pass up this opportunity. Now be quiet.'

Merari quietly came forward.

'Captain, on this occasion I agree with Mr Barok. I bow to your judgement, but I think it would be unwise to allow them any access to this ship or our technology.'

'Gentleman, your concerns are noted.'

Darrow turned back to the screen, signalling for sound.

'My apologies, we are making preparations to send you assistance. Kestrel out.'

A circular area began to glow to the rear of the main

fuselage of the Intruder ship.

Rendor was operating the scanner console. 'They have inadequate oxygen in their atmosphere, Captain. Breathing masks will be needed.'

'Noted. I will take Mr Hazeroth and Dr Dathan with me.'

Parks interrupted. 'Sir, it's my duty to point out the risk is too great. I should go.'

Darrow bit back a protest. Parks was right of course, he was getting carried away. He nodded.

'Commander. Wear suits, and take weapons. Stay in constant contact. Report everything you see and take as many readings as you can. At the first sign of trouble, get out of there.' He turned to Hoy. 'Contact sickbay and ask how Anna's doing, she must be receiving from them. We need her on the bridge to tell us what they're up to.'

* * *

In sick bay, Anna was trembling, she had woken up screaming to feel the nearness of the Intruders. The unexpectedness of their contact that had unnerved her. She wanted Ryan, but he was on duty elsewhere. Ky was checking her vital signs.

'I can't do it. They're so close, so close. I feel like they're inside my head.'

'Have they shown any indication of being aware of you?' Ky asked.

'No.'

'Then they're not in your head.' He took her by the shoulders. 'You must face your fear.'

'It's all right for you,' she said. 'You don't know what it's like.'

'We all have fears to face.' He looked away. 'My fear is the loneliness of retiring without my wife, my Rachel.' He brought his gaze back to her face. 'You must not give in.'

His confession shocked her. 'I'll try, Doctor. We'll try together.'

* * *

As the shuttle headed for the Intruder ship Anna arrived on the bridge with Ky, a little unsteady on her feet, but surprisingly collected. Ky was the one who looked nervous. Rendor gave Anna his chair and swung the console round to operate it standing. Ky stood behind and stared at the screen.

'I'm sorry, Captain,' Anna said, 'it's so strong it really shook me up. It's almost like being there with them, and I'm getting impressions from all of them. One is in great pain, and there's something about not being able to join the Great Mind that I don't understand. There's contempt, suspicion, and they're not happy they need help - they're very proud. They're going take what they need - use us.'

'Are they a threat?'

'Not at the moment, because they're powerless. But I don't know once they have power and strength again. They're not to be trusted, Captain.'

The representatives muttered to each other and nodded.

As the shuttle entered the ship, Parks' commentary began.

'The entry port is not a docking hatch, it's a force field - we just flew right through. We're landing now … It's dim in here, we're using our helmet lights. There's low gravity, and there seems to be a great deal of damage, there are components and conduits hanging loose everywhere - be careful there, Doctor … We're out in the corridor now and it's the same, except there's hardly any floor, just supporting struts. No wait, I don't think it *is* damaged, they just leave it that way. There is an atmosphere, but the doctor doesn't recommend we try breathing it. It's lighter ahead, we're heading for that. It's just round the corner - my God!'

'Parks! Are you all right?'

'Just a moment, Captain, we've made contact.'

For the next few moments they heard the conversation

between the team and the Intruders, which seemed to include ringing noises. There was a tense silence on the bridge, as they waited to make sense of it all.

Anna spoke up. 'It's all right, Captain. They were as surprised as we were. They've never actually spoken to any "solids". They were expecting us to be … less intelligent.'

'Stupid, you mean?' Rendor cut in. 'They've already called us primitive.'

'Yes,' said Anna, 'but the … revitaliser - I think they mean Dr Dathan - has impressed them.'

Parks came back to them. 'Everything's under control, Captain. These beings are almost pure energy, but they seem to keep a humanoid shape. We've had to turn our lights off in order to see them. The reason there's no floor in here is because they float! The ship provides an energy charge for them, but it can't at the moment. Dr Dathan has modified the power pack from one of our weapons to provide an energy charge for the injured crewman and he is already improving. They say their ship is partly organic and will regenerate itself. Sir, permission to bring them on board until it does?'

The four remaining representatives all protested. Anna cried out in horror at the thought of having "the terror" on board.

'Quiet!' Darrow shouted them down. 'What do you have in mind Commander?'

Hazeroth came on the comm. Given that Zoans do not show emotion, Darrow thought his voice was quivering.

'I am sending you their energy frequency, Captain. Use it to set up a containment field in sick bay and along the route from the shuttle bay. They say they do not need a special atmosphere, but you need to lower the lighting and add infrared to make them visible. We have given them assurances of safety but insist they be confined. They have agreed, but they will secure their ship against us. We will not learn much more *once we leave*.'

There was a heavy emphasis on the last three words, and

Darrow took the hint.

'Permission granted.' He turned to Rendor. 'Full spectrum scans, quick as you can. Record everything for later analysis.'

At the mention of sick bay, Anna turned to Dr Ky in horror. He quietly reassured her that of course she wouldn't be there with them.

Anna spoke tremulously. 'They don't believe we can hold them.'

She clutched at Ky and burst into tears.

Ky's caramel skin showed a pallor as he said, 'Please Captain, don't let the tokoloshe on board. Such an invitation could have terrible consequences.'

Darrow stayed calm. 'They are not tokoloshe, Doctor, and you are approaching insubordination. Your concern now is to take care of Anna. Do your job.'

Ky said, 'Take all precautions, Captain,' and rushed her away.

Darrow nodded. 'Close down all computer connections from sick bay into the main ship's systems. Lock out to my authorisation only. Mr Ehu, would you help Commander Blackwell with the containment field?'

Ehu nodded and left. Merari slipped into the comms seat. Darrow notified Blackwell, and then made a ship-wide announcement.

'This is the Captain. Clear all corridors. Remain in your quarters or at your current workstation until further notice.'

Within a few minutes they watched as the shuttle reappeared through the force field and returned to the Kestrel.

* * *

The representatives turned angrily on Darrow. He knew he was taking a big gamble, but the bridge was not the place to discuss it. He ordered everyone to the mess hall. As they reached the mess hall, they found Ky barring the door.

'Captain, in the eagerness to bring the Intruders on board, no one has considered Anna and Ryan, who were living in sick bay. I have packed them up and put them in here, so no one is using this room until they are found alternative accommodation.'

Darrow cursed silently. In all the excitement he had indeed overlooked Anna and Ryan, and the need to accommodate them. He was furious with himself for getting carried away. He was in danger of losing control of the whole mission. He was rescued by Blackwell, who approached just then.

'Excuse me, Captain, I've taken the liberty of adapting Trainee Enns' cabin in Engineering so Miss Anna can share with her. I thought maybe Dr Ky would allow Ryan to share with him temporarily.'

'Ryan can have my cabin,' Ky said, wringing his hands. 'I will not stay so close to these...' his voice trailed off under Darrow's stern gaze. 'I cannot!'

Blackwell came to the rescue again. 'Dr Ky is welcome to share with me,' he said. 'Although it will be a squeeze. It'll mean he's close to Anna too.'

'Thank you Commander,' Darrow said. He breathed a sigh of relief.

'Come on, Doctor. Let me give you a hand with their belongings,' said Blackwell, thumbing open the door.

'I'll meet with you in a few minutes,' Darrow said to the representatives, 'as soon as I've seen our new guests.' He rushed into sick bay before they could object. Reuel was guarding the door and he gave him instructions not to let anyone else in.

Parks, Dathan and Hazeroth were inside sick bay, putting the final corrections into the containment field. It was across the end of the L-shaped room, containing two beds. An Intruder was lying on one of the beds, glowing very faintly, and the three others were hovering around the bed in their energy state.

Parks murmured to Darrow. 'I'm sorry, Captain, there

wasn't time to consult.'

'I would have refused if I didn't agree,' Darrow replied quietly.

Darrow approached the containment field. Here at last were the beings he had been looking for for so long. Here at last was the proof that he was right. The Intruders floated towards him on the other side of the field. They looked at one another for a long moment. Darrow realised he had no idea what to say. He decided introductions were a good start.

'I am Captain Joseph Darrow. This ship is the Kestrel. We are part of the Planetary Alliance for Co-operation and Trade. Who are you?'

The Intruders continued to stare at him but made no reply. He tried again.

'We have offered you assistance. What do you need?'

No reaction.

'What help do you need to repair your ship?'

Silence. Darrow was frustrated.

'We have helped you. The least you can do is talk to us.'

One of the Intruders became solid and spoke. 'We will make use of your ship until our ship repairs itself. We require nothing else.'

'Well answer me this then: why? Why are you stealing our raw materials?'

'The strongest dictates, the weaker must concede.' The Intruder returned to energy and moved away. The other two followed it.

Darrow gave up, aware that the representatives were waiting in the mess hall. He gestured to Parks, Hazeroth and Dathan to follow him. Dathan insisted he needed to see to the care of the Intruders. Darrow had the feeling Dathan didn't cope well with conflict, and let him go.

Chapter 30

The first thing Tabitha knew of the drama was when Blackwell burst in through her curtain and told her to move her things.

'Sorry, my dear, you're going to have company,' he said. 'We need to get another bed in here. I think you had better sleep on the top bunk.'

Tabitha stepped back, the best she could do was stay out of the way as Blackwell and Stubbs bustled about, fixing a second bed on top of hers and bringing in another container to use as furniture. Stubbs winked at her as they left. She barely had time to gather her wits before Blackwell burst in again with Anna in tow. Anna was pale and wide-eyed. Tabitha felt for her straight away.

'Anna, this is Trainee Tabitha Enns. Enns, this is Anna. You're to look after her - any problems, call Dr Ky. He'll be along in a minute, he's moving his things into my cabin.'

With that, Blackwell rushed off and left them staring at each other. Tabitha estimated Anna must be about thirty, a bit younger than Chambers. She had shoulder length fair hair and an athletic figure, and was at least twenty five centimetres taller than Tabitha, but she didn't stand up straight. She seemed cowed somehow, and distracted. It made Tabitha want to protect her, but she didn't know where to start. Anna made the first move by bursting into tears. Tabitha put an arm around her and they sat on the bottom bunk together.

So this is the 'mystery woman,' she thought. *I don't know what I expected, but she's just another woman. I can deal with this.*

Anna stopped crying and looked around.

'It's not much, is it?' Tabitha said. 'I'm afraid you're stuck with me.'

'Better with you than with … them.'

'With who? Do you mean Ensign Ryan and Dr Ky? You were in sick bay weren't you?'

Anna nodded. 'The Intruders are in there now.'

'What? They're on board?' Tabitha jumped to her feet, not thinking that there was nowhere to run to. 'What happened?'

All sorts of scenarios went through Tabitha's mind. Most of them involved violence and getting boarded. 'Who's in charge?'

Anna took her hand. 'The Captain is in charge, I'm sorry if I frightened you. We found a crippled ship and the Captain invited the crew on board until their ship is repaired. They're in quarantine in sick bay. That's why Sam and I had to move out.'

Tabitha sat back down.

'Is it true you can read their minds?'

'Yes, but before it was a kind of collective thought through the ship. Now I can hear four different minds. It's like four people speaking at once, it's hard to distinguish between them and it gives me a headache.'

'You poor thing. You need to lie down while you have the chance. I expect the Captain will want to know what they're thinking soon enough.'

* * *

Darrow, Parks and Hazeroth joined the representatives in the mess hall. Darrow motioned for quiet.

'First, we will hear from the away team as to why they suggested bringing the Intruders on board.' He turned to Parks and Hazeroth. 'Who wants to go first?'

Parks stood. 'I will, I was in charge, I made the decision.' Everyone spoke at once, questions and protests. Darrow called for quiet again. Parks continued. 'The way I understand it, this mission is to learn as much about this species as possible. Their ship is badly damaged, and there's a real possibility they would have died if left on board. So the only way to help them was to bring them here.' He raised his hands to stop their protests. 'What better way to meet them than on our terms, on our ship?'

Hazeroth laid a hand on Parks' arm and stood up. 'We have a singular opportunity to meet them, find out about them, and tell them about us, without conflict. Without this accident, we would only have met them when we were at a disadvantage.'

'We are at a disadvantage now!' said Barok, banging the table. 'We don't know what powers they have. The force field may be nothing to them, they may be just waiting for the opportunity to take over the ship!'

'That is not the case,' said Hazeroth. 'They are almost pure energy, so they can be hurt by energy weapons - it was a circuit blow-out that injured the crewman.'

Ehu said, 'I have calibrated the field to their frequency. They cannot pass.'

'Captain,' Rendor said, 'first contact rules state…'

'I know what first contact rules say,' Darrow interrupted him. 'We're out here on our own, and this may be the only chance to avert a war. There are no rules to fit this situation, I'm doing the best I can.'

'No Captain,' said Hazeroth, 'you are using your years of experience in other situations to assess the best course of action.'

'Thank you.' He inclined his head in thanks to Hazeroth and pulled in a deep breath as he looked to the others. 'I know this is dangerous, but we have to try. I must remind you all that I am in charge of this ship and this mission, you are advisers only. The Intruders are here and I will not have them expelled, think of the message that would send. Now, let's have constructive comments as to how to proceed.'

There was a lot of dissatisfied muttering. The first to speak was Barok.

'I insist we return at once with our prisoners so they can be interrogated by the authorities, and their ship examined.'

'They are not our prisoners, Mr Barok,' Darrow said,

keeping his voice low. 'We hope to establish friendly relations and open up a dialogue.'

'Captain,' said Merari, 'they are confined behind a force field. What else would you call them but prisoners?'

'They must be!' Barok said. 'You are putting everyone on this ship at risk if they are not closely guarded. Any sign of trouble and they should be immediately executed!'

Darrow controlled his anger with difficulty. His head felt it would burst, things were happening so fast. 'I will not tell you again that our mission is to seek understanding between our species. If any of you are not willing to be part of that, and to take whatever risks are necessary, you are welcome to take one of the shuttles and leave for the nearest inhabited planet.'

Barok stormed out of the meeting.

Darrow turned to Parks.

'I want that man watched, he's going to be trouble.' He looked around the room. No one said anything. 'Mr Hazeroth, will you come to my office to discuss how to proceed?'

* * *

Darrow met with Hazeroth and Anna in his office. His heart was still beating fast with the enormity of the step he had taken, but he believed it was the right thing to do.

'The benefits may be enormous,' Hazeroth said. 'We can talk to them, show them we are sentient beings, reason with them.'

'But they are just four people from a whole race,' Darrow said. 'How do we know they will be able to influence their people, even if we convince them?'

'If we can convince four, we can learn how to convince the others. These are already reconsidering their preconceptions.'

'The decision has been made,' said Darrow. 'I take full responsibility for it. At the very least, this gives us a vital opportunity to find out as much as possible about them, their culture, and their weaknesses.'

They looked to Anna and she spoke hesitantly, but with growing confidence. 'I believe I have good news for you. It seems that what I reacted to before was a sort of collective mind, focussed through the ship. With the ship damaged, I am receiving their individual minds, which are not so strong. It's a bit confusing, but I am learning to focus - the way you can concentrate on one person speaking in a room full of conversations.' She took a deep breath.

'I can't understand the way they refer to one another, so I've given them titles based on their strongest characteristics. I call them the Leader, the Warrior, the Sage and the Scientist. The Leader plans to make a show of friendship in the hope we'll open up and give him valuable information to take back. He has to keep his honour and position, so must not be seen as weak. I don't know if they have sexes, but he seems to be male to me. The Warrior seems to be female, surprisingly, but she's like a lioness protecting her cubs. Her world, her people, come first. She has only contempt for us. The Scientist is the injured one. As he recovers he is excited at the thought of new technology and new life forms to study, although I don't think he would be willing to reciprocate. Our best hope is the Sage. He wants the best for his people but thinks negotiation may be a better way. I think he might be willing to talk to us.' She hesitated. 'There is one thing which worries me. Can they detect me? If they know I can read their minds, they won't like it one bit.'

Darrow squeezed Anna's hand.

'Don't worry,' he said. 'They can't get through the containment field, and we'll keep you well away from them.'

Hazeroth asked Anna, 'Are they telepathic?'

'No - no, I don't think so.'

'Right,' said Darrow looking at Hazeroth, 'how do we proceed?'

Hazeroth considered. 'First contact situations are always

delicate and the Intruders are already hostile and have the advantage of knowing more about us than we know about them. The big omission is, although they have spied on us, they know nothing of us as people, on a personal level. That is where we need to concentrate our efforts. I agree with Anna - the Sage is our best target. Meanwhile everyone who comes into contact with them should be friendly, kind and helpful, but absolutely firm about what they can and cannot do. We must not appear weak.'

* * *

Not only did Hazeroth have first contact experience, but he had the natural calmness which all Zoans exhibit. So much rested on these talks, including the continuance of Darrow's decision to offer them aid and bring them on board. Darrow was happy to let Hazeroth take the lead.

'Greetings,' Hazeroth began. 'Captain Darrow has already introduced himself. We have already met, as I was part of the team that came to your ship. My name is Hazeroth and I am a Zoan. Can you introduce yourselves please?'

There was a pause, then one of the Intruders said, 'That will not be necessary.'

'We have offered you assistance, maybe even saved your lives,' Hazeroth said quietly. 'It is a simple courtesy.'

'It is not necessary.'

'Very well, we shall proceed without it. You may have been surprised to see that the members of the group that came to your ship were from three different species. That is because we are in alliance with each other. We co-operate with each other. We have come all this way for the purpose of finding you and offering your people the same alliance. Once agreement is reached we may be able to provide what you need peacefully.'

The three Intruders turned to each other and made ringing sounds as colours flashed between them - dark green, turquoise and orange. Even the injured one joined in.

Eventually the ringing subsided and three of them turned white. The fourth one - the spokesman - turned back to Hazeroth.

'It is not necessary.'

Darrow was frustrated. '"The strongest dictates, the weaker must concede" eh? How do you know we are weaker?'

Hazeroth laid a hand on his arm and spoke to the Intruder. 'But if the weaker cooperates, the strongest becomes stronger surely? Is it not wise to obtain what you need with the minimum effort?'

'It is not -'

'Necessary,' Darrow interrupted. 'I know.'

Hazeroth bowed to the Intruders. 'We will speak with you again.' He pushed Darrow out of sick bay.

'Captain, you really must control your emotions. It does not give a good impression.'

Darrow sagged against the wall. 'I know. It's just so frustrating. I hoped they would respond to us for helping them, but they have only contempt. I have so much riding on this.'

'May I respectfully suggest that I speak to them alone in future?'

Darrow considered. His desire to get through to them personally warred with his frustration. 'Very well.'

Chapter 31

Everyone was on edge, everyone had their own opinion on the wisdom of helping the Intruders and what should be done next. There were discussions all over the ship. Some of the debates got quite heated, and Darrow and Parks had their work cut out keeping order. Even the two Altairians fell out.

'I am loyal to my captain,' Reuel said as they relaxed in their cabin, 'but it is madness to allow these creatures on board!'

'You are so limp,' said Rendor, which was a great insult on Altair. 'Why call them 'creatures' when they are a sentient life form? You just want to feel superior, and keep out of danger.'

Reuel jumped to his feet. 'I deny that! Working for PACT can be a dangerous business, but we should not have allowed them on board. They may escape and take over the ship, and we could be responsible for a great tragedy.'

Rendor leaned back and looked Reuel over. 'Perhaps it is fortuitous that I came on this mission, to be able to give you some perspective. I do believe you have softened during your time with the humans,' he raised his hand to still Reuel's protest, 'it is not necessarily a bad thing, but you should be aware of it.'

Reuel's cranial spines writhed. 'I was not aware you were here to examine me.'

'As a fellow clan member it is my duty to look after you.'

* * *

In the midst of the fuss, Anna was surprised to see Barok slip into the cabin in Engineering when she was alone. She was wary of the small, childlike figure with the imperious air, but he gave her a nervous smile.

216

'Please, do not be afraid. I simply want to talk to you.'
He stood in the curtain opening. 'Do you know what I am
thinking?'

'No, no,' she said, turning to face him. 'I can't read the
minds of anyone except the Intruders. And before you ask, I
don't know why.'

'You have no recollection of who did this to you?'

'No. Only memories …' she shuddered, 'of pain.'

He looked at her thoughtfully for a long time. It made her
feel uncomfortable, but not afraid. At last he sighed.

'I believe you. We Casparans have a lot of understanding
of what it means to be a victim. You have my sympathy.'

He bowed and left.

* * *

Tabitha's Journal

*We have four Intruders on board the ship! Some of the
representatives don't like it one bit, but they're all taking
advantage of it. I don't like it either. I was starting to feel at
home here, but now it feels, well, alien. I don't know the
details, but I don't feel very safe. We've been told what a
threat these aliens are, and then we invite them on board! I
can't get my head around it.*

*Anna, the mystery woman, is now sharing my curtained-
off corner of Engineering. They just shoved her in here to
make room for the Intruders, and told me to look after her.
It's nice to feel really useful though. Anna is so pleased to
have another woman to talk to. Not that we get much time to
talk, with her head full of the Intruders' thoughts all the time.
Luckily they seem to sleep, or rest, at regular intervals, so
Anna gets a break. She spends nearly all her time recording
the impressions she's getting, or trying to sleep. Sam spends
as much time with her as he can. He says Dr Ky has
assigned him to look after Anna, but I think he's sweet on
her. I think she might be sweet on him, if she had time to
think about it.*

It really bothers her that she doesn't remember anything from her past. I've been telling her what I'm learning about the different species, to see if it jogs any memories. She asks me questions about it, and Commander Parks said the standard of my reports has improved. Anna tells me things about them too, after she meets with them. She's very perceptive, and notices things I don't. She's telling me how the talks are going too, or rather not going. It seems it was a waste having them on board and causing all the fuss. They're just not talking.

* * *

'Captain to sick bay. Dr Ky?'

'This is Ensign Ryan sir. The doctor's not here, he may be with Anna in Engineering. Do you want me to find him?'

'You may be able to help me. I just wanted to know how Anna is coping.'

'She's struggling, sir. She feels a bit overwhelmed sometimes as she can't block their thoughts. They come at her most of the time, in waves, some stronger than others, and she's getting very tired. Dr Ky is prepared to sedate her if necessary, to give her some rest. She can't always be on duty!'

'I know, and I know you're concerned for her. But this must be kept absolutely confidential. Everyone on board thinks she is our safeguard to give us advance warning if they try anything.'

'I think she still is, Captain. She is working so hard to distinguish between the voices, and recording everything she gets. Mr Hazeroth has found it very useful.'

'I was not aware of that, it's a good idea. Thank you Ryan.'

Darrow checked the duty rota and found Hoy would be in hydroponics.

'Captain to hydroponics. Lieutenant-Commander Hoy?'

'Hoy here sir.'

'I want you to work with Mr Hazeroth and make summaries of what Anna is recording. She's putting down everything she gets from the Intruders, but it's going to be too much for everyone to read. Pick out the highlights and give them to Mr Barok for distribution.'

'Yes sir. Do you know where Mr Hazeroth is now?'

'I believe he's in his cabin preparing to speak to the Intruders.'

'Thank you sir, I'll see him straight away.'

* * *

'Miss Anna is recording all the thoughts she receives from the Intruders,' Hazeroth explained at a meeting the next day, 'and I am monitoring them through cameras set up in the sick bay quarantine.'

They were meeting in the mess hall as usual, the six representatives, Darrow and Parks. Hazeroth was trying to reassure those who were unhappy at having the Intruders on board.

'We should all have access to the camera feed,' said Rendor.

'It's on video channel four,' Darrow said. 'You can access it from the console in your cabin.'

'Thank you Captain.'

'What have you found out from them?' Merari asked Hazeroth.

'I have tried to speak with them on three occasions, but they are refusing to be drawn into any sort of discussion, except to tell us what they need.' He leaned forward over the table. 'It is a bit like our agricultural workers harvesting the fields and then finding the small creatures living in the crops were actually highly intelligent and civilised and objected to us taking what they viewed as their property.' He sat back. 'They are having trouble adjusting to the idea, and Anna says they disagree as to how to proceed. She reports that the Warrior and the Scientist want to disregard us and take what

219

they want. The Sage thinks negotiation might be an easier way. The Leader is still undecided, but is more concerned about what will make him look wise and bold than what is actually the best course of action.'

'So they *are* a danger to us!' Merari said, but was interrupted by Ehu putting a hand on his shoulder.

'I think not, certainly at this time. We have their frequency, and they cannot penetrate the shields around their quarantine. We are monitoring continuously to see if they can modulate their frequency or increase their power to override the force field. So far, it does not seem so. Besides, they have an injured crewman and their ship is not yet functional.' He paused and frowned. 'I have not seen any repair crews going out to the ship. I would be most interested to study it further.'

'Their ship is off-limits, as they said,' Parks said. 'It seems to be self-repairing. We did find some organic sections in the scans we took. Yesterday an opaque force-field appeared, blocking all further scans. It seems to be the first thing it repaired, so we can't see the rest.'

Hazeroth spoke. 'They seem to be in some sort of communication with the ship, because they reacted at precisely the same moment, and Anna recorded a surge of confidence. There are no signs of any equipment on them, so I do not know if it is telepathy, or they have equipment within themselves we cannot detect. Have you found anything, Doctor?'

Dathan stood up to report.

'They do seem to have organic components, but it is as particles held in suspension in their energy field. We know from the attack on Engineering they can generate a strong energy charge, but readings show it is an increase in amplitude rather than frequency. It also seems to tire them, as no single being produced the charge more than once. When I touched one of them I received a mild shock, but it affected the Intruder also. We are still analysing the dust from the dead Intruder, which we managed to retrieve. They did not seem concerned about it.'

'You see?' said Rendor, waving a hand, 'They do not have concern even for their own people. How can we expect to persuade them to have concern for our people? How do we know they won't break out and take over the ship? There is so much we do not know about them.'

He looked to Barok for support, as he had spoken against them before, but Barok merely nodded assent.

Barok is being unusually quiet, thought Parks. *What's he up to?*

'They do seem concerned for the wounded one,' Dathan said, shifting uncomfortably. 'The Scientist, as Anna calls him, needs his energy level recharging, which he is getting from us, but also, I notice, from his colleagues.'

Darrow intervened. 'Have we any more information about this energy charge? How they make it or how we could protect ourselves?'

'We cannot determine how the energy charge is produced, it could be they are able to create some kind of equipment from the particles within them.' said Dathan. 'It is simply beyond our technology.'

He looked to Ehu, who nodded. 'Since they are mostly energy, presumably an energy weapon could be set to the right frequency to disrupt them. I am already working on it. Any strong charge would probably kill them, but I hope to develop something a little more subtle.'

Barok was taking notes.

Dathan continued. 'We are also unable to determine the purpose of the second pair of appendages behind the shoulders, which Commander Blackwell speculated, from the attack on Engineering, may be wings or another pair of arms. My guess, if you will permit me, is they are some kind of antenna. What puzzles me is why they keep humanoid shape at all, it is not an easy shape, and seems unnecessary.'

'I asked them that,' said Hazeroth, 'and they simply said, "This is the shape we have always been." Some kind of race memory, I suppose. It is one of the few questions they actually answered. Most of the time I have tried to speak with them, they only tolerate me when I am giving them information.' He raised his hand to forestall those who started to express concern. 'And, as you will appreciate, there is little information I can give them, so our conversations have been largely fruitless.'

Darrow's heart fell. He had gambled that being friendly would get through to them. If they didn't respond, what could he do? He closed the meeting to forestall further comments.

'It's early days yet,' he said. 'Thank you for your efforts Mr Hazeroth, and Dr Dathan. We'll keep on trying to reach them. That's all gentlemen.'

Chapter 32

Dathan was working on his notes when Barok came into sick bay.

'Greetings, Mr Barok. How may I assist you?'

Barok glanced nervously across the room to where the Intruders rested behind the containment field. With no faces, he couldn't tell if they were looking at him. He dropped his voice and smiled ingratiatingly.

'I was wondering if you had completed the analysis of the dust sample from the dead Intruder. I am preparing a report for my government.'

'Affirmative. It contained most of the compounds common to the bodies of most species, but in minute quantities. Except for iron and silicon, which were proportionately very high. This is most interesting. I have the results over here.'

He moved away and instantly Barok raised an energy weapon.

'We will finish this now!' he cried, as he leaped through the containment field.

He fired at the nearest Intruder, the wounded Scientist, and the glow went out, leaving only dust. As he turned to fire again, Dathan flung himself in the path of the beam. Barok had forgotten the speed of the Kohathi, who were used to higher gravity. The beam caught Dathan high in the chest, and he staggered across the Leader in an attempt to protect him. The energy from the Leader surged into his body as they made contact and finished what the beam had begun. Dathan fell dead. At the same time the Warrior released a beam of energy that burned Barok to a cinder where he stood. Then the Warrior collapsed. The Sage reached out to share his energy with the other two.

The weapon discharge set off an alarm, and Balitoth, who had been standing security outside the door, arrived in time to witness the events, with Parks arriving at a run soon afterwards. Parks was so stunned at what he saw, that for a moment he didn't know what to do. All he could think of was the failure of their mission.

The three remaining aliens turned towards one another and spoke in their high, ringing tones, while dark blue, brown and orange lights flashed within them. Then they all nodded, and the Leader turned to Parks and said simply,

'We wish to talk.'

* * *

Tabitha was studying in her cabin while Anna was lying on the bed, quietly murmuring into the recorder all she received from the Intruders. Suddenly Anna screamed. Tabitha ran to her.

'What is it? What's wrong?'

Anna's eyes were wide with shock. 'Dead! They're dead!'

'Who? The Intruders?' Tabitha held Anna tight and called for help.

Blackwell pulled back the curtain.

'What's happening here?' He took in the scene with a glance. 'I'll fetch Dr Ky.'

Ky ran from the Engineer's cabin nearby. Tabitha helped Anna to sit up and sat with her arm around her. Ky checked her vital signs with a portable scanner.

'She is just in shock,' he said. 'Trainee, go to the mess hall and get her a hot sweet drink.'

Tabitha's head was swimming. *Who's dead? One of the crew? The Intruders must have something to do with it - were they dead?* As Tabitha reached the main corridor she saw Balitoth come out of sick bay and stand guard at the door.

'Excuse me sir, what's happened?' she asked Balitoth. 'Anna says there are deaths.'

Balitoth gave a nod. 'I will notify the Captain when he

comes. Is someone looking after Miss Anna?'

'Yes. Dr Ky and Commander Blackwell are with her. I must get to the mess hall.'

As Tabitha left the mess hall with the drink for Anna and passed sick bay again, Hazeroth was going in.

* * *

Parks contacted Darrow, who rushed to sick bay. Balitoth was sweeping Barok's ashes into a container. Dathan lay where he had fallen. The Intruders moved away towards the rear of the space. Parks bowed to them and stepped through the containment field to retrieve the body. Darrow helped him to lay Dathan on a bed and cover him with a sheet.

'Commander Parks,' Darrow said quietly, 'summon Mr Hazeroth. Lieutenant Balitoth, please resume guard duty.'

The tension was palpable, and the Intruders were glowing blue. Darrow, Parks and Hazeroth faced them through the containment field. The Leader spoke first.

'We wish to speak on equal terms, we will therefore become visible to you.'

Before their eyes, the three aliens ceased to glow and became opaque, their bodies having a golden, skin-like covering and their faces distinctly human, with golden eyes and high cheekbones. The appendages on the shoulders appeared to be vestigial wings. A small area on the chest still glowed and flickered different colours as they talked. They were completely hairless and their bodies featureless, but for the first time facial expressions could be seen. They all had furrowed brows.

Darrow smiled and said, 'We thank you for this effort. We communicate in part by facial expression and this will make it much easier for us. We are also honoured that you speak our language. How is this possible?'

The Leader touched his chest.

'We have translators. It was difficult, as much of our language is non-verbal. Please ask for clarification.'

'We will. What did you wish to discuss?'

'We do not understand the way you have behaved towards us. We Prin,' he made a ringing sound, 'seek to harvest your worlds. Our... research has caused disruption and suffering to your people and has terminated some of them. We have received communications that this vessel has already been attacked. We expected no... mercy when you found us, and would have given none had our situations been reversed. Yet the one called Barok is the only one who has behaved in this way, and the others... censured him. When you assisted us we assumed it was for your own ends and expected to be... interrogated.' He paused and bowed his head, as if to soften his words.

'But our wishes have been respected and your... menials even asked if we had customs regarding our dead when they came on board. We are especially surprised that the one you called Dathan would give his life-force to save us. We had not considered you to have such... moral principles.'

Hazeroth looked to the Captain for permission and then spoke. 'There is much about our peoples you do not know, and we are eager for dialogue so we may understand one another better. We value all life and seek to preserve it wherever we can. We explore the galaxy to seek out other species for mutual benefit. We have a great curiosity about life in all its forms, and believe we can learn from one another to grow and develop. As I explained before, we have on board representatives of the Planetary Alliance, a group of species who share knowledge and resources and protect one another. Dathan and Barok were also representatives.'

The Sage spoke. 'And you have come together to seek us out to try to dialogue with us in this way?'

The Warrior nodded, 'There is strength in numbers.'

Hazeroth replied, 'You are both correct. Our mission is to seek talks first, but defend ourselves and our home worlds if necessary. All the information we have gathered has gone back to our home worlds. So far, they see no option but to prepare for war. We hope to prevent that.'

The Leader replied, 'We did not expect we would receive any co-operation from you. We have need of many raw materials as our planetary system is old. We must consider this, and would speak with you again.'

'We too must consider how we should proceed and consult our leaders. We can talk again tomorrow. In the mean-time is there anything you need?'

'A little silicon powder would be welcome. There is one other thing we wish to ask. We wish to know of the one who touches our thoughts.'

Hazeroth was startled. 'You can detect her?'

'Ah, it is a female! We have not experienced this before. How is it done?'

Darrow interrupted. 'We don't know. We can't give you any more information at this time. We will speak again later.'

* * *

Darrow, Parks, Ryan and Anna met with the remaining representatives in the mess hall. The meeting was subdued, Anna was tearful. This time there were seats for everyone, with only four representatives. They had all reviewed the recording, and were shocked by the deaths of Barok and Dathan. Parks blamed himself for not keeping a closer eye on Barok and realising how extreme his views were. Merari also felt bad for goading Barok. It seemed everyone had pleasant memories of Dathan. He had gone out of his way to be kind. His gentleness and eagerness to learn about other cultures and their medicine, so he could better serve them, had touched them all. It was Anna who reminded them Barok had a good side too.

'I know nothing of the different species and their conflicts. Barok was afraid of me, of who I am - what I am. But he was dedicated to the service of his people, and he overcame his fear to come and speak to me and find out for himself. He felt I had been used against my will, as his people had been used by the Ochran...' She paused, looking embarrassed at Merari. He smiled.

'The Casparans were harshly treated,' Merari said, 'but we believed it was for their own good. Perhaps we were unwise. I begin to see how they felt, now that these Prin look on me in the same way. It is most uncomfortable and insulting to be regarded as inferior. But I fear Barok's action will bring his whole race into disrepute.'

'For that reason,' Darrow said leaning forward, 'I don't propose to report this until we see how things work out. He may yet be proved right. What we have to deal with right now is that his action has opened the way for talks, which we wouldn't have otherwise. We must now decide how to proceed.'

Hazeroth turned to Anna.

'May I first apologise for my clumsiness in allowing the Prin to find out about you. It was so unexpected that they were aware of you. I do hope you are not too alarmed.'

Anna shook her head. 'I didn't know they could feel my mind - I've just been receiving. You haven't revealed who I am, have you? How much do they know?'

'Very little, it seems. They were just aware of your touch, but nothing about you. I will try to find out more in future talks. The telepathy does not seem to go both ways, and they do not seem to be overly concerned.' Hazeroth took a deep breath. 'It would be helpful to me if you would be willing to monitor our discussions and indicate to me how they are reacting.' He turned to Parks. 'Perhaps Anna could listen in and we could have a hidden link in my ear.'

Parks nodded. 'That won't be a problem to set up, as long as Anna is willing.'

Anna nodded and asked nervously, 'Would it be all right if I had Sam with me? Sorry, Ensign Ryan.' She glanced at Ryan. 'I don't think I can cope with such concentration on my own. They won't know where I am, will they?'

Parks laid a reassuring hand on her arm.

'You don't have to be anywhere near them, as long as you can receive okay. You're protected at all times, and I'm sure the doctor will allow Ensign Ryan to be there.'

He looked towards Ryan, who nodded, 'I'm sure Dr Ky will give his approval.'

Darrow turned to Anna. 'What can you tell us about their reactions to the first meeting?'

Anna frowned. 'It came over as very mixed. The Warrior is suspicious. She feels Barok's behaviour may be a sign of how you all truly feel, and nice words don't make it right. The Sage is more willing to believe we have good intentions. The Leader is undecided, but will go along with it until he has more evidence on which to base a decision.'

Darrow placed his palms on the table.

'Now, we have to make detailed plans as to how we are to proceed. We have to decide what information we can give them to make them feel we are co-operating without jeopardising security, and we have to decide what we need to find out. We must also agree on how far Hazeroth can go in making agreements with the Prin without having to stop every few minutes to get permission.'

'If you will excuse us, Captain,' Ryan said. 'Anna needs to rest after her shock, before you begin talks.'

'Of course,' Darrow said, and Ryan shepherded Anna out of the room.

* * *

While all this was going on, Tabitha was left in suspense. With no one to talk to, she turned to her journal.

What's going on? Who's dead? Anna screamed, 'They're dead!' and when I went to the mess hall past sick bay there's all sorts of comings and goings. I tried to see in but Balitoth was guarding the door. I'm so scared. I wish someone would tell me what's going on. Things have been weird ever since the Intruders came on board. Anna says they're called Prin. Dr Ky won't go near the place - he seems scared of them.

He doesn't really like treating Anna either, I can tell. Probably because of her link to the Prin.

I wonder what they're really like? They must be dangerous, because they're locked up. I hope they don't get out. Maybe they have *got out and killed someone. No, there would be an alert if there was any danger, and sick bay was guarded. So who's died?*

At that moment, Anna returned with Sam.

'You must see that she rests,' Sam said to Tabitha, as he made Anna lie down. 'Do you want me to give you a sedative?' he asked Anna.

'Yes please,' Anna replied. 'I hope it silences the thoughts in my head so I can have some peace. I'm not going to be getting much peace in the days to come.'

Sam administered the sedative and left, and Tabitha sat on the side of Anna's bed.

'What's going on?' Tabitha asked. 'Can you tell me before you go to sleep? Who's dead?'

'Barok, Dathan and one of the Prin are all dead. Barok tried to kill them all and Dathan died trying to save them. Now the Prin have agreed to talk to us, so I have to rest.'

Anna closed her eyes and Tabitha sat there with her mouth open. It was too much to take in all at once.

Chapter 33

Hazeroth started the talks with the obvious questions.

'We have already told you a little about us, but we know nothing about you. Can you tell me about the Prin - who are you, what is your history?'

The Prin lights flashed rapidly dark blue and turquoise, and they made low musical notes. Anna said in his ear, 'You must be more respectful, they are very touchy.'

'Please understand,' Hazeroth said, 'we have never met any beings like you. We are eager to know about you, and will, of course, reciprocate.'

The flashing calmed, and the Leader gestured to the Sage, who became solid and spoke.

'I have been asked to tell you a little of our history. We are an ancient race. Our records tell us we used to be solid, like you, but evolved beyond that state. We now take our nourishment direct from the minerals and compounds on our planet. But our planet is old and its resources are finite-'

There were turquoise lights and shrill sounds from the Leader and the Warrior, and Anna confirmed they were warning the Sage not to reveal any weaknesses.

'The situation is the same on many of our planets,' said Hazeroth quickly, 'but we have resolved it by trading with each other. What one has in plenty can be traded for what they lack, and everyone benefits.'

'There is no need,' said the Warrior, flashing emerald, 'when one is superior enough to take what is required.'

'But the cost may be great,' said Hazeroth, 'if many lives and ships are lost in the taking. And it may lead to war. We have found trade to be a better way.'

'Change the subject,' Anna said in his ear.

'Could you please tell us about your government?' Hazeroth said quickly. 'We seek to make contact with your people, and we need to know who we should speak with.'

The lights faded into orange, and the Sage looked to the Leader and gained permission to speak.

'We are governed by the Great Council, and the Great Mind. Since we gave up our bodies it has been possible for those whose individual lives are ended to join together in one mind and live on, to watch over and advise the Prin people. We are directly governed by our wisest ones, who form the Great Council. If you come to Prin,' the others showed pale green in alarm at this, but he bowed to them and glowed deep amber, 'you would have to speak to the Great Council and satisfy the Great Mind. But it is unlikely you would be permitted to come.'

'I hope we can give you enough good reasons to convince the Great Council and Great Mind to allow us to meet them.' Hazeroth was pleased to hear hope from Anna in his ear, as the lights shifted to orange again. 'What is your planet like? For example, would we be able to come down to the surface without protective suits?'

Once again the Sage looked for permission.

'The atmosphere is the same as on our ship, which required you to have breathing assistance. Our sun is distant, and if the temperature here is indicative of your normal level, you would find it cold. There are, however, extensive heat sources from inside the planet. We no longer need warmth, but the heat sources are used for power.'

The lights flashed a turquoise warning, and he finished, 'More than this I cannot say.'

'The representatives of the other species would like to speak with you individually to tell you a little about each race and our mutual benefit in alliance.'

The Leader became solid briefly and said, 'Conversation in this manner is tiring. We will rest now.' They moved to the rear of the compartment, glowing emerald.

Anna reported to Hazeroth when he came to see her that there had been little change in their attitudes, and the Sage was being reprimanded for revealing too much.

Arrangements were made for each remaining representative to speak with the Prin, with Anna monitoring and advising them from a distance. Once talks were underway, Darrow turned his attention to other matters. Parks had been busy.

'Dathan's body has been put into stasis, so his people can perform the necessary funeral rites when we return,' Parks said when they met in Darrow's office. There was an awkward pause that screamed words they didn't dare add, "*If we return.*"

'I see you've changed the cabin arrangements too,' Darrow said.

'Yes, since there are now two free spaces, I've taken the opportunity to make people a little more comfortable. Lieutenant-Commander Hoy suggested it, actually. He volunteered to move in with Lieutenant Chambers so Anna and Trainee Enns could have his cabin. I thought it best to keep the women together, they seem to be getting on well.'

'I'm glad to hear it. Is Enns keeping up with her studies?'

'The schedule's a bit crazy at the moment for obvious reasons, but Enns has been teaching Anna what she knows and they've been researching together, when Anna can concentrate. It's only when the Prin rest that their thoughts go down enough for her to get some peace, poor woman.' He paused, frowning. 'There is a problem with Dr Ky though. He's petrified of the Prin and won't go near sick bay. It's not right, him sharing with Commander Blackwell, but he thinks it's beneath him to go into the makeshift cabin in Engineering. The best solution would be for Ensign Ryan to go in there, and Ky have his cabin back, but he won't hear of it. Blackwell is losing patience with him. I just hope there isn't a medical emergency, because with the state he's in, I doubt he'll be of any use.'

Darrow frowned. 'Leave it to me. Tell him I want to see

him, will you? Is that all for now? Dismissed.'

Parks left. Ky appeared a few minutes later. His face was pale and drawn. He almost forgot to salute.

'You wanted to see me Captain?'

'Yes Doctor, stand at ease. You realise you are responsible for all medical matters on board, now Dr Dathan has gone?'

'I understood I always *was* responsible, sir.'

'Don't think I didn't notice how Dathan did all the sick bay work once the Prin came on board. Are you sending Ensign Ryan in now?'

The doctor's eyes flicked about, as if looking for a way of escape. 'Sir, it's not possible…'

'It's perfectly possible, Doctor,' Darrow said. 'I told you before, your religion must not interfere with your duties. In normal circumstances I could have you replaced, but these are not normal circumstances. You are to move back into your cabin, and Ensign Ryan will move into Engineering.'

All attempts at control ended, as Ky burst into tears.

What have they landed me with? Darrow thought. *The sooner this man retires, the better.*

'Doctor, pull yourself together! This is disgraceful.'

'I cannot… I cannot…'

'Very well. You will move into Engineering and Ryan will undertake all duties in sick bay, unless there is an emergency. Speak to him and see what training he needs, and check in with him twice a day for reports. And Doctor - don't mention your theology to anyone. Is that clear?'

Ky nodded, wiped his eyes with the back of his hand and saluted.

'Dismissed.'

Darrow was tired. He was having to deal with issues with the crew on top of the strains of the mission. He hadn't slept much since the Prin came on board, and now he was worried about this latest development. *What good is a doctor too afraid to go to sick bay?* he thought. *And the Prin - there has to be a way to get through to them.*

* * *

So Tabitha and Anna got moved again, but this time to much better accommodation. Tabitha was relieved to see their new quarters, two real beds and proper storage. A real door for privacy. Hoy was meticulous in his neatness, Anna had no possessions, and Tabitha little, so it was the easiest move yet.

'At last,' Anna said. 'A proper cabin at last.'

Tabitha felt the two women were getting to know each other, but she found it hard to get used to Anna's divided attention. It was like being part of a three-way conversation when she had no idea what the third person was saying. Anna found it draining to have the Prin thoughts in her head all the time, but she did manage to have some conversation when talks were not going on.

'What's it like, having their thoughts in your head?' Tabitha asked.

'Oh, like being in a room where everyone is talking at once,' Anna said. 'It makes it hard to concentrate. And it's not like words, just images and emotions. Very hard to interpret,' she sighed. 'I hope I'm getting it right.'

'From what I've heard, the representatives seem to think so. Do you find it hard, being with the representatives while the talks are going on?'

'I just treat them all the same. I can't worry about individual customs or modes of address, it's hard enough as it is, especially when they start discussing what's going on. I had to threaten to work here if they wouldn't keep quiet.'

Tabitha laughed. 'I'll bet they didn't like that.'

Anna smiled. 'No, but Sam stands up for me. He doesn't care who they are, if they upset me.'

'I think he's sweet on you, you know.'

'I do know. I quite like him too.' Anna scowled. 'There's no time for that at the moment. I'll be glad when the Prin go back to their ship. Good riddance, I say.'

'Will that be the end of it then? Our mission, I mean.'

'It depends if the Prin can be persuaded to let us go to their home planet.'

'What?!'

* * *

The first chance she got, Tabitha sought out Chambers. Since the Kestrel was stationary, there was more free time, so she found Chambers alone in his cabin.

'Andrew, can I talk to you a minute?'

He beckoned her in and sat on the lower bunk. She took the chair.

'How's things?' he asked.

'Things were going quite well before these Prin came on board,' she said with a grimace.

'But I heard they moved you and Anna into Lieutenant-Commander Hoy's cabin. I thought you'd like that better than Engineering.'

'Oh I do, and I'm getting on OK with Anna. Have you heard anything about the talks?'

Chambers shook his head. 'Not much. I'm not really interested.'

'Not interested? But that's why we're out here!'

Chambers shrugged. 'I've got enough on my plate. Leave the Captain to worry about the Prin.'

'The reason I came to see you was because Anna says the Captain is trying to persuade the Prin to let us come to speak to their government.'

'No more following wake trails then.'

'Is that all you've got to say?' She thumped his arm. 'We were supposed to be finding out about these people and then taking the information back home, not going right into their clutches!'

Chambers grabbed his arm. 'Be careful, that hurt!'

'Sorry, but I'm frightened, and you don't care what happens to us.'

'Listen, I look at it like this: I signed on to serve in the fleet. That means I do as I'm told. Captain Darrow takes some chances, but never with the lives of his crew. If he thinks we should go, that's good enough for me. It's no good worrying over something you can't do anything about. Just do your job.'

Tabitha was quiet for a while. 'I never thought about it like that. Thanks Andrew.'

Chapter 34

The talks were recorded, and everything was sent back to PACT, but the distance to the last relay made the delay too great for ongoing instructions from them. The representatives watched the talks live on a monitor set up in the mess hall, so they could discuss progress as it happened. Even when talks were not in progress, they seemed to have taken over the place, or half of it, anyway. Darrow joined them as much as he could. That left one table for everyone else who needed to eat. The crew ended up taking their meals back to their cabins - the senior officers turned a blind eye to this breach of regulations. Around the representatives' table there was much discussion about tactics, especially when Hazeroth took a break.

'It is necessary we impress upon them our strength,' said Ehu. 'They have to realise we will not allow these raids to continue, and if they do, it will mean war. Which they cannot win.'

'Are we so certain of that?' Merari asked. 'How do we fight an enemy we cannot see? No, we must persuade them trade is a better alternative.'

'We have only met individual ships,' said Rendor. 'We have no idea how many ships they could muster in a war.'

'Let us not discuss war so soon,' Hazeroth held up his hand. 'You are rushing ahead. We must deal with the current situation. Once their ship repairs itself there will no longer be any reason for them to stay. We have to convince them to let us meet their leaders.'

'Maybe they are not the ones we should be speaking to,' said Ehu slowly. 'Perhaps they are too lowly to have any influence back home. Maybe we should just take them back with us for examination.' He looked around at them. 'Maybe the Leader isn't much of a leader at all.'

'Then why are we wasting time on them?' said Rendor.

'I think I see your point, Mr Ehu,' said Hazeroth. 'Instead of trying to reason, we should try appealing to their pride.'

* * *

'I see your ship is progressing well with repairs,' Hazeroth said to the Sage.

'Yes, we will not need to stay here much longer,' came the response.

'I am sorry we have spoken to you so much. We realise now we misunderstood your status.'

'What do you mean?' said the Leader.

'We were hoping to persuade you to convince your government to talk to us, but you obviously do not have access to them. You are probably just a scout ship, and we expected too much from you. My apologies.' Hazeroth bowed.

The Prin lights went pale green and then dark blue. Their ringing language rang out between them and Anna reported they were shocked and angry, and there was disagreement between them as to how to respond.

After a few moments, the Leader said, 'You are mistaken. When our ship is ready, we will contact the Great Council. There will be no further discussion.'

'What has he done?' said Merari, watching in the mess hall. 'He has ruined everything!'

'No,' said Ehu, smiling. 'He has been very clever. To maintain his pride, the Leader must persuade their Great Council to see us.'

'See us?' Rendor interrupted. 'There has been no discussion of actually going to their home world. It is out of the question!'

'We cannot go to their world, it would be suicide,' said Merari, slapping the table. 'And that would lead to war, which we are no means certain of winning. If their Great Council agree to meet us, it must be in neutral space, just their representatives and us.'

'I would remind you gentlemen,' said Darrow, getting to his feet, 'that I am in command of this mission. If going to Prin is the only option, then we will go. The safety of our worlds may depend on it.'

Darrow walked away. He didn't want to stay and hear any more arguments. *This mission is getting out of hand,* he thought. *I don't want to go to Prin either, but I don't see any other way.*

* * *

Darrow had only been back in his office a few minutes when there was a knock at the door. It was Hazeroth.

I was afraid I wouldn't get away that easily, Darrow thought with a wry smile as he invited him in.

'Captain,' Hazeroth began, 'we have discussed your decision, and are not all in agreement. I have been sent to request you to meet us for further discussion.'

'I don't see that it would be … helpful to discuss it. I am in command and my decision is final.'

'We know that Captain, and do not seek to undermine your authority. What we need is to hear your reasoning and to ensure you have considered the full possible consequences. Nothing more can be done until the Prin are able to return to their ship. If you would meet with us it may save … trouble later.'

Darrow sighed. 'Very well. Can you tell me - are any of the representatives with me?'

'At least one,' he gave a little bow, 'but even he would like your reasoning explained. I think it best if you aim to win us all to your side.'

Darrow gave a hollow laugh. 'Very diplomatic, Mr Hazeroth. Lead on.'

Hazeroth hesitated, looking round the room. 'May I suggest we meet in here where it is more private? There are members of the crew having food in the mess hall.' He looked around. 'There are enough chairs in here. I do not think it wise to stand.'

Darrow nodded and Hazeroth went to fetch the other three.

He studied the representatives closely when they came in. Hazeroth, of course, showed no emotion, but Darrow felt he had been with him so far. Rendor's cranial spines were rigid and erect and his face stony - probably against. Merari looked afraid, Ehu was frowning, neither of which helped him decide on their likely opinions. He almost longed for Barok, who was so clearly against everything that you always knew where he stood. But then, they had all misjudged him too. They ignored the chair opposite him at the desk, and took the four chairs around the walls. It felt like a bench of judges. No one spoke, so Darrow decided to start once they were all seated.

'Mr Hazeroth has said you wish me to explain the reasoning behind my decision to meet with the Prin leaders. I did not make the decision lightly, I assure you.' He took a deep breath. 'Let's look at the situation from the other perspective. If we just let the Prin return to their ship and go - then what?'

'We follow them to their homeworld and gather what information we can before returning home,' said Rendor. 'This is a fact-finding mission, not a first-contact mission.'

'Too late, we've already made first contact. Besides they will warn their homeworld against us, and we don't know what weaponry they have,' said Darrow. 'In fact, we don't know what weaponry their ship has. How do we know they won't turn on us as soon as they get back on board?'

Merari jumped in. 'I was not warned this mission could be dangerous. I would not have come if I had known.'

'You're in a space ship in the void of space, there's inherent danger just in being out here,' said Darrow. 'None of us knew what was waiting for us. We have to make the best use of every opportunity which presents itself.'

'I believe the modifications Commander Blackwell and I have made to the Kestrel's weapons will give us some protection,' said Ehu. 'But the reaction of the Prin from the crippled ship shows the only thing they will understand is war. I do not believe they will accept peace.'

To deflect their attention away from himself for a moment, Darrow looked across at Hazeroth. 'With your first-contact experience, how do you think we should proceed?'

Hazeroth shifted in his seat and looked away. 'I do not know,' he said. 'This is beyond my experience.'

'Explain yourself!' said Rendor, his spines thrashing. 'How much experience do you have?'

There was a long silence.

'I have only been in first-contact situations twice before,' said Hazeroth. 'Once as a junior and once as a senior team member.'

'You have never dealt with such alone?' said Rendor. 'You have deceived us!'

Darrow intervened. 'That is of little relevance now. My case is, if they get permission to take us to meet their government, it's too good an opportunity to miss. Frankly it could itself be considered an act of war, a snub to their honour and grace in giving the initial agreement. I hope the Great Council can be won over in the same way as these Prin were. The idea of trade doesn't seem to have occurred to them, and that may be the key.'

Ehu cleared his throat. 'I am still unsure of the wisdom of your decision, but I will support you. I agree that going to meet the Prin is now the best option. It is not wise to show yourself weak before your enemies.'

'My report will show you are reckless, Captain,' said Rendor. 'You were wrong to become involved with the crippled ship in the first place.'

Merari nodded, but said nothing. Darrow looked at Hazeroth.

'I will do my best to assist you, Captain,' Hazeroth said.

'Thank you.' Darrow looked solemnly around the group. 'Your comments have been noted and you are free to express your opinions in your reports, but I would ask you to present a united front to the Prin and the crew.'

The representatives seemed to take this as a dismissal, and left. Darrow leaned back in his chair and rubbed his tense neck muscles. *I thought I was going to have a mutiny on my hands there for a moment. I admit I may have got carried away with this opportunity, but I can't let them know that. I just hope it works out for the best.*

* * *

The Kestrel's crew watched in amazement as the Prin ship repaired itself, 'growing' new parts as they were needed and feeding on energy provided by the Kestrel under the Leader's guidance. After three days the iridescent glow began in the bow, the butterfly's head, and spread over the ship. The spars once again became butterfly wings. It was a beautiful sight.

Anna reported the Prin ship was ready, at the same time as the Prin signalled they wanted to speak to Darrow. He went to sick bay.

'We thank you, Captain, for your assistance,' said the Leader, glowing red. 'We must now return to our ship and contact Prin.'

'You are welcome.' Darrow said. 'I'm sure you understand we must take precautions for your journey through our ship to the shuttle ...'

'That will not be necessary, Captain. If you will turn off the force field, our ship will retrieve us.'

'How is that done?'

The colour showed flashes of turquoise warning. 'We cannot say.'

Darrow nodded and went to the intercom. 'All stations, alert. Our guests are leaving. Cancel the sick bay force field.'

The moment the force field went down, the Prin simply disappeared. Darrow raced to the bridge, waiting to see if they would attack. Within minutes there was a message from them.

'Captain,' the Leader said, 'I have informed Prin that we are escorting your ship to meet with representatives of our government. How soon can you be ready to leave?'

'Very quickly,' Darrow said, 'But where are we to meet them? Do you have a location in mind?'

'On Prin, of course. Our Great Council never leave the planet. It would be highly inappropriate.'

Darrow's mind whirled. Despite what he had said to the representatives, he had never intended to go to Prin, just close enough for a meeting. Well, he had said he would go, so now his bluff had been called.

'We will be ready shortly. Stand by, I will contact you.' He cut the communication and opened the intercom. 'Prepare to get underway. We are following the Prin ship to their homeworld. Commander Parks to the Captain's office. All representatives meet with me in the mess hall in five minutes.'

When Parks arrived Darrow closed the door and studied his face.

'Friendship aside,' Darrow said, 'I need to know now if you support my decision to go to Prin.'

Parks sighed. 'You have my support, Captain. You don't need my opposition, you're going to have your hands full. I can see why you made your decision, I just hope we don't regret it.'

'Thanks, it means a lot. Take the bridge and get us moving. Contact the Prin ship when we're ready. I'm going to face the representatives.'

Parks left for the bridge. Darrow took a deep breath before he went down the corridor to the mess hall. The four representatives were there all talking at once.

'Excuse me gentlemen, can I have silence please?' he began in a quiet voice. They all sat down in silence and looked at him.

'I understand your concern, and believe me, this situation

is not what I wanted. But if we don't take this opportunity, we may never have the chance again. We *have* to go, for the sake of peace. You're here to represent your governments, and I have welcomed your input and your expertise. We are already preparing to go and I will brook no argument. You should all take some time to accept the situation and consider how you can best serve your people in the coming meeting. Thank you.'

The representatives looked at each other in stunned silence. Darrow turned and left. As the door closed behind him he heard Ehu burst out laughing.

Is that with me or at me? he wondered.

Chapter 35

Darrow made a similar announcement to the crew once they were under way. He knew if he allowed dissent he could have a mutiny on his hands. He still wasn't sure he was doing the right thing, but he had to show confidence, now the decision was made. The only one he softened with, was Anna. When he visited her in her cabin with Tabitha, he was shocked to see how tired she looked.

'Oh, I'm alright,' she smiled, sitting up in bed, 'I just didn't want to miss anything.'

'She was recording for hours every day,' Tabitha cut in. 'Dr Ky tried to get her to rest, but she wouldn't.'

'Speak when you're spoken to, Trainee,' Darrow said.

Tabitha blushed and stood to attention.

Anna waved Tabitha quiet. 'I can rest now. Their ship unites their minds, so there's not much I can do.' She hesitated. 'We're going to their world, aren't we?'

'Yes,' Darrow said, sitting on the edge of the bed and taking her hand. 'We must. If we don't take this opportunity to try to convince them to trade, it could mean war. I'm sorry to put you through this, but we really need your help.'

The intercom chimed, and Darrow rose from the bed and answered. It was Ryan.

'Captain, Dr Ky wants Anna to come to sick bay for a check-up.'

'That's fine, Ensign. Ask the doctor to speak to me after he finishes with Anna.'

'Yes sir.'

'Go now,' he said to Anna. 'I'm sure Dr Ky will do everything he can for you. Thank you again for all you're doing.'

Anna stood up and gave a little smile. 'Maybe I'll finally find out who did this to me.'

Tabitha's Journal

Well, the dead are Mr Barok, Dr Dathan and one of the Prin. Mr Barok's attempt to kill them and Dr Dathan dying to save them made the shift in their minds. We're actually going to the Prin planet. Somehow they've agreed to talks. But we have to go to them. I think it's crazy.

I'm not really sorry about Mr Barok. He took matters into his own hands instead of consulting the others and he was a murderer. He wasn't very nice anyway and didn't even try to get along with people. When I had to meet with him he was really put out, like it was beneath him. It was really hard to be polite. When I asked him about the Casparans he just moaned about the Ochrans all the time, and how they oppressed them.

I am sorry about Mr Dathan though. He was so sweet. He gave me lots of good advice and told me stuff about the different species that I could put in my reports. He was fascinated about the adaptations in my body for high gravity - I never thought about it before. He was kind and gentle and so eager to learn. He didn't seem like he was over a hundred years old at all. I'm going to miss him.

During the time the Prin were on board, Anna kept to our room. Although she knew they were confined, she could never quite get over the initial terror she had felt at the touch of their minds. Now they've returned to their ship, which focusses and unites their minds, she can no longer tell them apart. Their touch returned to the nameless terror of before. As we follow the Prin ship, she is finding her meditation exercises help her to cope with the constant lower level of thought she receives, but she's nervous about the approach of a whole planet-full of minds. I'm trying to reassure her, but what do I know?

* * *

'We are now out of range of the nearest relay, Captain,' Balitoth reported. 'Communication with PACT is no longer possible.'

Parks looked around from the helm and whispered, 'We're on our own now, sir.'

Darrow reflected that whatever happened, he would have to make the decisions that would affect not just his crew but the lives of countless people on every inhabited planet in the known galaxy.

'Tell the representatives to prepare final reports and we'll send them via probe before we get close to Prin. That way, if anything happens to us, PACT will have all our data.'

As the days passed, the tension got to everyone. Mostly they kept it to themselves, but Tabitha found it particularly difficult to cope. Parks had been trying to keep her busy, filling her time with training and study, but the representatives had told her about themselves and didn't know what else to say. She became despondent and began neglecting her duties. When Parks called her in for a reprimand, she exploded.

'I can't do it! I quit!' She lost any idea of standing to attention.

'Calm down Trainee, we can work it out.'

'Work out more rubbish for me to do you mean.' She stamped her foot like a petulant child. 'It wasn't supposed to be like this…' Her voice tailed off and she turned away.

Parks' anger evaporated, and he ignored the lapse in protocol. He had dreamed of going out into space too, but at least he had experienced it for some years before he was grounded. He knew what it could be like. His voice softened.

'It's a wonderful dream, getting out among the stars, with nothing but space around you. Seeing strange places and meeting strange people.'

Tabitha turned back, her face twisted. 'But it's just a dream, nothing like the reality. You said I could make a difference. You said that the different species were just people and I should get to know them, but they're busy with these Prin, and some of them are obnoxious. The only one who was really kind to me is dead.'

'I forgot, Dathan spent a lot of time with you, didn't he? You must miss him more than anyone.'

'He was so patient, and didn't think I was stupid not to know things. He encouraged me to keep on learning. He said that with my background I would have a fresh perspective on things. What am I going to do now?'

Parks latched on to her memories of Dathan. 'Honour his memory by keeping on as he wanted you to. Look on this as a golden opportunity - you'll probably never have so many species together, so accessible. They're not so busy now, for a while. Think of how much you can learn.'

Tabitha's face brightened a little. 'Would it be all right if I asked Hazeroth about the Prin? No one outside this ship has even heard of them.'

'That's the way. There are good times as well as bad, you know. We have kind of dropped you in the deep end. It's not all like this.'

Tabitha scowled.

'But in the mean-time,' Parks said firmly, 'you have to pull your weight, and you have to finish your reports. It will get better, I promise. Now, attention, and salute.'

* * *

Ryan was increasingly concerned about Anna.

'Doctor, what can we do for Anna if she can't cope with a whole planet full of Prin minds?' he asked Ky. 'Do you think it would still affect her if we sedate her?'

'I'm afraid I don't know. I still don't understand how the receptor in her brain works.' Ky handed him a hypodermic shot. 'Carry this with you at all times, but only use it as a last resort. And don't tell Anna.'

'Why not? Surely it would reassure her that we're prepared?'

'I don't think so. Remember what she said in the beginning about doing things to her?'

'I'm still not sure...'

'It's not your job to pass judgement, young man. Just obey orders.'

'Yes sir.'

Ryan spent as much time with Anna as his duties would allow. He wanted to be with her anyway, needed to be with her, even though he knew he couldn't tell her how he felt. She was so vulnerable, it wouldn't be fair. It was unethical too - she was his patient. Why couldn't they have met under other circumstances? Maybe she wouldn't have looked twice at him under other circumstances. Was he taking unfair advantage?

The first touch Anna felt of the collective minds of the Prin home world, they were still six hours travel away. Tabitha called him and he rushed to their cabin.

'I'm all right,' Anna told him, with little smile, 'but it's like a huge crowd in the distance, all talking at once.'

'Now's the time to start doing those meditation exercises Dr Ky taught you. Concentrate on your breathing. Do you want to sit or lie?'

He so wanted to help her, but couldn't think of anything to do. Anna soon reported it became a deafening babble inside her head and a feeling of intense pressure. Ryan contacted Ky, who wanted Anna to move into sick bay, but she insisted on staying in her cabin, with Ryan and Tabitha for support. Ky set up a portable medical monitor to track her vital signs and brainwave activity. The meditation exercises designed to help her focus and keep calm became impossible as the planet drew nearer. Eventually she became hysterical and Ryan applied the knockout shot, hoping it would be enough to spare her any more suffering. But it was not to be. Even unconscious, she was restless, then moaning and eventually feverish.

Suddenly Anna convulsed, just once, and lay still. Ryan called Ky, who arrived at a run. They watched in despair as the monitor readings slowly fell … and stabilised at normal levels! They couldn't believe their eyes. Ky quickly examined her.

'It looks as though the receiver in her brain just shut down! I don't know whether it was programmed to do that or if it overloaded, but I think she's going to be all right. Let's hope there's no brain damage.'

Ryan almost wept with relief.

When Tabitha arrived after her duties they were able to tell her the hopeful news.

'Can we wake her?' she said. 'I want to be sure she's not harmed.'

'I won't give her a stimulant,' Ky said, 'but we can counteract the sedation and she should come round soon. She must be made to rest. I'm sure you and Ensign Ryan will be happy to see to that.'

Ky smiled. Ryan's feelings had been plain to Ky for some time. He was pretty sure Anna felt the same way. Now she no longer had to worry about the telepathy, perhaps her feelings would start to show too.

Ky thumbed the intercom. 'Captain, good news! It looks as if the receiver in Anna's head just switched off. She won't be bothered by the Prin again.'

'Thank you, Doctor. Though it does mean she won't be able to interpret their minds for us either.' Darrow said. 'I have some news for you too. While you've been preoccupied, we have arrived. They've escorted the Prin ship off for debriefing and are sending us an escort into orbit. I want everyone on standby until we see how they welcome us. I'm not making any assumptions.'

Chapter 36

The Prin language was largely non-verbal. They communicated with coloured lights and thoughts, to augment their musical, ringing words. It was quite beautiful to watch and listen to, but impossible to learn if you were not a Prin.

The Prin whom Anna had called the Leader faced the Great Council. The colours were turquoise and blue for warning and tension, flickering to dark blue signalling anger, and the lights were dim. He knew there was going to be trouble. The Great One, leader of the Great Council, spoke.

'You are under discipline for three reasons. Firstly, for negligence, that you allowed your ship to be caught in the meteor storm, endangering the life force of your ship and crew. Secondly, for accepting assistance from a lower species, thus putting yourselves in their debt and compromising security. Thirdly, for treachery in making an alliance with these lower species and daring to bring them here.'

The Leader spoke up, glowing amber in an appeal for understanding.

'O Great One, the ship will tell you the storm was upon us without warning, and you will see from our report we have greatly underestimated the solid ones of the Planetary Alliance …'

A Council member shouted him down, glowing turquoise warning and white loyalty.

'How dare you call into question the wisdom of the Great Council! We will not have trade with lesser races, we will use them as we see fit.'

The Leader glowed amber, pleading. 'We do not presume to question either the Great Council or our Prin heritage. We seek to enrich our people through new technology, new ideas, and the raw materials we need without the need for war.'

'There will be no war! We are superior, our ships are superior, and we will take what we require.'

'That has always been our way, but these solid ones are different. We can benefit much from their co-operation.'

The Great One interrupted before there was another outburst. 'You and your crew will be taken for examination. Perhaps you were affected by the meteor storm. All things will be taken into consideration. The original plan will proceed. We will, however, examine these solid ones whom you have brought us, and their technology, to learn what we may use against them. They have no weapon we should fear.'

Guards came to lead him away, but the Leader spoke once more, with a turquoise warning. 'They can read our thoughts!'

The whole room fell silent and green with the shock.

'This was not in your report! Are they listening now?'

'I do not know. We were able to find out so little information that it is only a small part of our report. They cannot all do this, they have a female with them who has the ability. We believe she was able to tell them how we felt about them and whether our promises were sincere. That is all we know. They would not discuss it with us and we never met her.'

'Remove him to a secure area, and do not allow him to communicate with anyone. We shall use the others to lure the solids here.'

The Leader was escorted from the chamber and a multi-hued discussion escalated.

* * *

As soon as the Kestrel was close enough, they took scans of the planet. They confirmed the atmosphere wasn't toxic, but thin on oxygen, so they would need simple breathers. The light level was low due to the distance from their sun, but they would be able to see where they were going. They would need warm clothing. Gravity was similar to Earth. Beyond that it was difficult to tell. Since the Prin were energy beings, it was impossible to see if there were any weapons or technology down there, as there were energy signals everywhere. Darrow met with the representatives to discuss the next move. He wanted to stay in orbit and send an advance party down in a shuttle craft.

'Captain, I understand your caution,' said Hazeroth, 'but I am concerned the Prin might take this as an insult. I strongly recommend that we land.'

'No!' Merari said.

Ehu looked up from the electronics he was working on with Parks, and growled. 'You do not give your enemy your ship.'

'But Captain, we have spent so long winning their trust…' said Hazeroth.

'The ship will not be left unguarded,' agreed Rendor. 'You can still select your landing party, and the rest of us will stay with the ship. But we must land, surely.'

Parks looked up from his task and raised his eyebrows at Rendor's change of attitude. Darrow caught his expression and nodded.

'Gentlemen,' Parks said, 'I fear your excitement is outweighing your caution. Leaving the ship in orbit would be far safer. Who knows what forces they have down there?'

Rendor bristled at this, and Darrow jumped in to prevent any trouble.

'We also have to decide who goes in the landing party,' Darrow said. 'Myself, of course, and Hazeroth because he has *some* first contact experience.' Hazeroth looked down. Darrow said, 'Are you willing?' and Hazeroth nodded. 'Do we have any other volunteers?'

There was an uncomfortable silence.

'Well, I have to go,' said Parks. 'I have to be there for security.'

'But surely,' said Ehu, 'we cannot risk losing the Captain

and the First Officer?'

'What other senior officers are there?' said Parks. 'The Captain shouldn't go on his own. Dr Ky won't leave the ship, and, with all due respect, I don't think Commander Blackwell is built for running.' He turned to Darrow. 'Unless you want to take Lieutenant-Commander Hoy?'

Darrow shook his head. 'I'd rather have you at my back. I think we can trust Hoy to take charge up here.' He raised a hand to silence any objections. 'Yes, Kestrel will remain in orbit. I expect you all to give Lieutenant-Commander Hoy your full cooperation. If we do need rescuing, I don't want him fighting you as well as the Prin.'

Hazeroth spoke up. 'I think there should be another representative in the landing party.'

Again there was no response. Merari and Rendor looked at the floor.

Ehu sighed. 'If you need rescuing, I will be in the rescue party. I know little of diplomacy, but I know how to fight.'

'Thank you,' Darrow said. 'I will allocate crewmen to be with you.'

The contingency rescue team was also hard to put together. Ehu was persuaded, but the other representatives didn't want to fight, preferring to leave it to the crew. If the two most senior officers were captured, Darrow was torn ... His instinct was for Hoy to lead the rescue team, but who would stay in command on the bridge? Blackwell solved the dilemma by volunteering for command. He would also take over weapons, releasing Balitoth. So the team consisted of Hoy, Ehu, Balitoth, and, despite what he had told Tabitha about not having to fight, Stubbs. That would leave no one in Engineering , but Blackwell would route the important systems to the bridge.

The call came through from the Sage with the invitation to land and be their guests. This was further complicated by a specific request, from the Great One himself, to meet Anna. After much discussion, the Sage agreed to persuade the Great Council to accept an initial group of leaders *and*

Anna. Her presence was not negotiable. Darrow explained she was unwell, and the Sage made it clear they would wait if necessary, but she must come. So it was decided the initial party should be Darrow, Anna, Hazeroth and Parks.

'I'll stay in the background,' Parks said, 'and while they're making a fuss of you, I can keep my eyes open.' He held up a tiny box with a thin wire dangling from it. 'This goes in your hair - it's the last place people think of looking for a tracer. If anything happens, just touch it and it will activate. That will set off an alarm on the bridge and allow them to track you.'

They would all carry ordinary communicators as well. They didn't need environment suits, only warm clothing and breathing masks. Dr Ky said there was enough oxygen and other gases that they could even manage for a few minutes without breathers, but didn't recommend it. The one thing Hazeroth insisted on was no weapons.

'We have to at least look as if we trust them. We have access to the Kestrel's fire power if we need it.'

Parks nodded. 'She's going to be in geo-stationary orbit right above - assuming we all stay together.'

In consultation with the Sage, they also decided to take as a gift some of the compounds needed by the Prin, and some music as an example of their cultures. With their ringing, musical language, they hoped the Prin would appreciate it.

Parks went to prepare the gifts and sent Tabitha and Stubbs to check over the shuttle. While everything was being prepared, Darrow went to see how Anna was.

* * *

Tabitha was nervous about working with Stubbs again, but Stubbs wanted to put things right.

'Look, I'm sorry I came on to you. It was just a bit of fun,' he said with a shrug.

'Well it wasn't fun for me,' Tabitha said, clenching her fists. 'I've got enough to cope with, without that.'

'I'm sorry. Relationships between crew members are frowned on, anyway,' he admitted. 'Can we just be friends?' He saw her wary look. 'Next time we kiss it'll be your offer.'

She smiled. 'It'll be a long wait, then.'

'Come on, we've got to go through this checklist quickly. I've done it before, it's not hard.'

Tabitha relaxed. As they worked, she thought about the Prin. 'Isn't it great that the Prin turned out to be friendly?'

He frowned. 'Don't jump the gun. Just because we're going to meet them doesn't mean they'll like us. There's a lot riding on what the Captain says and does once he meets the leaders.'

'Oh, I wish I could be there to see it. To be one of the first to meet a new species.'

'You've changed your tune! What happened to the Alphan suspicion of all things alien?'

'That was my parents. I always wanted to know more. Now I've met all the representatives, I'm keen to meet more.' She stopped work. 'You don't suppose the Captain...?'

'No way! You're only a trainee. Captain Darrow won't take any chances. Check there's four suits in that cupboard in case they're needed.'

She checked the cupboard and found four lightweight spacesuits hanging up. 'Check. If the talks go well, will we be allowed down to the planet then?'

Stubbs sighed. 'Of course not! First contact negotiations are very delicate. They won't allow visitors for a long time. It's not going to happen, Tabs, forget it. That's it,' he said, turning off his pad. 'Back to your duties now.' They left the shuttle. 'See you around.'

Tabitha had a faraway look in her eyes. 'See you. I'll just be a minute.'

Stubbs left the shuttle bay. Tabitha turned and went back into the shuttle. There was room for her to hide in the spacesuit cupboard. She hesitated for a minute, half turned away, then made up her mind and climbed in.

Anna woke up shouting, 'Oh no! No! We've got to turn back.' She struggled out of bed, and Ryan tried to calm and restrain her. Her hair was dishevelled, her eyes wild, but she had lost the haunted look she had had for so long.

'Oh Sam, my head is sorted! I finally know who I am, and I know about the Prin.'

At that moment Darrow arrived. Anna rushed towards him.

'Captain, I'm so glad you're here, you have to keep away from Prin. It's a trap!'

Darrow grasped her by the arms and sat her down on the bed. He sat with her and looked into her eyes.

'I'm listening. Now calm down and explain. But we've already arrived - and they want you in the landing party.'

She sagged, then took a deep breath. 'Well, if we *have* to go, at least you can be prepared. Captain, it was not other aliens who altered me to hear Prin thoughts - it was the Prin themselves!' She paused to allow the shock to register. 'I'll try to keep my story brief. Last year, my father and I were captured by the Prin when our research ship strayed into their space. They ... examined us,' she shuddered, 'in order to find out about humans, because they were interested in our part of the galaxy. To make communication easier, they ... adapted us to be able to hear their thoughts.' Her voice faltered. 'My father died.'

Ryan put his arm around her. He was horrified, but fascinated at the same time. 'How did you get away?'

'There's no time for that now.' Darrow said. 'Is there anything you can tell us that would help us fight them?'

Anna tried to remember. 'They can't cope with very high sounds - they didn't like me screaming. They have no sense of smell. Their language colour for extreme threat is violet, so ultraviolet would be terrifying. It wouldn't work for long, but if you shine ultraviolet at one or two of them, they will instinctively run from it.'

Darrow thumbed the intercom. 'Parks, get something inconspicuous rigged up to emit a high pitched noise, and something to emit ultraviolet light. I'll explain later.'

Anna said, 'Oh Captain, one more thing - I can still hear their thoughts. This thing in my brain didn't switch off, it just clicked over into normal operating mode.'

'What does that mean?' Ryan interrupted.

She laid a hand on his arm. 'I can filter out the thoughts, concentrate on one, several or many,' she said. 'And now I remember, now I know, the terror has gone. Now there's just the desire for revenge.'

Ryan pulled back at the new edge to her voice.

'So you can confirm what they're thinking,' Darrow said. 'Tell us if it *is* a trap.'

'Not from up here, there's too many. But it must be a trap, I'm sure of it. Down on the planet I will be able to distinguish individuals. That's why, if you're going, I have to go with you,' she stood up, 'even though they'll probably recognise me and want to kill me.'

'No!' said Ryan. 'Captain, you can't make her do this. We must escape in the Kestrel, you can't go down to the surface.'

Darrow shook his head. 'I'm afraid it's too late. They probably have other ships around - we'd never get away.' He turned to Anna. 'Are you well enough to meet with us and discuss the best way to proceed?'

Anna nodded. 'Just let me tidy up.'

'Meet us in the mess hall.'

Darrow left. Ryan grabbed Anna.

'You can't go down there, it's too dangerous!'

Impulsively, he kissed her hard. For a moment, she softened, then she pulled away. 'You can't stop me, Sam,' there was a new and determined steel in her voice. 'Maybe I can save the landing party, where I couldn't save my father. I'm going to pay the Prin back - if I die, it'll be worth it.'

Ryan checked her vital signs, looking for a reason to keep her, but she pushed him out of the door. She quickly washed her face and combed her hair. She tidied her clothes, and as she put on her jacket she checked the pocket, and went out.

* * *

As the cabin door closed behind him, Darrow slumped against the wall and balled his fists. The corridor was empty, so he dropped his guard for a second. *I was wrong about the Prin*, he thought. *I wanted to believe the best. I let my enthusiasm run away with me. Stubborn, arrogant fool!* He quickly recovered himself when the door opened and Ryan came out.

'How is she?' he asked Ryan.

'Medically - just tired, sir. Emotionally - wrung out. Captain, please, is there any way to keep her out of this?'

'I'm afraid not. The Prin insist she comes to meet them. We'll do all we can to protect her, I promise.'

'Thank you, sir.' He hesitated. 'Sir? If it *is* a trap, you'll need a rescue party. Can I come? You may need a medic, and I have weapons experience - we used to shoot vermin in the fields back home.'

'Very well, I'll notify Lieutenant-Commander Hoy to include you. Dismissed.'

Ryan headed to sick bay. Darrow took a deep breath and went into the mess hall where Parks and the representatives waited. *I don't blame them if they rip me to pieces,* he thought.

'How is Anna?' Hazeroth asked.

'Conscious, and her memory has returned.' He paused. 'She is convinced it's a trap.'

'That is unfortunate,' Rendor said calmly.

'I have not seen much in the way of planetary defences,' Ehu said. 'It may be they are so used to being superior in this region that they have not developed any.'

'We're definitely going to need those tracers,' Parks said. 'Shall I go to fit one on Anna, sir?'

'No need, she's meeting us here,' Darrow said. 'I must

say, you've all taken this very calmly.'

Rendor smiled. 'As you have reminded us several times, Captain, you are in charge. Even though we do not entirely agree, your reasons for coming here have been noted. Now we are here, what is there to do but proceed?'

Darrow sighed and thought to himself, *I didn't expect that. I'll probably have to face the music back home, but it makes things much easier now.* 'Thank you gentlemen,' he said, with a bow of his head.

The door opened and Anna entered.

'Well,' she said. 'What do you want to know?'

Chapter 37

When all was ready, the shuttle flew down into the thin atmosphere and was met by a guidance beam, bringing them safely into land in a large open space in the middle of the city. Darrow found it hard to think of it as a city, as the 'buildings' were mostly open structures of various shapes and sizes, whose functions were not clear. There were no corners anywhere, everything curved and flowed. The colours were all towards the red end of the spectrum, every shade of pink, red, orange and plum. Details were hard to see in the low light. The landing party put on their breathers, took the gifts, and left the shuttle.

There appeared to be an honour guard and a small group of officials outside the nearest structure, but it was difficult to tell because the glowing shapes all looked so similar to non-Prin eyes, and he wasn't sure what the different colours meant. Darrow realised how many species rely on clothes to identify status and roles - official robes, uniforms, quality of the cloth etc.

As Darrrow and the others disembarked the shuttle, the entire waiting crowd became opaque. It was an amazing sight, and now he could see the distinctions. The 'honour guard' of eight figures were white, and the group in the centre were four blue with two figures red.

Hazeroth leaned towards Darrow and muttered, 'The two red figures are the Sage and the Warrior. I am happy to see them, as they are already used to us.'

Two white figures came forward with the Sage who said, 'They wish to check you have no weapons. They will not hurt you.'

Reverting to energy, the two figures reached out to them. They all tensed, but the Prin's touch only tingled, and they didn't detect the tracers in their hair. After the search, the Sage and the Warrior came forward and greeted them. The white figures parted and the blue figures turned and moved towards a low, arched structure.

'Welcome to Prin,' the Sage said, 'we are so glad the Great Council has agreed to meet you. They go ahead of us and will greet you officially inside. Please come with us.'

Darrow glanced at Anna, who said, 'They're tense, but that's all I'm getting.'

They went in.

Parks began to mutter to himself, broadcasting a commentary to the Kestrel via a hidden transmitter. The archway proved to be the entrance to a large circular area just below ground level. There were shafts spaced around the edge that presumably led to lower levels. Great pillars supported the roof, which was a fretwork of arches and windows, letting in what little light there was. The Sage explained the atmosphere could be controlled inside, so they could remove their breathers.

'Now why would they want to do that?' Parks muttered. 'Unless they've had other races here before.'

Once inside, the walls began to glow in intricate patterns of scarlet, white and pink.

'The colours of friendship,' Anna murmured.

Darrow's heart lifted. Maybe it was going to be all right after all.

He gazed around in wonder as they were led towards the blue figures, who waited several metres inside. The white figures entered behind them and filled the entranceway, a small group coming forward to stand behind the landing party. As the Sage made the introductions, the Council members bowed to each in turn. They returned the bow and offered their gifts, Darrow explaining what they were. The Sage took the gifts and laid them on a raised surface near the Council members, reverting to energy and translating the explanation into the ringing, flashing Prin language. Darrow watched Anna carefully while the Sage was speaking, and she tensed and shook her head. The Council members' colour was growing darker.

'It's a trap,' she said, 'we walked right into it.'

The Sage and the Warrior turned pale green in shock at her words, and started forward towards the Council, glowing an amber appeal. Darrow looked around at Parks and Hazeroth and casually lifted his hand to stroke his hair, setting off the hidden alarm. The others did the same, but Anna didn't see the signal, she was too distracted. At that moment the 'honour guard' became the 'prison guard'. Without warning they changed back to their energy state, their colour turned turquoise, and they encircled the group. The Sage and the Warrior were also taken. Darrow reached out as if to reassure Anna, and activated the alarm in her hair. The rest of the Prin group reverted to their energy state and began to move away.

Parks switched on the high-pitched noise and all the nearest Prin recoiled and became solid. Parks shouted 'Run!' and, smashing the nearest solid Prin, he broke out of the circle, herding the others ahead as they dashed towards the exit. But they forgot about the Prin ability to fire an energy beam, and Parks was brought down by two simultaneous hits. His thick clothing saved his life, but it caught fire.

Darrow shouted 'Down!' and they all threw themselves to the ground.

Darrow knew they didn't stand a chance against the energy beams, and was desperate to put out the flames on Parks.

'Tell them we surrender!' Darrow shouted to the Sage, who translated.

'You must go with the guards,' the Sage said. 'Captain, I am sorry, I did not know…'

Four of the guards led the Sage and the Warrior away. Hazeroth put out the flames on Parks' clothing using his own jacket, while the remaining guards confiscated and destroyed the high pitched noise emitter and their communicators. Then Hazeroth and Darrow carried the unconscious Parks as they were all taken away in another direction. The archway they were led through wound down, underground.

* * *

When the landing party left the shuttle, Tabitha came out of the cupboard and crept to the window. She drank in the graceful flowing buildings and gasped when the welcoming committee became solid in their various colours. She had not been allowed to see the Prin when they were on board the Kestrel, so this was all new. As the group moved away into the building, she opened the shuttle door and stepped out. No one noticed her. She immediately became aware of the thin atmosphere - she hadn't thought to bring a breather.

How stupid of me! she thought. *Acted on impulse and now I'm unprepared.* She hesitated. *It's not too bad, I can have a quick look around and get back to the shuttle before I run out of breath.*

She tiptoed towards the building the group had entered and peeped in to see tall Parks over the heads of the Prin. He removed his breather, so she stepped inside and flattened herself against the wall in the shadow. Now she could breathe more easily. Her heart was thumping with excitement as she watched the gifts being handed over.

This is a historic moment, she thought, *that I'm witnessing!*

What happened next turned her excitement to horror. She didn't understand at first why some of the Prin changed colour and some moved away. Then Parks shouted and the landing party ran. For a second she didn't know whether to run away or stay hidden.

If I show myself, I'm in big trouble with the Captain, but if I don't ... what if the landing party make it to the shuttle and leave without me?

But then Parks got shot and the landing party was taken captive. She was frozen in indecision. Should she go or stay? Could she help the landing party or would it just cause more trouble?

I shouldn't have come.

As the hall started to empty, she crept further inside and followed the landing party through the archway and down the slope. She couldn't just leave them, even though she didn't know what she could do. Maybe there would be a chance to help them escape.

* * *

On the Kestrel bridge the four alarms from the landing party went off one after the other. Ehu left the bridge and Hoy surged to his feet.

'Red alert! Mr Rendor, I want the tracers monitored continuously. I want to know where they are at all times. Co-ordinate with the helm to stay with them. If they split up, stay with the majority. Ensign Reuel, monitor all communications frequencies for a message from the landing party, or anything from the Prin that will help. And get me online with the Pri-!'

Hoy's words were cut short as the ship lurched to the left, Chambers' quick reactions saving them from a beam emitted from the planet. Everyone buckled their harnesses. Hoy saved himself by grabbing his chair. Merari wasn't so lucky, and picked himself up from the floor. He pulled down the seat for the navigator next to Chambers, and buckled himself into it.

'Tractor beam,' reported Rendor, 'targeting now.'

Rendor missed, as Chambers moved the ship as he fired.

'No response from the Prin,' Reuel reported.

'Did you record Parks' commentary?' Hoy demanded.

'Yes sir,' said Reuel. 'It stopped so suddenly, I hope he is all right.'

'Put what you've got through to the shuttle for review, and make full scanner sweeps. Send a message back home via probe that the Prin are hostile. Mr Rendor, watch out for other Prin ships. We need all the information we can get.'

Blackwell arrived to take command and Hoy left for the shuttle.

266

* * *

One thing they didn't teach in the Academy was how to show confidence in front of your crew, even when you didn't feel it. Every Captain had to learn the hard way. Now, Darrow's confidence, real or otherwise, deserted him. He looked back over the mission and knew himself for a fool.

I should never have let Admiral Keever talk me into it, he thought. *This mission was bound for disaster. When we encountered the damaged ship, it was madness to bring the Prin aboard. And what was I thinking, to come to Prin? I've led my whole crew on a suicide mission!*

He turned to the Prin guards. 'Take me, but let the others go.'

Anna laid a hand on his arm. 'They don't understand you, Captain. Only the Prin on the ship had translators.'

'I'm sorry I got you all into this,' he said.

'You should not take all the blame, Captain,' said Hazeroth. 'We all agreed to come on this mission.'

They reached a junction in the passageway, and two of the guards indicated Anna should go with them. Darrow pushed Parks on to Hazeroth and grabbed Anna's arm.

'No! We all stay together!'

One of the guards turned from turquoise to dark blue and touched him, causing a shock to run up his arm. He let go of Anna and they separated her from the other captives. She gave him a sad smile as they led her away. Darrow and the rest were taken to a lower level, into a room where two Prin hovered by a table with restraints. Darrow and Hazeroth exchanged looks - this was obviously prepared for solid beings. Darrow thought back to the little Anna had told him about her captivity.

'They've done this before,' he said.

At the end of the room was a wall of what appeared to be toughened glass, making a secure area. There was no furniture. They went in and lay Parks down on the floor.

Before the guards closed the door, the two Prin in the room indicated Darrow should come to the table. Darrow shook his head and began to help Hazeroth make Parks comfortable on the floor and check on his condition. He had burns to his back and one temple, but was already starting to regain consciousness. One of the guards came into the glass room and touched Darrow's arm again, but this time the shock was much stronger. Darrow gasped as his arm went numb and his knees started to buckle.

While they were in their energy state, the Prin couldn't hold him, so the guard became solid to grab him. Darrow heaved himself upright and struck out with his good arm. There was very little resistance, like breaking a chocolate egg at Easter. The guard smashed to dust and a shimmer of energy shot out of the room. Darrow slammed the glass door. They were trapped but safe for the moment. Darrow leaned his back against the door to hold it shut and rubbed his arm. The other guard simply dropped to the floor and flowed under the door. It was only Hazeroth's shout that warned Darrow to move before his legs were shocked. The door swung open and the guard returned to his full height, staying in the doorway in his energy state. For a moment he paused and Darrow looked at him defiantly. Then the guard fired an energy bolt at Darrow's leg and gestured threateningly towards Hazeroth and Parks.

'Wait!' Darrow shouted. 'I'll come.'

He staggered over to the table, and the two other Prin became solid in order to strap him down. The guard remained threatening Hazeroth and Parks to ensure Darrow offered no resistance. Once the straps were fastened, the guard scooped up the dust from his comrade, locked the door and left the room. There was equipment suspended above the table that looked like an emitter of some kind, and the Prin positioned it over Darrow.

Parks blinked his way back to consciousness.

'Ow! Boy, they pack a punch without even touching you! Where are we? What's happening? Where are the others?'

'One question at a time, my friend,' replied Hazeroth. 'We are two levels below the area where we were captured. You and I are secured behind a glass wall and the Captain is strapped to a table over there, despite his resistance. We will find out any moment now what they are going to do to him. Miss Anna has been taken away.'

'Then we need to get out of here, quick,' Parks said, taking a quick look around and sitting up with his back to the glass. He searched his clothing and pulled out an assortment of wires and components. He spoke in a low voice. 'Lean over towards me, as if you are holding me because I am weak. Shield me from view while I put this together.'

As he worked, the equipment above Darrow emitted a wide beam that began to move slowly up the captain's body. Darrow flinched in pain. Whatever the beam was, probably some kind of scanner, it was intrusive to human flesh.

I came to find out about them, he thought, *and they're scanning me. I don't see a way out of this, I hope the Kestrel probe got through with all the data.*

The despair was almost more painful than the scan. As the beam reached his head, the pain became severe. Darrow groaned and gritted his teeth, but kept still as movement only intensified the pain. Eventually it was over. The Prin operators removed the restraints and backed away, ushering him over to the holding area. One of them made a ringing noise and the guard returned and unlocked the door and then moved away. None of them made any move to help Darrow, he had to manage on his own. His head was swimming, with a blinding pain behind his eyes, and he was unsteady on his feet. Parks quickly hid his construction, as Hazeroth jumped up to assist Darrow.

At that moment the main door opened and the another guard brought in Tabitha and put her into the glass chamber.

'Enns!' Parks cried. 'What are you doing here?'

Darrow looked up and gasped in surprise.

Tabitha hung her head. 'I wanted to see the new aliens. I

was going to stay out of sight.'

'You stupid girl!' Darrow said, and Parks added, 'Keep out of the way.'

She backed against the wall as Hazeroth helped Darrow into the chamber. The Prin operators pointed at Hazeroth. It was a dangerous moment. If the guards approached, they might discover Parks' handiwork. Hazeroth leaped through the door and ran for the exit, only to be stopped by the guards moving to block the way, but the distraction was enough cover for Parks, who reached up and pulled Darrow down beside him. Hazeroth raised his hands in surrender and moved to the table, and the guards locked the glass door and left. Darrow looked up groggily, and saw the Prin strapping Hazeroth to the table.

'Hey, wait, he's not human!'

He lunged towards the glass, and Parks used the distraction to resume his work. He finished quickly and spoke into his hidden communicator.

'Parks to Kestrel, do you read me?'

'Good to hear you,' Blackwell responded. 'What's your situation?'

'They didn't bother to search us, so I've put together my patent lock-pick. Hopefully it can find the right frequency. The Captain and I are locked up, but they're doing some kind of scan on Hazeroth, and it doesn't look too pleasant. The Captain's already had a turn, and he didn't enjoy it at all. We're ready to bust out of here. Can you give us backup?'

'We're dodging Prin fire up here, but there's a shuttle on the way. Leave your channel open so they can home in on you. Hold.'

Parks heard some exchange.

'The rescue crew will be landing in two minutes.'

'Okay on that. Tell them we're two levels down. Out.'

Chapter 38

When Anna was separated from the others, she knew this was not the time for escape: there were two guards and she had not been in this part of the city before. She waited in the hope she would get to more familiar territory. She tried to concentrate, to identify the different thoughts from the two Prin guards. The most indoctrinated guards displayed a white light, showing few thought patterns, just loyalty and obedience. Anna watched and 'listened', and found that while one guard was white, the other wavered into emerald: subtle changes reflecting his thoughts of doubt about what was going on. She knew there was no point in talking to him, as he wouldn't have a translator, but she had learned some of the Prin gestures and sounds, and signed to him for help and understanding. In reply he simply gestured towards the other guard.

To her surprise, neither of the guards seemed to know who she was, or why she had been separated from the others. However, as she approached a doorway she detected the unmistakable thoughts of the Great One himself. The feeling of terror stirred in her, with the memories of the last time she saw him. But she swallowed them down. She was lucky really. She had been hoping she could argue her way through to someone important, but here was the most important person on Prin, waiting to speak to her. And he had a translator. The door slid open and he spoke even before she was in the room.

'Why have you returned, and why bring these others?'

A good question, Anna thought. *I was so determined to warn everyone about the Prin, and get revenge for my father, but now…*

Memories crowded in and her courage wavered. She took a deep breath, she mustn't give in to the terror. She walked towards him, the guards remaining outside.

'To warn them about you and to stop you from taking what belongs to them,' she said.

There was a laugh in his thoughts, and she realised his plan all along was to trap them, examine them, and take the Kestrel. It would allow the Prin, with free reign, into Alliance space.

'What right do you have to set yourselves above the other species?' she said. 'The reason the Kestrel came here, with representatives from all the major species in our galaxy, was to talk to you, to discuss providing you with the materials you need by trade, to share knowledge and technology. These species have formed an alliance, and they all work together, so everyone benefits. You could be a part of that.'

She kept on speaking, moving gradually towards him, all the while fumbling her hand in her pocket and hoping he wouldn't notice. Sensing his thoughts of contempt, she began to make gestures and sounds, the same as she had done towards the guard. She was glad he couldn't read her thoughts, as she withdrew her hand from her pocket. Around her finger was a twist of wires, which drew energy from her own body via her blood. She stabbed it home with her other hand, and the blood ran down her finger.

It produced a sound almost too high for human hearing, but the effect on the Great One was dramatic. At once he became solid in appearance, as he pushed the particles swirling inside towards the outside, making a shell. Anna knew this, and as soon as the Great One's shell appeared, she pulled off her shoe and threw it at him.

The shell shattered, there was a shriek, a flash of energy, and the particles drifted to the floor. Anna ran to him and bent low over the dust. Yes, she could make out a faint glow of energy. She knew from her previous escape that some Prin died of shock when you shattered them, but some did not, and given time and help, could gradually regenerate their energy and re-absorb the particles. The Great One dead was no use to her - she would never get past the other Prin.

The shriek was heard by the guards outside the doorway,

and she just had time to turn it off and retrieve her shoe before they rushed in. She made the gesture and sound for defiance and raised her hand, showing the ring and making a clear threat towards the remains of the Great One.

'Get a translator!' she shouted, and prayed they would understand.

* * *

Hoy was a good pilot, but with the Kestrel manoeuvring to avoid the beam, take-off was tricky. He waited for a move to end, then shot from the shuttle bay, away from the ship and the beam. As soon as the shuttle launched, they encountered weapons fire.

'This is the same kind of beam that shut down the Kestrel's engines,' said Ehu with a smile. 'Watch this.' He fired.

A blue beam from the shuttle intersected with the Prin weapon beam and flowed down it to the source. The beam cut out with a flash and a cloud of blue smoke from the surface.

'Just a little something I have been working on,' he said. A second beam was similarly dispatched.

Blackwell's voice came over the comm. 'Recommended landing site is alongside the first shuttle. There seems to be no one about and Commander Parks has been in touch and said they are two levels down in the original building they entered.'

'Message received.'

He flew a long, curving course to bring them down through the atmosphere, low over the city, and back to where the first shuttle had landed. The purpose of at least some of the strange structures was now clear, as one was still enveloped in blue smoke, and another erupted as the Kestrel finally located the beam chasing them and destroyed it. Some Prin came out of surrounding structures and the Kestrel began to fire in support of the shuttle.

As the shuttle swooped over the landing site, Ehu

directed another beam across the open space. This beam, based on the force field they had used to contain the Prin on board, sent all the remaining figures flying for cover. Although they floated above the ground, they never rose more than a metre or two into the air, so it seemed the shuttle was safe from aerial attack unless there were any Prin ships within the atmosphere. None had been detected.

They landed, and Hoy gave them last-minute instructions as they adjusted their breathers. 'We don't know how long we have before those Prin return to the landing site, so we need to move quickly. If we get separated, rendezvous back here in one hour, or if this is not safe, at that oval shaped structure to the north. We also have no idea how many others there may be, but Ehu has modified our hand scanners to detect the Prin energy signature, so you will have some warning of them coming. A direct hit from our standard lasers will kill them.' He checked the display. 'Homing in on Parks' communicator, our people are two levels down inside that opening. Try to stay together, and good luck!'

* * *

As Anna waited, she thought back on the last few weeks. It seemed like a dream. Or a nightmare. The memories came to her as a kaleidoscope of emotions: fear when she was captured, terror at her adaptation, grief over her father's death, and then anger, determination, and terror again at her escape. Since she escaped her world had been shifting: confusion, understanding, resignation. And where was she now? Standing over the remains of the Great One, waiting for the chance to change the minds of a whole race. Could she persuade the Prin not to ravage the galaxy?

When the Sage arrived she was relieved - at least he had had time to think about the issue. She bowed to him.

'Thank you for coming to speak to me. I feel we know each other a little already. You have seen the truth while you were with us. We will not accept Prin domination. All we

274

have discovered about you has been sent home. If the Prin persist, there will be war. Many people on both sides will cease to exist and there will be great suffering. Please, you must persuade the Council to change their minds.'

She saw the colours change: purple fear, orange understanding and emerald doubt. She felt the shift in his thoughts. He agreed with her, but was not confident he could persuade the Council. He spoke.

'I will try, for the sake of all our people. May I give the Great One some life energy before I go?'

'I'm sorry, but I don't know what they're doing to my friends. This needs to be settled quickly, so the Great One must stay in jeopardy as long as my friends do.'

The Sage hesitated, he didn't want to leave the Great One like this, but he looked at her with a flash of amber pleading and turquoise threat, knowing his thoughts would be known to her. She was glad he could not read her thoughts: the desperation and the fear. She set her face and met his gaze steadily. Which way would he go? Would she have time to react if he decided to rush her?

Then he bowed and left, and she let out a long sigh. The guard who had gone to fetch the Sage came back into the doorway, but the other guard moved to intercept him, and with a tinge of turquoise, refused to allow him in. She realised this was the guard who had shown emerald as well as white, and he was thinking for himself. She could sense his thoughts weighing up what he had witnessed, trying to make sense of it without understanding the words. *Well, I've got one convert, at least,* she thought to herself.

Her senses felt sharpened, as if her memory wanted to capture every detail for the last time. Even the pain in her finger was intense. If this didn't work, she didn't know what else to do.

Being back here brought back so many memories. She closed her eyes for a moment, and opened them quickly as she caught a thought from the guard: he still wanted to stop her. She needed to stay alert. Then, she paused as she realised this guard was showing orange and amber - a plea for understanding. Too late, she realised that the first thought was not his, but those outside the doorway.

Without warning, the guard outside rushed into the room, along with three others, glowing shades of turquoise and blue. They swept the other guard aside, and fired an energy bolt at Anna. At the last second, Anna had sensed their thoughts and sidestepped as she activated the ring. She cursed herself for not staying alert, as the beam burned her leg, and she fell. The activation of the ring caused everyone in the room to become solid. Two of the new guards ran into one another and shattered, but there were still three standing - the two original guards and one of the new ones.

To Anna's surprise, the sympathetic guard ran to the others and stood between them and her. She understood from their thoughts that 'her' guard was telling the others it was in the hands of the Council now and they should not interfere. Her leg was painful and the ring was drawing strength from her, so she shut it off, and the guards became energy again. The sympathetic one was a threatening turquoise, the others blue with anger. She was afraid she wouldn't be able to carry through her plan. She looked down to check on the Great One and saw that the energy beam had caught him too, and he was gone.

She cried out in despair. Now she had no bargaining power. The guards followed her gaze and went green with shock and recoiled. At that moment the Sage arrived, with three members of the Council. He took in the scene and demanded to know what had happened. There followed a blaze of lights and a confusion of ringing tones Anna found hard to follow. The pain in her leg and her despair at the Great One's death made it hard for her to concentrate. One of the Council members made a loud noise and everyone fell silent. The Council member spoke to the Sage and indicated he should speak to Anna.

'We have heard what the others say, now we will hear you.'

She took a deep breath. 'The Great One questioned me in private, and I smashed him to force an opportunity to put my case to the Great Council. I never intended he should cease to exist.' The tears in her eyes were real, but she allowed them to draw their own conclusions. 'The attack on me caused his end.' She had an idea. 'This ability to hear your thoughts was forced on me when I was a captive here before.'

The Sage signalled her to stop and translated. The Council members turned green with shock and then dark blue with anger. She could tell they knew nothing about her captivity.

'My father died when they operated on him,' she said. 'Now I fear they are doing the same to the people from the Kestrel.'

The Sage translated again, and the Council members became very animated.

'I have told them also you wish to discuss trade rather than war,' the Sage said to her. 'It seems they know nothing of this.' He bowed, and the Council members bowed too, glowing amber in appeal. 'All hostilities will cease and the Council will listen to you and your friends.'

Chapter 39

Parks checked that Darrow could stand, and picked the lock. As the door opened, they heard explosions - the Kestrel taking out the beam and offering covering fire to the shuttle as it landed. They staggered out and Parks pulled out the ultraviolet light and shone it towards the Prin operators, who recoiled as Anna had said. Parks gave the light to Darrow and pulled a slim tube from the back of his neck - a miniature laser. In the circumstances, he didn't think Hazeroth would criticize him for carrying a concealed weapon after all. He used the laser to take out the scanning machine and released Hazeroth from the table. The scan had not completed, so the Zoan was in a much better condition than the Captain. Parks was suffering with his burns and Darrow was still unsteady on his feet. Tabitha stepped between them to support them both.

The ultraviolet light only worked as an initial shock, and as Hazeroth climbed off the table a crackling sound reminded them that all Prin could fire energy bolts. Luckily it missed. One of the operators had already overcome his fear, so the other was likely to recover soon. They heard the sound of shooting from outside then Hoy and Stubbs burst through the doorway.

The other operator launched an energy bolt that caught Stubbs on the arm. Hoy eliminated the two operators and ran to assist Darrow. He started when he saw Tabitha, but Darrow shook his head. Ryan rushed in, desperately searching the room with his eyes.

'Where is she? What have they done to Anna?'

Hazeroth laid a hand on Ryan's arm. 'She is not here, they took her away. Do not despair, we will find her.' He turned to Hoy. 'Let us go.'

'Wait,' said Darrow. 'What's the situation out there?'

'We met with surprisingly little resistance,' said Hoy. 'I

don't think they're set up for a fight.'

'All the more reason to act quickly,' said Hazeroth, 'before they organise a counter-attack.'

'You and Ryan get the Captain, Commander Parks and Enns back to the shuttle,' Hoy told Hazeroth. 'Stubbs, you'd better go with them. We'll look for Anna.'

'But sir!' Ryan said.

'I know you're concerned about Anna,' Hoy said, 'but your place is with the wounded. Keep your weapon ready.'

'This way,' Hazeroth said, 'I will show you where Anna was separated from us.'

They headed out into the corridor, where Ehu and Balitoth were standing guard. Tabitha helped Darrow and Ryan supported Parks. Ehu led as they cautiously picked their way down the corridor.

Energy bolts smashed into the wall from around a corner. Ehu jumped back, pushing the others behind him to safety. He risked a look, but only withdrew in time to avoid another bolt. The energy zinged past them. There was no getting to the junction Hazeroth indicated was Anna's route.

Without a word, Tabitha leaned Darrow against the wall and reached up and tore a panel off the wall with her bare hands. Holding it in front of her as a shield, she ran around the corner. Her action was so unexpected that for a split second, nobody moved. Then Ehu and Balitoth crouched behind her as she charged up the corridor and smashed into the Prin. Those who had been firing were quickly killed and Ehu called back for the others to join them.

'Thank you, Trainee,' said Ehu with a grin. 'I will take the shield. Do you think you could provide Lieutenant Balitoth with the same?'

Tabitha gave a shy grin and reached up and ripped another panel from the wall.

* * *

As they braced to attack the next corner the firing stopped abruptly, and Balitoth called back.

279

'Sir, they have withdrawn and there is a Prin here who wants to speak to the Captain.'

Parks pushed himself upright from the wall where he was leaning. 'You're not fit, sir, after what they did to you. They can speak to me.'

'No, Nate, it's all right,' Darrow said. 'I can manage.'

Hoy agreed with Parks. 'You both need medical attention, sir.'

Darrow waved him off and put a hand on the wall for support. Two Prin came round the corner, one of which Darrow recognised as the Warrior. She was glowing orange, the colour for understanding. She became solid and bowed.

'Greetings Captain. I am instructed to bring you to meet with members of the Great Council.'

Ryan moved forward. 'Where's Anna, is she all right?'

Hoy held him back, but they all wanted to know.

The Warrior bowed again. 'She is being brought. She will confirm all to you.'

Darrow raised a hand. 'Wait a minute. What's going on? Why the sudden change?'

There was a long pause.

'The Great One is no more.' She flickered back to energy for an instant, a deep brown sorrow, and then stabilised. 'The Council has agreed to listen to Anna ... and to you. You will please come.'

Two more Prin arrived, guiding a platform on which Anna sat, leaning to one side to ease her leg. They lowered the platform to the ground. Ryan ran to her, his lips already forming questions, but she shook her head.

'Not now, Sam, I have to speak to the Captain. But can you do something for this burn?' Ryan opened his med kit, and Anna turned to Darrow. She took a deep breath and it all came out in a rush. 'Captain. I managed to take the Great One hostage, to try to get them to change their minds. The Sage came, and brought some of the Council. When the Great One died, I thought it was all over, but he was the obstacle to change all along. And the Great Mind...'

'Wait, wait!' Darrow said, holding his head. 'Slow down a bit, you're losing me.'

Anna sighed, and then winced as Ryan ripped her trousers and spread cream on her leg. 'I'm sorry, but it's all happened so fast, and I'm scared the Prin Council will change their minds.'

'Well, let's cut to the chase. Is this offer to speak to the Council genuine, will we be safe?'

'Yes,' she said, 'to both questions. At least,' she swallowed, 'we're safe while they listen. Some want me tried for murder, and even if not, they may refuse us.'

Darrow turned to the Warrior. 'You must allow us to treat the wounded. Ryan, that's your department. Do you need me to send for Dr Ky?'

'Captain,' Parks interrupted. 'You and Anna are needed for the negotiations right now, so Hazeroth, Stubbs and I are the only ones Ryan can help at the moment. If the Warrior can give us a guarantee of safety, why don't we go to the shuttle with Ryan and wait, and Hoy can go with you to meet the Council?'

Darrow looked at Hoy, who was astounded. Darrow thought, *Holland would never have allowed anyone to take his place when there was something exciting going on. Well done Parks.*

Darrow nodded, and Parks turned to Ryan. 'Treat the Captain and Anna, quickly.'

'Sir, Anna needs a regenerator on this burn, and I don't know what I can do for the Captain.'

'Just give me pain killers,' Darrow said, 'and bandage her leg.'

Ryan swallowed hard. 'I really recommend you both return to the Kestrel for treatment. Can't the talks wait a while?'

Anna grabbed his arm and said, 'We daren't wait, in case they change their minds. I'm the only one who can confirm what the Prin are thinking, so I *have* to go to meet the Council.'

Ryan put a temporary dressing on her leg, and gave her and Darrow something for the pain. Tabitha stood by, not knowing what to do. They seemed to have forgotten her. No such luck.

Darrow turned to her. 'You, young lady, are in big trouble. Go with Ryan and I'll deal with you later.'

Anna interrupted. 'Please Captain, you're all going to need your attention for the Prin. Can Tabitha stay with me?'

Tabitha's heart was in her mouth as she waited for Darrow's reply. He shook his head. 'I can't put her in any more danger.'

To Tabitha's surprise it was Ehu who spoke up. 'Captain, I think she has proved her usefulness, even if she acted without orders.'

'Please Captain,' Anna repeated. 'I know you can't spare Sam.'

Darrow sighed. 'Very well. But Enns - you are to look after Anna and not make a move without orders.'

'Yes sir.' Tabitha's voice came out as a squeak, but her eyes were shining.

'It seems we are on the verge of achieving our greatest goal,' said Hazeroth. 'In view of the importance of this meeting, I think that the other species should be represented. However, since they were singularly reluctant to endanger themselves, except for Mr Ehu here.' He bowed to the Anak. 'May I suggest that he and I also come with you?'

'Are you fit? You were scanned too.'

Hazeroth waved his hand dismissively. 'They did not finish. I am well enough.'

Darrow considered. 'Yes. I will take Lieutenant-Commander Hoy, Mr Hazeroth, Mr Ehu, Anna and Trainee Enns. The rest of you go to one of the shuttles and stand by.'

Chapter 40

The Warrior and her companion went into the Council chamber, asking the others to wait in an anteroom. The two Prin who were controlling Anna's platform lowered it to the floor and stationed themselves in the doorway. Tabitha found it hard to keep her eyes off them. She stooped beside Anna and could see she was struggling. She thought the burn on her leg looked painful, and wondered what Anna's ring had done to her when she saw the trail of dried blood down her hand.

She hugged her. 'Hold on,' she whispered. 'They need you.'

The Prin seemed to have forgotten Anna could read their thoughts, so she was able to give the Kestrel team a running commentary of how the discussion was progressing. Occasionally, voices were raised, and they could hear what sounded like a cacophony of birdsong, but the team tried to concentrate on what Anna was saying.

'There are actually three parties in the discussion, those on the Council who still agree with the Great One's idea of Prin superiority, who want me executed for killing the Great One. The others are annoyed there have been things going on they were not aware of, and are interested in the idea of trade. But there's a major third party - the Great Mind. When a Prin dies, their essence, their personality I suppose, is collected into the Great Mind. On Prin ships there's a temporary collector in case anyone dies, which is downloaded when they return.'

She winced and shifted her position with difficulty. Tabitha tried to help, but Anna trembled and breathed deeply.

'All Prin have the right to consult the Great Mind over anything,' she continued, 'but it's especially part of the Great Council. There has been a communication problem for some time, but they are trying to find out what it thinks about all this, as well as debating between themselves.'

Darrow asked, 'What's the general mood in there? Can you tell which way it's going?'

Anna frowned. 'It seems to be pretty even at the moment. The Sage has been asked to speak about what he discovered on our ship. I think he likes us. The Warrior agrees … Oh, but some of the Council are furious. They say they have been brainwashed by us, and it's all a plot to steal their … I think they mean technology and such.'

She paused again, listening, her breathing ragged. She whispered to Tabitha, 'I'm so tired.'

'It's getting pretty heated.' Anna continued. 'There's a strong desire to maintain their status. Some of them think it would demean them to have help from others. The other side are trying to say it would be a relationship of equals.' She turned to Ehu and Hazeroth. 'You need to tell them that it doesn't destroy your dignity, or make you subservient.'

Ehu opened his mouth to speak, but at that moment, Anna sagged.

Tabitha caught her. She opened her eyes and gave a wan smile.

'Sorry Captain, I guess I'm weaker than I thought. Ah, they're coming for us.'

* * *

The Sage appeared in the doorway and beckoned for them to follow him. Darrow raised a hand to stop it, but Anna said, 'We must go, Captain, now!'

The guards operated Anna's platform and took her in. Tabitha walked beside her holding her hand. Darrow, Hoy, Ehu and Hazeroth followed. The Council Chamber, far from being the grand room they expected, looked messy, with conduits snaking about and an uneven floor.

Ehu leaned towards the others and murmured, 'Just like their ship.'

Tabitha looked around and drank it all in. The Council members appeared to be resting in cup shaped pedestals arranged in a semi-circle in several rows. As the Kestrel party looked around they saw, on the opposite wall to the Council, a large panel glowing brown, around which several Prin seemed to be working. Two of them were solid and working with tools.

Anna indicated the panel and whispered, 'The Great Mind.'

The Sage showed them where to stand, to one side of the centre of the semi circle, so they could face the Council and the Great Mind. He addressed Anna first.

'The Council wants to know why you can touch our minds. I will translate.'

Anna started. 'What! How come they don't know?'

The Sage hesitated, emerald in confusion. Anna hurried on.

'My father and I were captured by a Prin ship and brought here. We were … operated on to be able to hear your thoughts, to make communication easier. Unfortunately it didn't work both ways, and the process killed my father. I was questioned by the Great One for a long time. I thought the Council were aware of this.'

Darrow didn't need Anna to interpret the Council members' reactions when the Sage translated. There was a clear difference in the lights.

Some knew and some didn't, he thought. *What's the significance of that, I wonder?*

Anna had stopped in surprise. The Sage seemed flustered. His lights flickered through many colours. He spoke to Darrow.

'We need you to explain your planetary alliance, and your proposal to us.'

Darrow took a deep breath to ease his tension. The whole mission depended on what he said next. He stepped forward, making sure he could see Anna out of the corner of his eye, for feedback.

'Greetings. We are honoured to be able to speak to you.' He bowed. 'My name is Joseph Darrow, and I am the Captain of the Kestrel. I am here as a representative of the Planetary Alliance for Cooperation and Trade, which we refer to as PACT. This is an agreement between the species to share their learning and their resources with one another for the benefit of all. I ask my companions from two other species to speak about what it's like to be part of PACT.'

He deferred to Ehu and Hazeroth, and Hazeroth stepped forward. Darrow moved to stand with Anna and Tabitha so he could hear what Anna was murmuring as she attempted to pick up the Council members' thoughts, which still seemed to be mixed opinions.

'My name is Hazeroth, of Zoa. One of my race is the communications officer aboard the Kestrel, which works for PACT. All species work together on these ships. My people were part of the original group that created PACT. Great care was taken to ensure no judgements would be made about each species' form of government, religion, or culture. For example, there are things in my culture that humans do not agree with, but PACT is only about sharing and learning, and we have all benefited greatly. Should you join us we will not interfere in your way of life.'

There were no extreme light flashes from the Council members, they were mainly orange and emerald. When Darrow checked with Anna, she explained the colours were for understanding and doubt. As he looked round, he thought the orange outnumbered the emerald. He realised he was holding his breath, and breathed out in relief. Hazeroth had done well. Now, what would they make of Ehu? Darrow had gained a new respect for the Anak, and Ehu in particular, during the mission, hopefully the tall Anak could convey some of the more respectful notions to the Prin. Hazeroth stepped back and Ehu came forward.

'My name is Ehu Pathrusim, of Anak. I am not part of the Kestrel crew but came, like Hazeroth, as a representative of my people in seeking you out. My people have a reputation for violence and aggression. We feared we would not be welcome in PACT, or they would invite us in, only to take advantage of our planetary resources. This has not been the case. Because of our trade agreement with PACT, my people have been able to return to a peaceful existence. By joining PACT you would be able to gain all the materials you need without the need for attacking or killing. Believe me, the cost of trade is far less than the cost of aggression.' As they spoke, the Sage was translating, and it was interesting to see the colours flashing in the Council members as they considered what they heard. Anna told them that the Council were not yet convinced. Darrow pulled himself up straight and stepped forward again.

'While I am authorised to speak with you about future relations between your world and all of ours, our main mission was to seek information about you. Everything we have learned has been sent home. I must warn you that all the planets in our alliance, and others that we have relations with, can only act on what they have seen of you so far, which, to be blunt, is nothing but thievery and aggression. You are a threat, and threats lead to violence, not peace.' He paused to emphasise his point, and the colours of the Council were tinged with the green of alarm. 'We will resist you if you seek to take what is ours. But we will also welcome you if you come in peace. I do not know why you need the things you have taken from us, but trying to take any more will cost you dearly, and still you may not get what you need. Work with us, and we can help each other.'

A high-pitched shriek came from the lighted panel of the Great Mind, which had turned dark blue with anger. It was so loud everyone recoiled. The Prin flickered into solids, and when they returned to energy they were all bright green with the shock. One of the Prin who had been working on the panel appeared to have been killed, and a fine cloud of dust settled to the floor as his energy flowed into the panel. The panel gave a rapid burst of sound and turquoise and dark blue lights, and the Kestrel group turned to Anna for understanding, only to discover she had passed out in Tabitha's arms. Hoy immediately pulled out the med kit he had brought with him.

They stood in confusion as the Council and the Great Mind spoke back and forth. The Sage was moving to and fro as if pacing.

After several minutes there was an obvious difference in the lights. The majority of the members became green and dark blue, while several were amber and white. The larger group at once produced energy beams directed at the others, who flashed out of existence. Their energy rushed towards the panel, which went dark blue and blocked it, the energy dissipating with a shriek.

Silence fell, and the Council, as one, became dark brown with sorrow. They turned towards the Sage and Darrow and there was a short burst of ringing language. The Sage shimmered emerald in uncertainty for a moment and then spoke.

'We have received grave news, Captain. Communication with the Great Mind has been difficult for some time, and the Great One assured us everything was being done to remedy this. The Great Mind informs us it was actually the Great One and his like-minds who were preventing it from communicating, because of its opposition to their plans for the domination of other worlds. Our technicians just found the inhibitor and removed it, and it was regrettable that one was terminated by the Great Mind's rage. As you saw, the Council have dealt with those who were working against the common good, and the Great Mind has refused to absorb them.' The Sage faltered, and his lights ran through many colours. 'Such a thing has never happened before in our history. This is a great tragedy.' He faded to dark brown.

'I am sorry to hear this,' Darrow said. 'What does this mean for us and our mission?'

'The Great Mind has told us we must be less... arrogant, and it is time for us to learn from others in order to grow.' The Sage spoke slowly.

'Then you'll discuss trade agreements and call off the raids?'

'We cannot give you an answer immediately, Captain, but there will be no more raids. All ships are being recalled, as there is much to discuss. But we will assist you, and heal your wounds before you leave.'

Hoy looked up from leaning over Anna. 'It may be too late for Anna, Captain, I fear she may have brain damage.'

Tabitha gasped and held her tighter.

Darrow's emotions crashed. To come so far, but lose Anna … The Sage bowed as they turned angrily towards him.

'Please, Captain, we have discovered the Great One has been analysing other species for some time, and the technology he has had developed can also be used to heal them. We can treat all your wounds, including Anna's. The implant to enable her to hear our thoughts was ruptured by the outburst of the Great Mind. Do not fear, we will do our best to see she recovers.' He glowed amber in pleading and bowed deeply. 'Believe me, we will not harm you.'

Chapter 41

While the Sage made arrangements for the machine he said could heal them to be set up, Hoy contacted Ryan at the shuttles.

'Ensign Ryan, can you leave your patients at the shuttles? We need you here straight away.' There was a pause as Hoy consulted the Sage. 'Someone will come to escort you.'

'Yes sir. Is Anna all right?'

'You'll see when you arrive. On second thoughts, bring Commander Parks with you and anyone else who is injured. The Prin say they can heal them.'

Parks volunteered to go first. The Prin treated his burns, which should have taken days to heal, in just a few minutes. During the procedure, they discovered his damaged shoulder and repaired that as well. He seemed to be unconscious, which caused some concern until he came round and Ryan confirmed he was not only unharmed but appeared to be completely healed.

Nevertheless, Hoy asserted his right to be in command until Dr Ky declared him fit for duty. Only then did the others agree to be treated. Except for Stubbs, who point blank refused to let the Prin anywhere near him.

The injuries were treated so well there weren't even any scars. Darrow collapsed completely. The Sage consulted the Prin operators and reported that the scanner could cause tissue damage, so the regenerating beam had a lot of work to do, which was especially difficult on the brain.

Anna woke briefly, and then passed out again, but the operators told the Sage to assure the group treatment on the brain always caused restorative sleep. The whole process took less than two hours.

Back on board the Kestrel, Darrow slept for ten hours and when he awoke in sick bay, railed at Ky for not waking him sooner.

'Keep your voice down, Captain,' Ky said. 'Anna is still asleep.'

Darrow glanced across to where Anna lay. She looked very peaceful.

'How is she?'

'I can find nothing wrong with her, not even internal scarring from the accident. But I don't think it wise to wake her.'

'You're probably right. I must admit I needed the rest, even though it's frustrating to be out of the loop.'

'What *was* that beam?' Ky asked him.

'Some kind of scanner, but it probed pretty deep. Felt like hands moving my guts around, prodding and poking my brain.' He winced at the memory. 'What's the news of the Prin?'

'Mr Hazeroth is waiting to see you. He's been talking to them while you were recovering - they wouldn't wait for you to come round.'

'I'll call him now.' Darrow began to dress.

'Don't go tiring yourself. You'll be a little weak.'

Darrow laughed. 'Thanks Doctor. I'll check in with you later.'

*　*　*

Once the crisis was over, Chambers could be relieved at the helm. As he left the bridge, Tabitha called to him from her cabin door.

'Andrew! Over here. Is it really over then?'

'Looks like,' Chambers said. He leaned on the corridor wall. 'I guess the Captain found some reasonable Prin after all.'

'I know, I was there.'

'What! Why did you do such a stupid thing?'

Her face went red. 'I just wanted to see the Prin and their planet. I didn't know they were going to take us all prisoner, did I?'

'That's the point! Oh Tabs, you're going to have to learn to obey orders, or you'll be out of the service.'

She blanched. 'I've learned my lesson, but I've got to face the Captain, when he recovers.'

'Good luck with that,' Chambers said doubtfully.

She quickly changed the subject. 'The shuttle came back with the Captain and Anna on stretchers. Dr Ky rushed them into sick bay. I hope they're all right. Are you all right? I'm looking for an excuse to go in there to see how they are.'

Chambers smiled, then paused to consider. 'Do you know, I'm actually a lot better than I was. When the Prin turned nasty I didn't have time to think, and the old reflexes just kicked in. I still don't like being helmsman, but I think I'll cope a little better now.'

'Oh Andrew, that's great! And you sorted that thing with Mr Merari over your grandfather. I wish you'd tell me about it.'

'You, Trainee, are much too nosey for your own good!' He tapped the tip of her nose. 'Have you made up with Stubbs yet?'

She shrugged. 'Yes, he actually apologised, but he won't bother me again. I've got the measure of him now.'

'Hark at you! Slotted right in, haven't you.'

Now it was Tabitha's turn to consider. 'I guess I found my feet, in more ways than one.'

* * *

Darrow went to his office and called Hazeroth and Parks to him. Parks, when he arrived, was grinning from ear to ear. He was so excited he forgot his normal insistence on protocol.

'Joe, the Prin made me good as new!' He flexed his shoulder as proof. 'Dr Ky has passed me fully fit for duty -

space, here I come!'

Darrow grabbed his arm. 'That's great news!' He looked serious. 'Want to stay?'

Parks flopped down into a seat, a look of hope on his face. 'Can you fix it?'

'Well, I still need a new First Officer, so I'm pretty sure I can. What about Greta and the kids?'

Parks shook his head. 'The kids are growing up and Greta knows how much it means to me. I'd love to stay.'

Darrow shook his hand. 'Done!'

Hazeroth had been quietly watching, and now leaned forward.

'Captain, if I may?'

'Sorry, Hazeroth. What's the news on the Prin?'

'They are impatient for us to be gone.'

'What?'

'I told them you would consider it an insult if you were not given the opportunity to speak to them. That is the only reason we are still in orbit.'

'Surely you've spoken to them about the many benefits of a relationship with us?'

Hazeroth nodded slowly. 'I have tried every persuasion I can think of, Captain. They are not against the idea, but insist they have to sort out their government first, before they can consider our offer. I think they are also embarrassed that we know about their problems. First contact with a whole group of new species is not the time when you want to appear less than your best. They are also concerned that giving us new technology would be interference in our development.' He raised a hand to still Darrow's reply. 'You must speak to them yourself, of course, but I do not believe you will persuade them to move any faster.'

Darrow sighed. 'I'm sure you did your best.' He turned to Parks. 'How are the crew?'

'Everyone is fine. The Prin healed everyone's injuries who was *willing to let them*.' He pulled a face.

'Who?'

'Stubbs.'

Darrow nodded. 'How serious are his injuries?'

'A minor burn. Ensign Ryan treated it down on the surface, and Dr Ky says he'll be fine tomorrow.'

'Any damage to the ship?'

'None. We got off lightly, all things considered.'

'Well, might as well get it over with, then. Do we go down to the planet or talk on screen?'

'Just on screen, Captain, they don't want us down there, and we haven't been able to scan much either - they insisted we stay in geo-stationary orbit.'

Darrow sat before his console and put in the call. It was the Sage who answered. He became solid for a moment and showed a sad smile.

'Thank you, Captain, for your part in helping us to uncover the truth. Even though it is painful for us.'

'Thank you for being open-minded enough to bring us here,' Darrow replied. 'I hope the rest of the Great Council will also be open-minded.'

The Sage reverted to energy and glowed a deep sorrowful brown. 'I believe they will, in time. There is much to do here first.'

'I understand. What shall I tell our governments? They will want to know if you are still a threat.'

'We have considered this. Since you brought gifts, when we finish speaking, some gifts we have prepared will arrive on a small ship. One for each of your governments and one for you, Captain. When we are ready to begin discussions, a single ship will travel to agreed coordinates in your part of the galaxy, broadcasting a message of friendship. It will not approach any planets, but will await a reply. If no reply is received after some time, or there is any violence threatened, we will withdraw, but there will be no attack.'

Parks hissed in his ear, 'Won't it be attacked on sight?'

Darrow considered for a moment. 'Tell them to broadcast my name as part of the message, Joseph Darrow,

Captain of the Kestrel. I'll do my best to spread the word to watch for your Emissary.'

'Thank you, Captain. Once your gifts arrive, please leave. We have much to do.'

The transmission ended. Balitoth came on the intercom from the bridge.

'A small ship is approaching from the surface, Captain.'

'Allow it to dock and accept the cargo,' Darrow said.

He rose from his seat, beckoning to Parks and Hazeroth. 'Let's see what they've sent.'

* * *

The moment Tabitha was dreading had come. She was summoned to the Captain's office.

'Trainee Tabitha Enns reporting, sir.' She saluted and stood at attention.

Darrow looked up from his papers. His voice was low and measured. 'Do you realise the seriousness of what you did? You could have been killed. More to the point, you could have got others killed.'

'Yes sir.'

'As a trainee, and even when you complete your training, there will be lots of situations you're left out of. You can't just take the law into your own hands.'

'No sir.'

'The charges against you are very serious, and if you were a member of the crew I'd throw the book at you.' He thumped the table. 'As it is, I am responsible for you and should have had you more closely supervised. You betrayed my trust, Trainee.'

Tabitha was devastated. She finally realised the full enormity of her impulsive act. She had been making up excuses, but now she could see how useless they were. Tears came to her eyes but she swallowed hard. Her voice came out very quiet.

'I didn't think...'

'No, you didn't,' Darrow snapped. 'When you're more experienced you will be able to think things through before you take action. But until then, you just obey orders.'

Tabitha hung her head. There was nothing to say.

Darrow returned to the papers on his desk. There was a long pause. 'When you charged at the Prin, weren't you scared?'

Tabitha collected her thoughts. 'No sir. I was just mad at them for shooting at us.'

Darrow gave a little smile. 'Well next time you get mad, talk to your superior officer first. You were a great help to us, but once again you acted without thinking or recognising the chain of command.' Darrow's smile vanished. 'What would have happened if no one had followed you round that corner? That is reckless behaviour! This will all go in your report, you know, and it's a shame because overall we've been very pleased with you.'

Tabitha sighed. 'Thank you sir.'

'When they read my report, it will be up to your teachers at the Academy whether they allow you to continue in the programme. I hope they do. Meanwhile you have some hard lessons to learn on the way home. Dismissed.'

Tabitha saluted and left, allowing the tears to fall. She had wrecked her chances. It was all over.

* * *

Before they broke orbit, Darrow called a general meeting in the mess hall. It was cramped with everyone present, but no one wanted to miss out. Even Tabitha managed to squeeze in. Her eyes were red from crying and she hoped nobody would notice. She saw Stubbs come in with his arm bandaged, and wondered why he hadn't been healed by the Prin. She wasn't going to ask him though, he was bound to comment on her eyes. As she looked round the room she noticed neither Ryan nor Anna were there.

Darrow stood on a bench and called for quiet. 'I want to

thank you all for the parts you played on this mission. It wasn't easy to live together in these cramped quarters, however I think you did very well.'

There was nervous laughter.

'The Prin have given us gifts to take back to each of our governments.'

He opened the small box he was carrying, and removed a delicate object of intricate curving pieces twined around each other. It echoed some of the shapes they had seen in the city. Holding the base in one hand, he gently twisted the top to make it spin. The room was filled with a series of musical notes that blended into wonderful harmony. At the same time, its dun colour changed to a rainbow of rippling colours. There was a collective gasp, and a disappointed sigh as Darrow stilled it and the sound ceased. He seemed reluctant to break the silence.

'I need everyone to file your version of everything you saw and experienced. I would like to continue our cooperation and agree to share all reports with all governments.' He paused, and looked around. No one objected. 'Thank you. The scanner reports will be cross-indexed and catalogued, and Mr Ehu is going to talk to his government about sharing the weapons modifications. I understand Commander Parks has spoken to all the representatives about Mr Barok.'

He motioned to Parks to speak.

'It has been agreed all reports will show Mr Barok in a favourable light. His action opened the way for dialogue, and he was right about the Prin being dangerous.'

Everyone nodded, and Tabitha smiled at that. Anna had talked to her about him, and made her see he was just out of his depth, and not really bad. Parks gave way to Dr Ky.

As Parks sat down, the door opened and Anna squeezed in with Ryan. Tabitha was relieved, and the whole room cheered. Anna smiled and looked to Darrow for permission to speak. Tabitha thought she looked different somehow.

'Thank you all for your kindness to me,' Anna said. 'I'm

fine now, and my memory is restored. My name is Anna Mason, from Earth colony Delta 5.'

Darrow raised a hand as everyone started to speak. 'There'll be plenty of time to ask questions.' He turned to Anna. 'The success of this mission is largely down to you. We owe you our lives. We can return you to Delta 5 as soon as we get back. I'm sure you'll be glad to be going home.'

He beckoned to Ky to speak.

'As you can see, I'm pleased to report Anna has recovered,' Ky said. 'Also, in memory of Dathan, all the species are co-operating in building a database of their biology to be shared among the Alliance.' He paused and gave a rare smile. 'On a personal note, after talking to Ensign Ryan about his colony world, I've decided it would be a good place for my retirement.' There was a small round of applause. 'It will be good to be useful, and it will also leave Ensign Ryan free to qualify as a doctor and go out into space, which is what he really wants.'

Ryan smiled and took Anna's hand. 'But first, I'm going to Delta 5.'

There was a round of applause and Darrow dismissed everyone. Tabitha went back to her cabin to think about her future. It would take some time to get home and she was determined to prove her worth on the way.

###

Thank you for reading this book. I hope you enjoyed it.

Reviews are an author's lifeblood. If you enjoyed this book, please go online to Amazon and leave a review.

FREE BOOK!
Join her mailing list and receive this free book and monthly updates http://eepurl.com/bbOsyz

Amazon Reviews of Intruders:
My interest varies when it comes to reading Science fiction but I was totally absorbed, more so as the book progressed and the plot thickened. I could really identify with Tabitha, the main character of the story, especially as her curiosity gets the better of her, and this drew me further into the book. The author uses Tabitha's journal as a clever way of giving us the "real" story – it was a bit like getting the gossip as opposed to the formal report. The plot is well constructed and flows smoothly from introducing us to new worlds to a tense finish. As a history and travel buff, I liked the references to the different cultures and the history of the representatives – so much that I'm sure a spin- off series would be a success . I think that there is a good mix which

means that there are things that would appeal to people who were not necessarily sci-fi fans. Well done for a first Sci-fi novel, I look forward to the next book and to discover what happens next! (5*)

This is a well paced, imaginative science fiction novel, not normally my favourite genre but the author brings it alive with a huge cast of characters, many of whom are curious off Earth species who unite in trying to defeat a mysterious alien civilisation the Prin who is preying on all their natural resources. It moves at a cracking pace, piling incident on incident and kept my attention for several hours I was so keen to finish it and find out whether the heroine Tabitha Enns, the new Alphan space cadet, survives despite her inexperience and occasional lapses from protocol. M/s Thomas has created an exciting, well researched action novel. I particularly enjoyed the 'mind-reading' and use of colours for emotions and the battle sequences. (5*)

Flight of the Kestrel is a series of space adventures, so I hope you'll stick with it.

Continue the series:

Alien Secrets: Flight of the Kestrel book 2

On a failed mission to look for a secret weapon, Shom Reuel of the Kestrel saves a man – twice. It seems everyone wants him, but is he a friend or a deadly enemy? And will the shock of his identity cause Reuel to reveal his people's greatest secret?

Crisis of Conscience: Flight of the Kestrel book 3

Can Captain Joseph Darrow of the spaceship Kestrel commit theft and murder to save the lives of his crew? Is Second Officer Daniel Hoy right, that the ends justify the means? Are there some lines you must not cross?

Can they persuade the Zoan lizard woman Raven to tell them her father's secret?

Newly qualified Ensign Tabitha Enns steps straight into peril. Can she prove her worth?

And look out for book 4: *Planet Fail*

www.ingramcontent.com/pod-product-compliance
Lightning Source LLC
Chambersburg PA
CBHW051411170626
46809CB00006B/2118